IN THE DARK OF THE NIGHT

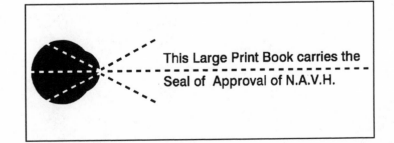

This Large Print Book carries the
Seal of Approval of N.A.V.H.

IN THE DARK OF THE NIGHT

JOHN SAUL

WHEELER PUBLISHING

An imprint of Thomson Gale, a part of The Thomson Corporation

THOMSON

GALE

Detroit • New York • San Francisco • New Haven, Conn. • Waterville, Maine • London • Munich

Copyright © 2006 by John Saul.

Thomson Gale is part of The Thomson Corporation.

Thomson and Star Logo and Wheeler are trademarks and Gale is a registered trademark used herein under license.

Wheeler Publishing Large Print Hardcover.

The text of this Large Print edition is unabridged.

Other aspects of the book may vary from the original edition.

Set in 16 pt. Plantin.

LIBRARY OF CONGRESS CATALOGING-IN-PUBLICATION DATA

Saul, John.
  In the dark of the night / by John Saul.
    p. cm.
  ISBN 1-59722-336-0 (hardcover : alk. paper)
  1. Teenage boys — Fiction. 2. Spirit possession — Fiction. 3. Serial murderers — Fiction. 4. Large type books. I. Title.
  PS3569.A78715 2006b
  813'.54—dc22   2006022007

ISBN 13: 978-1-59722-336-2

Published in 2006 by arrangement with The Ballantine Publishing Group,
a division of Random House, Inc.

Printed in the United States of America on permanent paper
10 9 8 7 6 5 4 3 2 1

For Liz, with love . . .

PROLOGUE

The man pulled hard on the oars, every muscle in his body burning despite the chill of the autumn night.

He ignored the pain, pulling the boat out toward the middle of the lake, where the water was the deepest.

Deepest, and coldest.

Yet despite the iciness of the water and of the night, perspiration trickled from his brow and from his arms and drizzled down his chest.

Urgency spurred him onward and he pulled again, straining on the oars. His biceps spasmed in protest, but he ignored the pain. Just as he ignored the voices in his head. The ones that commanded him to turn the boat around.

But he wouldn't do that. No matter what happened — no matter how much strength the voices gained or his muscles lost — he would stay the course he'd set.

He focused on the objects that lay toward the bow in the bottom of the boat. An old crawfish trap, its mesh torn but still strong enough to serve its purpose.

The float for the trap, even older than the trap itself, was secured to the trap with far too short a length of cheap polypropylene line. That wouldn't matter, either — the trap would be heavy enough to pull the float down.

Especially after he added the two concrete blocks he'd brought along, just to be sure.

Just to be absolutely sure.

The voices in his head were shouting now, with one voice rising to a shriek so loud he felt his skull might burst.

He pulled on the oars one last time, then let the boat drift. As it slid silently through the water, it rocked gently, and somehow the quieting motion silenced even the voices in his head.

Then the rocking stopped and the voices roared back to life. As if sensing what was about to come, they rose once again in a raging howl of protest.

But the man continued to carry out the plan he'd rehearsed so many times in his head and twice again in the boat itself.

He shipped the oars and reached into his coat pocket.

With trembling fingers, he pulled out a heavy piece of metal and rubbed his thumb across its edge.

The sharpened steel glinted in the autumn moonlight, shining as if from a fire deep within its core.

As if it had a life of its own.

One of the voices — the woman's voice — rose once more, but he closed his mind to it, willing himself not to give in. His hands shaking now, he dropped the glittering steel into the bottom of the trap. The voices shrieking ever louder, he closed and latched the trap's cover.

"No one will ever find you again," he whispered.

The voices heard, and the keening swelled in his head, hammered at his soul, threatened to tear his mind asunder.

"Stop," he whispered, "please stop." But he knew begging would only make it worse.

They would sense his weakness.

They would think they were winning.

They would not win.

Quickly, he threaded the end of the rope first through the frame of the trap, then through the centers of the two cement blocks in the bottom of the boat. Finally, he turned the rope back on itself to secure the free end in a series of half hitches, but the

voices tore at him as he worked, distracting him from what he was doing, and in the cold of the night his hands began to go numb. The rope slipped from his fingers, and he groped in the darkness until he found it again.

He shook himself violently, trying to rid himself of the voices as a dog would a coat full of water. The boat rocked wildly, and for a moment he thought he might pitch over the gunwale into the depths of the lake, but his hand closed on the oarlock at the last moment and he steadied himself. Still trying to shut out the screaming voices, he worked faster, fumbling with the rope, twisting it first one way, then another.

Then at last he was done, and he yanked the last knot so tight he heard himself gasp.

And in that gasp, he heard his own voice.

His last scrap of humanity.

It had been a long time since he'd felt human.

Since he'd had even a memory of who he really was.

The cacophony of screaming voices had long ago drowned out all but the last vestiges of the man he had originally been.

Yet now, with the rope still burning in his fingers, those final vestiges of his humanity gave him strength to resist the commands

of the voices. Keeping the boat carefully balanced, he lifted the crayfish trap and the cement blocks so they were balancing on the gunwale.

Sensing what was about to happen, the voices rose once more, the woman's voice towering over the rest as she roared her fury at what he was doing.

He felt his resolve weaken, and reached for the trap as if to pull it back inboard. Then, in the instant before his fingers closed on the trap's mesh, he found one last scrap of strength. "You . . . will . . . not . . . win," he breathed, and with a quick shove, tipped the trap and the blocks into the water.

The rope followed the blocks overboard, its coils racing into the depths, and he felt his entire body throbbing to the pounding of his heart.

He'd won.

But even as he felt the flush of victory, the rope went taut and he felt it jerk on his waist. Before he could react — before he could reach for the oarlock that had saved him a few moments ago — he plunged over the side and into the freezing water.

Too dark! It had been too dark, and when he'd fumbled with the rope, he'd somehow tied it around himself!

"Too bad," the woman's voice mocked. *"We*

11

told you not to! We told you! But we don't need you. There are others. There will always be others."

Others? Had he not stopped it all? Had he not stopped them forever?

He began tearing at the rope that was bound around his waist, his cold fingers clawing at the wet hemp, but he couldn't even find the knots, let alone untie himself.

He was going down too far, and far too fast. Pressure was building in his ears, a pressure that exploded into a piercing pain, as if an ice pick had been plunged into his head.

He gasped and choked as the dark, cold lake water rushed into his throat.

And now the woman was laughing.

Then, just when he thought it was too late — at the instant when he would have plunged irrevocably into the darkness — he thought he felt the coils around his waist begin to loosen. . . .

CHAPTER 1

The hands on the classroom clock were crawling far too slowly toward the weekend. Eric Brewster fidgeted in his seat as Mr. Smallwood reiterated the English assignment, but Eric wasn't paying much attention. Everybody in class — everybody in school — had spring fever, including the teacher, and Eric was certain that nobody intended to do much homework, any more than Mr. Smallwood expected it would get done. Not tonight, not this weekend, not next week, which was the last week of school before summer vacation.

When the bell rang, Eric was out of his seat, out the door, dodging fast-moving bodies as he made his way to his locker to dump his books. Long summer evenings weren't made for studying, and he was already thinking about the possibilities when Kent Newell started working the combination to the locker next to his. Which meant

13

that Tad Sparks, the third member of the triad that had formed in kindergarten and was still thriving in the next to last year of high school, wouldn't be far behind. When any two of them were together, the third was sure to be close by.

Except in summer, when the Newells and the Sparkses headed for rented summer houses in Wisconsin, while the Brewsters sweated it out in Evanston, just barely north of Chicago, and, where they lived, not quite close enough to Lake Michigan to catch whatever cool breeze the water might conjure up. But maybe this summer would be different. This summer his parents were looking for a summer rental, too. Of course, so far the looking had proved futile. It seemed every house at Phantom Lake had been rented months ago, and the ugly possibility that he might be stuck without his friends for another summer was starting to seem like an even uglier reality.

As usual, Kent Newell read his mind. "Your folks find a house yet?"

Eric shook his head, and memories of the single week he and his parents had spent at the lake with Kent's family last summer rose up to taunt him: fishing, swimming, water-skiing all day; barbecuing fresh trout or steaks outside in the evening while pretend-

14

ing the mosquitoes weren't nearly as bad as they were. Walking into town after supper to get an ice cream cone or just hang out ogling the local girls. Eric had loved it all, and so had his parents, even though all they'd done was sit around in chairs on the lawn or on the dock in front of the Newells' house, just talking.

But this year, with a lot of convincing from Kent's mom, his parents had decided they should rent a house of their own for the summer. At least, Eric's father was convinced.

His mother was a different story. All she kept talking about was how nervous she'd be, all alone in a house in the middle of the woods. Except that it wouldn't be the middle of the woods. It would be on the lake. And she wouldn't be all alone at all. He'd be there, and his sister Marci would be there, and every weekend his father would be there, too.

If his mother stopped dragging her heels, that is, and actually found them a house.

"Your mom's got to find a place, and she needs to do it quick," Kent said.

Eric nodded. "Yeah."

Tad Sparks arrived then, and was greeted with one of Kent's arm punches, which had grown more painful over the last year, since

15

Kent had spurted past six feet and put on twenty pounds, all of which was muscle. "This is the summer," Kent said, grinning slyly at Tad. "I can feel it."

"Feel what?" Tad said.

"You're gonna get laid, man. You're finally going to do it!"

Tad's face reddened as he followed Eric out into the already humid midwestern afternoon.

"Those girls up at the lake are just waiting for you," Kent went on, nudging Eric. "I mean, they are going to be *hot* for you this year. And Eric's gotta be there when you finally give it up, so we've got to get his mom in gear. I mean, there's got to be one house left, doesn't there? A cancellation or something?"

"But it's got to be in The Pines," Tad said. "You've got to make sure it's in The Pines."

Eric sighed. "Right now I don't care where it is, just so it's close to you guys."

"Which means The Pines," Kent said, rolling his eyes.

"We'll go fishing," Tad said.

"You'll dance naked with girls," Kent added, winking at Eric. "There's a dance every Friday night in the pavilion. If Tad can't get laid there, there's no help for him at all."

Eric groaned. "So far all Mom says is she can't find anything. Except I've got a feeling she's not really trying."

Kent Newell's brows arched, and his voice dropped to a conspiratorial level. "Ah, but you see, I've got an ace in the hole."

Eric eyed him. "Yeah? What?"

"*My* mom," Kent declared. "She knows some people up there. Hell, she knows *everybody* up there. And believe me, if there's a place at The Pines, she'll find it. And she'll talk your mom into taking it."

They paused at the corner. "I gotta get home," Tad said. "See you guys later."

"I'm going to go work out," Kent said to Eric. "Want to go to the gym?"

Eric hesitated, then shook his head, his good mood now long gone. If his mother was scared about being up in Wisconsin without his father during the week, then that would be that. And given that his mother was scared of practically everything, the possibility that she'd wind up just refusing to go even if someone did find them a house was all too real. "I think I'll just go home, too," he said.

Once again Kent read his mood. "Ah, who needs the gym," he said, clapping Eric on the shoulder. "Let's grab a Coke, then go over to my house and see if my mom's

found your folks a house yet."

Eric shrugged. Better to hang with Kent right now than go home, where he might well be stuck with his ten-year-old sister all summer, once again spending endless days mowing and trimming the lawn while his mom went out to lunch with her friends and his father worked and Marci would stick to him like glue, constantly asking her ten-year-old's questions while he was thinking his sixteen-year-old's thoughts.

While his friends were at Phantom Lake, fishing and swimming and waterskiing.

And getting laid.

Without him.

Falling in beside Kent, Eric felt the summer already slipping away even though it hadn't yet actually begun.

Merrill Brewster was just turning the last bag of the week's groceries over to Marguerite when the kitchen door slammed open — making Marguerite almost jump out of the maid's uniform she insisted on wearing, even though Merrill had pleaded with her not to. Ellen Newell appeared in the doorway, a grin spread across her face and something hidden behind her back.

"Guess what I have!" Ellen demanded. "You're going to love it."

18

Merrill's eyes narrowed as she ran through the possibilities. With Ellen, everything was always wonderful, and everyone was always going to love everything, so she could be talking about almost anything. Except that whatever it was, was small enough to be held in one hand.

Ellen Newell's hands, of course, were larger than most, and stronger, too. Even though she was nowhere near her son's size, she was just as good an athlete as Kent, and could still beat him at tennis without even breaking a sweat. If Ellen weren't one of her best friends, Merrill knew she could have hated her. As it was, Merrill just held out her hand. "Give," she said.

Rolling her eyes at the other woman's refusal to play a guessing game, Ellen surrendered the contents of her left hand to Merrill, then winked broadly at Marguerite, who was just pulling a carton of yogurt out of a bag. "Better check the expiration date on that," she said. "If it's less than a week from now, Merrill will be afraid she'll poison everyone if she serves it."

"I will not!" Merrill protested. "Besides, I already checked. It'll be okay for another week." Then, as her best friend and her housekeeper shook their heads in despair at what she knew they considered neurotic

overcautiousness, but which she herself thought of as mere common sense, Merrill turned her attention to the sheet of paper Ellen had surrendered.

An e-mail printout, from someone named Rita Henderson.

"She rents houses up at the lake," Ellen explained as Merrill scanned the page. "A house just came on the market this afternoon, it's available for the entire season, and she's holding it for you until five o'clock!"

Merrill looked at the kitchen clock. "It's four o'clock now!"

"Which gives you an hour! Merrill, it's the only chance left! This house has never been rented before, and Rita says she has a dozen people who will snap it up in a second. It's in The Pines, and it's right next door to us! It's perfect!"

Merrill's eyes shifted from the e-mail to Ellen. "Do you know the house?"

"Well, of course I do!" Ellen said, bracing herself to fight off every ridiculous objection Merrill might come up with. "It's called Pinecrest, and it's a fabulous old place. It's been vacant for a while — some legal snafu about the estate of the last owner."

"There's an attachment to this file," Merrill said, her eyes fixing accusingly on Ellen.

"It's a jpeg file, which I assume means it's a picture of the house. Is there a reason you didn't bring that, too?"

Ellen snatched the e-mail back, and for the first time saw the attachment line. "Oh my God, I got so excited at the message I didn't even notice there was a picture. Come on!" Grabbing Merrill's arm, she half dragged the other woman out the kitchen door, down the steps of the back porch, across the large backyard, and through the gate that had been installed years ago, when Kent and Eric had first become friends and Ellen and Merrill had discovered they were as compatible as their sons.

Except that today Ellen was completely excited about a house that Merrill, without knowing anything about it, was already fairly certain she wasn't going to agree to rent. Not, at least, in the hour she had to make up her mind.

Then they were in the Newells' kitchen, and Ellen was at the Mac that sat on the built-in desk that had replaced the table when she'd converted the breakfast nook into her office. *Why not?* Ellen had declared. *I'm not a housewife, anyway — I'm a family CEO, and I need an office.* Now, she was manipulating the mouse with the expertise of a teenager, and a moment later an image

filled the computer screen. "There," she said triumphantly.

Merrill found herself gazing at a photograph of what looked like a haunted house. It was a huge Victorian gothic, and nothing at all like the charming — and comfortably small — lake houses in The Pines that the Newells and the Sparkses had been renting for years.

"Good Lord," she breathed. The house was two stories tall, its roof pierced with gables. Built of granite that had blackened with age, it presented a stern countenance not at all softened by the sweeping front lawn that spread down to the water. Nor was the house the only building on the property; there was a dock and a boathouse, and what looked like what was once a large carriage house.

"Pinecrest was the original house on the lake," Ellen explained. "I think some Milwaukee beer baron built it, and the estate covered the whole south shore. It got split up into what's now The Pines back in the thirties after the beer guy went bust. Anyway, it's been closed up for years, and Rita says they're basically going to rent it this summer, and then put it on the market along about August." She hesitated, then decided there was no reason not to tell Ellen

the whole truth. "The reason they're renting it is so it won't seem unlivable, and you'd have to agree to let Rita show it if someone wants to see it. But not until August."

Merrill gazed at the oddly foreboding facade, tried to imagine what it would be like living in the house.

And keeping it clean, especially if it had to be shown.

"It's big, but it's not unmanageable," Ellen said, reading Merrill's expression. "And imagine the views from the second floor bedroom! Come on, Merrill — this is the chance of a lifetime! And it's just one summer — it's not like you're buying the place!"

Merrill told herself that Ellen was right — that it was a great opportunity, and that if she turned the house down, there wasn't going to be another one. Still, she hesitated. "Let's forward the e-mail to Dan, and I'll call him. But I have to say, I don't think I like it. It's so —" She hesitated, searching for the right word, then shook her head. "I don't know — it looks like a witch's house."

Ellen groaned, then glared at her friend. "You've been afraid of a lot of things over the years, Merrill Brewster. But *witches?* For God's sake!"

As Merrill leaned over the computer and hit the Forward button, the back door burst open and Kent and Eric came in. Kent threw his gym bag toward the dining room table, missed, but didn't bother to pick it up before coming over to see what was on his mother's computer. "Jeez," he breathed as he gazed at the picture. "Pinecrest? They're actually *renting* Pinecrest?"

"What's Pinecrest?" Eric asked. Then his eyes fell on the computer screen and widened. "Jesus — look at that place!"

Instead of responding, Kent looked up at his mother. "So what happened? Did the owner finally show up?"

Ellen's eyes bored into her son, and she tilted her head toward Merrill, but it was already too late.

"Show up?" Merrill repeated. "What are you talking about?"

Kent glanced from his own mother to Eric's, then back to his own, and it was finally Ellen who answered.

"It's no big deal," she said. "The house has been tied up for years because the owner simply vanished." As Merrill started to say something, Ellen held up a hand. "Merrill, I'm telling you, it's nothing for you even to think about. It's just that the owner's boat washed up on shore one

morning years ago, and the assumption has always been that Dr. Darby — he owned Pinecrest — had gone out fishing and fallen overboard. But since they never found his body, they've just had to wait to have him declared legally dead. It's not like he was murdered, or even died in the house or anything like that. So before you start getting all panicky —"

Her words were cut off by the beep of the computer announcing incoming e-mail, and a moment later all four people in the Newells' kitchen were staring at the message from Dan Brewster:

Just called Rita Henderson and took the house. Start packing — we go up the 17th. And I reserved a table for ten at Le Poulet Rouge at 7:30, so call the Sparkses. Might as well celebrate. See you in a couple of hours.

— Dan

Merrill read the message twice.

So the deal was done — Dan had taken the house.

Eric and Kent were high-fiving each other, Ellen was grinning like a Cheshire cat, and Merrill supposed she should be as happy as everyone else. But even as she told herself it

was going to be a wonderful summer, all she could think about was what had happened to the house's owner.

There had to be something else.

Something Ellen wasn't telling her.

People didn't just disappear.

Merrill Brewster tried to concentrate on what Ashley Sparks was saying, but despite the fact that everyone else at the table seemed to think the summer festivities had already begun, her irritation with Dan for renting the house without consulting her was a distraction.

And the irritation itself was fast congealing into a dark anger. What had he been thinking of? She *never* would have taken a house without consulting him!

Dan himself was at one end of the long table, talking golf with Kevin Sparks and Jeff Newell; the three boys had their heads together at the other end of the table; and she was seated in the middle with Marci, Ellen, and Ashley. The division of the genders, she thought. Just like it will be all summer. Ashley had her appointment book open and was talking about the four "girls" taking a day trip from Phantom Lake up into Door County for a binge of antiquing. Merrill made herself smile, nodded, and

agreed that that would be fun.

The problem, though, was that she wasn't at all sure she wanted to leave her own house for the whole summer, and here the rest of them were already planning getaways from their rentals. Is it possible that I'm already homesick? she wondered. But it wasn't just some kind of silly before-the-fact homesickness. She loved her home, loved watching it through the seasons, loved watching the ever-changing gardens she'd spent years planning.

And spending most of every summer executing the new plans she'd made for the garden over the winter.

But this summer she'd have to sit and stare at the lake.

Read exactly the kind of trashy romance novels she hated.

Go shopping with the girls, which she didn't hate at all.

Relax.

It all sounded great in theory, but if it was really going to be that great, why wasn't she looking forward to it?

"Okay, Merrill," she heard Ashley Sparks say, as she put her pen and book aside, folded her arms across her chest, and gazed darkly across the table. "Give. Start with

the list of worries, so we can all get it behind us."

Merrill flushed, forced herself to grin, and quickly searched her mind for something other than the truth. "Okay," she finally said, "how's this for starters: Is there a good grocery store up there? A pharmacy? A clinic in case somebody gets hurt?"

"And an ambulance!" Ellen Newell chimed in. "Don't forget an ambulance."

As everyone at the table started laughing, Jeff Newell chimed in from the far end: "And a hearse, too! Might as well prepare for every eventuality."

"They've got it all," Ashley said. "It's not the wilderness, Merrill. Phantom Lake is a whole town, for heaven's sake."

"They've got a great health food store," Ellen offered.

Jeff Newell's voice rose above his wife's. "If Dan weren't so cheap, the Brewsters would have joined us at the lake years ago. However, better late than never, I say." He raised his wineglass. "Here's to watching Merrill learn to water-ski." Everyone laughed, and Merrill felt her face burn as she realized they all knew there wasn't a chance in the world that she'd risk breaking her neck behind a speeding boat. Even Marci was grinning at her.

"Well, maybe I'll surprise all of you," she said, deciding it was better to go along with the joke than get upset. "I could water-ski!" As the laughter at the table grew louder, she added four more words: "When hell freezes over!"

"Well, I think a summer at Phantom Lake will be good for you," Ashley Sparks said when the laughter finally died away. "Maybe you'll finally realize that ninety-nine percent of the things you worry about never happen."

"But they might," Ellen declared in a voice that almost perfectly mimicked Merrill's.

Merrill waited until the latest wave of laughter started to die, then held up her hand. "It's not just the waterskiing," she said. "What about the plumbing? What about the electricity? My God, we could all drown in darkness, without even any water to put out an electrical fire. Don't you people think about *anything*?" She leaned back in her chair and smiled. "There! Did I leave anything out?"

"Actually, Pinecrest is probably the solidest house —" Kevin Sparks began, but his wife silenced him.

"She was joking, Kevin! *Joking!*"

"But he's right," Ellen Newell said. "Rita Henderson isn't going to rent a house that

29

isn't in perfect condition."

"Any house that's been empty that long has to have something wrong with it," Merrill began. "Empty houses —"

"Aren't always abandoned houses," Ellen Newell cut in.

"It'll work, hon," Dan said, seeing the uncertainty in his wife's eyes. "Jeff and Kevin and I are going to share a float plane and fly up on weekends."

"A plane?" Eric said. "Cool! Can I learn to fly it?"

"Maybe," his father replied in a tone that said no.

And Dan will be alone at home in Evanston all week, Merrill thought, and nobody will be there to clean up after him, and — and I'm being an idiot! she silently declared, breaking into her own thoughts. They're all right. I worry too much about too many things, and it's going to be a great summer, and that's that.

As the waiter came over to take their orders, she raised her glass. "To all of us," she said. "To all of us, and to Phantom Lake, and to a perfect summer." As everyone started to put their glasses to their lips, she added, "And one more thing — to all of you telling me when I'm worrying about nothing and making mountains out of

molehills and trying to protect everyone from everything. This summer, I intend to stop worrying and have a great time."

As everyone clinked their glasses and drank their wine, Merrill decided that maybe the words she'd just uttered in an act of pure bravado weren't as false as they'd sounded to her. Maybe, after all, everything was going to be okay.

Except that so far no one had been able to tell her why Pinecrest's owner had disappeared.

Disappeared without a trace.

As she turned her attention to the menu, all the brave words of a moment ago once again rang as hollow as when she'd first uttered them.

CHAPTER 2

Dan Brewster clicked off the late news, but instead of rising out of his favorite chair immediately, he sat in the dark for a moment, wondering if there was any way of avoiding the anger he'd felt simmering in his wife from the moment he came home that day. But of course there wasn't, and she was right — he shouldn't have taken the house without even consulting her. Still, he wasn't totally in the wrong, either, since he'd assumed when she forwarded him the e-mail that the house was fine with her. But the house wasn't the real problem anyway. The real problem was his wife's fear of practically everything, and she didn't seem to be getting any better. In fact, she seemed to be getting worse, and he was starting to wonder if she might be turning into the kind of agoraphobic who'd wind up never leaving her house.

Deciding he might as well face the music,

he heaved himself out of his chair and moved slowly through the house, turning off the lights and rechecking every door in what had become a habitual response to his wife's paranoia. Except it's not paranoia, he silently corrected himself. She just worries too much.

He climbed the stairs and paused in front of Eric's door, listening to the tapping of his son's keyboard for a moment before rapping on the door, then opening it. "Good night, sport," he said. "Don't be up too late, okay?"

"I'm just online with Kent and Tad," Eric replied, barely glancing away from the glowing monitor on his desk.

"Who you just saw at the restaurant," Dan observed.

"So?" Eric countered, finally grinning at his father. "What's that got to do with it? We're talking about going to the lake."

Dan didn't bother to point out that for the last several hours Eric and his friends had been discussing exactly that topic in person. "Okay, then. Sleep well."

But Eric had already gone back to his computer, offering only a distracted " 'Night" as Dan quietly closed his door.

Across the hall a pink glow from Marci's bedside lamp shone through his daughter's

33

partially open door, and Dan pushed gently on it to see his wife sitting on the edge of Marci's bed.

Tippy, the orange tabby who had adopted Marci three years ago, was nestled under Marci's arm, and Moxie, the West Highland terrier who was supposed to be Eric's dog but had fallen in unrequited love with Tippy the day the cat had appeared, was stretched between Marci's legs, his eyes fixed adoringly on the cat.

Though both animals ignored him, at least Marci seemed pleased to see him.

"Hi, Daddy."

"Hi, yourself, sweetheart."

"Can we take Tippy and Moxie to the lake?"

"Of course." He moved closer to the bed, standing next to Merrill, and put a hand on her shoulder, but pulled it away when he felt her body stiffen. "The whole family's going. Even Marguerite."

Marci grinned happily, and Merrill smoothed a lock of hair from the little girl's forehead, then kissed her. "Okay, now. To sleep with all three of you."

Dan bent over and kissed his daughter, too. "Sweet dreams," he said, clicking off her bedside lamp.

" 'Night, Daddy," Marci said. "Leave the

door open a little bit, okay?"

Dan followed Merrill out of the room and carefully left the door open just enough to leave a reassuring shaft of light running across Marci's floor.

And then, in their bedroom, his wife finally released the anger he'd felt her bottling up all evening.

"I can't believe you rented that house without even consulting me," she said as the latch on their door clicked closed.

Dan put his arms around her and brought her close, feeling her anger in the wooden unresponsiveness of her body. "Come on, honey," he said, using the soothing tone he'd often used to turn a jury that was about to rightly convict one of his clients. "Let's talk about what this is really all about, okay?"

"It's about you renting a house without —" Merrill began, but Dan pressed a gentle forefinger against her lips, silencing her.

"Now, come on," he went on. "Be fair, honey. We've all been wanting to rent a summer place for years, but you've been nervous about it. So we've stayed home. But this year you need to put your fears aside — by next summer, Eric will be working and getting ready to go to college, and if we're ever

going to do this as a family, it's now or never."

He felt her freeze, but then, slowly, her hands reached around his back, and then she was hugging him tightly, pressing herself against him. "You're right," she whispered. "I know you're right. But it's so hard for me."

"I know." His fingers gently stroked the hollow of her back, just where she liked it. "But you want to be a trouper, don't you?"

She leaned back and looked at him, a twinkle in her eye. "I'm still mad at you," she said.

"I know you are," he said, and kissed her.

"You better stop that," she whispered, wriggling closer to him in a manner that belied her words.

Later, as they lay cuddled in bed, Merrill could tell by Dan's breathing that he was on the verge of sleep. "Honey?" she said.

He shifted his weight. "Hmmm?"

"Tell me everything's going to be all right."

He pulled her closer, brought her head to his shoulder, and stroked her hair. "It's going to be better than all right," he whispered. "It's going to be great."

And finally, with her husband's arms

wrapped around her, Merrill put her fears aside.

Yet even when the clock downstairs softly struck three, she hadn't quite drifted into the easy sleep everyone else seemed to find with no trouble at all.

It's me, she decided. It's just the way I am, but I have to get over it. I'm not going to let it spoil the summer. Not for me, and not for my children. For once, I'm not going to be afraid of everything I see.

And finally, as the clock struck three-thirty, she slept.

CHAPTER 3

Rita Henderson checked the first item off her schedule for the morning as she pulled her two-year-old Mercedes out of the Phantom Lake High School parking lot and headed for Pinecrest, certain that Nathan Humphries would find the right crew for the cleanup job that not only had to be done right, but quickly as well. Rita had been cultivating the high school guidance counselor for five years, and today she'd told Humphries she needed the best three boys he could find. The Brewsters were due to arrive in just over a week, and not only did she need the grounds in perfect condition, but she had to open the house, get seven years of musty air out of it, and take an inventory of everything inside.

Pinecrest was going to look its best for the Brewsters, not only because they were friends of at least two of her best summer clients, but because at summer's end she

wanted Hector Darby's heirs to give her the listing to sell the house. Given the market, the commission on that sale alone could keep her going through the rest of the year, with plenty left over to add to the retirement fund she swore to start using every year, but never did.

Being the number one Realtor of the entire region gave her far too much pleasure to simply give up working, even at the age of seventy. Besides, it wasn't really like work anyway, since she loved everything about Phantom Lake. The name, the town, the lake, the people, the seasons — every bit of it. And her job kept her in the middle of all of it.

As she drove over the ancient wooden bridge that crossed Muskrat Creek, she waved to Gerilyn Evans and Carol Stauffer, who were sprawled on a blanket spread out in the park, watching their toddlers trying to catch the squirrels, who in turn were trying to cadge food from Gerilyn and Carol. Farther out in the ornate old pavilion that was built on pilings over the lake itself, the daily chess games had already begun, and Amos Carrier was bent over a board, studying his game with the intensity that Rita reserved only for the analysis of a property she was about to list. And Amos was actu-

ally a year younger than she was.

Unconsciously gunning the engine of the Mercedes, Rita left the park behind and sped toward The Pines, not slowing down until she came to the discreet granite block that marked the entrance. The Pines encompassed two hundred acres of lakefront forest that had been subdivided into ten acre parcels half a century ago, none of which could ever be divided any further, and each of which could never hold more than a single house and "appropriate outbuildings," as the master plan for the development read. Though that plan, of which Rita Henderson heartily disapproved, didn't specify exactly what "appropriate outbuildings" were, it did specifically say that they could not be for "human habitation" except for a guest house that would sleep no more than four people. For the forty years she'd been involved in Phantom Lake real estate, Rita Henderson had been trying — and failing — to find a way to break the master plan for The Pines, and as she calculated the increasing value of the land every year, she also increased her efforts to find a way to cash in on it.

Making a mental note to remind Tim Graves to have his crew trim the overgrown shrubbery around the granite marker, Rita

turned down the road that had once been Pinecrest's private driveway but now gave access to all twenty of the houses scattered through the acreage. Half a mile farther she turned into the long, circular drive that led to Pinecrest itself, and made another mental note, to talk to Tim about getting the trees trimmed. Just cutting back the limbs of the maples lining the drive would brighten the whole place up a bit.

A moment later she came around the last curve in the drive, and the house itself came into view. Pinecrest had always been her favorite house in the whole area, and this morning it looked almost majestic, with its granite walls supporting the gabled slate roof, all of it looking almost as good as the day it was built. Indeed, not only the house, but the carriage house, the boathouse — even the potting shed — had been built the same way, out of carved granite blocks on foundations sunk to the bedrock below the rich topsoil. None of the roofs sagged, none of the porches were even slightly askew.

Still, seven years of emptiness showed everywhere; the detritus of the surrounding forest had blown into the angles of the vaguely Victorian house, built up on the windowsills and accumulated on the steps and the porch, giving the place an air of

abandonment. But once the crew from the high school had swept that away and cleaned out the big stone fountain in front of the house, all that would change.

Rita parked by the front door, scribbled a few notes in the pad she always kept handy for just this sort of occasion, then stepped out of her car. Climbing the six steps that led to the heavy oak front door, she put the key in the lock, turned it, and swung the door open.

Even after the hundred years that the house had stood there, the hinges gave no hint of a squeal, and the door hung true.

Ahead was a marble foyer and vaulted ceilings, beyond which was the living room, its huge picture window perfectly framing a view of the lawn and the lake beyond. As Rita shut the door behind her, the silence of the big house, undisturbed all these years, closed in and she found herself moving noiselessly, as if even a single sound would disturb the tranquility of the place. By the time she got to the living room, though, her notebook was in her hand and she was ready to work.

Pulling all the sheets and dust covers off the furniture, she made a pile of them in the foyer. The furniture seemed to have held up just fine, but of course it had been good

furniture to start with: most of the pieces that weren't original had come from Carol Langstrom's shop in town, and Carol didn't deal in any antiques but the finest.

The kitchen had been updated ten years ago, and its granite countertops and stainless steel sinks still looked essentially brand new, as did the appliances. She ran the water and the garbage disposal, flipped every light switch she could find, and found herself pleasantly surprised: no drips, no leaks, no problems. Not even a burned-out lightbulb.

She continued on through the house, making a note to have the chimneys swept and inspected.

Ditto for the smoke detectors, which didn't fit the decor at all, but without which the house would be unrentable.

Then she went up the big staircase to the four bedrooms and as many baths above, searching for any signs of a leaking roof, or invading raccoons and squirrels.

Nothing — another pleasant surprise.

The bathrooms were in good condition — the toilets flushed, the water pressure was good. No rust came from any of the faucets. She slipped the sheets off the furniture in the bedrooms, pulling aside the heavy draperies and opening the windows in each

of them. The house didn't smell bad, just musty, the way unoccupied houses get. A family of four would change that within a day or two.

The master bedroom looked much the same as the rest of the house; there was a slightly masculine aura about everything, with heavy, dark wood furniture, and hunting prints everywhere. Rita tried all the lights and this time found a bedside lamp missing a bulb.

She made a note.

As she slipped the sheet from the dresser, she found herself looking at a picture of Hector Darby. His eyes, even in the picture, had the same piercing quality they'd had in person, and as she gazed at the photograph, Rita found herself wondering what had really happened to the man. There'd been so many rumors over the years — rumors made up, for the most part, out of whole cloth — and now she wondered if any of them could be true. Indeed, as she looked at the picture, she felt a shiver run through her, as if even from the old photograph, Hector Darby was looking deep inside her, searching for her darkest secrets.

Ridiculous, she told herself. It's just a picture, and all that happened was that he fell out of his boat and drowned. Yet still

she found herself putting the picture away on the top shelf of the closet where none of the Brewsters would have any reason to look for anything.

Finished with the house, Rita went on to have a quick look in the large garage, easily big enough to accommodate three cars in the space where once a collection of carriages, buckboards, and wagons had stood. She decided it needed little more than a good sweeping out, and perhaps some oil on the door hinges, then made a quick tour of the rest of the carriage house. The stalls and the tack room had long ago been converted into workshops and storage spaces. She made as careful an inspection of the grooms' quarters upstairs as she had of the house, then moved on to the boathouse and potting shed.

Less than an hour after she'd arrived, Rita Henderson was finished with her inspection.

Finished, and pleased.

Of course, the inventory would take two full days for both her and her secretary, but at least Darby's personal effects had already been packed up and moved out of the house, even if only into one of the storerooms in the carriage house, which is what she suspected had happened.

But in a week the place would be ready for the Brewsters, and within two weeks the last feeling of mustiness, emptiness, and disuse would be long gone.

And that, Rita knew, would make all the difference later in the summer when it would be time to show the house to prospective buyers.

Empty houses — especially abandoned ones — were hard to sell.

But Pinecrest, once it was filled with fresh air, bright sunlight, and a young family, would sell quickly.

Quickly, and for the high price and commission she intended to get for the old place.

Getting back in her Mercedes, she started the engine, then hesitated, remembering the picture of Hector Darby she'd left on the top shelf of the closet in the master bedroom. Maybe she should take it with her, and give it to the attorney for the doctor's heirs. On the other hand, what was the point, at least right now? If they'd left all the rest of his stuff in boxes in the storerooms, why would they want his picture?

Gunning the engine, Rita sped down the driveway, making one last mental note:

With a load of gravel spread over the

driveway, Pinecrest would be perfect.

Late that afternoon Rita Henderson wasn't feeling nearly as sanguine about Pinecrest as she had a few hours earlier. The three boys Nathan Humphries had sent over were lined up in front of her desk, and as she eyed them dolefully, she decided the counselor might need some counseling of his own.

In all fairness, Ellis Langstrom wasn't a bad choice; he'd at least worked in his mother's antiques store on and off since he was in grade school, and never complained about anything. Adam Mosler and Chris McIvens were something else, though. Neither had ever been known to work any harder than they absolutely had to, and Mosler, particularly, seemed to be in trouble more often than not. Still, beggars couldn't be choosers, and the work needed to be done now, so she turned on her best professional smile.

"Everything you'll need is in the trailer," she said, tilting her head toward the box trailer she had bought five years ago and stocked with every tool any cleanup job could demand, and which was now parked in the drive in front of Pinecrest. "Rakes, brooms, ladders, a couple of saws, leaf

blower, mower. If there's something you need that isn't here, call me and I'll have it brought out to you. There's even a cooler with some bottled water so you won't have to go in the house." She pointed to an open area about twenty yards from the trailer. "Pile everything over there and I'll send someone out to haul it away." When there was no response from the boys, she dropped the smile. "Okay?"

They nodded, and Rita Henderson turned the smile back on.

"Start at the top, with the roofs of all the buildings. Clean out the gutters, make sure there aren't any birds nesting in any of the chimneys, check the slates. And be sure to use a safety line — I don't want to have to find replacements for any of you. Sweep the eaves, and don't leave a single cobweb, then hose off the house." She droned on, giving them detailed instructions on what needed to be done to every building, but knowing she'd have to repeat everything she'd said tomorrow, and the day after that, and every day until the job was done. But at least if she laid it all on them now and they didn't quit, they couldn't start griping later that they hadn't known what they were getting into. "Got all that?" she asked when her recital was finally finished

All three of them nodded, though she was pretty sure only Ellis had paid attention. At any rate, she'd told them.

"Okay," she said. "I'll leave you to it. You'll each get paid a week from tomorrow, and I'll be checking in on you now and then to make sure everything is getting done. Okay?"

More nods.

"Then have fun."

As she walked to her car, she heard the rattle of tools and the first of what she was certain would be a steady stream of grumbling. Still, the boys knew as well as she did how important the summer people were to the town, and Ellis, at least, would do his best. With luck, he'd keep Adam and Chris in line. And, of course, she would show up every day, just when they were least expecting her.

Adam Mosler took a rake from Ellis and leaned it up against a tree. Ellis, standing in the trailer, handed Chris the leaf blower then tossed a coil of electric cord to Adam. "Who wants to start on the roof?" he asked.

"Not me," Adam promptly answered. "I got acrophobia so bad I'd fall off in a second. Besides, you're the one who was so excited about taking this job. You do it."

"Hey, it's money, right?" Ellis shot back. "And I've got no problem going up on the roof, so just give me a hand with the ladder, okay?"

A few minutes later, as Ellis tied one end of a nylon rope to himself and the other around the chimney, Adam took a bow saw and a pair of pruners and went to work on the clutter of dead branches that had fallen from the trees over the last seven years. He knew Ellis was right; he could use the money as much as Ellis, but he was still pissed off about having to work for a bunch of rich people whose kids would arrive in their L.L.Bean clothes with their Jet Skis and speedboats and spend the summer acting like they owned the whole town.

And everybody in it.

He picked up a bunch of branches and hurled them onto the growing pile of trash, his anger at the injustice of it growing steadily. None of those Chicago kids were going to be cleaning up stuff like this — their fathers would just peel off bills from the wads in their pockets and hand over the keys to the Range Rover or the Escalade, or whatever fake sport utility vehicle the rich people were driving this year.

Adam dumped another load of brush onto the pile, and felt a stab of pain as a long

sliver drove deep into the palm of his right hand. Cursing silently, he sat down on the patio and pulled his jackknife out of his pocket, pried the smaller of the two blades open, then realized it wasn't going to work: he was right-handed and he wouldn't be able to get the splinter out himself. "Chris!" he yelled.

A moment later Chris McIvens appeared from behind the greenhouse, pushing a wheelbarrow full of broken glass. He dumped it onto an old tarp they'd found in the trailer and spread out next to the rubbish pile, then inspected Adam's hand. "It's gonna hurt," he said as he took the knife from Adam. "You sure you want me to do it?"

Adam nodded grimly. "I'm only doing this for the money, and I can't do it with a freakin' log in my hand, can I?"

"Okay," Chris said. "Here goes." He poised the blade of the knife over Adam's palm, then carefully sliced through the skin over the sliver as Adam gritted his teeth against the pain. A moment later Chris lifted the fragment of wood out of the open wound, and Adam instantly began sucking on the cut, which, now that the operation was over, didn't really hurt all that much.

"Lucky it wasn't a nail," Chris observed

as he wiped the blade of the jackknife, then closed it and handed it back to Adam. "Coulda gotten lockjaw."

Adam rolled his eyes. "They got shots for that, *idiot.*" Then his eyes moved out past the house and down the lawn toward the lake. Shadows from the forest were creeping quickly across the lawn, the glassy water rippling where the fish were starting their evening feed. If it wasn't for who was going to be living here, this could be a nice place. Then he heard Chris talking to him.

"I was thinking we ought to do something out here."

"Yeah?" Adam asked. "Like what? Mow the lawn in a goddamned diamond pattern?"

Now it was Chris who rolled his eyes. "No, *idiot,*" he said, giving the second word the exact enunciation Adam had used only a moment before. "I meant like we should set a booby-trap or something."

Adam eyed Chris with new respect. "Like what?" he said again.

Chris shrugged. "I don't know yet. There's got to be something. And we've got a whole week to think about it."

The leaf blower suddenly roared to life above them, and a moment later a shower of filth rained down on their heads.

Adam jumped up, shook the moss and dirt out of his hair, and looked up to the roof, but he couldn't see Ellis, and knew Ellis wouldn't hear him over the roar of the blower even if he yelled until he ruptured his larynx. His eyes met Chris's. "Okay," he said. "Let's think of something. But we don't tell Ellis, right?"

Chris nodded, knowing as well as Adam that no matter how harmless whatever they came up with was, Ellis would talk them out of it. So now he and Chris knocked their fists together in a gesture of solidarity — if not actual conspiracy — and went back to work, Chris to the greenhouse, and Adam to cleaning up the yard so it could be mowed.

But now both boys felt an energy about the work that hadn't been there before.

They'd clean this place up, all right. But that wasn't all they'd do.

"Ya ready, boy?"

The words came out of the old man's mouth as little more than an indistinct whisper. Not that it mattered; the old dog's ears had failed three years ago. There wasn't anyone else to talk to, though, so the old man just kept on talking to the dog. Not that there was much to say, either, since the

53

old man's mind had become almost as indistinct as his voice. Nowadays, he only remembered the important things. His name for instance.

Logan.

He still knew his name was Logan, and he knew he had a first name, too. Or at least he'd had one a long time ago, before the bad times.

Now, as the sun began to drop toward the horizon, Logan gently lifted the bony old Labrador and settled him carefully onto a pile of rags in the bottom of the boat near the bow, where the dog could rest his head on the gunwale next to the rough wooden cross Logan had mounted on the boat's bow sometime in the past. If anybody had asked Logan why the cross was there, he wouldn't have been able to say. "Following Jesus," he'd probably have mumbled. "Can't be too careful, can you?" Nobody, however, had ever asked, and even if they had, they wouldn't have paid much attention to his answer.

Except the dog. The dog always listened, and the dog always understood. "Good boy," Logan sighed as he transferred the weight of the animal from his arms to the floorboards of the skiff.

Sensing more than hearing the sound of

his master's voice, the dog managed a thump of his tail as Logan stepped into the boat and used an oar to push off from the shore. As the boat drifted through the cattails and marsh grasses that choked this part of the lake, the dog managed to sit up, his grizzled muzzle lifting so he could fill his nostrils with what little breeze there was.

Logan used one of the oars to pole the boat quietly from its hiding place in the tangle of growth out into the open water thirty yards away.

The dog's head swiveled, his nose pointing directly across the lake toward the small town nestled on the opposite shore, and an eager whine bubbled up from his throat. "Not today, boy," Logan whispered. "We're just watching tonight. Just watching . . . just making sure."

The dog turned its all but totally blind eyes toward his master's voice, and a warm wave of affection — affection mixed with sadness — broke over Logan. The dog wasn't going to be around much longer, and Logan was pretty sure that when the dog died, he'd die, too.

He could keep watch for only so long.

He and the dog could protect things for only so long, and after that someone else would have to keep watch.

But who?

Nobody else knew what he knew.

Nobody else had lived what he had.

Nobody else understood the way things really were.

Nobody.

Nobody but him.

Logan rowed quietly as the setting sun painted the sky a shade of red that made him think of the hell he was certain waited for him on the day he died, and the pines turned to skeletal silhouettes that looked like fingers reaching desperately for salvation.

A salvation that Logan knew was far beyond his reach.

Turning away from the hopelessness of the sky, he pulled slowly on the oars, keeping close to the shoreline as the rowboat cut silently through the water. He could hear the faint putting of idling outboard motors drifting across the lake, and knew that people were still on the water, especially fishermen.

At dusk, though, the chances of his being seen were slim.

The inlet stream was choked with spawning ciscoes, flipping and slapping on the water, and Logan brought his oars in and let the boat drift soundlessly over the top of

them. "S'all right," he whispered. "Not after you. Not tonight, anyway."

Away from the mouth of the stream, he began rowing again, and a few minutes later he came around the end of a point. The house was ahead now, on the far end of the gently curving bay formed by the point he'd just rounded and the next one, but still hidden by the thick woods that bordered its lawn.

Just a few more strokes of the oars and he would be there.

Yet when Pinecrest came into view, Logan sensed that something was different.

Something had changed.

Then, as he shipped the oars to let the boat drift silently, he saw them.

Three boys.

Three boys sitting on the front lawn.

But that wasn't the problem. The problem was the house.

The house was different.

The house looked as if it were somehow expecting something.

As the dog tensed in the bow, the old man dipped the oars once more and turned the boat so the cross mounted in the bow stood between him and the looming stone structures that were Pinecrest.

What was going on?

Had Dr. Darby come back?

No — that was impossible — it couldn't happen!

Could the house have been sold? Were people moving in?

These boys, maybe?

But that could never happen, either.

He couldn't let it happen.

Nobody could ever live here again.

Using the oars so gently there was no sound at all, Logan slipped the boat closer to shore, careful every foot of the way to keep the big wooden cross between himself and the old estate.

The dog sensed his apprehension and shifted restlessly on his nest of rags.

"Easy," Logan whispered. "It's okay. We just have to figure out what to do. That's all. Just figure it out."

He peered through the failing light as the three boys rose from the lawn, dusted off their pants, and started toward the house. A moment later they were gone, disappearing toward the driveway. Soundlessly, Logan moved forward until the bow of the boat touched the shore.

He could feel it now — someone was coming to live in the house.

And it was as if the house itself were excited.

As if the evil knew it was about to be released once more.

Logan crossed himself and backed away with the oars, keeping the cross in the bow between himself and Pinecrest until the entire property began fading into the gathering night then finally disappeared behind the point around which he had come only a few minutes ago.

"It's all going to start up again," he whispered, as much to himself as to the dog.

Falling silent, he turned the skiff toward home and rowed into the dark of the night.

CHAPTER 4

The day had finally arrived, and after the first excitement of leaving Evanston behind for the summer died away, and the first three of the six hours it took to drive to Phantom Lake passed, a silence had fallen over the Brewsters.

Merrill was paging through what she thought of as her mental worry book, examining each item, assessing its current threat level. In the privacy of her own mind, she rarely lowered a level, while publicly she did her best never to admit they existed at all.

Did her best, but usually failed.

Still, for today at least, the calm of the rolling Wisconsin farmland was lulling her a bit, and none of the current worries seemed overwhelming.

If she'd left the iron on — had she turned it on at all? — Marguerite would turn it off and put it away.

If she'd forgotten sunscreen, there would be a store in Phantom Lake where she could buy some.

If she'd failed to pay a bill, Dan would take care of it when he got home.

If she forgot to pack — What? What could she have possibly forgotten to pack? The LX470 was filled to the brim with suitcases, pet carriers, blow-up water toys, kids, and . . . *stuff*. Stuff that would probably prove useless, but that she couldn't resist taking along anyway. There were even bags of food wedged in the backseat between the kids, in the unlikely event that somehow supermarkets didn't exist in northern Wisconsin.

She tried not to think about Dan, who sat beside her, driving — that he'd be gone all week every week.

In the backseat directly behind her mother, Marci was counting animals. She'd already decided Wisconsin was the best place she'd ever seen, and had spent the first hours trying to make up her mind whether to marry a farmer when she grew up or have her own farm, which would be filled with cows and horses and pigs, and no brothers at all. But then, as the farms began to give way to wilderness and she caught glimpses of deer — and even what she was sure was a wolf, though Eric said it

was just a dog — she decided maybe she'd be a forest ranger instead and live in a log cabin in the woods, with wild animals coming to eat every day.

Finally, she turned around to check on Tippy and Moxie, and found both of them sleeping happily in their carriers, Moxie burrowed deep into the towels in his cage, and Tippy sprawled out on top of her own nest.

Satisfied that the cat and dog were doing fine, she went back to her count, adding one more deer and a squirrel to her list, and trying to decide if the dead possum they'd passed a little while ago counted.

Eric, next to Marci, was listening to his iPod, tapping out rhythms on his knees, anticipating the summer with far more excitement than he would admit to anyone, let alone his parents and sister. When the trip began a few hours ago, the sun had already been too hot, the heaviness of the air telling him the afternoon was going to be miserable. If it was already that hot and sticky just in June, what was August going to be like? But he wasn't going to be there in August, so what did it matter?

He was going to be in northern Wisconsin, in a house on Phantom Lake, with his best friends only a few hundred yards away,

spending every single day swimming and fishing and waterskiing and hiking.

About the time they reached the halfway point, black clouds began rolling in from the west. The highway was already thick with SUVs and big pickup trucks pulling boats and camping trailers, and Dan Brewster unconsciously sat up a little straighter in the driver's seat, took a tighter grip on the steering wheel, and hoped his wife wouldn't notice the deteriorating weather.

A couple of heavy raindrops splatted onto the windshield, and Dan shot Merrill a quick glance. Sure enough, she'd noticed.

Merrill pretended she hadn't seen Dan's quick glance at her, but of course she had. And of course just the few drops of rain that hit the car had started a whole new page in the worry book. *What if it rained all summer? What if the roof of the house leaked? What if . . .*

Dan flicked on the wipers. "Looks like we're in for a little weather," he said. He took another quick glance at Merrill, then spoke again, doing his best to inject as much optimism into his voice as he could summon, given that every car coming toward them had not only their wipers on, but their headlights as well. "Probably just a squall — won't last more than a couple minutes."

The sky grew darker.

As Dan slowed and turned on his own headlights, he could feel Merrill struggling not to say anything, and began laying mental odds on how long she would be able to hold out. Given the blinding mist all the SUVs with their boats and trailers were throwing at the windshield, it wouldn't be long.

Merrill gazed out her side window, determined to concentrate on the scenery around her rather than the increasingly threatening sky above her, but then a bolt of lightning seared the sky, thunder clapped right behind it, and the clouds seemed to open up. Dan switched the wipers to full speed, but they couldn't keep up with the torrent of rain, and suddenly the road ahead was nothing more than a blur of red taillights.

"Maybe we should stop," Merrill said.

"Wow," Eric said from the backseat. "Almost thirty seconds since it started raining. I didn't think you'd be able to hold out more than ten."

"I was figuring fifteen," Dan said, giving Merrill a quick wink. "Thirty's a new record, isn't it?"

Merrill tried to glower but couldn't quite pull it off. "Oh, shut up, both of you. All I meant was —"

But before she could finish, they heard a strange popping sound and the car swerved. Marci squealed, and Merrill reached out to brace herself against the dashboard. Dan, though, simply pressed gently on the brake, flicked on the turn signal, then eased the now thumping SUV across a lane of traffic and onto the shoulder of the highway. "Flat tire," he announced as he switched on the hazard lights.

He turned off the engine, set the emergency brake, and for a moment the family sat silently in the car, listening to the rain pound the roof.

"So here are our options," Dan said, breaking the silence a moment before his wife could. "Either Eric and I change the tire, or we call Lexus and let them do it." He peered out through the streaming windshield. "And Lord only knows how long it will take them to get here in this weather." He unbuckled his seat belt.

"For God's sake, Dan, wait a few minutes," Merrill pleaded, reading her husband's intentions perfectly. "Maybe it'll blow over."

Dan stared at her, his eyes twinkling. "Do I know you? Since when do you ever think something's going to blow over? Who are you, and what have you done with my wife?"

"You could both drown out there!" Merrill protested, ignoring the jibe as Dan opened the door a crack.

"Ready, Eric?" he asked. "On three. One . . . two . . . three."

Both doors opened and both male Brewsters leaped out into the deluge. A moment later the back hatch was opened and Dan fumbled with the latch to the small tool storage compartment, cursing softly as one of the suitcases toppled out onto the shoulder of the road. Then he released the catch that allowed the spare tire to drop from its spot below the floorboards onto the pavement beneath the car.

As Marci and Merrill did their best to watch what was going on through the downpour, Eric and Dan jacked up the car, manhandled the flat off, put the spare on, and maneuvered the bad tire into position in the compartment beneath the Lexus. Twenty minutes after they'd begun, they were finished.

Soaked to the skin, but finished.

"There's a towel in the red tote," Merrill told Marci. "The one behind Tippy's cage."

Marci got it out, handed it to her brother, then found another one for her father.

"Wasn't that fun?" Dan asked Eric as he toweled off as much water as he could.

"Makes you want to be a mechanic, doesn't it?"

"Or not," Eric responded. "Think I'll still plan on college, at least for now."

"Remind me to drop that tire off as soon as we get to Phantom Lake," Dan said.

"I don't know —" Merrill began.

"Don't know what?" Dan asked.

Merrill frowned, and glanced out at the continuing downpour. "Maybe this whole thing is a bad idea. Maybe we should just turn around —"

"Mom!" Eric said. "Come on!"

"It's just a flat tire, honey," Dan said quietly. "And it's fixed, and the storm will blow over. It's going to be a great summer, so just relax, okay?" He started the car and eased his way back into traffic, and five minutes later the storm was over as suddenly as it had come upon them. The sun came out and the sky was clear and deep blue as far north as any of them could see. "See?" Dan said. "A beautiful day."

"I'm hungry," Marci said. "And Moxie needs to tinkle."

"How much farther?" Eric asked.

"A couple more hours," Dan said, giving Merrill a smile. "We'll stop for lunch at the first spot we come to, okay?"

Merrill smiled back and nodded.

Two more hours — three, including lunch — and summer would officially begin.

Rita Henderson turned the key in the massive oak door of Pinecrest, picked up the vase of wildflowers Camilla Bonds had delivered to the doorstep earlier in the day, and carried it inside, setting the arrangement in the most natural place — the center of the round mahogany table in the foyer. Stepping back, she eyed the blossoms critically and decided they were perfect.

Next came the fruit basket Camilla had also delivered, which went into the living room.

As always happened, Rita was instantly distracted by the view of the lake framed by the living room window, and for a moment she simply stood still, gazing at the panorama before her.

Two bald eagles soared over the water, fishing. The lake twinkled and sparkled in the sun, and a cloudless sky hung over it all like a turquoise dome. No matter how many times she saw it, she never tired of the view, and now she took a few moments just to savor it before turning her attention back to the task at hand.

She set the basket of fruit on the coffee table, adjusted it until it was perfect, then

took a long and very careful look around the room, which, though she would never admit it to anyone, she had never imagined could look this inviting.

Margie Haines's cleaning crew had aired the old house out to the point where barely a trace of mildew remained. In fact, the room smelled good, the lemon oil she had instructed Margie to use on every inch of wood in the house giving the whole place a fresh scent. Knowing Margie's girls would have done their job, but climbing the stairs anyway just to check, she found the bathrooms spotless, with fresh towels on every bar.

Brand new linens were on the beds, along with equally new pillows and quilts.

The kitchen had been stocked with good quality cookware, dinnerware, flatware, and everything else a renter could need, and in Rita's car a bag of groceries was still waiting to be brought in. She'd brought coffee, filters, cream, sugar, milk, and two kinds of cereal — the works. Along with the fruit basket, there would be plenty of food to see the Brewsters through until they could stock up.

Moving outside, Rita was forced to admit that the boys had done a better job of cleaning up the grounds than she had imagined

they would. The greenhouse was tidy, if not perfect, and the lawn was mown short and was vibrantly green. The terrace had been swept, as had the patio near the boathouse, where new sand had been put in the fire pit and a good supply of well-dried wood and kindling placed in a neat stack nearby. The chairs ringing the fire pit had been freshly painted, and new cushions were on their seats. The dock was in, with several new planks replacing old ones that had rotted out over the years of disuse, and two ducks and a throng of ducklings were using the dock for sunbathing, and possibly the ducklings' first diving lesson.

Ellis, Adam, and Chris had earned their money and a good tip on top of it, and Rita made a mental note to called Nate Humphries and give them a glowing recommendation. By the time she was back in the house with the groceries, she'd already thought of two other places that needed some work, and if they wanted the job, she could keep them busy all summer.

The grandfather clock in the hallway came to life as she stepped through the front door again, striking two. Rita checked her watch: two, right on the dot. The old clock seemed to be working just fine, which meant she needed to get the groceries unpacked and

put away and get back to the office; the Brewsters were due sometime around three.

As she drove out of the driveway a few minutes later, she cast one last glance back at the house. The roof was clean, the driveway freshly graveled, the old fountain scrubbed and actually operating. Rita passed through the gates, turned left, and headed back to her office, satisfied that the house was ready, never noticing the old rowboat with the strange cross mounted in its bow that had been all but hidden in the shadows near the boathouse.

CHAPTER 5

Though Eric had spent a week at Phantom Lake last summer, everything looked a lot better to him this year. Since the storm had cleared, the weather had steadily improved, and there wasn't a trace of the humidity that had begun smothering Evanston as they left that morning. But it wasn't just the weather that was different; the whole village looked better than he remembered it. Coming in from the south, they'd turned right at the flashing red light — which he didn't remember at all — and half a mile farther they were in the center of town.

To the right was the village itself; to the left, a long narrow park lay between the road and the lakeshore, widening out at the eastern end to a large pavilion built over the water. The buildings of the village, brightly painted and in perfect condition, seemed lifted directly out of a previous century.

"It looks like a movie set," his father said.

"Maybe it is," his mother replied. "Maybe they only put it up for the summer, and stow it away in a warehouse somewhere all winter."

"Can they do that?" Marci piped, then reddened as Eric rolled his eyes and groaned. "Well, they *could,* couldn't they?" she insisted in a futile attempt at recovery.

"I was only kidding, honey," her mother said.

Turning back to the window, Eric gazed out at the summer party going on in the park. The swimming beach to the west of the pavilion was filled with splashing kids and dogs, and every kid in the water seemed to have either an air mattress or some other kind of floating toy. Farther out, beyond a rope limiting the swimming area, ski boats crisscrossed the water, some of them with Jet Skis playing in their wake. There were enough blankets spread out on the huge expanse of grass behind the beach to turn the lawn into a giant patchwork quilt, and at least half a dozen barbecue fires were burning.

And there were girls everywhere. In the water, on the lawn, and on the bike path at the edge of the road. "I love it here," Eric heard Marci say, but he didn't take his eyes off a blonde on Rollerblades who was wear-

ing nothing but a bikini.

"So do I," he replied, with a note in his voice that made his mother turn around, see what he was looking at, and glare at him.

"Eyes front," she said.

"It doesn't hurt to look," his father said.

"Look at what?" Marci asked.

"Never you mind," her mother said. Then, to distract the little girl from pushing the subject, she pointed out the window on the other side of the car. "Look, an old-fashioned ice cream shop!"

They were in the heart of the village now, and next to the ice cream and candy stores they saw a small movie theater, a cluster of T-shirt shops, and a fish-'n'-chips restaurant. In the next block there was a tiny pharmacy, a dry cleaner, a small courtyard complex that seemed to be occupied by nothing but art galleries and gift shops, and an antiques store.

Merrill pointed to the next street. "Third Street," she said. "That's where we turn, and the real estate office should be on the right."

Seconds after Dan slid the Lexus into a spot right in front of Rita Henderson's office, the entire family was on the sidewalk, stretching. "This'll take a few minutes," Dan told Eric. "Why don't you and your

74

sister take Moxie for a walk?"

Marci got the leash out of the car, opened the dog's kennel cab, and had just hooked the leash onto Moxie's collar when the dog managed to slip past her and leap to the sidewalk. Moxie shook himself violently, then strained at his leash, trying to search out a patch of grass. Marci half ran after him, with Eric after her, the two of them following the dog toward the park. No sooner had they crossed Main Street than Moxie started to sniff, decided on a spot, and squatted.

As Eric and Marci waited for the dog to finish his business, two boys about Eric's age stopped on the sidewalk a few yards from them and stared at him.

Eric hesitated. Did he know them? Had he met them last summer when he was staying with the Newells? "Hi," he finally said, "I'm Eric Brewster."

"Who cares?" the shorter boy replied.

The uncertainty on Eric's face dissolved into a frown. "Is something wrong?"

The taller one shrugged. "Dunno yet."

Moxie, no longer squatting, was crouched at Marci's feet, a low warning growl rumbling in his throat.

"C'mon, Marce," Eric said. "Let's —"

Before he could finish, the bigger of the

two boys spoke. "Aren't you going to pick up after your dog?" he demanded, his eyes narrowing as they fixed on Eric.

Eric saw Marci looking up at him, and was sure she was about to burst into tears. "We're going to pick it up," he said. "I've just got to get a bag."

"Yeah, right," the other one said. "If you were gonna pick it up, you'd've brought a bag."

"We just got here —" Eric began.

"Who even wants you here at all?" the boy interrupted. "So pick up after your damn dog, okay?"

A knot of anger forming in his belly, Eric took his handkerchief out of his back pocket and picked up Moxie's droppings. As the two boys watched, he looked around, spotted a trash barrel, and dropped them in. Not wanting to put the handkerchief back in his pocket, he dropped that into the barrel, too, and turned back toward the two boys.

They were already halfway down the block, laughing loudly. As Eric watched, one of them wheeled around and raised a hand, middle finger erect. "Asshole!" he yelled. "Who needs you? Why don't you go back wherever you came from?"

Eric's jaw clenched but he said nothing.

Still he knew he wouldn't forget. The faces of those two boys — and their words — were burned into his memory. And if they wanted to start something —

He cut the thought off, telling himself they weren't going to start anything. Yet even as he tried to reassure himself, he knew he was wrong.

They *had* started something, and if they pushed it, Eric knew what would happen. Kent would want to finish it, and in the end, he and Tad — neither of whom had ever been much for fighting — would back him up.

And the two boys, whoever they were, would be sorry.

A half hour later the Brewsters drove around the last bend in the freshly graveled drive and found themselves staring at the dark stone facade of Pinecrest.

Merrill gasped in spite of herself. "Good lord," she breathed. "Are you sure this is it?" But even as she asked, she knew this was, indeed, the house they'd rented, though it looked much larger than it had in the e-mail attachment.

"Of course this is it," Eric said from the backseat. In fact, he'd seen it before, if only briefly, and only from down at the lake, last

summer. "Pretty great house, huh?"

"It looks like a witch's house," Marci declared, her voice quavering and her words echoing what Merrill had been thinking as she'd gazed at the house at the end of the drive. Her first impression when she saw it on Ellen Newell's computer was that the house looked haunted. As she gazed at it now, nothing she saw changed that impression; in fact, it looked even more like a haunted house.

"Don't be an idiot, Marci," Eric said, glaring at his sister. "It's cool. In fact, this might be the coolest house on the lake."

"Either way, it's ours for the summer," Dan Brewster said as he braked the car to a stop at the foot of the front steps. "Let's unload the car, unpack everything, and then go exploring."

He popped the hatch and turned off the engine. Eric was out of the car before the engine even died, but Merrill was still gazing through the window.

"This is way too much house for the rent," she said, still making no move to get out of the car. "Something's wrong."

"Nothing's wrong," Dan assured her. "We got a good deal is all."

Merrill wasn't convinced of that, and as Dan and Marci got out of the car, she sat

where she was, staring at the big stone house.

"If you're not even going to get out of the car, then you better let me have the key," Dan said.

Finally, Merrill got out and handed the key to him — a single key on a pewter Phantom Lake Real Estate fob — as if the act of relinquishing it might somehow absolve her of any responsibility for having rented the house.

Eric was already unloading boxes and suitcases and taking them up to the front porch. "C'mon, you two," Dan said to his wife and daughter. "Marci, why don't you help Tippy and Moxie get adjusted?"

Merrill followed him to the front door, and when it swung wide, she gasped again. But this time it wasn't so much at the house itself, but at the panorama of the lake visible from where they stood.

"Wow," Eric said. Picking up two suitcases, he stepped into the foyer — actually more like an enormous entry hall — and gazed in awe at the ornately carved mahogany woodwork, the marble floors, and the arched ceilings.

"Okay," Dan conceded, grinning at Merrill. "You're right. It's a lot bigger than it looked, and a lot fancier. But the rent's been

paid, and they can't raise it. So let's just count our blessings and spend the summer pretending it's a hundred years ago and we own a railroad or something. S'pose there's a butler hiding around here somewhere?"

Merrill advanced to the foot of the broad staircase leading to the second floor. "Why don't you go up and find your room," she said to Marci.

The little girl shook her head. "I don't want to go up there by myself." She had let Moxie and Tippy out of their cages, and now snapped the leash on Moxie's collar to keep him close, while Tippy began prowling through the room, sniffing everything, her tail twitching. "Tippy doesn't like it here," Marci announced.

"Tippy's just poking around," Dan countered. "She'll love it as soon as she gets used to it. And so will you."

Eric grabbed both his bags and managed to hold one of his sister's suitcases under his right arm. "C'mon, Marci," he said. "Let's go up and find our rooms. First one upstairs gets first pick."

Unable to resist her brother's challenge, Marci dashed up to the top of the stairs and pushed open the first door she came to.

The room behind the door was larger than their living room in Evanston, and even the

view of the lake through the large picture window couldn't overshadow the huge four-poster bed that dominated the room. It was hung with heavy brocade curtains in a pattern of dark reds and greens that matched not only the bedspread, but also the drapes at the window, the cloth on the tables, the wallpaper, and even the carpet. A life-size painting of a man on a horse occupied most of one wall, and another was dominated by two enormous dressers made of the same heavily carved mahogany as the four-poster bed. Two large chairs and a chaise occupied the ample space left unfilled by the bed and its nightstands.

"Pretty neat, huh?" Eric said.

"I hate it," she replied. "It's too big."

"Don't be a baby. It's a great room!" Eric dropped her suitcase on the floor, then took his own bags to a room that differed from Marci's only in its hues: in this room there were dark blues and browns, rather than the reds and greens of Marci's. He went back out to the car for his parents' suitcases, took them up to the master suite, and set them at the foot of their bed, which was even larger than the four-posters in his and Marci's rooms.

Going back downstairs again, he helped his father bring the last load of groceries

into the kitchen, set them down, and started toward the door. "Okay if I go down to the boathouse?"

"Sure," Dan replied, starting to unpack the bags onto the huge counters where a chef and two assistants could easily have worked. "Maybe I'll be down in a few minutes."

Eric went through the dining room and out the patio door into the late afternoon sun. Shadows stretched across the lawn, and as he started toward the lake, crows cawed from the trees.

The old stone boathouse had the same architectural style as the main house, tall and faintly gothic. There was a small terrace in front of its main door, a few large windows set into its walls, and it was situated near the dock, with double doors that opened directly onto the lake. He and Kent had tried to look in the window when he was here last summer, but the windows were too dirty to see through and the door had been padlocked. Now, the windows were washed, chairs were on the terrace, the weeds had been replaced by flowering plants in an old oak wine barrel, and the padlock on the door was gone.

Inside, the boathouse was dark and silent, the only noise coming from the lapping of

the water against the old and badly dented aluminum boat that was utterly unlike the gleaming wooden runabout that Eric had been picturing. In the corners of the concrete walkway that ran around the three walls of the boathouse were old tackle boxes, crawfish traps, and some tools that he didn't recognize. A sling hoist with enormous wheels for raising the boat had been installed in the center of the structure, and seemed the only modern thing to have entered the boathouse in a hundred years.

The cover was off the boat's outboard engine, and a tool kit was open on the boat seat.

A fouled spark plug lay on a rag on the floor of the boat.

Clearly, he wouldn't be taking the boat out tonight.

The kitchen was bright and roomy, if a little dated, but surprisingly well stocked with better cookware than she had at home, and by the time Merrill had put all the groceries away, she was starting to feel better about the place. Except that the big kitchen and formal dining room seemed to demand something a lot more elaborate for dinner than the hot dogs and potato salad she had planned.

"I'm going to start the barbecue," Dan said as he came out of the pantry, heading toward the dining room and the terrace beyond. But the expression in his wife's eyes stopped him. "Are you okay?"

Merrill did her best to hide her misgivings, though she knew her whole family — and especially her husband — could read her like a book. "Oh, it's nothing, really," she sighed. "Just another of my stupid thoughts."

"Which one this time?" Dan asked, coming over and slipping his arms around her.

Merrill sighed ruefully. "A really stupid one. Namely, should we be eating hot dogs and potato salad in that gorgeous dining room?"

Dan laughed out loud. "Absolutely not. So we won't — we'll eat our hot dogs and potato salad out on the terrace like the civilized people we are. And we'll save the dining room for formal occasions."

"I don't intend to have any formal occasions," Merrill protested.

"Then we'll ignore the dining room," Dan told her. "That's the nice thing about renting — since we don't own the house, we don't have to use any of the rooms we don't like. It's not like we bought the place and have to get our money's worth. So figure

out which rooms you like, and ignore the rest."

He continued out of the kitchen, and Merrill took the hot dogs from the refrigerator and cut the package open. If only it were that simple, she thought. Then she decided to put her worries aside. He's right, she told herself. All I have to do is ignore the rooms I don't like. It's only for the summer. It's not forever.

Marci stood at the window with Moxie in her arms and watched Eric enter the boathouse, then turned around to eye her room suspiciously.

She didn't want to open the closet.

She didn't want to open the dresser drawers.

She didn't want to unpack.

And she didn't want to be a baby, either. But her room at home had all her stuffed animals, and her books, and her pictures and all the rest of her stuff. She liked her bed, which wasn't nearly as big as the one in this room, but was just the right size for her. And she liked her bedspread, and her heart-shaped pillow, and the bird feeder that hung in the oak tree outside her bedroom window. Her room at home was *hers,* and

this wasn't. This was someone else's room. Someone old.

And she hated it.

She knew she'd never get used to it.

Setting Moxie on the floor, she started casting around in her mind for some way not to have to sleep there.

Maybe she could sleep with her mom when her dad went back to Evanston for the week.

And maybe she could go back home with him and just come up on weekends, too.

Or maybe —

A movement in the reflected image of the lake in the mirror over the dresser against the far wall caught her eye, and Marci turned back to the window itself. Something *was* moving out there, barely visible through the tops of the trees, almost out of sight.

She shifted her gaze to the boathouse, but Eric was still inside.

Then she saw an old rowboat creep slowly into view, with something standing straight upright at its front end. As she watched, the boat slowly turned until it was pointing straight at the house, and now Marci could see that the thing in front was a big cross, like the one on top of the steeple of the Methodist church where she went to Sunday

school. And sitting behind the cross, holding the oars, was an old man with a long beard.

And he was staring right at her.

Marci held still for a second or two as the man's eyes seemed to bore right inside her, then she wheeled around and ran toward the stairs, already yelling. "Mom! Mom!"

Merrill met her at the bottom of the stairs, and as Marci flew into her mother's arms, the tears that had been building up since she first saw this horrible house finally spilled over.

"There's a man outside in a boat. A boat with a big cross in it! And he was staring at me."

Merrill hugged her daughter and smoothed her hair. "A boat with a cross?" she asked, then turned and looked through the living room and its picture window, down the front lawn to the water.

She could see nothing but a ski boat speeding across the far side of the lake. "Honey, what are you talking about?"

"I hate it here!" Marci wailed. "I want to go home!"

Merrill knelt down and put her arms around the sobbing child. "It's just going to take some getting used to," she said. "We're

going to have a wonderful summer, you'll see." Sitting on the stairs, she pulled Marci close. "We're going to have a barbecue tonight, then Daddy will build a campfire and we'll toast marshmallows and make s'mores. That'll be fun, won't it?" Marci sniffled, then nodded, her face still buried in her mother's shoulder. "And tomorrow we'll go to town and do something even more fun. Girl stuff."

Marci's sobs slowed and turned to hiccups.

"Okay?"

Marci nodded.

"You want to help me set the table?"

Marci nodded again.

The crisis over, Merrill kissed her daughter on the forehead and dried the tears from her cheeks, and a moment later Moxie, who had followed Marci down the stairs, jumped up into Marci's lap and licked her face.

"That's my girl," Merrill said, taking her hand and leading her toward the dining room and the kitchen beyond.

Just before she passed through the dining room door she glanced once more through the living room window, but everything seemed normal, just as before.

A boat with a cross? What on earth could Marci have been talking about? But what-

ever it was, it was gone now.

Or had never been there at all.

CHAPTER 6

Cherie Stevens rinsed out the sticky bar towel after wiping down the tables in the ice cream shop for the last time and was about to hang it on the faucet to dry when she heard the ding of the door chime.

She'd forgotten to lock the door, and now another customer was coming in. But when she saw who it was, the frown she'd been preparing morphed into something that wasn't quite a smile but wasn't quite not one, either.

"Hey, Cherie," Adam Mosler said as he swung onto a stool at the counter. "Can I get a root beer float?"

"We close at eight on Sundays," Cherie said, tipping her head toward the clock on the wall that clearly read eight-seventeen, and wondering why she didn't like Adam as much as he liked her. But she knew why, really. Though he was cute, he could also be a complete jerk. Tonight, though, he didn't

seem to be in one of his completely jerky moods. In fact, he seemed to be in a good mood.

"Okay," he said. "So you're off work?"

"Soon as I sweep up." Cherie dried her hands, lifted one of the little wrought-iron chairs, and put it upside down on top of one of the round tables.

"I can do that," Adam said, sliding off the stool and beginning to take care of the rest of the chairs while she started sweeping. "What are you doing after you're done?"

Cherie shrugged. "I don't know — going home, I guess."

"I was going to take my dad's boat over to the south shore."

Cherie glanced at him, then shrugged again. "It's kind of late."

"Not too late," Adam countered, putting the last chair on a table. "And it's really nice out. Come with me."

"What's on the south shore?" Cherie asked, her mistrust of his motives clear in her voice.

Adam spread his hands dismissively. "Nothing. It's just a ride." Sensing her indecision, Adam put on his best smile — the one he'd practiced in the mirror to the point where it looked utterly uncalculated. "Come on. It's really warm tonight."

"Let me call my mom," Cherie said, not quite agreeing, but handing him the broom as she went to the phone behind the counter.

Adam finished the sweeping while he listened to Cherie's side of the conversation and heard her promising not to be home late.

"Good night, Mr. Evans," Cherie called into the back room as she hung up the phone. "See you tomorrow."

Adam opened the door and held it for her.

"You smell good," he said as she passed.

Cherie rolled her eyes. "I stink like sour ice cream, and we both know it. Don't push it, or I'll walk home right now. In fact, maybe I'll just do that anyway."

"Come on!" Adam pleaded. "Jeez, can't a guy say anything nice to you at all?"

Relenting, Cherie let him lead her down to the marina near the pavilion. Rows of boats floated quietly in the dusk. A few low-flying birds were still out scooping insects from the surface of the water, a few fish were still competing with the birds for the insects, and somewhere across the lake a loon was calling.

Everything else was quiet, their footfalls sounding unnaturally loud on the wooden planks of the dock. In a slip near the end,

Adam's father's bass boat was gassed up in preparation for an early morning fishing expedition. Adam helped Cherie in, then cast off the lines, jumped into the driver's seat, turned the key, and fired up the powerful outboard. Switching on the running lights, he backed the boat out of the slip. "Ready, babe?" he asked.

Cherie decided to ignore the patronizing endearment rather than just shove Adam overboard, and pulled her long hair up into a ponytail, fastening it with a rubber band as Adam idled out of the marina. When they were past the buoy holding the NO WAKE sign, he pushed up on the throttle. The bow rose in the water as the stern dropped, and a moment later they had leveled on the plane and were flying across the glassy surface of the lake.

I called her "babe" and she didn't even tell me to shut up! Adam thought. This was going to be the summer he nailed Cherie Stevens.

Cherie leaned back in the seat and concentrated on the feel of the evening air on her face as they ran across the lake. The town was behind them now, and the first of the summer houses were coming into view, spread along the south shore of the lake like

jewels on a necklace. Lights were on in some of the houses already, and if Adam were just idling along instead of racing like a nutcase, she knew she'd be able to hear people laughing on patios and around the small fires burning in the outdoor hearths.

Someday she wanted to live in one of these big lakefront houses; the only question was which one, since every one of them always looked even more beautiful to her than the last.

Adam took a sweeping turn along the shore, then abruptly decelerated the engine. The boat instantly dropped back, its own wake quickly overtaking it and threatening to swamp it.

"Adam!" Cherie cried as the wake splashed on her back. "What are you doing?" He turned off the running lights. Cherie braced herself, ready to push his hand away the moment he tried to touch her. A boat ride was one thing, but if he thought she was going to —

"Look!" Adam whispered, his voice breaking her thought as he pointed toward the shore.

"At what?" Cherie asked, her voice dropping to match his.

"Pinecrest," Adam whispered. "Look. Someone's living there."

Sure enough, lights were on all over the big house, which had been dark for so many years Cherie could barely remember when it was anything but a dark silhouette against the night sky. Tonight, though, it glowed beautifully in the twilight.

As Adam idled the boat up to the Pinecrest dock, Cherie reached out and grabbed one of the cleats. Adam turned off the motor. "I heard that someone rented it for the summer," she whispered. "But I didn't know they were already here."

"Want to go see if we can look in the windows?"

Cherie glared at him in the fast-fading light. "You mean like be a Peeping Tom? You're weird, Adam!"

Ignoring her words, he stood up on the seat of the boat and peered up the front lawn toward the big house, and suddenly Cherie understood. "Is that why we came out here? So you could spy on these people?"

"You don't have to spy," said a voice from the shadows by the boathouse. "Just come to the door and knock."

Nearly losing his balance at the unexpected sound, Adam sat heavily back down, rocking the boat violently.

"Hi," Cherie said. "We didn't mean any-

thing." She glanced at Adam. "At least *I* didn't."

A boy about her own age emerged from the shadows and walked down the dock, a spark plug in one hand, a greasy rag in the other.

"I'm Eric Brewster," the boy said.

"Hi. I'm Cherie Stevens. This is Adam Mosler."

"I already know him," Adam said. "His dog shits all over town."

Cherie turned and stared at Adam. "Excuse me?"

"It was only once," Eric explained. "And I picked it up. With my handkerchief. Your friend didn't think I'd come back if I went for one of those plastic bags."

Cherie gasped. "So you used your *handkerchief?*"

Eric shrugged, doing his best to act if it had been no big deal. "Well, it was either that or have your friend and his buddies take a swing at me. And handkerchiefs don't cost much."

Abruptly, Adam twisted the key in the ignition, and the outboard roared back to life.

"Hey," Cherie said, raising her voice over the rumble of the engine. "Doesn't Kent Newell stay out here somewhere?"

"Yeah," Eric said. "Next door."

"Fuckin' coneheads," Adam muttered.

"Coneheads?" Eric repeated, finally shifting his gaze from Cherie to Adam.

"It's stupid," Cherie said. "Because you're in The Pines, you know? Pinecones? Coneheads? And it's from some old movie they did a hundred years ago." She turned her head to stare directly at Adam. "It's stupid."

Adam, his jaw tightening, said nothing. He put the motor in gear, but Cherie tightened her grip on the cleat that was bolted to the dock. "Do you know about the dances at the pavilion on Friday nights?" she asked.

Eric nodded. "Kent and Tad told me."

"They start next week," she said. "Maybe I'll see you there."

Adam pushed harder on the throttle, and Cherie was finally forced to let go of the cleat. She waved back at Eric, who stood silently on the dock, watching them go.

"You were pretty rude," she said to Adam when they were far enough from the dock so Eric wouldn't hear her.

"Why did you tell him about the dances?" Adam shot back, ignoring her question.

"Why shouldn't I?" Cherie countered. "They're for everybody, aren't they? And

besides, he already knew. So what's the big deal?"

"They're summer people," Adam said, his voice taking on a hard edge. "They're coneheads. I hate them."

"Well, I think you're an idiot," Cherie said, sitting up straight in the stern and crossing her arms over her chest. "And I thought he was cute."

Adam threw the throttle forward so quickly that the boat's surge almost tossed Cherie into the lake. When they got back to the dock, she ignored his hand, easily stepping out of the boat unassisted.

"And I think I can walk myself home, too," she said, turning and marching up the dock before Adam had even the first of the boat's four lines secured to the dock.

Furious, he watched her go. This wasn't how the evening was supposed to end, and he knew whose fault it was.

Eric Brewster's.

And if he had anything to do with it, Eric Brewster would get exactly what was coming to him.

That, and maybe a whole lot more.

The old dog moved restlessly in the bottom of the boat, and the even older man put a quieting hand on his flank. "Shhh," he said

gently to the animal, who settled down with a tired sigh.

Logan parted the branches of the over-hanging willow he had slipped into when the loud fishing boat came charging around the point from town. It was a good thing, too. Yes, it was a good thing, because a boy had been in the boathouse, and he hadn't known that.

Hadn't known that at all.

But now, peering between the willow branches, he could see the faint light of the bare bulb in the boathouse, and as he watched, it went out. A moment later the boy closed the boathouse door behind him and walked up the lawn toward the house.

Logan waited a few more minutes, then quietly rowed around the overhanging tree just far enough so he could see up the lawn to the house.

The old mansion was ablaze with light; a warm, yellow light.

The house looked happy.

And if the house was happy, then the evil was angry.

"Mercy," Logan breathed softly, his eyes shifting from the house in the distance to the cross he'd mounted in the bow of his boat. "May the Lord have mercy on us all."

He bowed his head and prayed silently for

a moment, then looked up again. But what was he supposed to do now?

Keep watching — that was it! Keep watching, and see what happens!

Then maybe he'd know what to do — maybe the answer would come into his head like answers sometimes did.

But the answer, when it came, would be bad.

He was pretty sure of that.

In fact, he knew it.

Sighing almost as tiredly as the dog had a moment ago, Logan quietly dipped the oars into the water and brought the boat right up to the shore at the edge of the property. He secured the bow line to a branch and touched the dog on the head to reassure him, then stepped out into the shallow water and moved slowly up the bank.

He edged up the property, staying out of the light, keeping to the shadows of the trees.

Making sure he was invisible.

Soon he was close enough to the house to see people inside, and the sight of them drew him on.

His heart began to pound, and his head throbbed. He tried to turn back, tried to go no closer than he already was, but he couldn't help himself. He wanted — he *had*

— to see what they were doing inside.

And who they were.

There was a boy inside, he knew that.

But who else?

As he edged yet closer to the house, he glanced over toward the carriage house that seemed almost like it was trying to hide behind the larger building. But it looked all right — dark and safe, although even from here he could feel the pull.

But it was all right.

He could resist, at least for now.

For now, he was safe.

But he couldn't resist the family inside the big house.

He crossed the lawn to the steps, slipped silently up onto the terrace, and peered in through the big living room windows.

A fire burned in the fireplace.

He remembered another fire burning in that fireplace.

There was a woman reading in Dr. Darby's leather chair in front of that fireplace.

He remembered Dr. Darby reading in that chair.

As Logan watched, a little girl appeared, carrying a bowl of popcorn.

No! No little girls! No boys, no little girls!

Danger . . . so much danger.

It was happening again. It was all going to

start again! Soon!

Logan put his hands to his head, pressing hard. There was something he was supposed to do — something in case this very thing happened.

But what?

He couldn't remember!

A little white dog started to bark and jump at the window a few feet from where he was standing.

Panicked, Logan backed away from the window, then turned and ran back into the woods, making his way as quickly as he could down to the water.

Down to the water, and his boat.

His heart still pounding and his head still throbbing, Logan untied the line from the tree, got into the boat, and shoved off.

Careful to keep the big wooden cross on his prow between himself and the house, he backed slowly and silently away, until he was completely out of sight of the evil.

But out of its sight, he knew, didn't mean he was away from its influence.

Away from its force.

"Mercy," he whispered once more.

Praying silently, he began to row home.

"What's the matter with Moxie?" Merrill asked, looking up from her book.

"Something's out there," Marci said, her eyes narrowing as she gazed at the blackness beyond the window.

"Nothing's out there," Eric said, coming in from the dining room with a piece of pie, which he was piling on top of the s'more he'd already eaten. The dog was still scratching at the window and whining to get out, and though he'd just said there was nothing out there, Eric wondered if maybe Adam Mosler had decided to come back and do what he'd heard him suggesting to Cherie earlier. Except Adam Mosler hadn't had time to get all the way to town and back, and Eric was pretty sure that whatever Adam had in mind, Cherie wouldn't be willing to go along with it.

"Go take a look, okay?" his father asked, emerging from the den at the far end of the living room, which could be closed off with a set of sliding doors. "Set your mom and sister's minds at rest."

"Probably a raccoon or something," Eric said. "I better put his leash on him, or he'll get himself in trouble."

"Moxie could beat up a raccoon," Marci insisted.

"Yeah, right," Eric said, snapping the leash onto the dog's collar. "And Tippy could bring down a deer."

"I didn't *say* that," Marci shot back, injecting as much scorn into her voice as she could summon. "But I bet she could," she whispered as her brother opened the door and stepped out onto the terrace.

"Bet she couldn't," Eric tossed back. Glancing around and seeing no glowing eyes, he bent down and released the dog from the leash. "Sic 'em, Mox."

The dog ran barking down the lawn toward the lake.

Eric stood on the patio, gazing out into the night. The moon was just rising, and the light on the horizon threw the pine trees into silhouette and reflected in a faint silver tinge on the water's surface. The whole world seemed to be turning black and silver.

Then, from off in the distance, Eric heard the creak of an oarlock, and he saw a glittering splash of water. As his eyes adjusted from the brightness of the house, he thought he could see the faint form of a boat disappearing into the darkness. But almost as soon as it was there, it was gone.

Moxie continued to bark for another moment or two, then fell silent, and Eric could barely make him out, squatting at the edge of the lake. Finished with his business, the dog gave one more bark, then ran back up to Eric.

"Got that out of your system?" Eric asked, and picking the little dog up, carried him back inside the house. "Whatever it was, Mighty Moxie chased it off," he announced.

But later, as he was going to bed, Eric found himself gazing out the window at the lake, searching once more for the boat he thought he'd seen.

Where had it come from? It hadn't been there earlier, when he was talking to Cherie just before he came in for a piece of pie.

Or maybe he hadn't seen it at all.

Except he had.

He knew he had.

The memory of Eric Brewster was as vivid in Cherie Stevens's mind as she turned the corner onto Spruce Street and started up the last block toward her house as it had been when she'd walked away from the Moslers' boat, leaving Adam to tie it up himself.

Adam Mosler! How could she ever have thought that he might actually qualify as a boyfriend? Although to be absolutely fair, until tonight she hadn't realized just how much of a jerk he could be.

But Eric Brewster — now, he was something else. Even in the fading light of dusk she'd seen how cute he was, and though she

105

hadn't been quite able to tell for sure, she was still certain his eyes were blue. And not just any old blue, either, but the exact shade of turquoise that was her favorite color. All during the walk home from the marina — all eight blocks of it — she'd replayed the short conversation she'd had with Eric. He was so different from the boys at Phantom Lake, and the way he'd refused to rise to Adam's bait — or sink to his level — was so perfect. And she could just imagine how Adam and whoever had been with him must have treated Eric. But who had it been? Probably Chris McIvens, who could be just as much of a creep as Adam.

Cherie glanced at her watch as she came to her house, and quickened her step as she realized how late it had gotten. Seeing her father sprawled out on the couch with a beer in his hand, she braced herself for whatever mood he might be in.

Or whatever mood the beer had put him in.

" 'Bout time you got yourself home," Al Stevens growled as she opened the screen door and stepped into the living room. "Where you been?"

"Out with Adam Mosler. I called. Didn't Mom tell you?"

"Your mother's gone to work — it's late."

He glared balefully at her. "Too late for you to be out with a boy."

"It's not that late, Dad," Cherie began. "It's summer —"

"Don't matter," he cut in, his eyes shifting back to the TV. "Get yourself to bed."

Cherie opened her mouth to argue, then thought better of it. "Okay. I'm sorry." Going to her room, she took off her blue and white striped uniform, checked the closet to make sure she had a fresh one for tomorrow, then tossed the one she'd just taken off into the hamper. She dropped a thin nightie over her head, went down the hall to the bathroom to wash and cream her face and brush her teeth, then flopped onto her bed and called Kayla Banks, intending to tell her every detail of her encounter with Eric Brewster.

Kayla's cell phone rang seven times before a sleepy voice spoke. "Hello?"

"Were you asleep?"

"Yeah, I guess," Kayla sighed. "What time is it?"

"Not that late," Cherie told her. "Listen — I met the guy whose family rented Pinecrest. His name's Eric Brewster, and he's cute! I mean, like, *really* cute."

Abruptly, the sleep was gone from Kayla's voice. "Where? How'd you meet him?"

"I went for a ride with Adam in his dad's boat, and we pulled up to the Pinecrest dock."

"Adam Mosler?" Kayla asked. "Why were you out with him? You always said he was a jerk."

"Don't ask," Cherie groaned. "He *is* a jerk. But I told Eric about the dances in the pavilion, and he's going to come and bring Kent and Tad. You know, the guys from last year?"

"I remember Kent," Kayla said. "He called me once last fall after he got home."

"He did? How come you never told me?"

"Because he only called once. Besides, who cares? I'm with Chris now, anyway."

"But —" Cherie began, but before she could say another word, her bedroom door swung open and her father loomed in the hallway.

"To *sleep,* Cherie," he said.

As his eyes fixed on her, Cherie pulled the bedspread over the thin nightie that was all that covered her body. "I gotta go," she said to Kayla. "I'll call you tomorrow."

"Okay. 'Night."

" 'Night." As she folded the cell phone and set it on the nightstand she kept her eyes on her father. How much beer had he drunk? "It was just Kayla," she said. "I'm

going to sleep now, okay?"

Her father hesitated, and for a horrible moment Cherie was afraid he was going to come in and try to kiss her good night, getting his beery breath all over her pillow. But then he nodded, grunted a good-night that was reduced to a single almost unintelligible syllable, and closed the door.

Cherie clicked off her bedside lamp and slid under the bedspread and sheet. The crickets outside her bedroom window were the loudest she'd heard all summer, and every few seconds a frog croaked from the little pond down the road.

She wondered if Eric was listening to the crickets, too.

And she wondered if he was thinking about her the way she was thinking about him.

Logan threaded his boat through the tangle of cattails and willow branches as easily in the near-total darkness as he would have in full daylight, bringing the prow so gently to rest in the narrow channel that served as its berth that he barely felt it at all. Securing the bow line to a dead tree, he carefully lifted his old dog out of the boat and set him on the shore.

The dog staggered for a moment, found

its footing, and followed behind Logan as he moved through the thick brush to the cabin that was completely invisible from the lake, though it was barely two hundred yards from the shore.

Logan's feet felt heavy as he slogged along the path, and by the time they came to the cabin door, he was out of breath. The sack he carried, though only half full of the things he'd scavenged from the Dumpsters in town, felt heavy enough to stretch his arm.

He shouldered open the door and set the bag on the battered folding table he'd rescued from the dump so long ago he couldn't even remember when, fixing its broken leg with someone's discarded cane.

Home.

Safe.

Except he wasn't safe.

He would never be safe again.

Logan lit the stub of a candle that had half melted into a jar lid and set it on top of a stack of boxes so old they were starting to fall apart, held upright only by their contents. The light threw flickering shadows around the old trapper's shack, and for a moment Logan could almost imagine that he'd drifted back a century or two and was coming home from a night on the traplines

rather than another night of keeping watch on the lake.

The one-winged crow he'd found in the marsh a few years back squawked, hopped from his perch by the window to the box, and started tearing at the bag with its beak.

"Greedy critter, aren't you," Logan muttered, snatching the bag away as quickly as he could, but not quickly enough to avoid the bird's angry jab. "Dog first," he said, nursing his injured finger for a moment.

The ancient dog had collapsed on his jumble of rags in the corner. Logan squatted down and opened the bag. The old Labrador's nose twitched at the scent of scraps of half-eaten hamburgers he'd found in the Dumpster behind the drive-in, and piece by piece Logan hand-fed the dog. As the animal ate, Logan's eyes fixed blearily on the stack of boxes. "Keep the papers," he muttered softly. "That's what Dr. Darby said, isn't it? Keep all the papers."

So he'd kept them, and every now and then, as the years had passed by, he'd looked through them. There were all kinds of old papers in the boxes. Some of them came from Dr. Darby's own files, but that wasn't all there was. There were files from the hospital Logan himself had been in so long ago, after the trouble.

That was how he always thought about what had happened: the trouble.

The story of the trouble was in the boxes, too. The third box, the one with the yellow label that had finally fallen off a couple of years ago. Or maybe longer. But that was the box — it had all the newspapers in it, and the papers from the lawyers, and from the court, and then from the hospital where they'd put him.

Even now he wasn't sure how Dr. Darby had collected all of it, and Dr. Darby hadn't ever told him, either.

Before he was finished feeding the dog, the crow had dropped down to the floor and was pecking bits of meat and bun out of Logan's hand, off the floor, anyplace he could get to, even right out of the old dog's mouth.

"Why'd he want me to keep them?" Logan muttered. Maybe he should just burn the whole lot of them. But Dr. Darby had told him not to, told him that if he burned the papers, or threw them in the lake, or tried to get rid of them at all, they'd come and take him back to the hospital.

Logan didn't want to go back to the hospital. The hospital had been even worse than living out here in the old trapper's shack all by himself. So he'd done what Dr.

Darby told him to do, except for one thing.

The stuff in the old carriage house.

He should have gotten rid of it a long time ago, right after Dr. Darby —

— after Dr. Darby left, he finished, unable even in his own mind to think too much about what might have actually happened to Dr. Darby.

Dr. Darby had told him to do it. The very last time he'd seen Dr. Darby — at least he was pretty sure it was the last time, but there were things he just couldn't remember very well — things he didn't want to remember, Dr. Darby had told him — so maybe the last time he remembered wasn't really the last time he'd seen Dr. Darby.

But he remembered what Dr. Darby had told him. *Keep the boxes. But don't let anybody find the things in the back room.*

And so far, no one had. But no one had come to Pinecrest, either.

But now there were people there, and he wasn't sure what to do.

Logan stroked the old dog's head until the dog sighed and put his gray muzzle down on his paws. "I'll do my best," Logan said softly. "It's all anyone can do, isn't it?" The dog whined softly, and Logan nodded as if the animal had just confirmed his words. "And maybe nothing will happen,"

he went on.

The dog closed his eyes and relaxed into sleep, and Logan knew he should go to sleep, too. It was late, and he was tired, and before long another morning would be here. But he couldn't sleep — not tonight.

Tonight he had to look in the box — the box he hated most of all.

The box that held the story he still, even after all these years, couldn't quite remember.

The story of why they'd put him in Central State Hospital.

He knew the story, of course. He must have read it a hundred times — maybe a thousand.

And he knew the story was true.

Knew it when he relived it in his dreams, and woke up with his fingers flexing as if they were still around the girl's neck like they had been in the dream.

But when he was awake, it was like the girl didn't exist at all, and he couldn't see her face, or feel her body, or feel his fingers sinking into the flesh of her neck.

He'd told people he remembered. He'd told the doctors, and the lawyers, and even Dr. Darby, that he remembered.

But all he actually remembered was what he'd read.

What he'd read, and how he felt when he was at Pinecrest.

When he was close to the carriage house, where all the things were stored.

All the things he was supposed to guard, and keep anyone from finding.

The things that drew him, pulled at him, whispered to him in the night.

As they were whispering now, barely audible, nothing more than faint voices at the edge of his consciousness.

"No!" The word burst out of Logan's mouth like an explosion, startling the crow so badly that it leaped into the air, its single wing flapping madly, only to drop back to the floor a moment later, eyeing Logan balefully.

Even the dog, deaf for years, stirred slightly, and Logan scratched his ear to settle him down once more.

Only when the dog was once again sleeping peacefully did Logan move across the floor to his own bed, which was little more than a nest of tattered blankets on a worn mattress that lay in a corner of the tiny cabin. He held his head and rocked back and forth, trying to get the whispering to stop before the voices became clear and spoke to him distinctly.

Because once the voices started, once he

began listening to them, bad things started
to happen.

CHAPTER 7

Merrill went over the shopping list in her head one more time as she pulled into the parking lot to pick Marci up from the Summer Fun program that the Phantom Lake Elementary School was running, and that Marci had reluctantly agreed to try for the day.

"But if I hate it, I don't have to go back, okay?" the little girl had insisted for what seemed like the hundredth time when Merrill had dropped her off two hours ago. Merrill had gotten the message loud and clear that Marci fully intended to hate Summer Fun no matter what might be going on, but at least she'd given it a chance.

In the two hours she'd had to herself since then, Merrill had gotten better acquainted with the town. She had been to the grocery store — which was far better stocked than she'd anticipated — picked up the hot dogs and steaks at Vern's Butcher Shop, browsed

through the bookstore, found two art galleries that actually had decent things in them, and picked up all the odds and ends that were either missing from the house or she'd forgotten to pack. The rear of the Lexus was almost as jammed as it had been nearly a week ago, when they'd driven up from Evanston, and there was far more food than she'd need tonight when the Sparkses and the Newells arrived.

All that was left after picking up Marci was a stop at the hardware store to get some citronella candles.

As she braked the car to a stop at exactly the place she'd dropped Marci off two hours ago, she braced herself for her daughter's recitation of her objections to Summer Fun. But when Marci jumped into the car, her first words were the opposite of what Merrill had prepared for.

"Guess what, Mom? I get to be in the Fourth of July parade!" Merrill gaped at her daughter in utter shock, but Marci barely noticed. "We're going to do a red, white, and blue float, with flags and everything, and we have to start working on it Monday. It's going to be made out of tissue paper and, listen to this: I get to be the Statue of Liberty! Can you take Krissy and me shopping?"

"Who's Krissy?" Merrill asked, as Marci paused for a breath.

"She's my *friend!*" Marci replied, giving her mother the kind of scornful look only a ten-year-old can muster. "So can you? Take us shopping? We need to get stuff to make my costume."

"That's wonderful news, honey. Of course we can go shopping. We'll go next week."

"And can I go over to Krissy's house tomorrow?"

A wave of relief broke over Merrill as she put the car in gear and made the right turn down Main Street. "Shouldn't be a problem," she said once they were safely on the road. "So what do you think?" she asked as she scanned the block for the hardware store. "Did Dad and Eric get the boat running yet?"

Marci rolled her eyes. "Dad said that they don't know what they're doing."

Merrill pulled into a diagonal parking spot directly in front of the kind of old-fashioned hardware store that hadn't existed at home for as long as she could remember, feeling like she'd somehow slipped back at least half a century in time. "Want to come in?"

As Marci slid out of the car, Merrill scanned the window of the antiques shop next to the hardware store and stopped

short, her eyes fixing on a floor lamp with a stained-glass shade — exactly the kind she'd been looking for to finish Dan's study at home. She backed up two steps and looked at the sign on the store.

CAROL'S ANTIQUES

"Let's stop in here for a minute, okay?" She pulled the door open and Marci followed her into the small shop's air-conditioned interior. While Marci headed for a case filled with ancient dolls in faded dresses, Merrill went directly to the lamp.

Up close it was even better; Dan would love it.

"Hi," a cheerful voice said from behind her. "Can I help you?"

Merrill turned to see a smartly dressed woman about her own age whose smile actually seemed genuine rather than pasted on to impress a possible customer. "I just love this lamp," she said, realizing too late that she'd just undercut her bargaining position.

"Isn't it something?" the woman asked. "It just came in yesterday." She moved closer, holding out her hand. "I'm Carol Langstrom."

"Merrill Brewster. That's my daughter

Marci drooling over the dolls."

"Up for the summer?" Carol asked, putting on her reading glasses and peering at the tag on the lamp.

"Yes. We're staying at Pinecrest."

"Pinecrest? Really?" Carol took her glasses off and looked again at Merrill.

Merrill cocked her head. "You sound surprised."

"I *am* surprised. I didn't think it would be for rent."

Merrill's brow creased slightly. "Why not?"

Suddenly, Carol Langstrom looked uncomfortable. "Well, it's just that Dr. Darby was an odd sort of man." As Merrill's frown deepened, Carol Langstrom spoke more quickly. "It's not that I disliked him. I didn't. No one did. In fact, he was very well respected in town. And certainly one of my best customers — practically everything in Pinecrest came through my shop."

Merrill's puzzlement deepened. "Then what's the problem?" she pressed as Marci wandered back from the doll display.

"Oh, mostly it was probably small-town rumor," Carol Langstrom replied. "And perhaps I misspoke — it wasn't so much that Dr. Darby was odd as much as it was his interests that were —" She hesitated,

121

then spread her hands in a helpless gesture. "Well, they were *odd.* He worked with the criminally insane down at Central. You know, Central State Hospital? From what I've heard, he was doing some kind of experiments on some of his patients. New kinds of treatment or something, I suppose. But then to have him disappear like that! At the time, the stories were just incredible! I heard that one of his patients murdered him, and I heard that his experiments made him go crazy himself. I don't know — it was all just so strange. Kind of creepy, you know?"

Now Merrill was barely listening as some of Carol Langstrom's words echoed in her mind.

. . . *creepy* . . .

. . . *experiments* . . .

. . . *criminally insane* . . .

What had really happened at Pinecrest?

Merrill's mouth went dry, and she suddenly found she couldn't think of a thing to say to Carol Langstrom. For a moment she felt lightheaded, dizzy, almost afraid she'd faint. She put a hand out to steady herself against an oak armoire.

"Do you know Ashley Sparks?" she heard Carol Langstrom asking, and her head began to clear. "Ashley is a longtime cus-

tomer of mine. She could tell you about Dr. Darby."

Suddenly, Merrill found herself acutely aware that not only she, but a very wide-eyed Marci, was taking in every word that Carol was saying. "Well," she finally said, clearing her throat and deliberately trying to break the mood and change the subject, but not so obviously that Marci would see the ploy, "Pinecrest is a beautiful house, and we're enjoying ourselves very much." She put her hand on Marci's shoulder, trusting that Carol Langstrom would get the message. "And tonight we're having a barbecue." She squeezed Marci's shoulder. "Aren't we, sweetheart?" She herded her daughter toward the door. "And I'm serious about that lamp!"

"Then I'll hold it for you," Carol said. "See you soon."

Merrill stepped out onto Main Street, and now Phantom Lake didn't seem quite as delightful as it had only a few minutes earlier.

How could her friends not have told her what Carol Langstrom just had?

And how was she going to stay in a house where who-knows-what took place?

She walked quickly back to the car, foregoing the candles, already organizing her

predeparture packing in her head.

Then, as she started the car, she realized that neither she nor any of her family were going anywhere. They were going to be at Pinecrest for the summer, and no matter what Carol Langstrom had told her — or how she had let her imagination run away with her — she was once more looking for trouble where there was none.

She was being stupid, she told herself, and it had to stop. Right here, and right now.

"Mom?" Marci said as they started back to The Pines. "Do you think Dr. Darby was really murdered in our house?"

"Of course not, honey," Merrill said. "And I'm sorry you heard what Mrs. Langstrom said. Nobody knows what happened to him. It was a long time ago, and it's certainly nothing you need to worry about."

And if he had been murdered in the house, Merrill thought, we wouldn't tell you, because then you'd be afraid, and you'd have nightmares.

Which, she realized, was exactly why nobody had told *her* about the history of Pinecrest.

But now it was too late. Marci would be having nightmares.

And she wouldn't be the only one.

■ ■ ■ ■

Dan Brewster knelt on the concrete apron in the boathouse, leaned awkwardly over the old outboard engine, bracing himself with one hand while clutching a rusty screwdriver in the other, and twisted the set screw on the choke a quarter of a turn. "Try that."

Eric pumped the bulb on the hose that led from the three-gallon gas tank under the seat to the motor, then gripped the starter cord and pulled hard.

The ancient motor coughed out a plume of blue smoke, putted a couple of times, then died, leaving Dan coughing and choking. "Almost," he gasped as the smoke cleared. "Choke it a little, try it again, and if it catches, give it just a little gas."

Eric adjusted the choke and gave another pull. The little engine caught on the second try and began a tentative putt. Very carefully, Eric twisted the grip on the handle; the engine raced for a second, then threatened to die again. He quickly backed off on the throttle, and the engine coughed, then settled into an uncertain, irregular putting.

The motor was running, albeit roughly, and a great plume of exhaust was rising

from the boat's stern and quickly filling the boathouse.

"Not bad for a lawyer who flunked auto shop, huh?" Dan crowed, rolling back on his heels and holding up his hand in a clumsy attempt at a high-five. Eric managed to make his own palm meet his father's, then sat on the small seat at the boat's stern and began adjusting the choke and the throttle until finally the engine warmed up enough to settle into a smooth — and almost smokeless — idle.

"Let's take 'er out for a spin," Dan said. "Blow some of the carbon out of the cylinders."

Eric replaced the cover on the outboard. "Do we have time to fish?"

Dan checked his watch. "Don't see why not, at least for an hour or so." He scanned the boathouse, but the only fishing rod he saw was covered with cobwebs, and even from where he stood, he could see that the reel was corroded to the point of uselessness. "Why don't you check the garage for tackle? I'll take a look in the basement of the house." He cocked his head, gazing uncertainly at the boat. "Think we can risk shutting that thing off?"

"It's all warmed up," Eric replied. "It'll be fine."

Eric shut off the motor, climbed out of the boat, and headed toward the garage while his father started up the lawn toward the house. But even as he approached the old carriage house, he glanced back at the boathouse, still barely able to believe they'd actually managed to fix the old engine.

The boat — the *running* boat — meant freedom. Eric didn't have a car, nor was he old enough to drive one even if he did, but he knew that no license was required to drive a boat, which meant he could go to town — or anywhere else on the lake — whenever he wanted.

He could go to the dances at the pavilion that Cherie had told him about, without having to either walk or — worse — have his mother drop him off or pick him up. The boat might not be as nice or as fast as the one Adam Mosler had been in, but if he cleaned it up, it wouldn't be half bad. And already he could see Cherie Stevens sitting in the bow, her hair blowing in the wind as he took her out for a twilight ride.

The image still bright in his head, Eric turned back to the carriage house. One of the garage doors stood open, and he stepped into the gloom of its interior, snapped on the bare lightbulb that hung from one of the rafters, and looked around for any sign

of fishing rods. All he found, though, were some old jumper cables hanging from a nail, an old hydraulic jack whose orange paint was all but gone, and a collection of fan belts and old inner tubes that he was sure wouldn't go on any car built in the last forty years.

There was also a coiled, but rotting, water hose and some old lawn tools.

But the garage was only a small part of the old carriage house, and Eric shut off the overhead light, closed the door, and began exploring. On the side of the structure that faced away from the house, he found several doors, one of which opened onto a small foyer at the bottom of stairs that led to the old grooms' quarters above. Another door led into what must have once been a stable with enough stalls for half a dozen horses, but the stalls had long since been converted to other uses. At the back was the former tack room, still with a few old bits and bridles hanging on its walls. There was a long workbench backed by a pegboard full of tools, but still no sign of fishing tackle.

He moved on, coming to another door. Pulling it open, he found a room filled with a jumble of old furniture and boxes that looked as if they were about ready to split open.

He stepped into the room, gazing at the furniture. He could tell that some of the pieces were old — there was a mahogany table with a deep patina that told him it was at least a hundred years old, but some, like a chest whose white paint was chipped and stained, didn't appear all that old, and looked like it must have been junk even when it was new.

But what was it doing in here? Some of the furniture looked like it belonged in the house, but what about the rest? The stuff like the white chest?

Could it have been hauled down from upstairs, where the grooms used to live?

Moving slowly through the room, Eric let his hands brush over the pieces, his fingers almost tingling as they touched the surfaces. Most of them felt just like what they were — old wood. But some of them —

"Eric!" His dad's voice jerked him out of his reverie, and even through the walls of the carriage house he could hear that his father was angry.

"Coming," he yelled, his voice echoing oddly in the small room, though furniture and boxes crowded the floor. He quickly threaded his way out, closed the storeroom door behind him, and left the building, closing the outer door as well.

His father was standing in the driveway, a tackle box in one hand, two rods in the other. "Where have you been?" he demanded.

Eric cocked his head. "Looking for tackle," he said.

His father snorted. "It was in the basement — I found it half an hour ago. And I've been yelling for you ever since! Have you suddenly gone deaf?"

"Half an hour?" Eric echoed, staring at his father in disbelief. "I just went in there a couple minutes ago —"

"It wasn't a couple of minutes ago. It was —" He raised his wrist and looked pointedly at his watch. "— exactly thirty-two minutes ago. And Jeff Newell just called. They're going to be here in less than an hour, so if we're going to take that boat out, we've got to do it and get back so I can start the barbecue."

"I'm sorry," Eric said, his head suddenly swimming. "I can't believe I was in there —"

"Daydreaming!" his father finished for him. "So if we're going, let's go. Come on."

Eric took the poles from his father and followed him down to the boathouse. *Half an hour? He'd been in that storeroom for half an hour?* It didn't seem possible.

Dan stepped into the boat, set the tackle box on the middle seat, laid the rods on the floor, then sat in the bow. A moment later Eric had settled in the stern.

The motor started on the first pull, and as Eric released the stern line from its cleat, his father untied the bow line. Putting the engine in gear, Eric nosed the little skiff out of the boathouse.

As his father opened the tackle box and began searching through the jumble of hooks, lures, and sinkers inside, Eric headed onto the lake, but found himself turning to look back at the old carriage house.

Half an hour? He'd been inside for half an hour?

Even now it seemed he hadn't been in the place more than five minutes. Ten at the most. He'd taken a quick look in the garage and the workshop — it couldn't have taken more than two minutes. Then he'd gone into the storeroom and —

— and suddenly he couldn't quite remember what he'd been doing. Just looking at stuff.

And touching some of it.

The fingers of his right hand tingled slightly at the memory of it.

But that was all.

And it had been only a few minutes — he felt sure!

Except that now, as he gazed at the carriage house that was growing smaller as they motored out onto the lake, he wasn't so sure.

A moment later the building disappeared behind a screen of trees, and his father's voice once again pulled him out of his reverie.

"She's running fine," Dan said. "Why don't we hook up a couple of lures?"

But even as he began fishing, Eric's mind was still on the storeroom in the carriage house. Kent and Tad would be here soon, and maybe after dinner tonight he'd take them down there.

Suddenly, the idea of exploring the storeroom and finding out exactly what might be inside it was far more exciting than fishing.

With fishing, all he'd get was the occasional trout or bass or muskie.

But in that strange storeroom, there was no telling what he might find.

Ellis Langstrom dropped the last weed in the bucket, rubbed his aching shoulders, and finally stood up to assess his afternoon's work. The entire border of flowers around the Islers' summer house was weed free, the

soil dark with fertilizer, and the flowers —
whatever they were, which Ellis neither
knew nor cared to know — actually seemed
to be a few shades brighter now that there
were no weeds around them.

More to the point, Mrs. Henderson would
be happy, and so would the Islers, when
they arrived tomorrow.

The yard cleanup had been a bigger job
than he'd thought, and now he tried to
stretch the pain out of his back as he
searched for anything he might have forgotten.

There didn't seem to be anything — the
place looked great, and even Rita Henderson would have to admit it.

Ellis pulled off his gloves and tossed them
into the bucket on top of the weeds just as
Adam Mosler — stripped to the waist and
streaked with sweat and dust — came
around the corner of the house, using a
filthy bandanna to wipe a smear of dirt from
one cheek. The bandanna only made the
smear worse.

"It's raked," Adam stated, sounding more
resentful about having had to remove the
mown grass from the front lawn than
pleased to have finished the job. "Are you
done?" He scanned the patio area disinter-
estedly. " 'Cause even if you're not, I am."

"Thanks a lot," Ellis said, then realized the sarcasm would be lost on Adam. "Yeah, I think it's done."

"Yeah, well, you owe me."

"Hey, it's not like no one's paying you."

"There's still about ten million better things to do. I feel like a pig."

"Look like one, too," Ellis observed archly as he dropped down onto the cool grass and stretched out, feeling his aching muscles finally beginning to relax.

"Hey, check that out."

Ellis sat up and followed Adam's gaze, but saw nothing but two people fishing a few hundred yards offshore. "What?"

"That piece-of-crap tin boat? That's the one from Pinecrest. And that's the cone-head from Pinecrest in it. What a prick."

Ellis shook his head. "You think all the summer people are pricks. Just because you thought he wasn't going to pick up his dog's —"

"He wasn't!" Adam flared. "And he was hitting on Cherie Stevens right in front of me."

Ellis frowned. "Right in front of you? Okay, that's not cool. Definitely not cool."

Adam scowled, spat at the ground, then glowered out at the tiny boat in the middle of the lake. "His buddies arrive today. I

remember them. They're all pricks."

"C'mon, Adam," Ellis sighed. "Get real — they're not all pricks. My mom says —"

"You watch," Adam cut in. "Those three guys are going to hit on all the girls. And guess what? Just because they're rich summer kids who live at The ritzy-titzy Pines, they're going to get 'em!"

"Says you," Ellis snorted.

"Yeah, says me!" Adam shot back. "You should have seen Cherie — she was climbing all over herself inviting that jerk to the pavilion dances."

Ellis finally turned to face Adam, grinning. "Oh, really? I thought she was going with you."

"I thought so, too," Adam said, suddenly wishing he hadn't told Ellis that Cherie had practically dumped him. His eyes shifted back to the boat that was bobbing gently on the water. "If it wasn't for that prick —"

"Hey," Ellis cut in, seeing Adam's expression starting to darken into an ugly rage, which always wound up leading to some kind of trouble. "Come on. Let's go get cleaned up."

But Adam wasn't listening to him, his eyes still fixed on the boat. "I'll tell you one thing," he said, his voice so low that Ellis wasn't sure Adam was talking to him at all.

"If I catch him alone somewhere, he's as good as dead." Finally, he turned and looked Ellis straight in the eye. "Think I'm kidding?" he asked. "Well, I'm not. I'm not kidding at all."

Eric fed a little bit more line off his reel, feeling the spoon he was trolling drop a few inches in the water. The sun was low in the sky, fish were feeding near the surface, and he could almost feel a strike coming. Slowly, he began to wind the reel, bringing the lure in, drawing it closer to the surface.

And then his neck began to crawl, almost as if something was about to touch him.

Or was staring at him.

He turned around, half expecting to see another boat a few yards away — or even closer — but there was nothing. Then he saw two people on one of the lawns a few houses down from Pinecrest.

One of them sat with his arms around his knees; the other one stood with his legs apart and his arms crossed over his chest.

And both of them were staring directly at the boat.

At *him.*

But that was stupid — they were too far away for him even to tell exactly in what direction they were looking — they could

have been looking at anything. Another boat, or a bird, or —

But there weren't any other boats on the lake, and when he scanned the sky, there were no birds, either.

And he still had that crawly feeling.

He turned his attention back to his rod and reel, slowly drawing his lure closer to the boat, but the strange sensation on the back of his neck didn't ease up.

He turned again, and this time he recognized the one who was standing.

Adam. Adam Mosler.

He recalled the scene from his first night at Pinecrest, when Adam Mosler and Cherie Stevens had turned up at the dock. Adam had been pissed off, and now, as Adam kept staring at him, Eric knew that he hadn't gotten over it.

And suddenly he had a bad feeling about Mosler — a really bad feeling. He began winding the reel faster, and a few seconds later the lure broke through the surface of the water and glittered in the afternoon sunlight. Just as Eric raised the rod higher to swing the lure over the boat, a trout leaped, snapped at one of the lure's bare hooks, missed, and dropped back into the water.

"Fly fishing with a spoon," his father said.

"Don't think I've seen that one before." Then, as Eric laid his rod on the floorboards of the boat, he began reeling in his own line. "Ready to go back?"

Eric nodded, took the handle of the outboard, and made a sweeping turn toward home.

He'd talk to Kent and Tad about this Adam guy — maybe they knew the story on him.

He gunned the engine, and as the bow lifted and the skiff struggled to reach the plane, he glanced once again at the lawn where the two boys had been.

It was empty.

But the hatred Eric had felt emanating from Adam Mosler still remained.

CHAPTER 8

Ashley Sparks gazed dolefully at the enormous pile of cooked, peeled, and cubed potatoes that threatened to overflow onto the floor at any moment. "Merrill, do you have a bowl for the potato salad? Or can I just chuck it all in the trash and take everyone out for dinner?"

"In the lower cabinet to your left." Merrill pointed with the knife she was using to chop celery. "And no, you can't throw it out. The worst is over — all you have to do now is add the good stuff."

"Oh, come on, Merrill," Ellen Newell put in as she unwrapped the butcher paper from a dozen thick steaks and arranged them on a platter. "Ashley doesn't cook — she shops." Then, as Ashley tried to muster up a dirty look — and failed — Ellen gazed enviously around Pinecrest's huge kitchen. "Too bad we aren't all living in this place," she said. "I can't believe how huge it is."

Merrill glanced out to the terrace, where her friends' husbands were drinking beer while her own poked at smoldering coals in the barbecue. "Marci, would you take the meat out to your father?"

Marci finished drinking her lemonade, set the empty glass in the sink, then took the platter from Ellen.

As soon as she was out of the room, Merrill turned to Ellen. "So I hear this Dr. Darby used to do experiments on the criminally insane," she said, her voice as accusing as her expression.

Ellen and Ashley exchanged a quick look, then faced Merrill, expressions of mock guilt on their faces, and promptly dissolved into laughter. "That's the rumor, all right," Ellen said. "Hand me the mayo. Is it fat-free?"

Merrill pushed the jar of mayonnaise across the kitchen island. "Don't you think you could have told me?" Then, as both her friends looked as if they were about to start laughing again, she glowered at them. "Don't laugh at me!"

"Oh, honey, we can't help but laugh," Ashley said, sliding chopped pickles and onions from the cutting board into the bowl with the potatoes. "Look at this fabulous house — there's no way on earth you would have

rented it if you'd known about all those silly rumors."

"And that's all they are," Ellen said. "Rumors. Who did you hear that one from?"

"Carol something-or-other. In the antiques store."

"Carol Langstrom," Ashley said, testing the water for the corn on the cob, then setting the lid back on the steaming pot before turning to face Merrill. "Here's the story on Carol, and a lot of other people in Phantom Lake. Imagine being up here all winter long with ten feet of snow at forty below zero and really short days with nothing to do except gossip, spread rumors, and turn molehills into mountains. It's not just Carol Langstrom, but much as I love her, she *is* the biggest gossip in town."

"So, I have a plan," Ellen said, as she began mixing the salad with a big wooden spoon. "To keep all of us from the evil of dwelling on rumors, we shall keep ourselves active. Minds and bodies. There's a lovely little par-three golf course on the north shore of the lake, and there are public tennis courts over by the pavilion in town, and Jeff has the ski boat all tuned up. If we keep you busy enough, you won't have time to think about everything you're going to hear about this house. In fact, if I keep you re-

ally, really busy, you won't even have time to hear the stories, let alone worry about them."

"Not all of us are Barbie dolls, Ellen," Ashley Sparks observed dryly, patting her own ample rump. "Nor do all of us look good enough in swimsuits to actually put one on. So for me there will be nothing involving public displays of flesh, okay? I'll golf with you, but that's as far as it goes. And you'll go antiquing with me. Deal?" She lifted the lid on the pot again, where the water was now boiling. "I'm going to start the corn."

"Deal," Ellen said. "But from what I've seen so far, you could do a year's worth of antiquing right in this house."

"Don't I know it," Ashley replied, turning back to Merrill. "And I need a full tour right after we eat. I've wanted to get inside this house for years!"

"Maybe we should trade houses, and *you* can ignore all the stories about this one," Merrill suggested, then wished she could retract her words as she saw both her friends roll their eyes.

"For God's sake, Merrill," Ellen said. "Don't you think it's about time to give up the Queen Nervosa title? You're already over forty, and someday you're going to look

back on your life and see how much you've missed just by being afraid that something might happen."

Merrill sighed and nodded, and as her two friends began planning tomorrow, she looked out through the window at their three sons, who were throwing a football around on the big lawn while Moxie chased after them. Dan and the other two men were laughing around the smoking barbecue, and Marci had sprawled in the hammock with her cat.

All of it going on against the beautiful backdrop of the sparkling lake at the foot of the lawn.

Ellen and Ashley were right; it was, indeed, time to give up her title and stop worrying.

If every day turned out like this one, there would be nothing to worry about.

Eric passed the bag of marshmallows to Kent Newell, who expertly skewered three of them onto a single stick and held them just far enough over the glowing barbecue coals so they'd brown without bursting into flames the way his own marshmallows always did. The low murmur of their parents' voices floated out from the house, and the soft background chorus of chirping crickets was the only other sound that broke

the silence of the calm evening, except for the occasional croaking of a frog or the lonely call of a loon searching for its mate somewhere across the lake. As the daylight began to fade, he leaned back in one of the worn canvas camp chairs they'd found in the basement and decided that things couldn't get much better. Kent and Tad were both here, and the summer stretched before them, an unexplored territory with a new adventure waiting every day.

"I'm going to look up Kayla Banks tomorrow," Kent said, slowly rotating his marshmallows. He grinned at Eric and Tad over the barely flickering fire. "She's had all winter to think about me."

"Which could be good or bad," Tad pointed out, "depending on how hard you tried to get in her panties last summer."

"She loved it," Kent bragged.

"And assuming she hasn't already got a boyfriend," Tad went on. "You don't really think she's been doing nothing but dream about you all year, do you?"

"If all the guys up here are like the ones I ran into, they're all jerks," Eric said before Kent had a chance to defend his desirability.

Kent's gaze shifted from Tad to Eric. "Who?"

"Adam somebody."

"Mosler." Kent spat the name as if it tasted bad in his mouth. "Adam's an asshole. He and two other creeps hassled us last year." He grinned again, but this time there was a hint of maliciousness about it. "But this year it's three of us against three of them. No problem."

"Or maybe we ought to just steer clear of them," Tad said. "In fact, maybe we should just stay away from all the townies."

"No way," Kent flared. "I have an investment in Kayla from last year, and this year it's gonna pay off!"

"Jeez," Tad groaned. "You sound like you think she owes you something."

Kent's grin broadened. "She does. She owes me a piece of —" He cut his own words short as first one, then the second, and finally the third of his marshmallows dropped off the skewer into the coals and burst into flames. "Crap!"

As Kent reloaded his skewer, the boys lapsed into silence, watching the embers. The brighter stars were just becoming visible in the evening sky, and the pine trees on the hills across the lake were silhouetted points against a rosy background.

Fireflies winked around the yard.

Suddenly, Eric remembered the other night, when a boat bearing not only Adam

Mosler, but someone else as well, had shown up at the dock at just about this same time. "Do you guys know Cherie Stevens?" he asked.

"Sure," Kent said. "She's Kayla's best friend."

"I'm thinking maybe we should go to the pavilion dance next Friday," Eric said. "She practically invited me."

"I'm in," Kent said. "We'll all go, and maybe we'll all get lucky."

"We didn't get lucky last year," Tad reminded him.

"But that was last year," Kent countered. "I've got a good feeling about this year."

The kitchen lights went out and the dining room lights went on in the house, and Eric watched as all their parents settled in for a card game, which meant none of them would move for at least an hour. "You guys want to see what I found today?" he asked in a tone that caught both Kent's and Tad's attention. Setting down his marshmallow skewer, Eric rose from his chair, and a moment later the three boys moved soundlessly away from the terrace, across the lawn, and into the shadows of the old carriage house.

Eric opened the door and led the way down the darkened hallway.

"What is this place?" Tad asked, uncon-

sciously dropping his voice to a whisper.

"It's the garage now," Eric said. "But there's an apartment upstairs, and lots of other rooms from when it was a stable and carriage house."

He opened a door and turned on a solitary lightbulb.

Kent and Tad edged past him and they all crowded inside the cramped room Eric had discovered only a few hours earlier.

"Wow," Tad said, peering at the jumble of furniture. "Look at this stuff! My mom would go nuts if she saw all this."

As Tad ran his hands over the polished wood of one of the old dressers, Kent opened one of the boxes, peered inside, then carefully lifted a leather photo album out of the box, setting it on a desk.

He opened the cover.

"Look," he said. "It's old pictures of Pinecrest."

Eric and Tad moved closer and peered down at the page covered with deckle-edged photographs of the house. In one of them a young man in an old-fashioned suit was standing in front of the front door. "Suppose that's Dr. Darby?" Tad asked.

Kent turned a few more pages. There were more photographs of people at Pinecrest — people posing on the front porch, relaxing

on the back terrace, standing on the dock with a stringer of fish.

Some of the pictures showed people standing next to old cars; others depicted the interior of the house but with different furniture than it now contained.

Nowhere were there captions for the pictures.

Nowhere were there identifications of the people in them.

"Look at that," Tad said, pointing at a photograph of a man wearing wire-rim glasses, his hair slicked back, sitting in front of a small oak secretary. "That's a picture of this desk." It was clearly the same slanted-front secretary they had the photograph album resting on.

Eric and Tad leaned in closer as Kent turned the pages one by one. . . .

Ellen Newell peered dolefully at the pair of sevens that had first been dealt her, and made one last attempt to find the possibility of a winning hand in the five additional cards that had come her way. Finding nothing, she tossed the hand in. "Okay," she sighed as Dan Brewster raked in the pot, adding the last of her chips to the enormous pile in front of him. "I'm broke, and I'm tired, and I want to go to bed." She glanced

out the window, but all she could see was blackness — the last of the fire's embers had long since died away. "How about you go call your son?" she asked Jeff, who'd lost the last of his stake in a game to Dan two hands earlier.

"How come he's suddenly just my son?" Jeff asked as he stood up and moved to the French doors.

"Because I'm too tired to call him myself," Ellen replied, watching her husband step out onto the terrace to call Kent.

When there was no answer, Jeff called again, then crossed the terrace and moved down the steps onto the lawn. "Kent!" he called again. "We're leaving!"

When there was still no answer, he moved down the lawn to the fire pit, where a half-empty bag of marshmallows lay by one of the canvas chairs and three skewers — still sticky — were propped against the metal ring that contained the fire, which was no longer even smoldering.

But no sign of the boys.

Jeff felt his blood pressure rise as he walked down to the boathouse. If they'd taken the boat out after dark and not even bothered to tell anyone what they were up to, all three of them would find themselves grounded for a week.

But the boathouse was dark; Pinecrest's little aluminum skiff lay quietly tethered to the dock.

"Kent!"

But the lake and the woods were silent.

He stood on the dock and peered across the dark water. The moon was about to rise, and the eastern sky was taking on a faint silvery glow. But the lake was quiet, the shore deserted as far as he could see; there were no boys here.

Jeff looked back up the lawn toward the house, and for the first time saw a faint yellow light in a back window behind the garage.

The old carriage house? What were they doing in there? But of course he knew what they were doing.

Messing around.

Seeing what they could find.

And, of course, getting into mischief.

Jeff began rehearsing the speech he was going to deliver in about two minutes when he found the boys, letting them know exactly what would be expected of them this summer. He began mentally ticking off points.

Almost old enough to drive.

Going to be seniors in the fall.

Time to demonstrate responsibility.

And, last but far from least, they weren't going to ignore him when he called!

A door to the rooms behind the garage was ajar, and down the hall another door stood open, yellow light spilling out, illuminating the hallway. Jeff strode down the hall and stepped into a storeroom.

The three boys were huddled together, poring over something on an old desk.

"Kent!" All three boys jumped at the sound of his voice and whirled to face him. "Are you deaf?" he went on. "I've been calling you for at least five minutes. It's time to go home."

The boys looked at one another uncertainly. "You just started playing cards," Kent finally said.

Jeff scowled at his son. "We started an hour ago, and Dan's cleaned us all out. I'm down at least three dollars, and it's time to go. After you've cleaned up the mess by the barbecue pit," he added pointedly.

But the boys were barely listening. An hour ago? How was it possible? They'd been in the storage room only ten minutes or so. They couldn't have been looking at the album for more than that.

But as they stepped outside, they saw that night had fallen; there was no trace at all of the sunset that had still been bright when

they'd left the fire pit.

It was completely dark, except for the brightness in the east where the moon was coming up.

But how could it have gotten this late?

"I'm sorry, Mr. Newell," Tad said. "I guess we just lost track of time."

Jeff Newell's eyes narrowed. "What were you boys doing in there, anyway?"

"Looking at some old photographs is all," Eric said.

"For an hour?" Jeff turned, addressing the question directly to his son.

Kent only shrugged, and so did Eric and Tad.

"Okay," he began. "This is not how it's going to be this summer." He began ticking off all the points he'd laid out in his head a few minutes earlier, using his fingers to count them one by one. "And you're going to show some respect and have some consideration for other people. When I — or anyone else calls you —"

"Sorry, Dad," Kent cut in. "It won't happen again."

"See that it doesn't," the elder Newell replied as they came to the remains of the fire. "Now clean up those skewers and get the marshmallows into the house before a raccoon gets them. And your mother is wait-

ing. She's tired. We're all tired. It's time to go. So step on it, okay?" Without waiting for a reply, Jeff Newell wheeled around and headed back to the house, leaving the three boys to clean up their mess.

"You guys go if you want," Eric said. "I've got this."

"How did it get so late so fast?" Tad whispered.

Eric shrugged. He had no idea how it had happened, but he also knew that what had happened this evening was exactly what had happened that afternoon.

Only tonight it had happened to all three of them.

There was something about that room.

Something strange.

Something that, even now, seemed to be tugging at him.

But what was it? It was just a storeroom, wasn't it?

Or was it?

As he picked up the marshmallows and skewers and started toward the house, he suddenly turned and looked back at the dark mass of the carriage house, and even though he still had no idea exactly what had happened in there just now, there was one thing he did know.

He couldn't wait to go back in there again.

CHAPTER 9

Logan pulled on the oars, sending the boat silently through the water. Even the oarlocks seemed muffled this night as he skirted the edge of the lake where the moon had not penetrated the dark shelter of overhanging trees.

Near the bow, the old dog stirred restlessly on his bed, the scent of bones that Logan had dug up from the Dumpster behind the butcher shop strong enough to penetrate even his diminished nostrils.

"Soon," Logan soothed. "Just a little longer, then we're on our way home." He eased the boat around the point, turned it, then froze as he gazed at Pinecrest, his hands clenching the oars so hard his arthritic knuckles sent agonizing protests straight up his arms. But he was barely conscious of the pain as he gazed at the windows of Pinecrest, almost all of them ablaze with light.

He had hoped that the people would go away. He had *wished* them away, focusing every fragment of his consciousness on his need to have Pinecrest — all of it — empty of people.

But they hadn't gone, and he knew he was failing at what Dr. Darby had commanded him to do before he'd . . . Logan groped in the cluttered depths of his consciousness for the right word. . . . Before he'd *left*. And now, after all these years, all the years in which he'd been able to do what Dr. Darby had asked — had demanded — he was failing.

How could he protect Dr. Darby's things when he couldn't go near them? For several long minutes he sat perfectly still in the boat, telling himself that maybe it would be all right, that maybe the people in the house would stay in the house and that, after all, the hidden things — the secret things — would remain exactly as Dr. Darby had left them. Finally, he began rowing again, heading for home.

He would feed the dog and feed the bird, and maybe the doctor's things would be safe, and the people in the house would soon be gone.

But as he eased the boat through the water and came abreast of the old carriage house,

his heart began to pound.

The light in the storage area was on.

The light was on, and he knew why.

The boy.

The boy he'd seen earlier.

That's who it had to be. The boy was inside the storage area, and Dr. Darby's things were not safe.

The boy was not safe.

No one was safe.

Once again Logan let the boat drift to a stop, hidden deep within the shadows cast over the lake by the tall pines for which the house had been named, trying to find the courage to go ashore.

Then he heard a shout and saw a man coming down the lawn. His heart skipping a beat, Logan backed into the reeds near the shore, where the shadows of the pines were so deep he could barely even see the dog, who had caught his master's anxiety and was now trying to rise on his rickety legs. To quiet the animal, Logan fished a knucklebone from the leavings he'd scavenged that night, and in an instant the dog had dropped back onto the floor of the scow and begun to gnaw.

Logan waited.

The man called again, went into the carriage house, then came out followed not by

one boy, but by three.

Not long after that, the lights in the house went dark.

Logan waited in the darkness, knowing it was finally time for him to do what he should have done years ago.

Careful to make no sound at all, he beached the boat, tied the painter to a branch, and stepped out.

And the moment he set foot on Pinecrest's soil, he felt it.

Felt the pull.

It was as if the things in the storeroom — the things Dr. Darby had told him to keep safe — had awakened and were somehow whispering to him.

Beckoning to him.

Luring him, as at dusk he sometimes lured the fish from the depths of the lake.

Now, as he crouched in the boat that was itself hidden in the shadows of the pines on the shore, he tried not to listen to the whispers.

Tried to resist the calling.

His heart pounded in his chest as he tried to decide what to do.

Almost against his own will, he stepped out of the boat and edged up toward the old carriage house, keeping to the fringe of the woods.

And as he moved, the voices in his head began to rise.

The whisperings became a cacophony of noise inside his head, each voice vying for his attention, each of them whispering what he must do.

But on one thing, all of them agreed: he must go through the door into the back room, through the door that had been hidden for so many years.

The door that should never be opened again.

As if to turn away from the voices themselves, Logan turned away from the old carriage house, and his eyes fixed on the red glow of the dying coals in the fire pit. And as he stared at it, an idea began to form in his mind.

He started toward the fire pit, the voices protesting with every step, but he ignored them until he was near the glowing coals.

A few feet from the pit itself he found a can of charcoal starting fluid and a box of matches.

The voices in his head rose as he picked them up.

He forced himself to ignore the voices, steeled himself against the hard knot of fear gnawing at his belly.

The voices grew louder, clearer.

"Come to us."

A strangled whimper of protest bubbled in his throat.

"We know what you want."

"You know what we want."

Logan tried to close his mind to them, tried to concentrate only on the structure that lay a few paces ahead now, and the objects in his hands.

The objects that could be his salvation if only he could find the strength to disobey the voices.

"Remember how good it felt to have your fingers around her throat?"

Logan tried to focus his mind on nothing more than emptying the can in his left hand onto the evil structure, then setting it ablaze with the matches that were all but crushed by the pressure in the fingers of his right hand.

"You can feel it, can't you? You're feeling it even now."

He was at the door of the carriage house.

"Come in. See if all is as it should be. Make sure our treasures are safe."

The voices were nearly overpowering now, and Logan felt what little courage he'd summoned begin to fail.

What could it hurt? And it had been so long since he'd been inside the room.

Dropping the matches, he reached for the doorknob.

His fingers were no more than a fraction of an inch from the cold metal when a tiny spark of reason flared in his mind for the briefest of moments.

Dropping the can of lighter fluid, Logan turned and fled, shambling away into the darkness of the night.

Only when he was back in his boat and it was slicing once more through the smooth waters of Phantom Lake, did he dare to take a deep breath and finally look back at Pinecrest.

For now, at least, he and everyone else was safe.

But for how long?

Tad Sparks filled the top drawer of the bureau with his underwear and socks, closed the drawer, and dropped his finally empty duffel bag on the floor of the closet. Flopping onto the bed, he looked out the open window at the lake. The water seemed almost to be glowing from deep beneath its surface rather than merely reflecting the light of the moon.

He'd forgotten how silent it was here at night, and how loud the frogs sounded

when they broke the stillness with their calls.

Then another sound broke the silence: his father's voice calling from downstairs. "Tad!"

Tad slid off the bed and went to the top of the narrow stairs. "What?"

"Did you roll up the windows in the car and lock it?"

He couldn't remember. "Coming." He took the stairs two at a time, and headed through the living room where his father was watching a baseball game while his mother knitted a sweater Tad secretly hoped wasn't intended for him.

"Might rain," his dad said, barely glancing away from the TV screen.

"Okay." Tad grabbed the keys from the little table by the front door and went out into the night.

The sky was clear and the canopy of stars hung so low that it seemed he could reach up and touch them.

No way was it going to rain.

Not that it mattered. Better to just do as his father asked than try to argue, since arguing had never worked. Besides, even if it didn't rain, a raccoon could get into the car, and then his dad would really be mad.

The car was next to the house, and for a

moment Tad considered putting it in the garage, but then thought better of it — the garage door was narrow, and he didn't want to think about what his father would say if the car got even a single scratch. Better just to roll up the windows and lock it. His father could move it into the garage tomorrow.

Tad slid into the driver's seat, inserted the key in the ignition, turned it to activate the electrical system, and was about to close the windows when he heard something.

A faint but rhythmic squeaking noise.

Frowning, he got out of the car and listened closely.

The sound seemed to be coming from the lake.

Oars?

Was someone out on the lake at night, rowing?

The moon was now paving a silvery pathway on the lake, which shimmered with ripples. A moment later the silhouette of a man rowing a boat slid into the bright moonlight.

The boat turned slightly, and Tad saw what looked like a giant crucifix rising from its prow.

But it couldn't be — it had to be something else. A trick of the light.

Something that just looked like a crucifix.

He reached in through the window and flicked on the headlights.

The boat was closer to shore than it appeared in the moonlight, and as the headlights flashed out of the darkness, the man rowing the boat turned, staring into the light like a deer caught on the highway at night.

He was dressed in what seemed to be rags, with long hair and an even longer beard, and though he froze for an instant, he immediately came back to life, sinking his oars deep into the water and pulling hard so the boat turned away and Tad was staring at his back.

But even though the man's face had vanished, the memory of it was etched clearly in Tad's mind. The man looked like one of the crazy homeless people he'd seen in Chicago plenty of times.

The kind of man who was never seen at all in Evanston.

So what was somebody like that doing in Phantom Lake, let alone this part of the lake?

And why would he have a wooden crucifix on the bow of his boat?

Leaving the headlights on, Tad ran a few steps toward the house. "Dad!"

Though the window he could see his

father, who was still watching TV. He went to the front door. "Dad, there's a really weird guy out on the lake."

Finally, his father turned away from the screen. "What do you mean, out on the lake? It's almost nine —"

"Come look," Tad broke in. "Hurry."

Kevin Sparks heaved himself out of his chair and followed his son back to the car.

The headlights still shone brightly on the lake, but only the still water was visible.

They walked down to the lake, but even from its edge there was nothing to be seen.

No boat.

No man.

No sound of anyone rowing.

Not even the tiniest ripple of a wake at the water's edge.

It was as if it hadn't happened at all.

"Jeez, that is so creepy," Tad said. "He was just here."

Kevin slung an arm around his son's shoulders as they both stared out over the silent, empty expanse of water. "Well, if there was anything there at all, it's gone now," he said. "Come on, let's get back to the house."

As his father went back to the baseball game, Tad closed the car windows, shut off the headlights, and locked it.

A few minutes later, back upstairs in his room, he found himself not only shutting his bedroom door, but locking it as well, and before he went to bed, he closed and locked the window, too.

Despite his father's words, he was certain that not only had he seen the strange man in the boat — and the madness in his face — but that the man hadn't gone anywhere at all.

He was still out there somewhere, hiding, waiting, in the dark of the night.

CHAPTER 10

"Right here," Kent Newell said. "This is where I caught six trout in less than an hour last summer."

"Yeah, right," Tad groaned. "It was three, and we were out for two hours at least." He looked around, finally spotted the dead tree he'd been looking for, and smirked at Kent. "And it wasn't right here, either." He pointed east, where the sun was still rising in its morning arc. "It was over that way. The dead tree was lined up with that real tall pine at the top of the hill, remember?"

Kent spread his hands in mock helplessness. "So sue me! This is close enough, isn't it?"

They'd taken the boat out nearly two hours ago, tried three other spots where Kent had insisted the fish had been biting like crazy last summer — or the summer before — and failed at every one of them. As Tad shook his head at Kent's refusal to

rise to the teasing, Eric killed the motor and let the little boat glide slowly to a stop almost precisely at the point where the dead tree on shore lined up with the tall pine at the crest of the hill that rose a few hundred yards beyond the lake's shore.

Kent, his line already rigged, dropped his baited hook over the side, made sure the red and white bobber was doing its job, then turned to help Tad get his line ready.

Eric snapped a jig onto his own line, threw it over, and started moving the tip of his pole up and down in the theoretically enticing motion that Kent still insisted was the only way to lure a fish, despite the fact that so far none of them had gotten even a nibble.

"Hey," Tad Sparks said in a tone that caught both Eric's and Kent's attention. "I saw something really weird last night." He hesitated, certain that Kent, at least, would tell him he'd only been imagining what he'd seen, but even when the sun had come up three hours ago, the strange image was still fresh in his mind. Besides, it was too late to change his mind now — both Eric and Kent were looking at him expectantly. "There was this old guy in front of our house," he finally went on. "He was rowing a wooden boat with a huge cross on the bow. And he

looked crazy."

"Old Man Logan," Kent said, snapping a small spinner onto the swivel on Tad's line, then passing the rod to Tad. "Here. Cast and retrieve."

"Old Man Logan?" Tad said as he took the rod. "Really? You think it was him?"

"Who's Old Man Logan?" Eric asked, his own rod no longer jigging as he gazed at his friends.

"Crazy old guy who lives in the woods," Kent said, shrugging indifferently.

"Crazy?" Eric asked, frowning. "You mean really crazy, or just weird?"

"Really crazy," Kent replied. "I heard he killed a girl a long time ago."

Eric's eyes narrowed suspiciously, certain that Kent was up to something. "Come on. If he did that, how come he's not in prison?" he asked, his eyes locking onto Kent's as if daring him to push the story any further. But it wasn't Kent who replied.

"Because he was crazy," Tad said. "At least that's what we've heard. He was locked up for a long time, but they finally let him out."

"When?" Eric demanded, certain that neither of his friends would have an answer.

"Maybe ten years ago," Kent replied.

"So if they let him out, he must not be crazy anymore, right?" Eric pressed.

Kent shrugged. "From what I've heard, he's still nuts even if he's not dangerous. I mean, who else but a crazy guy would mount a cross on the bow of his boat?"

Eric turned to Tad. "So what was he doing at your place last night?"

"Probably looking for someone else to kill," Kent said before Tad had a chance to answer.

Once again Tad pictured the wild-eyed man with the scraggly beard, and suddenly his appetite for fishing evaporated. "All I know is that I saw him last night," he finally said. "I don't know what he was doing, but it was really creepy. Creepy enough that I made my dad come outside, but by the time he got there, the guy was gone. I mean like he just disappeared. It was like he hadn't been there at all, but I know he was."

"Jeez," Eric whispered, scanning the lake as if in search of the apparition Tad had just described.

Abruptly, the wind picked up, and a dark cloud covered the sun. Goose bumps rose on Eric's arms, and then even blacker clouds were closing in. What had been a perfect morning only moments ago was quickly turning into a storm, and already whitecaps were kicking up on the choppy water.

"Maybe we better go in," Tad said, zipping up his windbreaker.

Eric nodded, reeling in his jig and laying his rod on the floor of the boat, then moving back toward the outboard. The engine started on the first pull, and Eric turned the boat toward the dock in front of Pinecrest, the little skiff rolling violently as the wind hit it broadside.

"Jeez," Kent howled, grabbing the cleat near the bow to keep from pitching overboard. "What are you doing?"

"Trying to get us back to the dock," Eric called a moment before a bolt of lightning ripped across the sky, followed immediately by a crash of thunder.

The boat steadied as Eric headed it directly into the wind, and he twisted the throttle, sending the skiff's bow steeply upward, crashing into the trough beyond the wave they'd just crested. Water cascaded over Kent, who swore loudly, and Eric throttled back, afraid of swamping the boat.

Then, with no warning whatever, the motor died.

Eric pulled on the rope.

Nothing.

Another pull.

Still nothing, but this time he felt an ugly metal-on-metal grinding.

The motor would not be running any time soon.

"Get the oars," he said.

As Tad dropped the oars into their locks and began to pull, the first raindrops began to fall, and by the time they tied up at the Pinecrest dock nearly half an hour later, all three boys were soaked to the skin. Then, as Eric was tying the last line to the cleat on the dock, the rain stopped as abruptly as it had started, the sun came out, and raindrops sparkled everywhere.

"So now what?" Tad asked, stepping out of the boat and peering up at the sky.

"Fix the motor," Eric said. "The boat's our only transportation, remember?"

"Then let's fix it," Kent said, rubbing his left biceps, which was still sore from his fifteen minutes on the oars. "I don't want to row all the way to town and back Friday night."

They crossed the lawn toward the carriage house, but stopped short at the door leading to the workshop.

Lying on the ground and glittering in the sunlight almost as if it were begging to be seen, was the can of charcoal lighter fluid they'd used at the barbecue the night before.

A couple of feet away from it lay the box

of matches they'd used to light the fire, now sodden from the recent rain.

"How'd these get over here?" Eric breathed. "Didn't we leave them by the fire pit?"

Tad shrugged, but Kent nodded. "So now we know what Old Man Logan was doing last night," he said. "He was going to burn your house down."

As Tad's eyes widened at Kent's words, Eric again felt goose bumps surging up his arms.

Then Kent grinned. "Kidding, guys," he said. "Just kidding."

But neither Eric nor Tad made a move toward the carriage house door.

"C'mon, you wusses," Kent said. When neither Eric nor Tad made a move, he pushed between them, pulled the door open, and stepped through it into the gloom inside.

Nearly half a minute passed before first Eric and then Tad reluctantly followed him.

The door to the workshop where the tools were kept stood open in front of them.

A few yards farther down the passageway was the door to the storeroom they'd spent a few minutes exploring last night.

Or had it been an hour?

None of them, not Eric, not Tad, not even Kent, made any move to step through the open workshop door. Instead, all three of them stood perfectly still, staring down the hall at the closed door to the storeroom.

Kent finally broke the silence. "That was weird last night." When neither of his friends spoke, he looked first at Tad, then at Eric. "I told my dad we were just looking at old pictures, but it seems like . . ." His voice trailed off, then: "I don't know. It was like I was feeling something. Or hearing something."

The face he'd seen caught in the headlights last night flooded back into Tad Sparks's mind. "Let's just get the tools and go fix the outboard, okay?" he said. Though he'd tried to control it, there was a hint of a stammer in his words, and now Kent was staring at him, his eyes glinting.

"You chicken?" the bigger boy asked. When Tad hesitated, Kent turned to Eric Brewster. "What about you?" he asked. "You scared, too?"

Though Eric's heart was suddenly beating faster, he shook his head.

"Then let's go see," Kent said softly.

The workshop suddenly forgotten, Kent led the way to the storeroom door, opened it, and turned on the light.

As they stepped through the door, a strange feeling of familiarity — almost of welcome — came over Eric. It was as if the room itself was glad to have him back.

Or something in the room.

He looked around.

Nothing had changed since last night.

The photo album sat open on the small slant-topped desk exactly as they had left it.

With Kent and Tad following him, Eric wound his way through the maze of stacked furniture and cartons until he was once more gazing at the still open album. He could feel Kent at his right side and Tad at his left.

The old white-bordered photographs in the leather-covered album were held to its black pages by little triangular paper corners.

Without thinking, without even looking at the image before him, without even realizing what he was doing, Eric turned the page and found himself gazing at a photograph of a small office, a ledger open on its desk. An octagonal window over the desk let in a ray of light.

"That's this room," Tad breathed.

Eric and Kent looked up to see the same octagonal window half obscured by a dresser that sat atop a table.

But in the photograph there was a small door in the wall opposite the little window.

A wooden door with what appeared to be a hand-forged iron handle and latch.

Kent pointed at it, then looked at the wall where that door ought to be, but saw instead a sheet of plywood propped against the brick wall.

As if by unspoken agreement — or drawn by some unseen force of which they weren't quite aware — the three boys moved toward the sheet of plywood, moving the stacks of cartons and jumble of furniture just enough so that when they finally reached their goal they could slide the plywood a few feet to the left.

And there was the doorway they'd seen in the picture.

Except that the wooden door with its iron hardware was gone.

In its place were bricks.

But not the kind of bricks with which the carriage house had been constructed. These were newer, and not nearly as well laid and neatly mortared. Rather, whoever had bricked up the doorway had done it poorly.

Or perhaps too quickly.

The bricks had been shoved into the opening haphazardly, and were only lightly and unevenly mortared.

"Why would anybody brick up the doorway?" Tad whispered.

"Want to open it?" Kent countered, not answering Tad's question, and already prodding at the bricks.

Something inside Eric wanted nothing more than to find some tools and go to work on the outboard motor. But there was something else inside him as well.

Something that wanted to take those bricks down and free whatever was hidden behind them.

As the two conflicting forces struggled within him, Kent Newell was already working a brick loose.

Mortar dust sifted to the floor.

The brick moved more easily.

"Wait," Eric said. "Let's do it later, when our parents are gone."

Kent stopped, his hands dropping away from the brick.

The three of them stood quietly, gazing at the makeshift wall, saying nothing.

None of them made any move to leave.

"We should go fix the boat," Tad whispered.

Kent and Eric nodded, but still none of them moved.

Instead they stood staring at the doorway.

Something behind the bricks — something

unseen — was holding them.

It was almost as if Eric could hear voices now, voices whispering to him, pleading with him.

Pleading for what?

"Now," he said, his voice preternaturally loud. "Let's go now."

Slowly, as if struggling against the unseen force, they backed away from the wall, through the maze of cartons and furniture, and out the storeroom door.

Eric turned off the light and closed the door firmly. Yet even as he turned away he could still feel the strange force from behind the bricks pulling at him, and he knew Kent and Tad could feel it, too.

He knew they could hear the same indistinct voices that were calling to him.

And he knew that soon all of them would answer that call.

Handing the heavy tool kit to Kent, Eric led the way out of the carriage house and back down to the dock. As soon as Kent took the cowling off the motor, Eric saw the problem: the frayed starter rope had slipped from the pulley and wedged itself underneath, making it not only impossible to pull, but impossible for the motor to run as well.

"Needs a new rope," Tad said.

"Which we don't have," Kent responded.

"I saw an extra one in the boathouse," Eric said. "It's hanging on a nail in the closet with all the old life jackets."

As Tad went to get the new rope, Eric grabbed a couple of tools from the box and went to work. Fifteen minutes later the old rope was gone, the new one — which was almost as rotten as the old one — was on the pulley, and the final screw was tightened. "All I need is one pull," Eric said as he put the tools back in the kit. "If it starts, let's go to the marina and get a new rope. This one won't last until tomorrow."

He crossed his fingers, gave the rope a pull, and the motor instantly surged to life. As Kent replaced the cowling, Tad cast off the lines.

"Let's go," Tad said as he threw the last line off its cleat.

Eric pulled the boat away from the dock and turned toward town.

The sun was now shining brightly in a cloudless sky, and the only reminder of this morning's squall was the leftover chop on the lake. Even that died out as they rounded the point that separated The Pines from the town itself. As the boat settled down to skim across the now glassy water, Kent finally began talking about the subject all three of

them had been thinking about.

Whatever it was that lay behind the bricked-up doorway.

"If we just stack the bricks inside that back room, nobody would ever know the door had been bricked up."

Eric's brows knit uncertainly.

"The photo shows the door," Tad said. "And if we slide that plywood back over it after we see what's there, nobody would even know we went inside."

"So what do you guys think is in there?" Eric asked, realizing even as he spoke that whatever they finally decided to do with the bricks and the plywood, the decision to find out what was behind them had already been made.

"Stuff that somebody doesn't want us to see," Tad said.

Kent nodded.

And despite the sun shining overhead, a shiver crept up Eric's back. Tightening his grip on the control, he held the boat on a steady course.

As he eased the boat up to the dinghy tie-up on the fuel dock at the marina, Tad tossed a line around a cleat, used it to pull the skiff snug to the dock, then waited for Kent to make the stern fast before dropping the fenders over the side and hitching the

bow line. It took them no more than ten minutes to find what they were looking for, but ten more to pay for it, and in the twenty minutes they were gone, something had changed at the marina.

A familiar figure was standing on the fuel dock, filling the tank of his family's boat. And the dinghy tie-up was at the far end of the fuel dock.

"Crap," Eric said quietly. "There's Adam Mosler."

"And Ellis Langstrom," Kent said.

"Ignore them," Tad said. "We'll just walk by."

But Adam wouldn't be ignored, and as the three of them approached, he centered himself squarely in the middle of the dock, feet spread, arms crossed over his chest.

"What are you dickheads — oops, I mean *cone*heads — doing on our dock?"

"Just leaving," Tad said.

"And it's not your dock," Kent added.

"In your little girlie boat?" Adam asked, ignoring Kent. "Better hurry or you won't make it all the way home before dark." His lips twisted into a sneering grin. "Bad things can happen to coneheads after dark."

Doing his best to ignore Adam, Eric moved quickly around the other boy, walked to the end of the dock, and tossed the new

180

rope into the Pinecrest boat. As he was climbing in, Kent and Tad caught up with him, untied the boat, and shoved it away from the dock before Adam had a chance to try to pick a fight.

Eric offered a silent prayer to the god of little outboard motors and pulled the rope.

Miraculously, it started.

He gave the engine a little gas and the boat moved away from the dock, leaving Adam glowering after them.

"Why does he want to be such a jerk?" Tad asked, neither expecting nor getting an answer to his question.

Eric guided the boat out of the marina and away from town, and as they pulled out into the open lake, he finally began to relax. Only a moment later, though, he heard the roar of a powerful outboard, and his guts told him what it was even before he glanced back over his shoulder. Sure enough, Adam Mosler was steering his father's runabout straight toward them, racing at full speed. Ellis Langstrom was standing behind Adam, hanging onto Adam's seat with one hand, clutching the boat's rail with the other. Only at the last possible moment did Mosler throttle back and let the runabout's bow drop into the water, bringing the boat to a stop alongside their little dingy.

"Going fishing, girls?" Adam mocked, then eyed the bait bucket on the floor of the dinghy. "Eeewww, worms!" he said in an exaggeratedly girlish voice. "Who's going to bait your hooks?"

Eric held his course steady, silently praying that Kent wouldn't try to pick a fight out here in the middle of the lake.

Once again his prayers were answered.

"Okay," Adam said, finally deciding that neither Eric nor his friends were going to rise to his taunts. "We'll leave you to your summer fun." He shoved the throttle forward; the motor roared, the boat surged, and Adam flipped the wheel and cut sharply away from Eric's boat, executing the maneuver so quickly that Ellis Langstrom nearly lost his balance.

The spewing rooster tail built so quickly that Eric had no time to escape it, and as Adam's boat shot away, a cascade of water poured into the dinghy. Tad Sparks instinctively tried to dodge away from the deluge, but succeeded only in slipping off the seat and banging his shoulder against the side of the boat as he fell. Soaked to the skin once more, the three of them could hear Adam laughing as he sped back toward town.

"Bastard," Kent said. "I'd like to kill that guy."

"Forget him," Eric said.

"I don't want to forget him," Kent said. "You okay?" he asked Tad.

Tad scrambled back onto the seat, rubbing his shoulder. "Yeah," he said. "I shouldn't have tried to duck."

"It's not your fault," Kent said. "What a jerk. Maybe we should go back to town, find him, and teach him a lesson."

"Or maybe," Eric countered as he turned the boat back on course toward Pinecrest, "we should just go home and forget about Adam Mosler." As Kent opened his mouth to argue, Eric grinned. "My folks are off playing golf, and Marci's going to that Summer Fun thing at the school. Which means we'll have plenty of time to unbrick that door and see what's behind it."

Kent looked once more at Adam Mosler's boat. "Okay," he said. "Besides, who knows? Maybe there'll be something in there I can use to get that loser."

Eric twisted the throttle and the boat picked up speed. A moment later they rounded the point, and Adam Mosler's boat disappeared.

But, though Adam Mosler and Ellis Langstrom were no longer visible, they were not forgotten.

Rita Henderson saw the sheriff's car pull up and silently rehearsed what she was going to say to the two boys who were sitting in the backseat. She didn't care much for Adam Mosler, and was fairly sure that sooner or later he'd take a wrong turn on the road of his life and wind up in prison, if not worse. But Ellis Langstrom was another matter, and when she'd recognized him in the boat with Adam, she called Floyd Ruston, who had been the sheriff as long as Rita could remember and was every bit as eager as she herself that nothing happen to dent the tourist trade that was all that kept the town alive. It had taken her no more than a minute to convince Ruston to throw a scare into the two boys, and no more than ten to bring them to her. Now Rita swiveled in her chair and made a few notes on her pad as she heard three car doors slam and footsteps come up the wooden porch steps to her office door.

She looked up when the door opened, then stood and held her hand out to Sheriff Ruston. "Thank you, Rusty," she said, deliberately using his nickname to make it clear to the boys just how close her relationship with the sheriff was.

"If you hadn't called, I'd have impounded that boat and arrested these boys," Ruston

replied, sticking perfectly to the script they'd worked out on the phone.

Rita set her mouth in a grim line and inspected the two who stood before her.

Adam Mosler was on the verge of a smirk — no surprise — but Ellis Langstrom looked positively terrified.

Good.

"Reckless endangerment," the sheriff went on, starting to tick off the boys' various offenses on his fingers. "Exceeding the five mile per hour speed limit in the marina. Ignoring the no wake rule."

Rita nodded.

"If it were up to me, they'd both spend the rest of the summer attending Power Squadron classes and doing a whole lot of community service. Not to mention the six hundred and twenty dollars Adam's father would have to pay to get his boat out of impoundment."

Rita noticed Adam's smirk fading. "Sounds like they both owe you a debt of gratitude for not doing all that," she said pointedly.

Ellis got the message in an instant and turned to face the sheriff. "Thank you," he said, clearly on the verge of tears. "It won't happen again. Really — I promise."

Adam mumbled his apology, and Rita

wanted to shake him, but she was prepared to settle for what little she could get, especially since Ruston hadn't actually seen any of what the boys had done himself, and wouldn't have wanted to risk Cleve Mosler's wrath anyway. Not with an election coming up in the fall.

A moment later the sheriff was gone, and it was Rita's turn.

"It isn't just the recklessness," she said, feeling her blood pressure rise as a smirk began to curl around the corners of Adam's mouth again. "I saw what you did — you were hassling summer people from The Pines."

Ellis looked at the floor, but Adam merely gave her an insolent glance.

"I'm so disgusted with both of you that I can barely stand to look at you," she went on. "Especially you, Ellis. How much do you think the local residents spend in your mother's store?" She barely gave Ellis a chance to speak before answering her own question. "Not much! Not much at all. It's the summer people and the tourists who put money in our bank accounts and food on our tables. They give you summer jobs." She moved directly in front of Adam to make her point. "Actually, *I* give you summer jobs on their behalf. Is that clear?"

She waited for a response.

An apology, maybe.

Or a thank-you for saving them from the possibility of criminal prosecution and juvenile court.

Anything.

But there was no response from either of them.

"Are you listening to me?" Rita finally demanded.

"Yes, ma'am," Ellis said.

Adam nodded.

"I saved your butts this time because I think you deserve a break. Once. *Once.* Next time, I'll let Sheriff Ruston haul you off and take your father's boat." Adam glowered at her, his face twisted with fury. "So you'd both better grow up and do something constructive with your time." She stared at Adam, who met her gaze unflinchingly. "Get it?"

"Yes, ma'am," Ellis said.

"Adam?" Rita demanded, her gaze unwavering.

After what seemed an eternity, Adam's eyes shifted to the floor. "I hear you," he said.

"Good," Rita said. "Now get out of here, both of you."

As soon as they were outside, Adam pulled a crumpled pack of cigarettes from his jeans pocket and took his time lighting one. He glanced back through the window at Rita Henderson, who was back at her desk but watching them. "Bastards," he said softly. "Maybe we should just kill 'em. All of 'em."

"Will you shut up?" Ellis said. "What if she hears you?" He walked down the steps to the sidewalk. "I'm going over to my mom's shop."

"You workin' today?"

Ellis shrugged, glancing at Rita Henderson, who was still watching them. "I think I'll just go help her out. It's summer — she'll be busy."

"So go," Adam said, his voice taking on a sarcastic edge as he sauntered down the steps, deliberately flicking the ash of his cigarette on the real estate office porch. "Go do what that Henderson bitch wants, and I'll think of a way to get even with those pricks."

"Why don't you just give it up, Adam?" Ellis started down the sidewalk, walking faster to put some distance between them. "It's not like they ever actually did anything to you."

"Who cares?" Adam countered as Ellis moved away. When Ellis disappeared around

the corner, he tossed his half-smoked cigarette into some bushes and spoke again,
more to himself than to anyone who might
be listening. "What they did isn't the point
— it's what they are. And I say they're a
bunch of snotty pricks, and I'm going to
teach them a lesson they'll never forget."

CHAPTER 11

Eric Brewster watched nervously as Kent Newell pried the first brick loose from the wall. His parents had barely disappeared around the curve in the driveway before he'd led Kent and Tad back down to the carriage house, where Tad had insisted on keeping a lookout at the door while Eric and Kent set to work on the wall. Within five minutes, though, Tad's curiosity had overcome his fear that Eric's folks might come back and catch them, and now he was hovering just behind Eric, seeming even more nervous than Eric himself.

The brick suddenly slid out. Kent handed it to Eric, who set it carefully on the floor, cradling it as gingerly as if it were a piece of crystal that might shatter in his hands, dust from the rotting mortar sticking to his moist palms.

Tad Sparks took the next brick, and within minutes Kent had removed enough of them

to make a hole they could look through.

"Hand me the flashlight," Kent whispered, lowering his voice as if something that lay beyond the bricks might hear him.

Eric passed him the broad-beam flashlight they'd brought from the house, then crowded close to Kent for a first glimpse of what was behind the bricked-up doorway as Tad Sparks tried to see over Kent's other shoulder.

The musty odor of mold and dust wafted through the opening, and for a second Eric felt oddly dizzy.

"More boxes," Tad said as Kent played the beam of light around the small room.

"And a bunch more old furniture," Kent added, clearly disappointed that the contents of the hidden room seemed to be more of the same stuff that filled the room in which they were standing.

"There has to be something different about that stuff, though," Eric said. "I mean, why is it in there instead of out here? There's got to be a reason why someone bricked up the doorway." Reaching over Kent's shoulder, he grabbed a brick and tugged hard.

It came away in his hand, loosening a dozen others, which tumbled to the floor in a cascade of clatter and dust.

The boys moved back, and Kent passed the flashlight to Eric. "Jeez, Eric — be careful!" he said.

Elbowing Eric aside, Kent moved forward again, and working as swiftly and as silently as he could, dismantled the rest of the doorway. When the hole was big enough to step through, Kent straightened up and handed the last brick to Tad. But then, realizing there was no longer any barrier between himself and the hidden room, he stepped back.

"You want to go in first?" he asked Eric.

As Eric gazed at the gaping hole where a brick wall had stood, his heart began pounding so hard that his breath caught in his chest. Even so, he gripped the flashlight tight and stepped over the few remaining rows of bricks into the dark room.

A feeling of utter isolation instantly fell over him. It was as if he were totally alone in a dark and cavernous place — a dangerous place — where unseen evil lurked in every shadowy corner. Turning away from the blackness, he ran into a veil of cobwebs that covered his face and nearly dropped the flashlight in panic as he clawed them away.

"This is so weird," Tad whispered, stepping through the doorway and moving close

to Eric. Eric reached out, closed his fingers on Tad's arm, and immediately regained his equilibrium.

Despite the cool of the chamber, perspiration burst from his forehead.

"It's bigger than I thought," Kent said as he, too, stepped through to join them.

Eric slowly moved the flashlight beam around the room, his heart still hammering, his hand trembling as he wiped bits of cobweb from his eyelashes and hair. The room was, indeed, much larger than they'd expected — it seemed almost the size of his bedroom up in the main house. Yet from the dimensions of the carriage house, he'd expected it to be only a few feet wide and deep, no more than a large closet.

And now that they were inside the room, they began to see that in fact it was different from the storeroom behind which it was hidden. This chamber was well organized, with a desk, a long table, and bookshelves, as well as stacks of boxes, some of which were beginning to slump with age.

And it was filled with a heavy odor that made Eric think of death and decay.

Tad's voice broke the silence that had fallen over them as Eric played the light around the walls. "This box is open," he said. "Give me some light."

Eric turned the light toward Tad, who lifted an old black leather valise out of a box and set it on the table.

"What is it?" Kent asked.

Tad gazed at the object for a second, then recognized it from something he'd seen in one of the antiques stores his mother had taken him to a couple of years ago. "It's an old medical bag. Maybe it was Dr. Darby's."

"What's in it?" Eric asked.

Tad unlatched the tarnished catch and stretched the bag's hinged mouth wide.

Eric shone the light inside.

Empty.

Turning away from the bag, Tad opened more of the boxes while Kent began exploring the drawers of the desk.

Eric went to the bookshelves and played the light over the titles, but many of the books were so old and worn that the printing on the spines was all but illegible. Still, he had a feeling that whatever the reason this room had been sealed up, the books were part of it.

"Look at this old lamp," Tad said, breaking Eric's reverie as he pulled a heavy, ornate lamp base from a box that was all but invisible in the dim light from the single bulb in the storeroom. He set the lamp on the table, which wobbled under its weight.

"Table's missing a leg," Kent said, pointing to the two small boxes that were all that supported one corner of the table.

Eric ran his finger along the dusty spines of the books, brushing them just clean enough to make out their titles. Most of them appeared to be old medical texts.

A row of jars with black screw tops and murky contents lined the top shelf, but in the darkness that was broken only by the flashlight and the spillover from the storeroom next door, he couldn't tell what was inside them.

Then his finger passed over a different kind of book, and he felt a strange sensation — almost like electricity. He pulled the volume from the shelf and laid it on the table. A single word was stamped on the front in ornate gold script: *Ledger.*

Eric looked up from the book to see that Tad had become fixated on the lamp base, turning it around and around as he studied the intricate scrollwork, and that Kent was lost in tracing the pattern of the cracked Formica on the tabletop with his forefinger.

"Look what I found," Eric said, and both their heads snapped up as if his words had startled them out of a deep sleep. As they moved closer, Eric opened the ledger to the first page.

Written in a fine, old-fashioned copperplate script were a variety of notes:

10/8 acq ladder fm M. Heuser. $17.
10/10 Saw R. Squireson .75 hr
10/11 Chimney swept. Hired F. MacIntosh
gardener.

Eric turned the page.

11/3 acq painting for dng rm fm H.H.$9.
11/5 acq chaise fm J. Sanders $6
11/7 weigh 177. Must stop dairy

He flipped to the middle of the book.

7/6 sld washbasin $4, acq 3/6 $47. No
energy. Suspect fraud
8/1 Saw R. Logan 1.5 hr.
8/5 Brkn window in boathouse fx'd.

Tad reached out and touched the second entry with his forefinger. "Logan," he breathed.

"And what's that mean?" Kent asked, pointing to the entry above the one that mentioned Logan. "Fraud on a forty-seven dollar washbasin?"

But Eric was eager to continue and kept turning pages, his eyes scanning each of them in turn, the whole process taking on

the same almost automatic, oddly hypnotic rhythm they'd experienced with the photo album in the other room.

Page after page contained strangely cryptic notes — words that didn't quite mean anything, or seemed oddly out of place — all written in the same fine hand.

At the end of the thick tome were half a dozen blank pages, but only when he was gazing at the inside of the back cover did Eric turn to the final entry.

I've acquired the final piece, but if I fit it to its mate I know my strength will fail. The power overwhelms me now — it is far stronger than I.

I shall therefore close this room, leaving all but one of the pieces inside.

Perhaps I should never have begun this venture, but I have the strength neither to continue the research, nor destroy what I have taken such pains to amass.

I pray that some day someone stronger will finish what I have begun.

May God have mercy on my wretched soul.

— H.D.

Kent whistled softly as he finished reading the entry, and Tad looked up to gaze straight

at Eric. "H.D.," he said. "Hector Darby. And that sounds like a suicide note, doesn't it?"

Instead of answering Tad's question, Eric played the beam of the flashlight around the room. "What is all this stuff?" he asked. His heart was beating faster again, and as the now fading beam of the flashlight hit each object, he felt a strange sense of excitement. Suddenly, he wanted to touch everything — to feel the objects — to experience them. It was almost as if the contents of the room had found voices and were whispering to him, calling to him.

But it was more than that, more than merely a need to look at the strange amalgam of seeming junk that filled the room.

No, it was much, much more. Eric — indeed, all three of the boys — were feeling an almost electric eagerness to absorb and understand everything in the room.

As the flashlight beam faded to a dull yellow, Eric hit it onto the palm of his hand. It flickered strong for a moment, then faded again. "What's the matter with this?" he muttered.

"What time is it?" Tad asked.

Eric glanced at his watch, then looked again. Disbelieving what his eyes were tell-

ing him, he tapped its face, then held it up to his ear.

Its ticking was faint, but definitely there. "Five minutes to five?" he breathed, making it more a question than a statement. He looked first at Tad, then at Kent. "How could that be? We've only been in here — what — a half hour?"

"We got here at one," Kent said. "I know — I looked at my watch."

"Crap," Eric said. "My folks'll be back any minute." Turning away from the room and its contents, he led the way back through the broken brick wall, leaving everything as it was, and together the three of them pulled the sheet of plywood back across the opening.

Eric put the flashlight back in the tack room, and they walked out of the carriage house into the bright afternoon sunshine. He felt strangely disoriented, as if the daylight was wrong, as if the outdoors was too big. He quickened his step as he headed up the lawn toward the house.

The message light was blinking on the phone when they came through the back door into the kitchen, and he pressed the button to play back the message.

"Hi, honey," his mother said through the tinny speaker. "The six of us had a great

round of golf and your dad picked up Marci from Summer Fun. We all decided to have dinner here at the club, and if you and the boys want to join us, Tad's mother says there's a taxi you can call. Or you can all go into town for a pizza if you want to. Just behave yourselves, and be careful, and be home by ten-thirty, okay? Eleven at the latest. Love you."

Eric looked at his friends, and could read the decision in their faces as clearly as it was in his own mind. If they went into town for pizza, they could be back in less than an hour.

And that would give them at least two more hours in Hector Darby's secret room.

"Let's go now so we can get back sooner," Tad said, voicing Eric's thought almost exactly.

Eric took a bite of pizza, even though he wasn't hungry. All he could think about was the secret room, and the stuff in it, and the ledger.

And the way he'd felt when he was in that room, every nerve in his body seeming to tingle.

Time vanishing away, leaving him feeling . . . how?

He wasn't sure. It was a strange feeling,

but not bad. It wasn't as if he couldn't remember everything that had happened, but somehow hours slipped away in what felt like minutes.

And then, at the end, just before they'd all left, there had been that strange sensation of hearing voices, but not really hearing them at all.

Now that he was sitting in the bright lights of the pizza parlor, it all seemed even stranger. Strange, but not really frightening. But shouldn't he be frightened? Shouldn't all of them be? Hours had passed, and none of them had been aware of it.

Maybe they should just brick up the doorway again.

Maybe —

"Know what I think?" Kent Newell said, breaking Eric's thoughts as he pushed his own uneaten slice of pizza away. "I think we should stop pretending to be hungry and go buy a couple of lanterns so we can get some decent light in there — you know, those Coleman ones that are almost as good as electric lights."

Tad nodded. "At least we'd be able to see what we're doing." He hesitated, then spoke again, avoiding his friends' gazes. "I mean, if we're really gonna do it."

"What do you mean, 'if'?" Kent flared.

"We already broke in — all we're doing now is finding out what that stuff is. And if we leave now," he added, "we can get another look inside that room before our folks get home."

"I don't want my dad to catch us in there," Eric said. "So let's pay a little better attention to the time, okay?" And even as he spoke the words, Eric knew he wasn't going to brick the secret room back up. Instead, he'd just agreed to go back into it tonight, and his excitement was starting to grow.

"There's something in there," Kent said softly. "Something big. Something important."

Tad flagged down the waitress to bring a box for the leftover pizza, and a few minutes later they were out of the pizza parlor and halfway down the block, heading for the sporting goods store. But before they came to it, Eric stopped in front of the ice cream shop. Inside, Cherie Stevens was behind the counter, loading a sugar cone with ice cream the same shade of pink as her apron.

"You guys go get the lanterns," Eric said. "Come back for me."

"Aw come on, Eric," Kent protested. "Not now!"

"I'm just going to say hello," Eric said.

"Go get the lanterns." And before either of them could protest any further, he pushed the door open and stepped inside.

The cool interior was filled with the sweet scent of ice cream and toasted cones. Cherie looked up and smiled at him as she finished with the couple at the counter. The only other people in the shop were a woman and a little boy who sat at one of the small round tables, eating dishes of ice cream. Eric walked up to the counter, suddenly feeling as if he were six years old. Instead of looking at Cherie, he found himself staring at the variously colored squares of fudge that were laid out in the case.

"Hi," Cherie said.

"Hi." Eric tried to look up, and failed. Now his heart was pounding even harder than when he'd been in the secret room that afternoon. Except that this afternoon it had been exciting. Now he just felt like an idiot. "I — I think I'd like some fudge," he stammered. "Is it good?" Is it good? he echoed silently to himself. Bigger idiot!

"It really is. Want a taste?"

Eric managed to nod, and pointed at a dark chocolate slab that was studded with nuts.

Cherie sliced off a bite and handed Eric a square of wax paper with the taste of fudge

on it. "I'll take a hunk of that," he said.

Cherie's brow rose. "You haven't even tasted it yet."

Eric felt himself blushing. "Don't need to. You said it's good."

Cherie rolled her eyes, but smiled. "How much do you want?"

Eric shrugged.

Cherie sliced off a chunk, wrapped it up, and put it into a little white bag. "On the house," she whispered as she handed it to him. "What are you doing later?"

"I'm going to — I've got to do some —" He fell silent for a moment, then: "Hey, do you know anything about Hector Darby?"

"Dr. Darby?" Cherie replied, and Eric nodded. "Sure." She wiped her hands on a white cloth and leaned in against the counter. "He used to own Pinecrest."

Eric nodded again. "Yeah, I know."

"So what do you want to know about him?"

The bell on the door dinged, and Eric saw Cherie's eyes flick to the door, then back to him, disappointment clear in her expression. "Uh-oh," she whispered, then stood up straight. "Hi, Kayla. Hi, Chris."

"Hey, Cherie," Kayla Banks said.

Eric turned to see a pretty brunette about his own age, holding hands with a tall,

skinny kid. Then he recalled that the skinny kid had been with Adam Mosler his first day in town, when he and Marci were walking Moxie.

Eric held up the white bag. "Thanks," he said, turning around to leave. But just before he reached the door, it opened and Adam Mosler himself walked in.

" 'Bye, Eric," Cherie called. "See you at the dance Friday night."

Eric's heart skipped a beat, but his gut knotted as he saw the expression Cherie's words brought to Adam Mosler's eyes. Then he decided he'd had enough of Adam Mosler. "I'll be there," he called back over his shoulder.

And Mosler walked right into him, bumping him hard with his chest, knocking him against a table, which tipped over onto a couple of chairs, then crashed to the floor.

The woman with the little boy looked up in alarm.

Wishing that he'd just kept his mouth shut and ducked past Mosler, Eric apologized to the woman and quickly picked up the fallen furniture.

Meanwhile, Adam Mosler regarded him with an evil sneer. "Oh, gee, excuse me all to hell," he said, his tone emphasizing the sarcasm of his words.

Eric saw Kent Newell and Tad Sparks walking up outside, carrying plastic bags from the sporting goods store, and he knew it would be better to get past Mosler before Kent decided to get involved. "Apology accepted," he muttered to Adam, and pushed the door open.

Too late. "Was that guy hassling you again?" Kent demanded. "I can kick his ass, you know. And I can do it right now."

"No. Let's just go."

"You sure?"

"I'm sure," Eric said. "Let's just not get into anything now, okay?" Before Kent could argue, Eric relieved him of the pizza box and started toward the dinghy dock at the marina.

Kent glanced back at Adam Mosler once more, but then turned and followed Eric and Tad to the dock. Though part of him wanted to punch Adam Mosler's lights out, another, far stronger, part of him wanted to get back into the secret room hidden in the carriage house at Pinecrest.

Already, Kent thought he could hear voices whispering to him.

Voices that wanted something.

But what?

Soon, he was sure, he would know.

All of them would know.

The tingling sensation began to come over Kent even before he'd stepped through the door into the hidden room, and by the time he actually followed Eric and Tad over the threshold, every nerve in his body seemed to be vibrating with an energy he'd never felt before. He set the lantern on the desk, pumped it up, then carefully lit it with a wooden match from the box they'd found in the kitchen. As he adjusted the flow of fuel, the orange flame around the mantle disappeared as the mantle itself began to emit a blinding white light that banished the shadows from most of the room.

A few seconds later Tad set the second lantern on the old three-legged table, lit it, adjusted the flame, then straightened up as the new lantern washed away what few shadows were left. Yet even though the room was now flooded with bright light, its feeling hadn't changed at all, and Tad shivered as a sense of anticipation flooded over him.

Something was about to happen.

He could *feel* it.

His eyes fixed on the ledger that still lay on the table, open to Hector Darby's final entry, and as he gazed at the thick tome, Tad felt as if he could almost hear Darby's

voice whispering inside his head. "It feels so weird in here," he breathed. "It's like I'm on a roller coaster that's almost at the top. Know how that feels?"

Kent Newell barely glanced at him, but Eric nodded. "Like you sort of wish you hadn't gotten on in the first place, but you don't really want to stop, either."

"So what do we do?" Kent asked. "Where do we start?"

Eric's eyes focused on the ledger. "Let's see if we can match any of the stuff in the room to what he wrote in the book." He rested his hand on the Formica surface of the broken table. "See if there's anything in there about this thing."

"How'm I supposed to know what I'm looking for?" Kent asked as he turned back the pages of the old ledger. "I can't even figure out what half of these things mean, and even if I find a table, how're we going to know it's the right one?"

Eric moved around the table, then bent down to look at its underside. Taped to the inside of the table's frame, he found a small tag. Pulling it loose, he stood up and held the tag so the light of one of the lanterns fell full on it. "It's from Plainfield," he said. "It's got some numbers on it, but I don't know what they mean."

"Let me see," Tad said. He peered closely at the tag, then: "It's an auction tag. I've been to some with my mom. They put these tags on everything. The number just means which lot it was at the auction."

"Well, here's something from Plainfield," Kent said, poring over the ledger. "But it still doesn't make any sense."

Eric and Tad moved toward Kent, flanking him on either side and peering over his shoulder at the entry in the ledger:

7/11 acq table (#36) frm est. sale Milwaukee $10,350. Bargain.

"Ten thousand dollars?" Tad said. "That can't be for this. It's gotta be for something else. Is that right?"

"Gotta be that table," Eric said. "Same — what did you call it? — lot number? Thirty-six is what's on the tag."

Kent reread the line, following it along with his finger. "That's nuts," he said. "Old Darby must have been some kind of wacko."

Eric went back to the scarred Formica table and ran his hands over its surface, feeling not only the cracks and chips, but something else as well.

A faint tingling feeling, the same feeling he got from the ledger when he first found

it on the bookshelf. Almost like electricity flowing from the table into his fingers. He stood perfectly still, savoring the odd sensation until Tad's voice broke through his reverie.

"What about this doctor's bag?" Tad said, and Eric finally moved away from the table and started pulling the drawers of the old Victorian desk open one by one as Kent thumbed through the ledger.

"Here it is," Kent said, pointing to a single line in the middle of one of the pages so Tad could read it as well.

1/5 acq phys valise complete frm J.Stackworth, GBR £34,670. Beauty.

"I don't get it," Tad said. He picked up the leather valise and shook it upside down. Nothing came out.

"He wouldn't have used something this expensive himself, would he?"

"He was a shrink," Kent said. "They don't even carry bags, do they? Besides, this one's got to be at least a hundred years old. And it's all beat up. What would make it worth that kind of money?"

"Wait a second," Eric said from behind them. "What's this?" He set a small bundle on the table. It was wrapped in layers of

black oilcloth and tied with twine so rotten that it broke apart as he put the bundle down. "It was in the bottom drawer of the desk."

"Open it up," Kent said.

Eric looked up at him for a long moment, and Kent thought he saw a flicker of something in Eric's eyes. Then, very slowly, Eric began to unroll the small bundle.

When he unfolded the last layer, a complete set of surgical instruments lay exposed, which, in contrast to the scuffed and battered bag on the table, lay shining and glinting in the lamplight as if they were brand new.

Kent picked up a scalpel, feeling its heft and balance. The curved blade flashed like a mirror in the light.

"Look at this old shot needle," Tad said, picking up a metal hypodermic casing, still with the enormous slant-ended needle attached. He touched it to the end of his finger.

"Be careful with that," Kent said.

"There's all kinds of stuff here," Eric said, picking up first a retractor, then a spreader. There was a whole array of instruments, as if someone had put together an entire surgical kit. As he touched each of them, Eric felt the same flow of energy that had come

from the table on which the instruments now lay.

"What's this?" Tad asked, reaching for a small bit of something brown and dried.

"No!" Eric said, and hit his hand away. "Leave it alone. And give me back the hypo. And the scalpel. They need to all be kept together." He looked over at the valise, which now seemed to have a glow emanating from it. "They need to be back inside the bag."

Tad pushed the leather valise across the table to him, and as Tad and Kent watched, Eric very gently, one by one, placed the instruments inside it.

When he was finished, Eric closed the bag and snapped the catch, but his eyes remained fixed on it.

"You okay?" Kent asked after several seconds had passed.

Eric finally looked up at the other boys and smiled. "I feel great," he said.

Outside, Moxie began barking.

"Jeez," Eric said with a shiver. "Moxie's out. What time is it?"

Kent looked at his watch, then looked at it again.

Once again they had lost track of the time.

"It's five to eleven," he said, his voice hollow.

"Oh, man," Eric said. "My parents are home."

Quickly, they doused the lanterns, pulled the plywood back into place across the doorway, and left the carriage house. Eric led them around the back of the structure and along the edge of the woods, so when they finally walked up the lawn, it would look to his parents as if they were coming up from the lake.

His mother was silhouetted in the kitchen light as she held the door open for his father, who carried a sleeping Marci in from the car.

"It's eleven o'clock," she whispered loudly as the boys came up to the house. "Time for you to come in the house, Eric, and time for Kent and Tad to go home."

Eric nodded a good-bye to Kent and Tad, who took off toward the lakefront trail that would take them to their houses, then stepped into the bright light of the kitchen. He didn't want to talk to his mother, but neither did he want her to wonder if he'd been out drinking by going too quickly up to his room. He compromised by moving to the refrigerator and fishing out a Coke.

"What'd you three do tonight?" Merrill asked.

"Not much. Went into town for pizza.

Hung out."

"You missed a good dinner at the club."

Eric shrugged. "It's okay," he said, picking up the Coke and taking a sip. "I'm pretty tired."

Merrill Brewster smiled at her son. "It's late. Why don't you go on up to bed?"

"Yeah," Eric agreed, moving toward the door. "Think I will."

Eric walked quickly and quietly up the stairs and closed the door to his room. He didn't want to wake up Marci, nor did he want to talk with his father. He just wanted to think about what he and Kent and Tad had found in the hidden room.

Junk — what looked like absolutely worthless junk — had been bought for unbelievably high prices, prices he could barely even imagine.

He kicked off his shoes, stretched out on top of the bed, and instantly felt as though his bones were melting right into the mattress. The moon was too high in the sky to see, but its silvery light sparkled on the lake and spread a calm light throughout his room.

How had it gotten to be eleven o'clock?

It seemed impossible.

Maybe he should call Tad or Kent on their cell phones. Or log on to see if they were

online to chat.

But what good would it do? They didn't know any more than he did, and all it would turn into would be a bunch of meaningless speculations.

But one thing he knew for certain: he was as exhausted after the hours he'd spent in the hidden room as he would have been if he'd been working hard all day long and all evening, too.

Too tired even to undress and get under the covers, Eric pulled his pillow out from under the bedspread, plumped it up under his head, and closed his eyes.

Chapter 12

He clutched the heavy wool cloak tight around his throat to ward off the bone-chilling fog. The street seemed empty, though he knew that wasn't true.

Somewhere nearby someone else was searching, too.

He felt safe in the fog, knowing that its cold, white shroud protected him from prying eyes.

He was on a narrow, cobbled street that he knew wound down toward the docks. He had hunted here before, and now the smell of the place — the water, the fish, the sewage, even the vomit — all stirred something deep in his gut.

Soon a new fragrance would be added to the mix, and his pulse quickened as he thought about it.

His whole body was tingling as if some kind of current were running through it.

He saw her.

She was barely visible, lurking in a doorway,

all but lost in the shadows. But still, despite the darkness and the fog, he knew.

She was the one.

She was perfect.

His hunger flared.

He slowed, feeling his excitement grow.

And feeling the emptiness of the streets around them.

They were alone.

Beneath his cloak, he slipped off a leather glove and slid his hand deep into an inner pocket.

His fingers closed on smooth, cold steel.

He was close to her now, and she spoke, her voice muffled by the fog. "Raw night, ain't it?"

The mounds of her breasts pushed vulgarly up from the top of her dress, but they were blushing an authentic red from the cold, not from the rouge pot.

Her hair was blond and crumpled messily on top of her head. Garish rouge and bright red lipstick turned what could have been a pretty face into a grotesque mask.

Her blue eyes were outlined with black that had smudged through the course of the night, giving her a look of ineffable sadness.

Sadness he knew he could cure.

"Yes," he said, moving closer to her. "Raw."

She offered him a twisted parody of a

coquettish smile, ruined by a missing tooth.

He held up a bill between two of the gloved fingers of his left hand, and she eagerly reached for it, but he pulled it back, holding the bill just out of her grasp.

"Someplace warm," he said.

"All right, then," she said, "whatever you say." She pulled her ragged coat closed at the neck. "This way." She turned and led him down a narrow cobbled alley, crooked and dark, lined with shadows.

He followed, outwardly calm but barely able to contain the excitement spreading through him.

His grip tightened on the object concealed beneath his cloak.

The scalpel.

The scalpel whose need to work seemed almost as great as his own.

Tippy lay curled on the chair cushion, her eyes wide in the moonlit darkness, her ears flicking to catch the sound of any movement the darkness might hide even from her sharp eye.

Suddenly her body tensed.

There it was! One tiny sound nearly lost in the cacophony of crickets and frogs at the water's edge.

Nearly lost, but not quite.

She knew that sound. She'd been waiting for it.

A mouse.

Silently, the cat stood, stretched, and jumped lightly from the chair to the patio, then stopped to listen again.

Her ears twitched, and caught the sound once more: by the woodpile at the edge of the trees.

Slowly, quietly, one soft step at a time, Tippy crept through the grass, ears forward, eyes trained on her destination.

She heard the mouse gnawing on something hard.

As she drew closer, she slowed nearly to a standstill, fixing the exact location.

A blade of grass moved.

She froze, sniffed.

Something else was in the night.

Something that caught not only Tippy's attention, but the mouse's as well.

A moment later the breeze wafted the scent of the mouse into her nostrils, and Tippy crouched, her tail twitching in readiness, her hind feet moving to find a grip on the damp grass.

The mouse, unaware of the danger nearby, went back to its meal.

Tippy slunk a step closer. Paused.

Another step.

She could smell more than just the mouse now: she could smell its nest as well. It wasn't far away — just under a nearby board.

The mouse stopped, sitting up to look out over the grass, its eyes glinting like two tiny beacons in the moonlight.

Tippy tensed, trembling as she readied herself to pounce.

And in the instant she began her spring, a pair of hands grabbed her from behind.

Tippy splayed her claws, ready to do battle with the unseen attacker, but before she could react, she was flipped over onto her back. She kicked out with her powerful hind legs but caught nothing with her claws.

Her mouth gaped open to utter a yowl of fury, but even as the sound began to form in her throat a searing pain sliced through her belly.

She heard, rather than felt, her skin rip as two hands pulled her apart.

Then she knew no more.

A few moments later the crickets and frogs resumed their nighttime chorus.

The mouse nosed its way out of its nest, smelled a new scent, but deemed it to be of no danger.

Safe, it darted through the grass to resume its meal.

■ ■ ■ ■

The room the woman had led him to was so cold he could see his breath plume out in a steaming cloud, and the only light came from a gas street lamp outside the window.

The skewed rectangle of light lay directly on the woman's bed.

The bed where she lay, her painted lips curled back in a grimace that could have been mistaken for a smile.

But there was no smile in her eyes.

Her eyes were fixed and empty and beginning to glaze as she stared into eternity.

From her neck to her groin, though, she was exquisite, her skin laid open to expose all the secrets concealed within her body. Her entrails steamed in the cold, and scarlet trickles of blood still spilled over the edges of the slash.

He tortured himself by watching and waiting, holding off, tantalizing himself with the pleasure that was soon to come.

But not yet. Not yet. Not quite yet.

He fixed every detail in his mind so that later he would be able to revisit this girl and savor the gifts she had to offer. He would visit her many times in his memory, and in his dreams.

Only when he had committed every detail of her exposed body to his memory, but before

the freezing chill in the air turned the best part cold, did he finally drop the scalpel on the bloody bedspread and plunge his bare hands into her warm viscera.

Eric jerked awake with a sob.

He sat straight up in bed, utterly lost in the dark, his mind still full of the nightmare that had gripped him a moment ago.

His heart pounded so hard he saw red orbs glowing in the darkness around him.

Red, like the blood that filled the corpse into which he'd plunged his hands.

He gagged, rolled off the bed, and dashed to the bathroom, groping for the switch by the door, finding it.

Bright white light seared his eyes but freed him from the terror of the dream. He squinted, blinked, then saw his own image in the mirror.

He was still dressed in the clothes he'd worn yesterday.

His mind began to clear.

It had just been a nightmare.

His relief drained his strength away and he leaned against the sink for a moment, staring at himself in the mirror. His face was ashen.

Dark smudges lay beneath each eye, and

sweat stood out on his forehead and upper lip.

His heart still hammered, and the details of the dream began to replay in his mind.

He needed to look at his hands, but he didn't want to, terrified of what he might see.

He could still feel the slimy softness of the girl's insides, could still hear the wet sounds his fingers had made as he'd plunged them into her torn body.

His stomach heaved and he barely made it to the toilet before his mouth filled with vomit.

When the nausea passed, he took a deep breath, steeled himself, and then finally looked down.

Looked at his hands.

Nothing.

No blood.

Eric raised his hands to eye level and looked first at his palms and then at the backs.

He examined his fingernails.

Clean. No trace of blood at all.

Yet he could so clearly remember the feeling of plunging them inside her —

"Stop!" he whispered out loud. "It was only a dream."

He splashed cold water on his face, filled

the water glass and drank it down, then closed the lid on the toilet and sat for a moment.

The cold hard tile on the floor felt solid beneath his feet, and finally his pulse began to slow.

He waited, putting off the moment when he would have to go back into the bedroom where the nightmare might be waiting to torture him once more.

But it hadn't been real, he told himself. It had only been a dream.

Yet even as he silently reassured himself, he could almost feel the cold steel of the scalpel in his right hand.

But it had only been a dream, he told himself once more. It couldn't have been real, any of it.

Could it?

CHAPTER 13

The smell from the kitchen greeted Eric as he opened his bedroom door. He stood at the top of the stairs, rubbing his eyes, listening to his parents talking with his sister as they made breakfast.

A breakfast of waffles.

His stomach rumbled just at the thought, and he headed down to heed its call.

" 'Morning, sleepyhead," his mother said as he came into the kitchen.

" 'Morning." He kissed her on the cheek.

"Please, Daddy?" Marci was pleading in the dining room. "Can't we look for Tippy now?"

"This place is paradise for a cat, honey," Eric's father replied. "She just went hunting last night, that's all. She'll be back. Cats always come back."

"What's going on?" Eric tipped his head toward the dining room as he poured himself a glass of orange juice.

Merrill handed him a plate of waffles, hot off the iron. "Tippy didn't come home last night."

Eric carried the plate to the dining room, where the morning sun streamed in through the big windows. At the foot of the lawn, the lake appeared to be paved with sparkling diamonds, and ski boats were already out taking advantage of the perfect morning.

In an hour, he thought, he would be out there, too, fishing with Kent and Tad.

"Tippy comes in every morning for breakfast," Marci pronounced, clearly on the verge of tears. "What if she got lost? What if she's on her way back to our house in Evanston?"

"If she's not here by lunchtime, we'll go look for her," Dan said. "Okay?" He took the plate of waffles from Eric and forked two of them onto his plate. "Hey, sport. Great morning, huh?"

Eric grunted a greeting as he took a chair.

"I can't believe there was a waffle iron here," Merrill said as she came in with the coffeepot, refilled Dan's cup, and then set it on the table. "What a treat."

"Do you *have* to go back today, Daddy?" Marci asked.

"Yep, tomorrow's a workday. The float

plane's coming to pick us up this afternoon."

"This afternoon?" Marci echoed, her eyes now glistening with tears. "You said you were going to help me look for Tippy!"

"And we'll find her," Dan reassured her. "And if she's not back by the time I have to leave, Eric will help you look." He fixed Eric with a look that Eric knew would brook no argument. "Right, Eric?"

"Sure," Eric said, pouring warm syrup on his waffles. He didn't want to wander around in the woods calling the cat all day, but he knew there was no point in trying to get out of it, either.

By the time he had consumed two waffles and refused a third, Marci was already outside, calling Tippy. His father kissed his mother's cheek, dropped his napkin next to his plate, and sighed heavily.

"Guess I'd better get out there and give Marci a hand," he said, looking longingly at the thick Sunday paper that was lying untouched on a sideboard.

Merrill shrugged sympathetically, picked up two empty plates, took them to the kitchen and started loading the dishwasher.

Eric finished his juice, then took the remaining plates to the kitchen and gave them to his mother. In exchange, she

227

handed him a white plastic bag of garbage. "Please?"

"No problem." Eric took the bag out the back door and around to the side of the house, where a steel trash container with a bear-proof lid housed two big garbage cans.

He lifted one of the covers, then stopped short.

All the shop rags — at least a dozen of them — lay on top of the trash from last night.

Had his dad cleaned up the boathouse and thrown away all the rags they'd used while working on the motor?

But his father had told *him* to clean up the boathouse. And why would he throw the rags away? He never threw *anything* away, not even a broken TV that had been in the garage in Evanston for as long as Eric could remember. And the rags were still good — they'd looked practically brand new when he found them last week, even though they'd been in the boathouse for years.

Frowning, Eric put the bag of trash on the ground and picked up one of the rags. There was some kind of dark stain on it, but it didn't look like oil. He pulled out more of the rags.

They were all stiff and sort of a dark brown. Whatever had been cleaned up with

it had dried.

But they could still be washed, and the way the motor was acting, he was pretty sure he was going to need them.

Eric reached deeper into the barrel and came up with a wad of others, all stuck together.

He pulled them apart.

In the center was what looked like a fresh piece of liver, and his stomach churned as he realized what the rags were covered with.

Blood!

Every one of the rags was soaked with blood.

Feeling his breakfast rise in his gorge, Eric dropped the lot back into the can, put the garbage bag his mother had given him on top, then replaced the cover and closed the lid.

Without thinking, he wiped his hands on his pants.

And suddenly the dream came back to him full force.

The dream in which he'd been standing over a young girl.

A young girl whose belly he'd ripped open.

His bloody hands were deep inside her, the scalpel cool and smooth to his touch.

But what did that have to do with these

bloody rags?

Nothing.

It was just a dream.

Right?

No.

Somehow, in some way he didn't understand, these rags had something to do with his dream.

With him.

And with the scalpels in the carriage house.

Eric looked at his hands again. They were clean. No blood.

And there was no way he could have been anywhere but in his bed all night long.

So somebody else had put these bloody rags in here.

Somebody else had wrapped them around the piece of liver, or whatever it was.

His first impulse was to tell his father.

Maybe this was somebody's idea of a joke.

It wasn't very funny.

"Tippy!" Marci's voice came to him from the woods on the far side of the carriage house. "Tippy, come here."

And then the bloody rags and their disgusting contents assumed a brand new meaning.

And he knew this wasn't something he'd tell his father. This wasn't something he'd

tell anybody.

He walked quickly back into the house to wash his hands.

Kent stapled a copy of Marci's flyer to a pole by the pavilion, a pole that looked like it was covered with confetti, it had seen so many flyers before. "How many more?" he sighed, silently thanking his parents for never having inflicted a little sister on him, at least not one who would get so upset over a cat running away that she'd make him spend the whole day putting up posters when he could have been doing something else.

Anything else.

Tad riffled through the dwindling stack of missing-cat flyers. "Six."

"What a waste of time," Kent muttered under his breath. "That cat didn't come all the way into town."

"You think I don't know?" Eric sighed, taking another flyer from Tad and stapling it to the other side of the pole. "But the sooner we're finished with this, the sooner we can do something else."

"Maybe we could get Mrs. Langstrom to put one in the window of her shop," Tad said.

"Good idea," Kent said. "And the ice

cream shop, too. That way at least Marci'll see the poster every time she has an ice cream cone." He looked at Eric and grinned slyly. "Now, I wonder which one of us should go in there and ask?"

"I'll do it," Eric said at once, not even bothering to pretend he wasn't hoping Cherie might be at the counter again.

Taking a couple of the posters, he headed across the street, but when he looked through the window, he saw a different girl in a pink apron serving the ice cream. Still, it wouldn't hurt to ask if he could put up a flyer anyway.

Or maybe they should call the job done and just throw the rest of the posters in the trash. But even as he looked around for a barrel, he remembered his father's lecture on that exact temptation and the consequences he'd face if he succumbed to it.

A full week without access to the boat.

With another sigh, Eric headed for the door to the ice cream parlor, and came face-to-face with Adam Mosler, flanked by Ellis Langstrom and Chris McIvens.

"What's this?" Mosler grabbed the posters out of Eric's hand. "Oooohhh," he said in mock sadness. "Somebody's missing a little kitty cat." His two friends snickered.

"Give me those," Eric said, and snatched

them back again as Tad and Kent started across the street.

"You losers are wasting your time," Adam said. "If your cat's gone, it's dead."

"You don't know that, jerk," Kent said, falling in on one side of Eric as Tad flanked his other side.

"Yeah, I do know that, asshole," Adam said. "Know how many things out in the woods eat cats?"

"A pine marten got ours," Ellis Langstrom said.

"Plus there's weasels, raccoons, bears, wolverines, and a dozen other things," Chris McIvens added, grinning as Tad Sparks's face paled.

"Yeah," Adam chimed in. "This is the Northwoods, coneheads. You really think some dumb cat who's never seen anything worse than a squirrel is going to survive more than an hour?" Eric started to turn away, but Mosler added, " 'Course, even a cat would last longer than any of you pussies."

Kent took a step toward Mosler, his eyes narrowing, his fist clenched, but Eric reached out and took his arm. "Let's just go, okay?" he said, his voice low.

Kent hesitated, and Eric could almost feel him making his decision as some of the ten-

sion left the other boy's arm.

As the three of them crossed the street, leaving the local boys behind, Kent said, "I hate that punk."

"I know," Eric replied. "But let's just finish this and get out of here." He took two more flyers from Tad and handed them to Kent. "We each get rid of two and we're done."

Kent took his two, but his gaze followed Adam Mosler and his friends as they moved through the parking lot toward the dock. "You think maybe those guys took your cat?"

Eric shivered, the memory of his dream and of what he'd found in the garbage can that morning still fresh.

His stomach churned.

"No," he said. "They wouldn't do that. Anyway, I don't think they would. Besides, it doesn't matter, because even if they did, we'd never find out. Let's just get these flyers up and be done with it."

"They'd do it, all right," Kent said, his eyes glinting. "They'd take her, kill her, and love every second of it."

"C'mon," Tad said, and pulled Kent toward the antiques shop. "The cat probably just took off. It could be back by the time we get home." He led Kent into the

shop, but Eric didn't follow.

Instead, he stood on the sidewalk, feeling a dark knot of guilt forming in his belly.

But he had nothing to feel guilty about. Nothing!

And yet the memory of the dream didn't go away.

In his dream, he'd used that scalpel on a girl.

He'd taken her, and killed her.

And he'd loved every second of it.

The float plane was waiting at the dock when the Brewsters pulled into the parking lot by the pavilion. The Newells and the Sparkses were already there, talking with the pilot, and as Merrill walked down the dock to join them, she wished there were some way she could convince Dan to stay a few days longer, at least until they knew what had happened to Tippy. If the cat wasn't back by this evening, Marci would be crying herself to sleep, and Dan had always been better at comforting their daughter than she was. But all her arguments had fallen on deaf ears. "Everything's going to be fine," Dan had told her only an hour ago. "Tippy'll come back, you'll have a great week, and I'll be back on Friday night or Saturday morning."

Now he was looking at his watch and smiling at her. "This guy doesn't mess around," he said, waving at the pilot. "Right on time."

Merrill managed a wan smile, and a moment later they came to the plane.

"Looks like we got everyone," the pilot said, taking Dan's computer case and putting it in the back of the tiny plane. "Two of you in the back, one up front riding shotgun with me."

Dan squatted down for a hug from an unhappy Marci. "Look at that lip," he said to her. "You better watch out or you'll trip on it."

"Don't go!" the little girl begged.

"I don't want to, honey, but I have to." He drew Marci close. "Tomorrow you'll be back at Summer Fun, getting ready for the Fourth of July parade." He pulled back and gave her a kiss on the cheek. "Before you know it, it'll be Friday and I'll be back. And next weekend we'll do something special. I promise." Jeff Newell and Kevin Sparks were already boarding the little orange plane, which rocked gently at its mooring, and Dan straightened up to give his wife one more kiss.

"Call me when you get home," Merrill said, hugging him tightly.

"I will." Dan reached roughly for Eric and

gave him the kind of uncomfortable hug that was all his teenage son would accept from him right now. "You're the man of the house this week."

Eric nodded.

"Take care of your mother and your sister, okay?"

Eric nodded again. "Don't worry, Dad."

"I won't." He kissed Merrill one last time. "And don't you worry, either." He gave them a final wave, then climbed the two-step ladder into the plane.

The pilot cast off the single line that held the float plane to the dock, pushed the little aircraft away, then went in and pulled the door closed. A moment later the engines started and the plane taxied slowly out into the lake.

A wave of panic came over Merrill at the thought of spending the evening at Pinecrest with Dan nowhere close, and she turned to Ellen Newell and Ashley Sparks. "You two doing anything tonight?" she asked.

"I'm driving over to my cousin's for dinner," Ashley said. "Her son's talking about joining the army, and she's hoping I can talk him out of it." She rolled her eyes. "The problem is, of course, being that he's such a jerk, the army would be the best thing for him. But what can I do? She's my cousin."

"I've got tennis this afternoon, and I promised I'd have dinner with my doubles partner," Ellen Newell said. "How about we all get together tomorrow?"

Merrill tried not to let her disappointment show. "Okay."

The plane's engine roared then, and it picked up speed and rose into the air. After looping once around the lake, it headed south toward Chicago.

As the sun set and the shadows of the evening crept over Pinecrest, Merrill moved methodically through the house, closing all the draperies, turning on all the lights, and locking every door and window.

An hour later Eric was sprawled on a large but lumpily uncomfortable easy chair, halfheartedly watching reruns on television, while Marci kept fidgeting on the couch as her mother read her a book. Except Merrill read the book only sporadically. Every time she heard any kind of sound she couldn't instantly identify, she put it aside and prowled through the house.

"I think it's bedtime," she finally announced at ten o'clock.

Eric shrugged, more than ready to go upstairs and spend some time on the Web, maybe talking with Kent and Tad.

"Can I sleep with you tonight, Mommy?" Marci asked.

Merrill nodded. "Of course."

"We should put some food out first, though, in case Tippy comes home," the little girl went on. "She'll be hungry."

"Good idea," Merrill said. "Eric will go out with you."

"Why can't she go by herself?" Eric groaned. "All she has to do is open the door and set a bowl of food out on the steps."

"But it's dark out there," Marci objected, not quite able to keep her voice steady.

When his mother gave him a look that reminded him that he was supposed to be the man of the house — at least while his father was gone — Eric sighed and hauled himself up off the chair. "Come on, then."

Marci poured a cup of dry cat food into a small bowl, and Eric held the door open while she carried the food and a bowl of water out onto the patio.

The sky was full of stars, and a soft, warm breeze tinkled the wind chimes his mother had hung at the corner of the boathouse that morning.

Then Eric's eyes were drawn to the carriage house, which sat silent and dark. He felt an urge to go over there, or maybe to sneak out of bed after his mother had gone

to sleep and open up the hidden room to see what else might be there. He'd have nobody to tell him when to leave, nobody to distract him from his exploration.

But even as he felt the strange urge — as if something in that room were actually pulling at him — he knew that for tonight, at least, he wouldn't give in to the impulse. The horror of the nightmare hadn't fully released its grip on him even now, and he knew that something in the carriage house — something in the hidden room — had caused it.

But what?

"Can we go back in now?" Marci asked, breaking into his thoughts of the carriage house and what might lie within its walls.

"Don't you want to call Tippy?" Eric countered, though he was already certain that no amount of calling the cat could possibly summon it back.

"No," Marci whispered.

Eric cocked his head. "Why not?"

Marci peered nervously out into the night. "I don't like it out here. I don't want to make any noise."

Eric's brow lifted. "Getting to be as nervous as Mom?"

Marci shook her head vehemently. "No. But it feels like someone's watching me."

"Maybe a raccoon," Eric countered, "waiting for you to go inside so he can eat Tippy's food."

"He can't!" Marci declared. "It's for Tippy!" She abruptly seemed to lose her fear, and looked out into the darkness once again. "If there's a raccoon out there, you can just go away!" she called out. "This food's not for you! It's for my kitty!" When there was no response from out of the night, Marcie turned and marched back inside the house.

Eric took another moment, and, like his sister, gazed out into the darkness.

Suddenly he wasn't eager to go to bed at all, for bed meant sleep.

And sleep meant that terrible nightmare might return.

But sleep was inevitable.

He looked again at the dark silhouette of the carriage house and at the woods beyond.

Maybe there was a reason his mother and sister were so nervous. Maybe something was, after all, out there.

Watching.

Lurking.

Waiting.

But waiting for what?

A shiver ran up his spine.

He quickly stepped inside the house and locked the door behind him.

CHAPTER 14

Logan shuffled restlessly back and forth in the tiny cabin, the walls seeming to close in on him with every pace.

Like the walls of the room at the hospital so many years ago. . . .

Every time he looked at the little bundle, wrapped in an old piece of burlap he'd scrounged from a Dumpster, his stomach hurt, and he thought about the hospital and what it had been like.

And why he'd been there . . .

But he couldn't think about that now. He had to deal with the bundle, and he had to deal with it soon, but he didn't know how.

"What to do," he muttered to the dog, who had long ago given up watching and had fallen into a twitchy sleep. "What. What. What to do."

Logan paused to touch the bundle that sat next to the candle stub, then resumed pacing. "It's the first," he whispered, more

243

to himself than to the sleeping dog. "Only the first. Dr. Darby. He'd know. He'd show me what . . ." His voice trailed off. Dr. Darby couldn't show him anything. Dr. Darby was gone.

He stood still now, his eyes fixed on the bloody bundle, and from somewhere deep in his subconscious, as if from some far distant place that was all but forgotten, a new voice whispered to him.

A voice he hadn't heard in years.

A familiar voice.

His mother's voice.

Logan stopped pacing and slapped himself on the side of the head. "Stupid!" he whispered, then repeated the word three more times: "Stupid . . . stupid . . . stupid!"

His mother's words came clear.

Follow Jesus, she had always told him. *Jesus has all the answers.*

"Jesus!" he echoed softly. That's what he had to do: follow Jesus.

Yes. And he knew how to do it, too. All he had to do was get in his boat.

A few minutes later, as the moon set and the darkness of predawn came over the woods, Logan rowed silently across the lake, his eyes focused on the huge cross he'd long ago erected in the prow of the boat so that no matter where he went, Jesus would be

his guide. The bundle lay on the floor between his feet, the ancient dog lay in his bed of rags.

"Please Jesus, show me what to do."

He kept rowing, letting the great cross be his guide, until he was at the dock in the town of Phantom Lake.

The marina was dark, utterly deserted.

He shipped the oars, drifted to a stop, and tied his skiff to a cleat. "Shhh," he said to the dog. "Wait." He stepped out of the boat, bundle in hand.

The old dog sighed and put his head back down.

Nobody was there to see him, nobody who might call the police. The town was empty and dark, except for the glow of streetlights.

One streetlight — which seemed brighter than the others — shone down on the ramp at the end of the dock.

The light, he remembered his mother saying. *Jesus is the light.*

Logan shuffled up the dock, cradling the bundle as if it were an infant in swaddling clothes.

The light shone down on a massive wooden piling by the ramp.

And on a white piece of paper stapled to the piling.

Logan edged closer to the light, closer to the paper.

LOST CAT.

Jesus had heard his prayers. "Follow Jesus," he whispered once again.

He pulled the flyer down, then moved up the ramp and onto the street, certain that somehow — if his faith was strong enough — Jesus would use the paper to guide him. A moment later he found another flyer, and took it down, too. He was moving steadily now, from one white flyer to the next, each of them reassuring him that he was doing the right thing.

He followed the trail eagerly, gratefully, the bundle safe in the crook of his arm.

The flyers led him to big glass doors with a silver star on them.

Another flyer was stuck to the glass, on the inside.

The inside, where he couldn't reach it.

LOST CAT.

This was where he was intended to come. He'd followed Jesus and been led here.

Logan put all the flyers he'd collected down on the black mat in front of the door and laid the bundle reverently on top.

Yes. This was right.

Maybe they'd listen. Maybe they'd heed his warning.

He shuffled back to the boat, where the old dog waited, shoved off and rowed home just as the colors of a false dawn edged the horizon.

"They have to listen," he said to the dog. "Please, Jesus, make them listen." He shook his head, trying to dislodge visions of carnage. "If they don't listen, it'll get worse. It'll all get worse."

The one-winged crow cocked his head at Logan and the dog as they came back through the cabin door, but seeing no food, he ruffled his feathers once, then went back to sleep.

The dog went directly to his corner, and was soon snoring softly.

Logan curled up on his own bed of rags, trying to imagine what the sheriff was going to do to stop it before it got out of control.

He wondered if the sheriff had the power to stop it, or if somehow he himself was going to have to do it.

He didn't think he could do it. And if he couldn't . . .

As early light came through the oily window, Logan closed his eyes, but sleep was as far away as that little bundle on the sheriff's doorstep.

Blood.

Blood was all he saw when he closed his eyes.

Blood in his past, and more blood in his future.

Blood.

Lots and lots of blood . . .

Merrill Brewster felt just plain fuzzy-headed as she nursed her first cup of coffee and watched her children eat their breakfast. She'd barely slept at all last night — every creak in the house had brought her back to full wakefulness, and no matter how many times she'd told herself that nothing was wrong, she still hadn't believed it. Well, maybe after she took Marci to Summer Fun, she'd catch a nap in the hammock.

The doorbell startled her back to reality, and she put the mug down. "I'll get it," she told the kids, then checked her clothes and ran her fingers quickly through her hair before going to the front door.

A man in a police uniform stood on the steps, a small box under one arm. "Mrs. Brewster?" he said.

Merrill nodded, feeling the blood drain from her face.

There's been a plane crash. Dan's dead.

Seeing the sudden panic in Merrill Brewster's face, the policeman spoke quickly.

"I'm Rusty Ruston, the sheriff?" He made the last two words almost a question, and Merrill nodded.

"Is — Is it my husband? Has something happened to Dan?"

Ruston quickly shook his head. "No, no, it's —" He hesitated, then blundered on. "Well, I'm afraid it's your little girl's cat. It — Well, someone left it — well, what's left of it, more exactly — on the steps of my office last night."

" 'What's left of it'?" Merrill echoed, her voice barely audible. "I — I don't understand."

"It appears that it met with some kind of animal — maybe a raccoon or something," Ruston explained, then reached out a hand to steady her, as Merrill appeared about to faint. "Mrs. Brewster?" he said, his voice rising. "You okay?"

Eric, hearing the alarm in the man's voice even from the kitchen, had risen from the table, but when Marci started to get up, too, he shook his head. "You stay here," he said in a voice that was every bit as commanding as the one his father sometimes used on him — the one that left no room for argument. As Marci sank reluctantly back onto her chair, he went to the open door and saw a policeman helping his mother sit down on

the front step.

"Mom?"

"She looks a little faint," Ruston said. "I'm the sheriff — I brought back the little girl's cat."

"She's dead," Merrill breathed. "Tippy's dead!"

Eric looked at Ruston, who nodded a confirmation.

"Someone left it on my front step — looks like it was killed by some kind of animal." He handed the box to Eric. "You might want to just bury it. It's not a pleasant sight."

Eric hesitated, his stomach suddenly churning, images of the dream he'd had rising up in his mind. But maybe it was a mistake — maybe it wasn't Tippy in the box. With trembling hands he lifted the lid.

It was not a mistake. There, resting on a filthy, blood-soaked rag, was what was left of Tippy.

Her eyes were open and glazed, her mouth stretched wide as if she were snarling.

Or screaming.

Her fur was matted with blood.

But worst by far was her belly.

Her belly was ripped open, and Eric could see her intestines spilling out of the wound.

He felt his stomach lurch. No wild animal

had done this. She'd been cut right up the middle.

Sliced open like she'd been cut with a knife.

Or a scalpel . . .

. . . like the woman in the dream . . .

Marci's scream ripped into his consciousness then. "No!" she was beside him now, howling, and before he could react, she snatched the box out of his hands. "No, Tippy!" she wailed, bursting into tears.

Eric pulled the box away from her. "Don't look, Marci," he said. "Don't look at her!"

His mother was on her feet now, grabbing Marci's hand, easing her down onto the top step of the porch, where she cradled Marci's head.

"I'm sorry," the sheriff said. "I can't really say exactly what happened to it, and whoever found it and left it didn't leave a note or anything. Just a bunch of those flyers you put up."

Eric tried to think of something to say, found nothing, then wondered what his father might say. Finally, words came. "Thank you for coming." He held out his hand. The sheriff hesitated a second, then shook it and started back to his car.

Before he got in, however, he turned back. "If I hear anything about what might have

251

happened," he said, "I'll let you know."

Eric nodded, the sheriff got into his car, and a moment later the police cruiser disappeared around the curve in the driveway.

"Tippy!" Marci wailed, but Eric barely heard her.

Adam Mosler, Eric thought. That's who it was. It had to be. But even as he clung to the thought, he knew he wasn't sure it had been Adam Mosler.

He wasn't sure at all.

A strange numbness falling over him, Eric sat down on the front step next to his sobbing sister, the box on his lap, his mother flanking Marci, rocking her.

"We'll have a nice funeral for her," Merrill said as she smoothed back the hair from Marci's forehead. "Eric will dig a little grave and you and I can make a headstone, okay?"

Marci nodded, her uncontrollable sobbing starting to ease a bit.

"It's okay, Marce," Eric said. "We can get you another cat. Okay?"

"I don't want another cat," Marci cried. "I want Tippy!"

Merrill wrapped her arms around her grieving daughter and looked at Eric over Marci's head. "Will you put Tippy someplace safe, please, until we can bury her?"

"Sure." Eric looked around, then fixed his

gaze on the carriage house. "I know a place."

Eric stood at the doorway to the storage room, Kent and Tad close behind him. He reached for the handle, but hesitated before his fingers closed on the cold brass.

Maybe he should just walk away right now, he thought. In fact, maybe he shouldn't have called Kent and Tad at all. Maybe he should have just buried the cat this afternoon and tried to forget the whole thing. But that was impossible, for as soon as he'd seen the mangled corpse wrapped in bloody rags, the terrible nightmare of the night before last had risen out of his memory and hung before him not so much as a dream, but of something half remembered, something that, though not coherent in his mind, was nonetheless real.

As real as the cat's body that lay behind the door.

His fingers trembled slightly, and he felt a strange excitement flow through his body, as if some kind of energy were flowing through the doorknob into his fingers. As that energy penetrated not only his body, but his soul as well, he knew he would not turn back.

He had to follow the energy.

Follow it to its source.

His fingers closed on the doorknob.

He twisted it.

The door eased open.

Eric's fingers moved from the knob to the light switch, and a moment later the glow of the naked bulb on the ceiling drove the darkness away.

Followed by Kent and Tad, he stepped through the door. Nothing had changed: the sheet of plywood still concealed the door to the hidden room.

Everything was as they had left it the last time they were here.

Except that now a box sat on the table where before there had been only the old photograph album.

Tad eyed the box warily, his tongue running over his lower lip. "Wh-Where'd that come from?" he asked, his voice quavering just enough to betray his uncertainty as to whether he wanted the answer to his question.

"The sheriff brought it," Eric replied. The three of them were standing at the table now, and Eric could feel the strange energy building inside him.

"You gonna tell us what's in it?" Kent finally asked when Eric said nothing more, nor made any move to open the box.

Eric's eyes shifted from the box to Kent Newell. "It's Tippy," he said, his voice barely more than a whisper. "She's —" His voice broke, then he took a deep breath. "Something got her," he finally managed.

As Tad Sparks unconsciously pulled away from the table — and the box — Kent's brows furrowed deeply. "What do you mean, 'got her'?" he asked.

Instead of answering Kent's question, Eric lifted the lid, and both Tad and Kent peered in.

"Oh, Jeez," Tad whispered, turning away as his stomach contracted so violently he could taste the bile rising in his throat.

"Christ," Kent breathed, his eyes fixing on the mutilated corpse of the cat. "What could've done that?" Even though his own stomach was starting to feel queasy, Kent leaned closer. "It's like part of her's gone. Like something ate part of her or something."

"Except look at the cut," Eric whispered. He reached out with a single finger, but couldn't bring himself to touch the corpse. "It's like it was cut open with a knife or something."

"Or a scalpel," Tad said in a hollow tone that made both Eric and Kent turn toward him. Tad's face was ashen; his eyes were

wide open and fixed on the grisly object in the box. "I had a dream," he whispered so softly that neither Eric nor Kent was certain he was talking to them. "I had a scalpel," Tad went on. "And I . . ." His voice trailed off, and finally his eyes shifted from the box to Eric. "Remember that movie we saw last year?" he asked. "The one about Jack the Ripper?"

Eric's own dream suddenly exploded in his mind once more, and when he glanced at Kent, he could see that Tad's words had touched something in him, too.

For the first time in all the years Eric had known him, Kent Newell actually looked frightened.

"It was just what we found," Kent said, his eyes fixing on Tad, but he sounded more as if he was trying to convince himself than Tad. "The old black doctor's bag, and all that stuff."

The look on Kent's face as much as his words told Eric the truth. "I had the same dream," Eric said. Kent's eyes widened. "And you had it, too." When Kent said nothing, Eric asked, "You had the same dream, didn't you?"

Kent hesitated, then tried to shrug it off. "I — I dreamed something," he finally said, his feigned nonchalance falling flat. His eyes

shifted back to the box. "And anyway, there wasn't any cat in my dream."

A silence fell over the room that seemed to stretch on for an eternity.

"So what do you guys think happened?" Tad Sparks finally asked.

Kent's eyes fixed on him. "Whatever happened, it wasn't Jack the Ripper. Jesus, Tad. All we did was have some dreams!"

"Dreams about Jack the Ripper," Tad said. "Except in my dream, I wasn't *watching* Jack the Ripper. I *was* Jack the Ripper."

"I was, too," Eric said softly. "And when I woke up I felt like I was all covered with blood."

Kent Newell's piercing gaze shifted from Tad to Eric. "What?" he demanded. "You're saying *you* killed the cat?"

"I don't know!" Eric said. "I don't think so, but —"

"But what?" Kent pressed. "So if it wasn't you, who was it? Tad or me?" When neither Tad nor Eric replied, Kent answered his own question. "Well, it wasn't. What'd one of us do? Sleepwalk down here, get the scalpels, go find the cat, kill her, and then go back to bed? That's just stupid!" Yet even as he spoke, Kent's voice once again gave the lie to the certainty expressed by the words themselves.

Once again the silence seemed to stretch into infinity.

"Okay," Kent said when he could stand the silence no longer. "Let's go take a look."

"At what?" Eric asked, though he already knew the answer.

"The stuff," Kent replied, and turning away from the table, he threaded his way through the jumble of boxes to the sheet of plywood and pushed it aside. "Let's see if the stuff is where we left it."

Wordlessly, Eric and Tad followed Kent into the hidden room.

The darkness seemed to Eric to be filled with whispering voices, but whatever words they might be speaking were lost on the edges of his consciousness.

He lit the lanterns.

The voices faded away.

The medical bag was still on the table, exactly where they had left it, seemingly untouched.

"Dr. Darby paid for those scalpels with British money," Tad said softly, his eyes fixing on the satchel. "Remember?"

Kent looked over at him. "So what are you saying? Those scalpels actually belonged to Jack the Ripper?"

Tad hesitated, then shook his head. "No-

258

body even really knows who Jack the Ripper was."

"Maybe Darby found out," Kent said. "Maybe that's why he paid so much for them."

Eric was barely listening. The bag, still closed, seemed to be drawing him to it. The fingers of his right hand were trembling, and as he stared at the bag, he could once again feel the cold metal of its contents in his hand. "I've got to see them," he whispered. "I've got see if there's blood on them." Finally, he managed to look away from the bag and turned to Kent and Tad. "And if there is, we're bricking this room up again, and we're never coming anywhere near it afterward." His eyes moved from Kent Newell to Tad Sparks, then back to Kent. "Deal?"

Kent and Tad exchanged a glance, then Kent spoke for both of them. "Deal."

Eric bent over the old medical bag.

"Go ahead," Kent whispered. "Open it."

Eric swallowed hard, trying to rid himself of the lump that seemed to fill his throat. The room suddenly seemed too small, too close, and despite the light from the lanterns, the indistinct voices were back, humming in his ears.

"Open the bag," Tad urged. Eric's gaze

flicked toward him, and in the split second in which their gazes connected, Tad saw something in Eric's eyes that made him take a step back.

Eric reached for the worn leather valise, his hands clammy, his fingers still trembling.

He drew it across the table until it was directly in front of him.

"Thirty-four thousand pounds," Tad said quietly. "That's a lot of money."

Eric took a deep breath, snapped open the catch, lifted the leather strap, and opened the hinged mouth of the bag until it yawned wide.

Kent lifted a lantern and all three boys peered inside.

The scalpels gleamed, their blades glittering in the light.

No blood.

They were clean and shiny.

As clean and shiny as if they were brand new.

Eric leaned against the table, his eyes closed, listening, trying to concentrate.

He could almost make out what the voices were trying to say to him.

Almost, but not quite.

"We've got to know all of it," he whispered. "We've got to find out what Dr. Darby was doing in here."

CHAPTER 15

Marci's chin quivered as she set a worn catnip mouse on top of the shoe-box casket and sprinkled a handful of soil on top of it, then slipped her hand into her mother's as Eric shoveled more dirt into Tippy's grave.

"We couldn't find anything to make a headstone with," Merrill said as the little grave quickly filled, "so we're scattering rose petals."

"I'm going to make a cross later," Marci said.

Eric nodded, and Marci picked up the basket of fresh rose petals she had spent the last hour gathering and carefully dropped them on top of the freshly turned earth, upending the basket to shake the last ones out. "Good-bye, Tippy," she whispered, and once more clung to her mother's hand.

"Good-bye, Tippy," Eric and Merrill echoed as Merrill stroked her daughter's hair.

"See?" Merrill went on, as Eric started toward the carriage house, the shovel held against his shoulder like a rifle. "Now Tippy will always smell the roses." She gave Marci one more squeeze, then raised her voice enough for Eric to hear. "Fresh chocolate chip cookies in the kitchen." As he waved an acknowledgment, she gently turned Marci away from the grave and started back toward the house.

A shiver ran through Eric as he came to the door to the storeroom.

He paused.

Maybe he should let Kent and Tad go to the library by themselves, while he spent the afternoon in the secret room, quietly exploring the contents of the boxes and trying to decipher the cryptic entries in the journal.

He reached for the doorknob, his fingers already tingling in anticipation of touching the hard brass.

On the edges of his consciousness he could hear a whispering sound, almost like voices. Though the words — if they really were words — were unintelligible, they seemed to be pleading with him.

Pulling him closer.

His fingers closed on the doorknob.

*The room — and the room beyond —
wanted him. . . .*

The shovel slipped from Eric's grasp, and
when it crashed to the concrete hallway,
startled him back to reality.

He checked his watch. It was only three-
thirty.

At least he hadn't lost track of time, and
Tad had said the library stayed open until
nine in the summer. Turning away from the
door to the storeroom, he hurried to the
tool room and replaced the shovel.

Back at the house, he found his mother
and sister having cookies and milk at the
kitchen table. He washed his hands, then
went over and picked up a cookie from the
plate in the center of the table. "I'm going
over to Kent's," he said, snagging two more
cookies, hesitating, then taking a fourth.
"For Kent," he added, though no one had
challenged his taking all but three of the
cookies left on the plate.

"Oh, honey," Merrill said, putting a hand
on his arm. "Couldn't you just stay here
with us?"

Eric turned back. "Why?"

Merrill's brow creased with worry. "Because of all that's happened. I just thought
it would be nice if you were here with Marci
and me." *And besides,* she added silently, *I*

don't want to be alone when it gets dark.

"But Kent and Tad and I were going to the library."

Merrill stared at her son. "The library?" she repeated. "I don't believe it — Tad Sparks, maybe. But Kent? The library? During summer vacation?" She eyed Eric. "What's going on?"

"Nothing," he replied quickly casting around in his mind for something his mother might buy. "Kent said a lot of girls hang out there," he finally said, though Kent had never said anything of the sort.

His mother seemed to accept it, but said, "I still think you should stay home today."

Suddenly he understood, and met his mother's gaze squarely. "You're just afraid something else is going to happen. And because you're afraid, I get punished."

Her gaze dropped away from his. "I'm asking you nicely to please stay home."

Eric slid into one of the kitchen chairs. "And I'm asking you to please let me go hang out with my friends. If Dad were here, I'd get to go." He could see his mother wavering. "Let's call and ask him."

Merrill hesitated, then reached for the cordless phone and dialed. She'd hoped Eric would have agreed to stay home, and then maybe her fears over being in the big

house at night wouldn't escalate into another series of horrible, interminable sleepless hours. She felt tears building up, but didn't want to cry in front of the kids.

And she sure didn't want to cry on the telephone to Dan, who answered on the first ring.

"Dan Brewster."

"Hi, honey." *Not bad! Barely a quaver.*

Eric bit into a cookie while Marci sat with her hands in her lap, a sad look on her face.

Merrill recounted Tippy's funeral and Eric's request to go out. "I just don't think I can do it, Dan. I can't be alone up here all summer while you're in the city." In spite of her efforts, her voice started trembling. "I'm thinking I want to pack up and come home."

"Slow down, sweetie," Dan said. "There's nothing wrong with Eric spending the afternoon with his friends. It's summer."

"But I'm afraid —"

"I know," Dan cut in. "You're afraid. You're nervous. But that's no reason to spoil everybody's summer. Call Ellen or Ashley and get together. Don't stay in the house. Take Marci and go somewhere."

"But I hate it up here alone," Merrill whispered fiercely.

"You've only been alone for twenty-four hours."

Merrill chewed her lip.

"And you're not alone. You've got the kids. Marci's having a great time, and so is Eric. It's sad about Tippy, but those things happen. You know that."

"I know, but —"

"We're not giving up the house," Dan said quietly. "I'll be up at the end of the week for the Fourth of July weekend. And Marci's going to be in the parade, remember? I know you, sweetheart — you don't want to spoil that for her."

Merrill sighed, not only accepting defeat, but knowing that her husband was right. "I don't," she finally said. "And I won't. I guess I just miss you."

"I know, honey. I miss you, too. Tell Eric to go have fun and be home by dark. And you find yourself something fun to do, too, okay?"

"Okay."

"Gotta run. Love you."

Dan clicked off.

"Love you, too," she said to the hollow silence of the broken connection. Composing herself, she pressed the Off button and turned to Eric. "Okay," she said, forcing a bright smile. "Just please be home by dark, all right?"

Eric paused on his way out to kiss her

cheek. "Thanks, Mom. And thanks for the cookies. They're good."

"You might as well take the rest for Tad." This time her smile was genuine.

Eric took the last three cookies from the plate and headed out the back door.

Eric and Kent followed Tad as he wound his way through the maze of heavy oak reading tables toward the archway that led to the large room that was filled to overflowing with row after row of tall bookcases. Beyond the last row, they came to the room that held the periodicals, including bound copies of the town's weekly newspaper, the *Phantom Lake Times,* going back ten years. They were just where the librarian had said they would be.

Tad ran his finger along the shelf of bound newspapers until he came to the large, heavy volume that was dated seven years earlier. He pulled it off the shelf and carried it to the scarred wooden table in the center of the room.

"Where do we start?" Kent asked.

Tad rolled his eyes. "At the beginning, of course. Except that if he went out in his boat, it had to be at least March or April, right? Otherwise the lake would still have been frozen." He opened the cover and

began carefully turning the pages until he came to the issue from mid-March. "And it'll be on the front page. Right? I mean, Darby was one of the most important people in town, wasn't he?" As Eric nodded, Tad continued turning the pages.

Nothing through March, or April, or May. June and July showed nothing, either.

Then, in August, Kent reached out and stopped Tad from turning the next page. "There it is," he said. "August eighth. Front page, just like you said."

The three boys huddled close and began reading.

PHANTOM LAKE MAN MISSING

Dr. Hector Darby appears to be missing after a boat belonging to him was found abandoned near Hunter's Reserve last Wednesday. Mr. Charles Spencer reported first seeing it on Monday, then again on Tuesday morning. Spencer himself thought he recognized it as belonging to Dr. Darby, and reported the boat's presence to Sheriff Floyd Ruston only after getting no response when he tried to contact Dr. Darby at Pinecrest, Darby's residence of the last twenty years.

Sheriff Ruston went to Pinecrest to

investigate and found newspapers piled in the doorway and an overflowing mailbox. Ruston entered the property, found no sign of Darby, but says he found no evidence of foul play. Though with no evidence of where Dr. Darby might be, Ruston is unwilling to launch a full-scale investigation, at least as of this date.

"Though Dr. Darby often stopped the newspaper and had his mail held when he left home, it wasn't a consistent habit," Ruston said. "Therefore, for the moment at least, I'm assuming that this time he simply didn't make the arrangement, and in his absence, the wind blew the boat loose. If he hasn't been heard from within a day or so, then of course I'll look further into the matter."

The boat was towed back to Pinecrest and secured in its boathouse.

When asked if there could be any connection between Dr. Darby's disappearance and the discovery of Tiffany Hanover's body found July 15, floating near Hunter's Reserve, Ruston brushed the question aside, saying only that "I don't even think that one's worth a 'no comment.' "

When he finished reading, Eric studied

269

the photo accompanying the story. Dr. Darby appeared to be an ordinary, nondescript man wearing glasses and a business suit.

"Weird," Kent said, rereading the last paragraph. "Go back to July fifteenth."

Tad flipped the pages back three weeks.

"What do you know," Kent whispered, staring at the headline for that week's paper. "I never even heard about this one."

BODY FOUND FLOATING IN LAKE

Fishermen reported finding the body of a young woman floating near Hunter's Reserve early this morning, according to Sheriff Floyd Ruston. She was not immediately identified, nor was the cause of death known.

"We've had no missing persons reports," Sheriff Ruston said, "but she hadn't been in the water very long. I'm sure we'll learn something very soon."

The girl's body was removed to the county coroner's office.

The boys scanned through the rest of the article, but there was no further information about the body; just a lot of warnings about water safety, not only from the sheriff,

but from half a dozen other people as well.

"So somewhere between here and August eighth, they identified her," Eric said when they'd all finished the story.

"Maybe she just drowned," Tad suggested.

"Or maybe something else happened to her," Kent said, and began slowly turning the pages once more.

They found the story in the issue from the following week.

BODY IDENTIFIED AS SUMMER VISITOR

The young woman found floating in Phantom Lake near Hunter's Reserve last week has been identified as Tiffany Hanover, granddaughter of Luther and Iris Hanover of Milwaukee and Phantom Lake. She had been spending the summer with her grandparents at their summer home on the west bank.

Tiffany, 18, graduated as valedictorian of her high school class last month and was slated to begin college this fall at Northwestern University in Chicago, where she had intended to enroll in a premed course of study.

Though sources close to the investigation say the cause of death appears to be drowning, the investigation of the case has

not yet been closed.

The Hanovers have returned to Milwaukee to be with their son, Robert G. Hanover, and his wife, the former Lynette Giles, also of Milwaukee.

Tad turned page after page as all three boys scanned each issue for a resolution to either Darby's disappearance or the girl's death, but they found nothing. Finally closing the heavy volume, Tad looked up at Eric and Kent. "We don't know much more about Darby now than we did when we got here," he said.

"No," Kent said, "but now we have Tiffany Hanover, too. And doesn't it seem weird that the paper would say her drowning and Darby's disappearance weren't connected? I mean, doesn't that make it sound like people must have thought they were? Otherwise, why even mention it?"

Eric suddenly remembered the woman behind the desk who had told them where to find the old newspapers. Certainly she looked like she'd been working in the library for a whole lot longer than seven years — in fact, she could have been the original librarian when the place had been built almost a century earlier. "How about asking the librarian?" he suggested.

They replaced the book and approached the big mahogany counter just inside the front door, where Miss Edna Bloomfield — identified by a neat brass nameplate set discreetly by the book-return box — was sorting catalog cards in a long narrow drawer.

"Are you boys finding what you're looking for?" she asked in a whisper, peering at them over the top of her wire-rimmed glasses. Though her hair was twisted up at the nape of her neck in a tight bun and she wore a long-sleeve dress that was buttoned all the way up to her chin, there was a glimmer of a smile in her eyes that belied the severity of her dress and hairdo.

"I'm living at the house called Pinecrest this summer," Eric said, "and we were interested in finding out something about Dr. Darby." He glanced at Tad and Kent, then spoke again. "I mean, like, what happened to him? Did he really just disappear?"

"And we're wondering about Tiffany Hanover, too," Kent added. "Did she really just drown?"

Edna Bloomfield gazed up at them, her eyes moving from Eric to Kent to Tad, then back to Eric, and Eric could almost see the gears turning in her head as she appraised them and decided how much — if anything

273

— to tell them. Finally, she leaned back in her chair, took off her glasses, and let them hang on a chain around her neck. "Well," she said, her voice rising slightly, "you boys seem to have happened onto the only two mysteries of Phantom Lake." She clucked her tongue sympathetically. "That poor girl." Now her voice dropped again, and she leaned forward, glancing in both directions as if to be certain nobody but the three boys was listening. "She was murdered, you know."

"Murdered?" Tad echoed. "But there was nothing about that in the paper. At least nothing we could find."

"This is a small town," Edna Bloomfield said. "We rely on tourism." She glanced around once more, and her voice dropped still further. "So sometimes everything doesn't get into the paper. But everyone knows she was strangled, even if Gerry Hofstetter at the paper didn't publish anything. And who can blame him? He didn't want to scare people. And why hurt the town? After all, it isn't like one of our people did it."

"Then who did?" Tad asked.

Edna Bloomfield waved her hand at the question as if it were a pesky fly. "Well, I'm sure I don't know. I don't think anyone

knows. Some reporter from Milwaukee came and poked around, trying to make everyone think it was one of those killers you hear so much about these days."

An image of Old Man Logan and his strange boat with the cross mounted in the bow suddenly rose in Tad Sparks's mind.

Miss Bloomfield put the index cards aside and leaned closer to the boys. "I heard he even suggested our nice Dr. Darby might have done it, just because he used to work with those killers at the hospital down in Madison. But none of us ever believed that, of course. Dr. Darby was such a fine man. He was a patron of this library, you know. Always in here, working on his research."

"What kind of research?" Eric asked.

"Well, his specialty, of course," Edna Bloomfield replied, as if Eric should have known. "Those terrible killers — what do they call them?" She glanced around distractedly, as if expecting to find the words she was looking for tucked away in some far corner of the library, then brightened as she found them. "*Serial* killers! Yes, that was it. My goodness — he used to come in every week, it seems like, always looking for new books about the psychology of murderers and all that sort of thing. Of course, I tried to buy all of them since he was so generous

to our library, but it seemed I could never keep up. He always knew of one I didn't have, and oh how I'd scramble to get it for him. Now, of course, he'd get them all on the Internet, but back then . . ."

Her voice trailed off and she seemed to disappear into another world. Then she straightened up in her chair, and when she spoke again, her voice was much brighter. "I always liked Dr. Darby. I considered him to be Phantom Lake's only genuine eligible bachelor. He was very nice and very well-respected. He had a fine mind." She took a deep breath, replaced her glasses on her nose, and smiled up at the boys. "But he's gone, and we'll probably never find out what happened to him, will we?"

As she picked up her cards and began shuffling through them once again, Eric saw a sadness replace the smile in her eyes.

The last of the twilight faded quickly as Kent walked off the road onto a path that seemed to plunge directly into the densest part of the woods. In moments the forest had closed around him like a shroud, and a veil of fog seemed to have come out of nowhere. Even though he was only a few steps ahead of Eric, Eric still found himself barely able to see the other boy's back as

they made their way along what both Kent and Tad had insisted was a shortcut home. Squinting hard, Eric kept his eyes on the ground to avoid the roots, rocks, and thick mulch of rotted leaves that it seemed were conspiring to trip him. The path appeared to be little more than a game trail, one so seldom used and so overgrown that even the animals seemed to have abandoned it.

Soon the darkness obscured even the path, and now Eric had to rely on the sound of Kent's footsteps in front of him — and Tad's behind him — to keep him on the trail.

His mother was going to be furious that he wasn't home yet.

Worse, she'd be worried, and once she started worrying, there'd be no stopping her. "Maybe we should have taken the boat to town," he said.

Before either Kent or Tad could say anything, a twig snapped.

Eric froze, and a second later Tad's hand closed on his shoulder, startling him so badly he whirled around, ready to defend himself.

"Did you hear that?" Tad whispered. "Someone's behind us!"

Unbidden — and unwanted — images rose in Eric's mind, and for a moment he

was caught once more in the dream he'd had only a few nights earlier, when he was prowling through the same kind of darkness and mist that surrounded him now. He tried to force the memory down, but even as he reminded himself that he was only a few hundred yards from home, something in his memory kept trying to drag him back to the streets of London.

London, and Jack the Ripper.

"There's nobody there," Kent said, his low, confident voice staving off the panic that had nearly overwhelmed Eric. "Just keep going." Then Kent increased his pace, leaving Eric to try to keep up, stumbling along in the dark, Tad close behind him.

But a few seconds later another sound came out of the darkness, this time from the other side of the path, and all the images Eric had banished came flooding back. Now Tippy's torn body floated in the night, and he could almost see bloodstained blades glinting in the darkness.

And what about the girl they'd read about only a few hours ago, who'd drowned in the lake?

If she'd really drowned at all.

What if the rumors were true?

What if someone had killed her?

And what if he was still out there?

What if he'd seen them in the library, and knew what they were doing?

Another twig snapped, closer this time.

From a few yards behind, Eric heard Tad utter a tiny yelp, and a second later Tad's hand clamped onto Eric's biceps so hard it sent a spasm of pain right down to his fingertips.

"Something's out there," Tad whispered. "It's —" Before he could finish, a low growl came from their right, instantly followed by a violent thrashing in the brush.

"Bear!" Tad yelled, shouldering past Eric and charging up the path at a dead run.

Eric's heart was pounding so hard he could barely breathe, let alone speak, but his horror at being left alone in the dark with whatever was hidden in the brush overcame the terror that was all but paralyzing him. "Kent?" he finally managed to squeal, no longer even able to see his friend. "You still there? Don't leave me!"

"Let's just get out of here," Kent called back over his shoulder, his voice trembling almost as badly as Eric's. "Come on!" He broke into a run, cursed loudly as his foot caught on something and he nearly lost his balance, then caught himself and once more bolted into the blackness. Eric followed, stumbling after Kent and Tad, low-hanging

branches slashing at his face, and brush catching at his clothes like claws trying to snatch him away into the night.

He could hear the predator clearly now, crashing through the brush off to the left. He could almost smell it, almost feel its fetid breath on the back of his neck as it charged toward him.

The bushes thrashed right beside him.

In another second it would be too late — the creature would be upon him, cutting him off even from the help of Kent and Tad.

Panicked, Eric leaped forward, racing through the darkness. He could feel the beast behind him, feel it rising up, poised on its hind legs, lashing out to smash him to the ground with a massive clawed paw. He could feel its fangs sinking into his flesh, feel it tearing at him, gnawing on his very bones. A howl of terror rose out of his throat, and then he'd caught up with Kent and Tad, and all three of them were flying through the woods, the lumbering, crashing beast following close behind.

Then, with no warning at all, they burst from the woods onto the road, and dead ahead of them was the floodlit entrance to The Pines.

And as suddenly as they were out of the woods, the crashing of the beast stopped.

Silence — a silence so heavy that Eric could actually feel it — dropped over the night.

"Wh-Where is it?" Tad Sparks stammered, gasping for breath. "Where'd it —"

His words ended abruptly as a rock hit him hard on the side.

"What the —" he began again, but his words were cut off once more, this time by the sound of laughter as Adam Mosler, Ellis Langstrom, and Chris McIvens emerged from the edge of the woods.

Mosler threw another rock, forcing Eric to dodge away. "Oooh, it's a bear," he said, his voice a mocking singsong.

"Don't leave me," Chris squealed, pitching his own voice into a girlish register and pitching a third rock that hit the pavement at Kent's feet.

"What a bunch of fags," Ellis sneered.

Eric felt his face burning, and out of the corner of his eye he could see Kent's hands clenching into fists. "Let's just get out of here," he said softly enough that only Kent and Tad could hear him. "Ignore them." He grabbed Tad and they walked quickly down the road toward home.

A moment later Kent reluctantly followed, but his fury was still palpable as he caught up with Eric and Tad. "I'm going to freakin'

kill that bastard," he grated, his breath still rasping from his charge through the woods.

"Maybe we should tell somebody about them," Tad said. "One of us could have really been hurt back there!"

"And if we report them," Eric instantly responded, "all that will happen is that my mom will make me go back to Evanston. Let's just leave it alone, okay?"

"Not okay," Kent shot back, kicking a rock out of the road. "I *hate* those guys."

Tad snickered. "You gotta admit," he said when Kent glared at him, "they really had us going."

"Yeah?" Kent growled. "Well, maybe you think it's funny, but I don't!"

Eric eyed Kent, whose eyes were almost glowing with anger, even in the darkness. "Come on, Kent — lighten up. What good's it gonna do to stay mad? Tad's right — they made us look like idiots."

"He's right that someone really could have gotten hurt, too," Kent said, balling his fists again. "And I'm not going to get mad — I'm going to get even!"

Five minutes later Eric was back at Pinecrest. He stood by the front door for a moment, checking his breathing and trying to shrug away the last tendrils of the fear that had gripped him only a few minutes

ago. When he was sure neither his breathing nor his expression would give away what had just happened, he finally went inside and found his mother and sister watching a movie.

A Disney movie.

The house still smelled like chocolate chip cookies.

A small fire was glowing on the hearth, even though the evening was warm.

The draperies were drawn against the darkness outside, and as he settled into the big easy chair, the last of his terror faded away.

Outside, hidden in the darkness, the old skiff with the crude wooden cross on its prow moved silently away from the shore and headed out across the dark water.

CHAPTER 16

The strange tingling sensation began the moment Eric stepped into the storeroom. It started in his fingertips, but spread quickly through his whole body as he and Kent pulled the heavy plywood away from the doorway to the hidden room. As he crossed the threshold, his mind as well as his body was suddenly filled with unfamiliar stimuli. Every one of his senses seemed sharpened, and he felt imbued with an energy he'd never experienced outside this tiny room.

An energy that filled him not only with excitement, but with disorientation as well.

Disorientation, and dread.

It was as if a force had gripped him, gripped him so tightly that he could not only feel it, but hear it, too. From somewhere far away, vague voices were again whispering darkly at the edges of his consciousness.

As the force tightened its grip on him, one

small part of his mind told him to resist it, to back away before it was too late. Yet even as this small inner voice spoke to him, the voice of the force whispered its siren song, and instead of turning to escape back into the bright light of the summer morning, he moved deeper into the darkness of the room.

He and Kent lit the lanterns and peered around the chamber almost as if expecting the answers to Phantom Lake's mysteries to be spread before them on parchment scrolls or etched on the walls like some modern Rosetta stone. Eric had known they'd be back in the room the moment he awoke that morning; he'd felt its pull like some sort of fate or predestination, and after breakfast, when his mother left for a crafts fair with Marci, Tad and Kent had arrived.

With no need of a single word being spoken, they had gone directly to the carriage house to find some answers.

"Darby specialized in serial killers," Kent said, gazing around the room at all the dusty boxes and strange half-broken objects. "So if he really managed to buy Jack the Ripper's scalpels —"

All their eyes turned to the medical bag that still sat on top of the three-legged Formica table, and Eric could feel the strange

energy that suffused the room increase as they focused on the dark object with its macabre contents.

"I'm not touching that thing," Tad breathed, his voice sounding oddly strangled.

Eric, though, moved forward and gently — almost reverently — picked it up and set it on a bookshelf.

"So if that really was Jack the Ripper's bag," Kent went on, "maybe the rest of the stuff in here belonged to serial killers, too." He moved to an old wooden lateral filing cabinet and tugged on one of its long, warped drawers. It didn't budge, held fast either by the warping of the wood or the lock.

"Maybe that's the difference between the stuff in this hidden room and the stuff out there in the storeroom," Eric mused.

"This room wasn't just hidden," Tad said, his hands drawn almost against his will to the ornate scrollwork on the lamp base that still sat on the broken table. "The doorway was bricked up, so Darby must not have wanted anybody to know about this stuff."

Kent shook his head. "If he really didn't want anyone to find it, why didn't he destroy it?" He grasped the handles of the stuck drawer again, preparing for a final assault.

"I have this weird feeling he left all this for someone to find. And we found it."

"Fate," Eric breathed, not even conscious that he'd spoken the word aloud.

Kent put his weight into a massive tug on the drawer. It held for a second or two, then the front panel split as the lock gave way. Kent staggered, then regained his balance and looked inside the now gaping drawer. "Okay," he said, reaching inside and pulling out a long, thin object wrapped in bubble wrap. "What do you suppose this is?" Before anyone could reply, he peeled away the tape, then unwound the bubble wrap. He held the object up, and all three of the boys recognized it immediately.

"The missing table leg," Eric said. "Weird! Why wrap it up like that?"

"And why lock it in a file drawer?" Tad Sparks added.

"Maybe he just never had a chance to finish putting it together," Kent said. "Here. Hold the table up while I move these boxes."

Eric took hold of the table, and instantly the flow of energy increased, as if the table itself were vibrating with some kind of excitement.

Kent slid away the two crates that held up the corner of the table and crouched low to

fit the leg. "It just screws into a bracket," he said. "Hold the table up a little higher."

With Eric lifting the corner, Tad steadied the heavy lamp base so it wouldn't fall.

A moment later the leg was attached and the table stood whole.

Eric felt a tingle in his scalp as the dark energy in the room — and in his mind and body — rose higher. As if guided by some unseen hand, he opened the ledger and flipped its pages back to the entry for the table.

He turned the book so Tad and Kent could again read the entry.

7/11 acq table (#36) frm JD est. sale Milwaukee. $10,350. Bargain.

As the words penetrated, Tad leaned against the table, his palms pressed against the Formica surface.

It felt oddly warm to his touch, as if some kind of energy were flowing directly from it into his hands. The energy seemed to heighten his senses, and suddenly he felt as if he could almost make out exactly what the voices that had been murmuring on the fringes of his consciousness were saying.

Almost, but not quite.

Tad's gaze shifted to the two crates that

Kent had moved out from under the table, and as it did, the voices seemed to encourage him.

It was as if they wanted him to open those crates.

But something inside Tad didn't want to open them. Indeed, he didn't want to know anything more about what else might be in this room.

He didn't want to have anything more to do with it.

Most of all, he didn't want to have any more nightmares.

Yet despite his instincts, Tad found himself moving toward the crates, following the pull of the energy, obeying the urging of the voices.

The voices murmured their approval.

He lifted the lid on the top crate.

Nothing but Styrofoam peanuts.

He scooped them away, reluctant to plunge his hand into the depths of the crate. But slowly, almost against his own will, his hand disappeared into the pool of packing material, and he felt himself groping carefully around inside.

His fingers touched something smooth and cylindrical. He pulled it out, shedding packing peanuts all over the floor. "Look at this," he said, gazing at the object as if his

eyes must be deceiving him. "It's just a roll of trash bags."

"Trash bags?" Eric looked at the roll of black bags in Tad's hand, then stepped over to the ledger, which was still open on the table. "Is there anything else in there?"

Tad put his hand into the box again, feeling all the way to the bottom, then felt something almost like an electrical shock as his fingers touched something else.

Something metal.

Warm metal.

"Wait," he breathed. "Yes." He pulled out an old rusty hacksaw, its blade missing.

"This is so weird," Eric said, slowly turning the pages of the ledger.

"Look at this," Kent said from the other side of the room, where he stood by a rack of metal shelving. He held up a rusty hacksaw blade. "It was just lying here. Not even wrapped or anything."

"And here's the entry," Eric murmured a moment later, after turning more pages in Hector Darby's ledger:

3/6 Acq. saw and bags from K. Wharton, LAPD evid rm. w/K&H docs. $4600.

"Are you kidding me?" Kent said, taking the saw frame from Tad and fitting the blade

into it. "You could buy this thing brand new at a hardware store for less than twenty bucks." He tightened the wing nut that locked the blade into place, and shivered as a peculiar stream of something almost like electricity flowed out of the tool and into his body.

His body, and his mind . . .

. . . and his soul . . .

He held up the completed saw, and suddenly its rusty spots were glowing red in the lamplight.

Bloodred.

"All the pieces fit together," Eric said slowly, his gaze wandering over the room. "The table. The saw. The bag and the scalpels." His eyes came to rest on Tad Sparks. "It's almost like this room is a giant puzzle."

"If it's a puzzle," Tad replied, his own gaze fixing once more on the shadeless lamp, "it sure is a creepy one."

A silence fell over all three boys, broken seconds — or perhaps minutes — later as Moxie began to bark outside the carriage house.

"Crap!" Eric said, the strange spell he'd fallen under shattered by the dog's racket. "Mom's home. What time is it?"

"Four-thirty," Tad said, his eyes widening

as he stared at his watch. "Jeez, how could it be that late already?"

Kent was already dousing one of the lanterns. "How come you sound so surprised? Isn't that what always happens in here?"

Leaving everything as it was, the boys pulled the plywood back over the opening and went out through the carriage house door. Then, though no words had been spoken, they turned away from the house and slipped unseen into the woods.

After supper that night, Eric went up to his room and turned on the computer.

With a few keystrokes he Googled "serial killers," and a moment later found himself staring at something called the Crime Library.

The images from Hector Darby's ledger were burned into his mind: JD . . . Milwaukee . . . K and H in Los Angeles.

A few seconds later he found it.

All of it.

JD in Milwaukee: Jeffrey Dahmer, who had killed young boys.

Killed them, and sat at his cracked Formica kitchen table, eating them.

Eric forced down the wave of nausea that rose in his gut, and kept reading.

K and H in Los Angeles: Patrick Kearney and Douglas Hill, the Trash Bag Murderers. They had killed young hitchhikers, dismembered their corpses with a hacksaw, packed their body parts into trash bags, and left them strewn about the Los Angeles area.

His hand trembling, Eric picked up the phone and began dialing, first Tad, then Kent.

His voice low, he began telling them what he'd found.

CHAPTER 17

Ellis Langstrom dug his toes into the sandy bottom of the lake and gazed dolefully out over the water, wondering why the liquor wasn't making him feel any better. Between them, he and Adam Mosler had swallowed almost half of what had been left in the bottle of Jack Daniel's that Ellis had swiped out of the cupboard where his mom put all the liquor after his dad left two years ago. And even if he took away the one swig Adam had talked Cherie into — which hadn't been much more than a sip, if she'd actually taken any at all — it seemed he should have had enough to feel a lot drunker than he did.

Wiping his mouth with the back of his hand, he turned away from the lake and started unsteadily toward the picnic table that the three of them had been sitting at for the last hour while he and Adam passed the bottle back and forth, both of them do-

ing their best to ignore Cherie's disapproval. He knew that pretty soon Adam would start trying to put the make on Cherie, and Cherie would get pissed off, and then Adam would get pissed off, too, just like he always did. And that, Ellis decided, was the problem. Everybody he knew — everybody in town — always did exactly what they always did, and tonight, with half a dozen shots of whiskey in him, he decided he'd had it with the whole thing.

"Know what I'm gonna do next year?" he asked as he handed the last of the whiskey to Adam. "I'm gonna get outta this stupid town."

"Yeah?" Adam said, raising himself up just enough to drain the whiskey into his mouth. Flopping back down onto the tabletop, he screwed the top back on the bottle and hurled it toward a clump of bushes a few yards away.

"You know, this isn't just *your* park," Cherie said, glaring at Adam as the bottle dropped to the ground five feet short of the bushes.

"Wha'd I do?" Adam whined as Cherie slid off the bench and went to retrieve the bottle.

"Just don't be throwing your trash around."

"Someone paying you to pick it up?" Adam shot back, then shifted his attention back to Ellis before Cherie could say anything else. "So, where you going to go? That's if you really split, which you won't."

"I don't care," Ellis said, wheeling around to peer across the park at the empty streets of the little town. "Somewhere. Anywhere. Just far away from here. I hate it here. I hate school, and I hate the summer people, and I hate —"

"Yeah yeah yeah," Adam interrupted, having heard it all before and wondering how much time he had to put the make on Cherie before she would decide she had to go home. "So if you're going to leave, why wait? Why not just go right now?"

"Maybe I will," Ellis said, his eyes fixing blearily on Adam.

"And maybe I should never have come out here with you guys," Cherie said, dropping the empty bottle in a trash barrel, then coming back to the table but not sitting down again. In fact, she was starting to wish she'd never come to the park with them at all. "You're both drunk."

"I'm not drunk," Adam said, reaching for Cherie, who rolled her eyes as she sidestepped his groping hand. "An' Ellis isn't drunk, either — he's just a loser." He ut-

tered a cackling laugh at his own words, which only elicited a glare from Cherie.

"You really think you're smart, don't you?" she asked, her voice edged with a sarcasm that was completely lost on Adam.

"Smarter'n Ellis," he said. His eyes drifted back to the other boy. "He doesn't even know when it's time to leave a guy alone with his girl."

"I don't want to be alone with you," Cherie said, crossing her arms over her chest. "And I'm not your girl."

Ellis weaved slightly as he stared at Adam. "You really want me to go away right now?"

"Yes, for Chrissakes," Adam said. "Go. Just go."

"Stop it, Adam!" Cherie said. "Just leave him alone." She turned away from Adam and started out of the picnic area. "Come on, Ellis. I'll walk home with you."

The alcohol he'd consumed was suddenly ignited by Adam Mosler's stinging words. Ellis wheeled on Cherie. "Why would I want to go home?" he demanded. "Why would I want to go anywhere with you or Adam? Know what I'm gonna do? I'm gonna do exactly what I said I was gonna do. I'm outta here. I'm done with all of it." He glowered foggily at Adam. "I'm done with you, Mosler. You're nothing but a loser!

When I'm long gone, you'll still be here in Phantom Lake, doing lawn work for Mrs. Henderson when you're eighty."

Adam sat up, felt a wave of dizziness, and quickly lay back down again. "So go," he muttered. "It's not like anyone wants you around here."

"Fine!" Ellis said. "And don't be surprised if you never see me again." He turned and stumbled off into the darkness, heading toward a path that led into the woods.

"What are you doing?" Cherie demanded of Adam as Ellis vanished into the night. "Ellis is your best friend!"

"C'mere," Adam said. He sat up again and reached for her, but Cherie backed away.

"No, Adam. Just leave me alone, okay?" She pushed him away, but he caught hold of her arm and jerked her closer to him. A moment later his other hand was on her breast and he was pulling her face close to his.

Then, just as his lips were about to press against hers, she slapped him.

Slapped him hard.

Startled, Adam lost his grip on her, and she whirled around and headed out of the park without so much as a backward glance.

Adam's fury rose as he watched her go. This was the night he was supposed to get

lucky! He'd been sure of it when she'd agreed to come to the park with him. All he'd needed to do was get Ellis to take off and leave him with the bottle, and he'd have had Cherie's clothes off in five minutes. But instead Ellis had drunk most of the booze himself, and then picked a fight.

And Cherie had sided with him!

With Ellis!

What the hell was going on?

Lurching to his feet, Adam felt the alcohol burning in his belly.

Ellis's fault.

That was it. It was all Ellis's fault.

His fury building, Adam staggered off into the darkness.

A dream.

It had to be a dream!

The tunnel was all around him, a tunnel so dark that nothing was visible — not even the walls of the tunnel itself. Yet he knew it was there, surrounding him, closing him in, giving him nowhere to go except straight ahead.

Ahead to what?

There was a feeling of menace in the darkness now, an undefined terror that seemed to emanate both from the walls and the air itself, making every breath a moment of fear as he struggled against the noxiousness that flooded

not only his lungs, but every cell of his body.

He needed to get to the end, needed to get out, needed to escape before what little air was left had vanished and only the deadly fumes remained.

He could see his destination now. Though it seemed impossibly far away, it hung in the darkness, gleaming and glittering, shining out of the blackness. He struggled to increase his pace, and now his raspy, fear-choked breath echoed off the close walls.

His feet felt as if they were glued to the floor, and he had to consciously pull them free. Each step made a hollow sucking sound, as if his own coffin were being pulled from a grave of viscous muck.

With every step, his panic grew. His chest heaved; his heart slammed against his ribs.

The air grew still heavier, and now he felt himself dying.

Dying slowly, vanishing into the blackness of the tunnel until nothing would be left of him at all.

Nothing but the pain in his body, and the terror in his soul.

Just as the last of his strength was being leached from his body, a sliver of light glinted from some invisible source, and he suddenly recognized the shiny objects at the far end of the tunnel.

Except that now the end of the tunnel was at hand, and the objects were almost within his reach.

Scalpels.

The blade of a saw.

A hacksaw.

They were on the ground in front of him, gleaming and glowing on the tunnel's floor, tiny blue flames dancing along their glimmering surfaces.

The blades were whispering now, speaking to him, inviting him to touch them, to pick them up.

To become the vessel of their evil.

He tried to draw away, but his feet seemed sealed to the ground.

Panic gripped him like a powerful serpent, its coils threatening to crush not only his body, but his spirit as well. He lashed out, flailing his arms against the tunnel wall.

And all he touched was plastic.

The tunnel was nothing more than a long, black plastic trash bag.

He ripped his way through it, his fingers tearing the tunnel to shreds, and abruptly it all fell away, as if it had never been there at all.

He was on a path.

A path in the woods.

But the menace — the terror — was still with him, closer now than it had been before.

The sounds of the night were all around him, but amidst the keening of the crickets and the calling of owls in the starlight he could also hear the whispers and taunts of formless beings.

Beings that had pursued him out of the tunnel . . .

But here, at least, he could breathe.

Here, he knew the path.

Here, he knew where he was.

Suddenly, the unseen menace was closing in on him, surrounding him.

He tried to shout, tried to scream defiance into the night, but his mouth felt stuffed with cotton and no sound emerged.

Now he tried to run, but his feet were mired in something even thicker than before, and each step threatened to imprison his foot.

Mud?

He looked down.

Blood!

It wasn't a path at all, but a roiling river of thick, sticky, coagulated blood.

Blood, with something floating on its surface.

He reached down, scooped it up.

Intestines.

The intestines of some kind of animal.

Then the face of a cat was hanging in the darkness, its dead eyes fixing on him, accusing him. . . .

The cold of the cat's own death dropped over him, and its intestines fell from his fingers back into the stream of blood whose babbling was the voices of the victims from whom the river's scarlet waters had been drained.

The menace was closing on him now; the faceless terrors hiding behind every tree, the river of blood growing deeper with every step.

He dare not stumble lest he plunge into the river of gore from which there would be no escape at all.

Something struck him from behind.

Something heavy.

A rock?

He turned, and suddenly felt a glimmer of hope. Only a step or two away was solid ground. If he could reach the bank — if he could climb out of the river of blood — he could run.

Run for his life.

Run to save his soul.

Another rock hit him, this time in the leg.

He managed to slog a step toward the shore, then another.

The menace drew closer. He could smell it now, even more putrid than the river itself.

One foot was on solid ground. He put his knee down and his hands on the cool, piney earth to pull his other foot free of the muck.

His hand fell on something hard. Something long.

A table leg.

A table leg that transformed itself even as he touched it into a stick.

A heavy stick with a great burly knot at its end.

A surge of power flowed into him as his fingers closed on the stick, and as he rose to his feet he knew he was finally ready to face the menace surrounding him.

Face it, and destroy it.

He could see the menace now, see it as clearly as if the darkness had suddenly lifted, driven away by the morning sun.

But there was no sun.

The night was still around him, yet at last he could see the menace that had been hidden a moment ago.

A menace that was no longer drawing closer, creeping up on him in the darkness.

No, the menace was running.

Running away.

Running from him.

He went after it, his weapon held high.

And as he ran, a strange thought flitted through his mind.

What if it wasn't a dream?

What if was real?

What if it was all real?

Ellis Langstrom was barely aware of the thigh-high brush as he slogged through the woods. He was still pissed at Adam Mosler, and the whiskey he'd drunk was making him a little dizzy, but it didn't matter — he'd been wandering around in the woods for as long as he could remember, and the path that would take him to his house on the far edge of town was only a little farther ahead, and there was plenty of moonlight.

Which was a good thing, since he didn't have a flashlight.

A branch lashed across his face, and Ellis swore under his breath as he pushed it aside, then swore out loud as he tripped over a root.

Where was the damn path?

It had to be here somewhere!

Except now that he thought about it — and now that the pain of the branch slashing his face had cut through some of the fog in his mind — it seemed he should already have found it.

He stopped and peered around, searching the darkness.

Nothing looked familiar.

In fact, he didn't recognize anything at all.

Could he have crossed the path without noticing it?

Or was he maybe going in the wrong direction?

He looked up, searching the sky for something familiar, and finally found the Big Dipper, then followed its line to the North Star. So now at least he knew he was going in the right direction. If he kept going straight, he'd get back to town.

But he'd actually get *home* a lot faster if he found the path, and as the beginning of a headache throbbed behind his left ear, the idea of going to bed sooner rather than later seemed pretty good.

Maybe he shouldn't have had so much to drink.

He started walking, getting pissed at Adam all over again; if Adam hadn't been such an asshole, they'd have just finished off the bottle, had a couple of laughs at the expense of the coneheads, and by now he'd be home and in bed instead of trudging through the woods trying to find a path that wasn't all that easy to spot even in daylight.

Abruptly, the woods gave way to a large open space, and Ellis stopped short as he saw a towering deadfall standing alone in the center of the clearing. Its leafless, barkless branches gleamed in the moonlight like

great lifeless arms reaching out to him.

Reaching out to touch him.

To close around him.

To crush him . . .

With a strangled cry, he took an instinctive step backward, tripped, and fell to the ground.

He scrambled to his feet, his eyes still fixed on the looming deadfall.

A deadfall he'd never seen before.

But that wasn't possible — he'd been everywhere in these woods. Everywhere!

Turning away from the tree, he started moving again, hurrying his step. He couldn't be that far from town, but what if he'd turned himself around?

What if he couldn't find the path?

He shivered as the idea of wandering in the woods all night long began to take root in his mind.

Maybe, after all, he should have walked Cherie home.

In fact, maybe he shouldn't have gotten pissed at Adam, either.

Somewhere behind him, he heard a branch crack and froze in his tracks, his breath catching in his throat as his heart skipped a beat.

Was it a branch falling from the deadfall?

Or was it someone stepping on a branch

that had already fallen?

Adam! That was it — Adam had followed him, just like he and Adam and Chris had followed those coneheads the night before last. "Adam?" he called out, taking a couple of tentative steps toward where he thought the path ought to be.

He heard the brush rustle behind him.

Once again he stopped short.

The rustling stopped.

Now his skin was starting to crawl. "Come on, Adam," he said, struggling to keep his voice from betraying the fear that was starting to spread through him. "This isn't funny. I'm not a conehead, you know."

No answer.

He started walking again, and as he did, the rustling in the brush began again.

He stopped. "Chris?"

No answer.

"Adam? Come on, man! I'm sorry, okay?" Ellis quickened his pace.

What if it wasn't Adam? What if it was a bear, or a mountain lion?

What if it was stalking him?

His fear suddenly threatened to explode into panic, and as he twisted his head around to peer into the blackness behind him, the toe of his tennis shoe caught on a root. He sprawled out hard, pine needles

stabbing his face and hands, a sharp pain shooting through his leg as his knee smashed onto a rock. He stifled the yelp of pain almost before it escaped his throat, then lay silent, listening, trying to breathe noiselessly through his mouth.

All he could hear was the pounding of his own heart.

As the panic — and the agony in his knee — eased, Ellis rose unsteadily to his feet.

And the sounds behind him began again as soon as he started limping ahead.

He tried to move faster, but couldn't, his throbbing knee threatening to collapse after every step. And then, a dozen paces farther, he found it.

The path, its features familiar even in the dark.

He began to run, ignoring the pain, wanting only to escape whatever it was that had been stalking him. But after only a few yards his knee threatened to give out and he fell back to a limping half trot.

And the footfalls behind him were there again.

He'd gained nothing by running; in fact, whatever it was seemed closer than ever.

Once more he forced himself into a run, even though he knew it didn't matter.

Whatever was chasing him was going to

catch him anyway.

But still he had to run.

Sheer panic drove him on until finally he could bear the pain in his leg no more, and his breath came in rasping gasps, and his heart felt like it was about to explode.

He could hear whoever — or whatever — it was breathing behind him now.

He reached deep inside himself, found one last hidden reserve of energy, and —

Something hard — something hard and heavy — crashed against the back of his neck.

Fireworks exploded in his head as he stumbled and fell to his knees.

He turned, wanting to see who — or what — had attacked him, but all he saw was a black silhouette looming over him, obscuring the faint moonlight.

The attacker raised what looked like a huge club high above him.

Ellis whimpered, cowering back, trying to drag himself away into the darkness.

And then, as the cudgel began arcing down on him, recognition flashed through his mind.

He knew who was killing him.

He knew, but it didn't matter.

It was already far too late.

CHAPTER 18

Eric knew something had happened the moment he saw Tad and Kent coming up the lawn the next morning, partly because it wasn't even seven-thirty yet and he knew that Kent, at least, never got up before eight unless he absolutely had to. But it wasn't just that Kent was up too early — Eric could see by the way he was walking that Tad was upset about something.

By the time they came to the steps leading up to Pinecrest's wide veranda, Eric was already outside, waiting for them. "What's going on?" he asked. Tad, his face pale, said nothing, and just as Kent was about to say something, the kitchen door opened and his mother stuck her head out as Moxie slipped through the crack and charged down the steps to throw himself on Kent.

"Breakfast in fifteen minutes," Merrill said. "You two want pancakes?" When both Kent and Tad shook their heads, she wid-

311

ened her eyes in mock surprise. "Teenage boys who don't want pancakes? It must be the end of the world!" Her eyes shifted back to Eric. "Will you keep an eye on Moxie, or shall I call him back inside?"

"I'll watch him," Eric replied. As the kitchen door closed again, he moved down the steps. "So what is it?" he pressed.

Kent tipped his head toward Tad. "Ask him."

Tad glanced around furtively, and when he finally spoke, he still didn't answer Eric's question. "Maybe we ought to go down by the lake or something."

You mean go somewhere where my Mom won't hear anything, Eric translated silently, following Tad and Kent toward the water as Moxie charged ahead.

"I had a nightmare last night," Tad said when he was certain they were out of earshot of the house. A strange feeling of something like déjà vu rippled through Eric as Tad added, "I mean, a really bad nightmare."

"What kind of nightmare?" Eric asked, the feeling of déjà vu deepening as a vague, half-formed memory of his own dreams last night began to creep up from his subconscious.

Tad finally looked up from the ground

he'd been gazing at and saw Kent eyeing Eric warily.

"You have one, too?" Kent asked.

Eric said nothing, for now another memory was recurring. Was it possible they'd all had the same dream again, like on the night Tippy was killed? Moxie, who had been sniffing along the lakeshore, suddenly headed toward the woods. Eric called after him, but the dog kept going, apparently on the scent of something.

"We better follow him," Eric sighed, knowing what would happen if he went back to the house without the dog. "So how come this dream's got you so worried?" he went on as they started through the trees.

"It was weird," Tad said. "I was being chased."

"Which isn't so weird," Kent said. "We were chased night before last by those yahoos from town, remember?"

Tad shot Kent a dark look. "It wasn't the same. It was like I was being hunted. Only then I was the hunter." He took a deep breath as he saw Eric and Kent exchange a glance. "Okay, I know it sounds stupid when I tell it, but it was really horrible. First I was in a tunnel, only the tunnel was made out of plastic garbage bags." Slowly, he recounted every detail of the nightmare —

the blades glinting in the darkness, the river of blood. And the table leg that turned into a club. When he finished, he gazed at the trees that now surrounded them. "It looked like this," he said. "Except it was dark. And when I —" His voice broke at the memory of the dream and what he'd been about to do, and he fell silent.

The faint chill that had come over Eric when Tad began describing his dream now seemed to wrap him like an icy shroud. But maybe he was wrong, he thought. Maybe he hadn't had the same dream himself last night — maybe it just *seemed* like he remembered having it. If he'd actually had it, wouldn't he have remembered it before Tad started talking about it? Then Kent spoke, and the cold shroud tightened around Eric.

"The thing is, I had the same dream. Like the other night, when we all dreamed about Jack the Ripper. Remember? And last night —"

"We just dreamed about what happened to us," Eric said, desperately wanting to believe his own words. "We found that table leg in the carriage house yesterday, remember? It was like a club, right? And night before last those jerks followed us through the woods and scared the crap out of us. So

of course we dreamed about it! Why wouldn't we? It's no big deal! It was just a dream!"

There was a long silence as the three boys remembered what happened after they'd all dreamed about Jack the Ripper.

"What if it wasn't," Tad finally said. "What if it was like the other dream we had? What if —"

Before he could finish, they heard a rustling in the brush to the right, immediately followed by Moxie growling.

"Moxie?" Eric called out. "Moxie, come!" Instead of bursting out of the brush, the dog only growled louder. "He must have found something," Eric sighed. "Now we have to go get him."

With Tad and Kent following him, Eric pushed his way through the brush, following the dog's now steady growling. Twice more he called out, but all he got in return was more growling and a single muffled bark. Then, ten paces farther on, they found the dog.

Moxie was crouched low to the ground, his jaws clamped on the end of a stick.

A heavy stick with one end much thicker than the other, like a club.

The boys stopped short, staring at the object.

All three of them had the same thought: *the dream.*

None of them spoke.

Eric glanced first at Tad, then at Kent, and finally moved closer, squatting down. "What is it?" he whispered. "What you got, Mox?" He reached out to take hold of the object and Moxie growled a warning. Eric jerked his hand away, then rose to his feet. "Drop it," he commanded. Moxie's ears flattened against his head, but he peered up at Eric. "I said drop it!" The dog stood up, hesitated, then finally let the thick stick drop back to the ground.

Now they could clearly see what Moxie had gone after: the knot at the end of the stick was covered with what looked like blood.

Blood, and strands of hair.

The details of his own dream flooded back to Eric. *But it wasn't possible — it had only been a dream!* So what if Tad and Kent had the same dream? It was still only a dream. It *had* to be only a dream! He tore his eyes away from the bloody stick and turned to his friends.

"It's like the dream," Tad whispered. "But it can't be. I mean, we were home. Asleep." His voice took on a desperate tone. "We were in our beds." He turned away. "I think

I'm going to be sick."

Eric's eyes fixed once more on the heavy stick. "You think maybe we better get rid of this thing?" he asked.

"Why?" Kent said, almost too quickly. "It doesn't have anything to do with us."

Moxie, who had barely been able to control himself since Eric had made him drop the stick, could contain himself no longer, and began slinking back toward it, whining eagerly as the scent of blood once again filled his nostrils.

"No!" Eric said, reaching down and scooping the dog up before it could begin licking and gnawing. "Let's just get out of here, okay?"

With Eric leading the way, they started back toward the path, none of them saying a word, each of them hoping that if they didn't talk about what Moxie had found, maybe they could just forget it. When they were a few feet away, Eric tossed the stick behind him.

But they knew that even if their memories from last night were nothing but a dream, the heavy stick Moxie had found wasn't.

It was real.

And it was covered with blood.

Carol Langstrom turned the rapidly brown-

ing sausages in the frying pan, lowered the flame, then put a lid on the pan and poured two small glasses of orange juice.

"Ellis!" she called. "Breakfast!" She listened for his usual sleepy-voiced response, but none came. "Ellis? We need to leave in ten minutes." When there still was no answer, she set the glasses on the breakfast bar, walked down the hall, and knocked on his door. "Ellis? I need you in the shop today, honey."

Still no answer. Which meant he'd been out way too late last night, and she distinctly remembered telling him to be in by midnight, and not a minute later. She turned the knob and opened the door.

Ellis's bed was still made, and she didn't even have to enter to know it hadn't been slept in.

So he hadn't come home last night.

He hadn't even called.

Which was very odd.

Carol went back to the kitchen, turned the stove off under the sausages, and checked her watch. If she wasn't going to be late, she had to leave for the store in ten minutes, and she needed Ellis today. The Fourth of July weekend was coming up, and it was her busiest of the year — people came from all over the county and even all the

way up from Illinois and Ohio for the parade, the fireworks, and the picnic that Phantom Lake had become famous for.

And all those people bought, which meant her shop had to be ready for the onslaught of antiques buyers, which meant she needed Ellis's help.

So where was he? She knew he hadn't told her of any plans to spend the night at Adam Mosler's place, because he knew perfectly well she would have said no.

And that, she decided, was precisely why he hadn't asked. But if he thought that by not coming home he was going to get out of helping her unpack the five crates of furniture that were waiting in the back room of the shop, he was dead wrong.

Carol picked up the phone and dialed Adam's number.

Cleve Mosler answered on the first ring with the kind of ragged hello that told her that he, at least, had had too much to drink last night. But that, fortunately, wasn't her problem. "Hi, Cleve," she said, trying to mask her disapproval of Adam's father with a voice that was a little too bright. "It's Carol Langstrom. Sorry to bother you so early, but does Ellis happen to be there?"

"Nope," Cleve Mosler said. "Adam came home about two this morning, and he and I

are going to have a little chat when I get home from work. But he came home alone, and he's still asleep."

"Okay, thanks." Carol hung up the phone, the first pangs of real worry beginning to sprout in the back of her mind. Adam came home at two in the morning? Had Ellis been with him? And if he was, what had they been doing?

Drugs?

Absolutely not. At least not Ellis.

A girl?

There'd been no evidence of a steady girlfriend. Not yet, anyway. At least, not that she knew of.

Drinking? She started to dismiss that possibility, too, then revised her initial "no" to "maybe."

But even if he'd been drinking, where would he have gone? Probably not back to Adam's house, because Cleve Mosler was the kind of drunk who was quite capable of taking a swing not only at his own son, but at anybody who happened to be there when he got angry. And, despite his own habits — or maybe because of them — Cleve Mosler wouldn't tolerate even a hint of alcohol on his son's breath.

Carol took a sip of coffee as she tried to decide what to do next. Other than his

friendship with Adam Mosler, Ellis had never given her anything to worry about. In fact, he was the kind of boy any mother would be proud of; he worked hard, and at least until now had always told her where he was going and with whom.

So for him to not call and not come home was totally uncharacteristic.

Which meant something was wrong.

Thoughts of an accident occurred to her. But if something had happened — something that could have put him in the hospital — someone would have called. And it was the same if he and Adam had done something that would have gotten them in trouble with the sheriff. Maybe in Milwaukee or Madison a teenage boy could get in trouble without anyone calling his mother, but not in Phantom Lake. In Phantom Lake, no news was definitely good news.

Then where was he?

Two possibilities came to mind: his father's house, or Chris McIvens's.

She picked up the phone again, but before she dialed, she caught a glimpse of the clock — she was now going to be late opening the shop.

She'd call Chris's house from work.

She finished her coffee, then wrote a note for Ellis in case he came home before she

found him. *Call me the minute you get home!!* She underlined the six words three times, stuck the note to the refrigerator with a woodpecker magnet, put the eggs back in the refrigerator, wrapped up the sausages, rinsed her coffee cup in the sink, then grabbed her purse and keys and went out the door.

But as she drove the few blocks to work, her feeling of worry kept growing, and no matter how much she told herself that nothing was wrong, that Ellis was just being a typical irresponsible teenager, deep in her heart she didn't believe it.

Ellis just wasn't the kind of boy who would have taken off for the whole night without calling her.

If he could have called, he would.

Something had happened.

Something bad.

CHAPTER 19

As soon as his mother left with Marci, Eric began loading breakfast dishes into the dishwasher. Meanwhile, Kent, who had gotten there just after Merrill and Marci left, picked up the telephone and dialed Tad's cell number. "Hey, you okay?" he asked when Tad answered on the first ring.

There was a moment's hesitation before Tad said, "I guess," and an even longer one after Kent told him to come back to Pinecrest. "If you guys want to go into that room again, go ahead," he said just as Kent was about to start the "Can you hear me now?" routine. "But every time I go in there, I have nightmares, and after the last one, I'm not sure I want to know anything more about what's in there."

"Don't you even want to find out why we're having nightmares?" Kent asked, but Tad didn't take the bait.

"No," he said, his voice taking on a desper-

ate tone. "I just want them to stop. Call me when you want to do something else," he finished, and hung up before Kent could argue with him.

Kent clicked off the phone and set it back in its cradle. "He's scared."

Eric shrugged as he rinsed the last plate and put it in its slot in the dishwasher. "Maybe he's right — maybe we ought to leave all that stuff alone."

Kent's eyes widened in disbelief. "Are you kidding me? We don't know the half of what's in there."

"Yeah, but —"

"But nothing!" Kent broke in. "So Tad's scared. Does that mean you have to be, too?" He paused, looked straight at Eric, and played his trump card: "C'mon, Eric — you turning into your mother?" Kent knew he'd ended the argument even before Eric spoke.

"Okay," Eric said, "but if it gets weird —"

"It's *already* weird," Kent shot back. "That's what's so great about it."

Eric added soap to the dishwasher, set it running, then followed Kent across the lawn toward the carriage house. But as he walked, his eyes kept moving back to the spot where they'd gone into the woods.

The spot where the bloody cudgel still lay

in the brush.

He tried to tell himself that it didn't mean anything — that they didn't even know what the heavy stick might have been used for. Maybe it hadn't been used to hit a human being at all — maybe someone had clubbed a rabbit, or a beaver or something. Yet even as he tried to reassure himself, he knew that it was something else, that however the bloody weapon had come to be there, it had some connection to their dreams.

And some connection to the hidden room in the carriage house.

First, the scalpels.

Then someone had left Tippy's mutilated body at the sheriff's door.

Now the bloody club . . .

But it didn't have anything to do with them — it couldn't have anything to do with them.

They'd been asleep.

Or had they?

Now he was remembering the time they all lost whenever they went into the hidden room. The time that had passed as quickly as if they'd been asleep. Yet they hadn't been asleep.

What if last night —

He put the thought out of his mind, unwilling even to think about what it might

mean. They'd all been at home, in their beds, asleep. Whatever had happened in the woods had nothing to do with them.

And besides, the stuff in the hidden room was just that — stuff! Old stuff that Hector Darby had probably collected because he was as crazy as his patients.

"I think I'm starting to figure out why Darby collected all this stuff," Kent said as they came to the carriage house door.

A chill passed through Eric as he realized that Kent's words seemed almost a response to a question he hadn't asked. "Yeah?" he said, consciously keeping his voice steady. "Why?"

"I think maybe he thought there was something about the stuff — like maybe there was a piece of those guys caught in the stuff they used when they killed people, you know? Sort of like voodoo, where you have to have something that came from the person you want to put a hex on. It's like maybe Darby thought if he had the stuff, he could figure out what was wrong with the people, you know?"

They were inside the carriage house now, at the door to the storeroom, and already the strange humming — the barely audible noise that sounded almost human — was beginning. Had Dr. Darby heard that

sound, too? And what if Kent was right? What if the voices on the edge of his consciousness really were coming from the things in the hidden room?

With the voices whispering to him again like a siren song, Eric helped Kent slide the plywood away from the hidden door. Then they went into the dark chamber and began the familiar ritual of lighting the lamps.

The voices were louder now, and Eric looked around at all the boxes, all the shelves filled with books. Where to begin? Where to start? There was too much, too many things to see, to touch. . . .

As the babble of the voices filled their minds, Kent began opening boxes.

The first two were full of more books, and he put them aside as he searched for more interesting artifacts.

Eric, though, lifted half a dozen books from the top box and scanned their titles. All of them were about serial killers. Some were texts on abnormal psychology, some were scholarly case studies.

Some were true crime paperbacks.

And from somewhere deep inside him, a craving arose.

He wanted to read these books.

He wanted to read them all.

He wanted to know exactly what Dr.

Darby had known.

And he wanted to know even more.

He opened one of the books and began to read, unconsciously sinking into Hector Darby's own chair. The book was a case study of someone named Andrei Chikatilo, who killed fifty-five people in Russia in the 1970s and 1980s. Chikatilo had ripped pieces of his victims' flesh from their bones with his teeth and swallowed them even before murdering them. Then, after they had died, he'd sometimes taken more, taken bloody souvenirs to eat on the way home.

It took fifteen years to catch Andrei Chikatilo, and at least one innocent man was tried, found guilty, and executed for one of Chikatilo's murders. "This guy was really weird," Eric said as he turned the last page on the strange case, but when he looked up, he realized Kent was no longer in the room.

"Kent?" he called out, rising abruptly from the chair and knocking it backward into a stack of boxes, which tipped over, sending something clattering to the floor.

He picked up the object.

The hacksaw.

The hacksaw they'd left on the table the last time they were here.

It had been clean then, but now —

"Give me a hand with this," Kent said,

jerking Eric's attention away from the hacksaw as he ducked back in through the door, carrying a lightbulb and the last few loops of a worn extension cord whose length disappeared back into the outer storage room. It wasn't until Kent began screwing the bulb into the ornate lamp they'd found a few days earlier that Eric saw the lamp shade that now sat next to it on the table.

And there was a new energy in the room — a new note in the hum of indistinct voices.

With the bulb in place, Kent plugged the lamp into the end of the extension cord. "Look up the lamp in the ledger," he said, his voice tense as he began fitting the lamp shade to the harp on the base.

Eric opened the ledger and carefully turned the pages until he found the entry:

2/25 acq. lamp (#63) frm E.G. est. sale Plainfield, WI. $35,250.

"Thirty-five thousand dollars," Eric breathed.

Kent said nothing as he finished fitting the shade to the lamp and twisted the switch.

A soft amber glow filled the room.

The voices seemed to sigh with the beauty of it.

Unconsciously wiping his hands on his pants, Eric reached out and touched his fingertips to the lamp shade.

It felt warm, and almost soft, like leather.

But so thin, so fragile.

He leaned closer.

It was, indeed, leather, but not like any leather he'd ever seen before. He could actually see veining in its grain.

He laid both his hands on the shade, and one of the voices in his head seemed to rise above the others as a strange energy coursed from the lamp into his hands and up his fingers and arms to flood his body.

He listened to the voices, and though he still couldn't understand the words, he didn't care.

He knew that something deep inside him — some part of him he was barely aware even existed — heard the voices perfectly.

Heard them, and understood.

CHAPTER 20

Merrill Brewster put down her fork and eyed her son. He looked pale, with flushed spots high on his cheeks, and as far as she could see, he hadn't consumed even a single bite of his supper. All he'd done was merely move his meat loaf and mashed potatoes around on his plate, but none of it had actually been eaten. "Do you feel all right, honey?"

Eric nodded, then put down his fork and sat back in the chair. "I guess I'm just really tired," he said.

Merrill cocked her head. "What were you up to all day?"

"Nothing," Eric said, shrugging dismissively. "You know — just hung out. Poked around in the carriage house, looking at some of the old stuff that's stored in there."

"Those aren't our things," Merrill said, frowning. "I think you'd better leave them

alone. If something breaks, we're responsible."

"I know. We're careful."

Merrill rose from her chair and picked up her plate, but before she took it to the kitchen she paused and felt Eric's forehead. "I hope you haven't picked up some bug," she fretted. "Ashley Sparks said Tad went back to bed this morning."

"I'm fine," Eric insisted, ducking his head away from his mother's touch. "I'm just tired, okay?"

Merrill pulled back almost as if she'd been stung. "You don't have to bite my head off! I'm just worried —"

"You worry about everything!" Eric broke in, rising from his chair. "I think I'll just go to bed, okay?"

"Fine," Merrill said, stepping back from Eric's outburst, and looking him over once more, noticing for the first time a stain on his pants. "What's that?" she asked.

Eric looked down to see dark rusty finger streaks, and the memory of the hacksaw he'd picked up from the floor of the hidden room flooded back. He thought quickly. "Rust," he said. "I found an old saw, and it was all over the blade."

"Have you ever heard of a rag?" Merrill asked, then shook her head and answered

her own question. "Of course not. Why would I think you would have? Just put those in the wash before you go to bed, okay?"

Though he was barely listening, Eric nodded. Rust? Why had he said that? It hadn't been rust — it had been sticky. Sticky, like —

He felt the blood drain from his face, and now his mother was staring at him.

"Honey? What's —"

"I'm okay," he insisted, managing to conceal his roiling emotions. "I'm just pooped — I'll be fine in the morning."

Merrill continued to eye him, and tried to tell herself she was just falling victim to needless worry again. "Okay," she said. "Marci and I are going to work on her costume for the parade for a while. She's going to be the Statue of Liberty."

Feeling his mother's appraising gaze still on him, Eric winked at his sister. "Tomorrow I'll see if I can find something to make a torch out of. Wouldn't that be neat?" Marci, still sitting at the table, bobbed her head happily, and he could see the worry start to drain out of his mother's eyes.

A few minutes later, after he'd once more loaded the dishwasher, he paused at the table where his mother and sister were put-

ting together something he was sure wasn't going to look anything like the Statue of Liberty's crown. "See you in the morning," he said as he kissed his mother's cheek.

To his relief, she barely looked up.

An hour later, after she'd tucked Marci into bed — the freshly glued and glittered crown sitting safely on the nightstand next to her — Merrill looked in on Eric.

He was sound asleep.

She smoothed the hair from his forehead and kissed him gently, careful not to waken him. He still felt warm, and little beads of perspiration stood out on his upper lip, but she decided he didn't look sick.

She tiptoed out and gently closed the door behind her.

As she moved through the quiet house, sweeping up wayward glitter, putting the lid back on the glue, folding up the newspapers, and disposing of the leftover cardboard and construction paper, she decided that her husband and family and friends had all been right.

Tonight, even without Dan here, she was actually enjoying being where she was.

She was enjoying the quiet of the lake and the house.

Before closing the drapes and locking the

doors for the night, she took a long moment to gaze out at the moonlight on the lake.

Peaceful. Serene.

Perfect.

How could she have been so nervous about coming here?

She pulled the drapes, then turned back to the room, where Moxie was sprawled on the sofa, one ear cocked in her direction even in his sleep, ready to accompany her upstairs and sleep on a real bed as soon as she gave the word.

Even Moxie wasn't worried.

And she herself felt calmer and more rested than she had in a long time.

She turned out the lights and headed upstairs, Moxie waking up to trot along at her heels.

Just as she slipped between cool sheets, the phone rang.

"Hi, honey," Dan said.

Merrill smiled in the quiet and darkness of the house and snuggled down in her warm bed.

Tonight, for the first time in years, she didn't have a single worry to tell her husband about.

Go home! Turn the boat around and go home!

But Logan knew he couldn't go home —

not yet. Not until he'd done what he came here to do.

The thing was, he didn't know what to do.

Not anymore.

Not since the people had come to Pinecrest.

He tightened his hands on the oars, squeezing them so hard his knuckles ached. In the bow, the old dog whimpered softly, and Logan clucked in sympathy. "Too old," he muttered. "Too old for any of this."

Go back! Go away!

The voice seemed to come from outside his head now, but Logan knew that wasn't true. The voices weren't real — they were only part of his own craziness! That was what Dr. Darby had said — that was what all the doctors had said. They weren't real, and he had to pretend they weren't there.

He pulled hard on the right oar, and the shriek of its lock ripped through the night. From somewhere off to the left a bird burst from its roost, flapping in indignation. Logan ignored it, concentrating instead on pulling the boat around and forcing its prow into the muddy bank.

The howling in his head grew worse, but he dragged himself out of the boat, pulling it farther onto the shore and making its

worn painter fast to a low-hanging branch.

Once on shore, the voices began to shriek at him. Gone were the soft, soothing tones that used to whisper to him, murmuring their approval as his fantasies became reality. As the voices howled, the long-buried memories crawled up from his unconscious, and once again he could feel it.

His enormous, coarse hands around her small, soft throat.

The sweet taste of her blood on his tongue.

All he'd had to do then was listen.

Listen, and obey.

But now —

The voices didn't want him here.

But why?

It didn't matter. It didn't matter what the voices wanted him to do.

He had to do what Dr. Darby wanted him to do.

He paced the shore, searching for the courage to do what he knew must be done.

His hands went to his head, trying to shut the voices out, but even as he pressed so hard he thought his skull might crack, the voices tortured him.

In the bow of the boat, the old dog struggled to sit up, and Logan stopped his pacing. As the dog's eyes fixed on him, a strange foreboding fell over him, and then

his skin began to crawl as if he'd just been touched by death itself.

But it wasn't death.

It was Dr. Darby.

Dr. Darby was inside the dog, and if he just concentrated — just focused his mind and kept his eyes on the dog — he would know.

Dr. Darby was stronger than the voices, and now, in the dark of the night, Dr. Darby would give him the strength to ignore the voices, too.

It would be all right.

He would find the strength.

Dr. Darby depended on him.

He had to keep everything in order, keep everybody safe.

Finally turning away from the boat — and the dog — he began slogging toward the carriage house, resisting the voices that pushed against him like the winds of a hurricane.

"I can do it," he whispered as he came at last to the door. "I *will* do it."

His hand touched the doorknob, and the cacophony of voices screaming at him to go away pounded so hard in his head that he almost fell to his knees.

Why weren't they luring him the way they used to? Why weren't they promising him

the fruit of his darkest desires?

Why didn't they want him anymore?

The answer bubbled up from the depths of his subconscious, groping its way through the fog in his mind.

They didn't want him here because they had someone new.

They had someone else to carry out their evil.

Now a harsh ray of jealousy ripped at the clouds in his head, and Logan's fingers tightened on the brass of the doorknob until he felt as if it must crumble under the pressure.

"Help me," he whispered, leaning against the door. "Help me, Jesus."

He turned the knob and entered the carriage house.

Logan stepped into his boat just as dawn was lightening the eastern sky. The old dog barely looked up when he shoved off from the weedy shoreline and began rowing toward home.

His back ached. His arms ached. His head ached.

And his soul ached even more.

He rowed with his eyes half closed, the little boat seeming to know the much traveled route even without his guidance.

He needed to rest.

He ached to put an end to his weariness.

Head hanging, he kept rowing, each long, torturous pull of the oars endurable only because it took him closer to home.

To sleep.

To blessed unconsciousness.

To freedom from the voices, even if only for a little while.

The dog moved restlessly on his nest of rags, and Logan opened his eyes.

Dawn was on the lake and they were almost home.

He put the last of his energy into the final strokes of the oars, and then the boat nosed into the hidden mud slip and came to a stop.

He secured the boat to a stump, lifted the dog onto the shore, and limped up the hill as sunshine blazed on the tips of the trees.

When he opened the cabin door, the one-winged crow greeted him with a hungry caw, and Logan realized he had failed to bring any food home.

The dog looked up at him with big, brown, expectant eyes, and Logan's spirits dropped even further.

They had trusted him.

Trusted him as Dr. Darby had trusted him.

And he had failed.

"Sorry," he muttered, his head hanging as he took off his jacket. Even the energy to talk had been drained from him, and all he could do was repeat the single word. "Sorry."

He hung the jacket on a nail and lay down on his bed.

The old dog went to his bed and collapsed with a groan.

But the crow jumped from his perch, hopped up a series of boxes to the jacket, and pecked at the pocket.

"Go, crow," Logan said, and waved an exhausted hand at it.

But the crow was insistent, and as Logan watched, it burrowed its head deep inside the jacket's pocket and emerged a moment later, a bloody chunk of meat clutched in its beak.

The meat fell to the floor, and the crow jumped to the ground and began pecking at it.

The old dog hauled himself to his wobbly legs and made his way over to the meal.

"Good," Logan whispered as he watched the two broken creatures rip and tear at the scrap. But then, as the meat slowly disappeared into the animals' mouths, questions began to drift through the mists in his mind.

He had no memory of scavenging that night.

He hadn't even been to town.

Then where had he gotten meat?

Didn't matter. The dog and the crow were fed.

And the fullness in his gut told him he, too, had eaten not long ago, even though he didn't remember that, either.

"Doesn't matter," he said, this time uttering the thought out loud.

He closed his eyes and let sleep overtake him.

Rusty Ruston fixed Adam Mosler with his meanest, most authoritative stare, the one that never failed to work on recalcitrant teenagers. Though Adam was a troublemaker, Rusty didn't think he was a bad kid, and he was pretty sure the stare would get the truth out of him. The thing was, Adam seemed utterly unfazed by being called to his office, and he certainly hadn't crumpled under any of his intimidation techniques. So either he was telling the truth about the last time he saw Ellis or he was so jaded by his father, who took the meaning of the word "mean" to a level Rusty could barely even imagine, that the stare truly didn't bother him at all.

Still, he had to take a final shot at it. "So tell me one more time what Ellis said when he walked away," he growled, doing his best to make his voice sound as threatening as possible.

Adam's sigh told Ruston he'd succeeded only in boring the boy, and Mosler's shrug was actually dismissive. "I've already told you a million times."

"Tell me once more," Ruston said, "and then you can go."

Adam rolled his eyes impatiently, but began the recitation one more time. "Ellis was drunk. Said he hated this town, and everybody in it. Said he was leaving and we'd never see him again. Then he left."

"Left for where?"

"Seemed like he was walking toward town." Adam hesitated, then: "But I don't really know — I was busy with Cherie."

Ruston leaned tiredly back in his chair. This was exactly the same story Cherie Stevens had already told him, except that of course Adam wasn't mentioning the part where she'd brushed him off. "Okay," he said. "You can go."

Adam stood up. "You want to know what I think?" he asked. Ruston shook his head, but Adam went on anyway. "You should talk to those summer kids out at Pinecrest."

"And why should I do that?" Ruston asked, once again fixing Adam Mosler with the stare. Almost to his own surprise, this time it worked; Mosler actually flushed slightly.

"Well, some of us were having a little fun with them the other night," he said, some of the bravado fading from his voice. "And they didn't like it."

"What do you mean, 'fun'?"

Mosler spread his hands dismissively. "They were walking through the woods and we made bear sounds and scared them."

"That's all?" Ruston asked, his eyes boring into Adam now. "You just made noises? Nothing else? Nothing at all?"

Mosler's blush deepened. "All right, maybe we tossed a rock or two. But it's not like we hurt them."

"But you figure maybe it made them mad enough to jump Ellis Langstrom?"

"Hey, I didn't say they did anything," Adam replied. "All's I said was you should talk to them."

"I will," Ruston assured him. "And I'll also ask them exactly what happened the other night, and you'd better hope their story matches yours." As Adam started toward the door, Ruston said, "I don't want to hear any more about you hassling the

summer people, Mosler, and you need to hear me good about this. I'm not going to put up with it. Not even once more. I'll bust you for criminal mischief, and you can spend some time in juvie hall down in Irma. That sound like fun?"

Adam shook his head, but didn't look too worried.

"Go," Ruston sighed, waving Mosler out of his office, and wishing he hadn't heard about Eric Brewster and his friends. The last thing he wanted to do was go out to Pinecrest and scare the summer visitors with a story about a missing kid. But now he had no choice — Ellis was definitely missing, and he had to follow up on Adam's story. And he had to do it gently, without getting the visitors, the town, or especially the mayor, riled up. He was going to have to muster a whole boatload of tact for this one.

Half an hour later — at precisely ten o'clock, which would mean he would be interrupting neither breakfast nor lunch — Ruston turned his cruiser up the long Pinecrest driveway, silently rehearsing the questions he wanted to ask Eric Brewster and consciously bringing a pleasant expression to his face.

He walked up to the front door and rang

the bell, and no more than fifteen seconds later Merrill answered.

Remembering their last encounter, where the sight of him in a uniform made her think that something had happened to her husband, Rusty offered her a smile and asked to see Eric. "He's not in trouble — I just heard a story about some of the town kids hassling him and his friends the other night and wanted to check it out."

Though Merrill's expression tightened slightly, she invited him in and led him to the dining room, where Ruston realized there was one meal he'd forgotten about: brunch. Gathered around the dining table were not only Eric and his little sister, but two other boys his age, and two women who he assumed were their mothers. He also assumed that the boys had been with Eric the other night, when Adam said he and his own friends tried to scare them in the woods.

Merrill made a quick series of introductions, then waited expectantly. Picking up his cue, Ruston got directly to the point, but decided to direct his first words to all three of the boys and see what happened. "I heard some of the boys in town tried to give you guys a scare in the woods the other night."

Three pairs of eyes darted toward one another, then Eric nodded. "Something like that, yes."

"All three of you?" He indicated the two other boys with a nod of his head.

Eric nodded.

"Anything come of that?"

"Do you mean did we kick their butts?" Kent asked.

Ellen glared at her son. "Kent!"

The sheriff, though, smiled at the three boys. "Basically, yes, that's what I'm asking. And I'm not saying you're in trouble if you did, either. From what I've already heard, it sounds like they had it coming to them."

"Well, we didn't," Kent said, "but we should have."

"You didn't come all the way out here just to ask my son if he was in a fight," Merrill Brewster said. "Something else is going on, isn't it?"

Ruston shifted his weight uneasily from one foot to the other, but saw no point in not telling them what they were bound to hear within a few hours anyway. "Ellis Langstrom has been missing since night before last."

Tad Sparks paled and slumped in his chair.

"Ellis Langstrom?" Ashley Sparks

347

breathed, her face as pale as her son's. "Carol Langstrom's son?"

"Yes, ma'am," Ruston said.

"Oh, dear, that's terrible." Ashley said, sinking into one of the empty chairs at the table. "Poor Carol. I'd better call her." She looked back up at the sheriff. "Where is he? I mean, what happened to him?"

"That's what I'm trying to determine."

"Well, we sure didn't have anything to do with it," Kent said. "All that happened was that they were trying to scare us the other night in the woods," Eric explained. "You know — cracking twigs, and growls and moans and all that kind of stuff. And it worked — we got spooked and they got their laugh. But that was it — it was nothing, really." He looked at his mother, who was frowning at him as if there must be something he wasn't talking about. "Really. Nothing happened at all!"

Kent turned to the sheriff. "And if I was gonna make someone disappear, it'd be Adam Mosler, not Langstrom."

"Kent!" Ellen Newell looked like she might slap her son, and Ruston quickly smiled at her. "Some of our kids can get kind of frisky in the summer. School's out and they don't get much supervision from their folks."

Tad was still slumped in his chair, staring into space. Nothing about either his posture or expression suggested guilt. In fact, he looked more scared than anything else, and none of the boys showed any obvious cuts or bruises on their faces or their hands. At least not the kind they would have had if they'd gotten into a fight with Adam Mosler and Chris McIvens, and he was sure that Kent Newell's remark about going after Mosler rather than Ellis Langstrom was absolutely true. Ellis might have gone along with Mosler's harassment, but if it came down to a fight, Ellis was far more likely to run than stand. Which, in Ruston's book anyway, at least made him smarter than his two friends.

"Well, I guess that's it for now, then," he said. "If you hear or see anything, give the office a call, okay?"

"Of course," Merrill said. She walked the sheriff out the door to the edge of the porch, then put a halting hand on his arm. When she spoke, he could hear the fear in her voice. "You don't think an animal did something to him? I mean . . ." Her voice trailed off, her eyes shifted to a spot near the woods, and after a second or two she spoke again, though her words were barely audible. "I was just thinking about our cat."

He followed her gaze to a makeshift cross over a little plot of cleared earth near the garage, and a shiver ran the length of his spine as he remembered the way the cat had been ripped open, gutted, and left on his doorstep.

Surely there couldn't be any connection between that and —

He cut the thought short, unwilling to complete it. "I think some kind of animal got your cat," he said quietly, "but between you and me, I still think Ellis took off for Madison or Chicago or someplace. I'm pretty sure his mother will hear from him within a few days."

Merrill shook her head sadly. "Every mother's nightmare. I'm not sure I could stand it at all."

"Sorry to have bothered you," Ruston said. "Try to enjoy your day, okay? I'm sure everything's going to be just fine, and you can be proud that your boy and his friends were big enough to just ignore Mosler's crowd. I wish we had more kids around here like yours."

Merrill managed a smile and stepped back to the doorway, staying there until he had driven out of the driveway. He could still see her in his rearview mirror as he made the turn toward the highway.

There was a woman, he decided, who worried too much. Today, though, he couldn't help but wonder if maybe she wasn't right to worry.

What if the same thing that had happened to the Brewsters' cat had, indeed, happened to Ellis Langstrom?

Rusty Ruston didn't even want to think about it.

CHAPTER 21

Tad Sparks peered uncertainly around the small clearing. It looked sort of like the one where Moxie had found the heavy stick the day before yesterday, but so had the two others they'd already explored in the hour since they escaped from their mothers. But he wasn't sure whether he wanted to find the stick or not.

"It's got to be here somewhere," he heard Kent Newell say. "I know it was right around here. It was under a —"

"That's the third time you've said that," Tad cut in sourly. "We all know it was under a bush, but all the bushes look alike." He turned to Eric. "You sure you just dropped it, or did you throw it?"

Eric shrugged. "I thought I dropped it, but now I'm not sure."

"Even if we find it, what are we going to do with it?"

Kent looked at Tad as if he was an idiot.

"Tell the sheriff, of course. I mean, what if someone used it to kill that kid?"

"Doesn't it seem like maybe if we were going to do that we should have done it the day before yesterday?" Tad countered.

"Well, it doesn't matter anyway, because it's not here." Kent sighed. "Who knows? Maybe a bear found it and started gnawing on it or something."

"Or whoever left it here came back for it," Eric suggested. "And even if we found it, so what? I mean, it's not like the sheriff even said someone killed that kid —"

"Can we talk about something else?" Tad broke in as the memory of his nightmare — the nightmare in which he himself had killed someone — rose up in his mind.

"How about the room?" Kent asked, and saw a flicker of fear in Tad's eyes. "You know, the one you won't go into anymore?" When Tad's face reddened, he took another jab: "The one you're too *chicken* to go into?"

"What about it?" Tad asked, trying to keep his voice casual, but not quite succeeding.

"Remember the lamp we found in there?"

Tad tried to shrug, but again didn't quite succeed. "Yeah, I remember."

"You should see the lamp shade that goes on it."

Tad knew Kent was baiting him, and part of him wanted to simply ignore it. But there was another part of him, too, which was suddenly far stronger. "You found it?" he breathed. "You really found the lamp shade?"

Kent nodded.

"Where is it?"

"Where do you think it is?" Kent countered.

"What does it look like?"

Kent and Eric looked at each other as if deciding whether to tell him, but then a strange, puzzled look came into Eric's eyes. "I can't really remember," he said, his voice so soft it was almost a whisper. "That's weird."

"It was —" And now Kent, too, looked uncertain. "I can't remember, either. All I remember is that I never saw anything like it before. It was —" He shook his head, and Tad could see him groping for the right word. "It was amazing."

As Kent spoke the words, Tad felt his resolve never to go back into that room crumble. He was going to go back into that room after all, even though the mere thought of it made his heart pound and filled his mouth with cotton.

"Okay," he breathed. "Let's go."

Kent led the way into the carriage house, then helped Eric move the sheet of plywood, while Tad hung back in the storeroom, gazing at the darkness beyond the hidden doorway. Deep in his gut, he knew he'd come to some kind of point of no return, and now as he stood gazing into the depths of the room, a small voice inside him still cried out, pleading with him not to cross that threshold — not to step into the darkness — again.

As he hesitated, Kent and Eric stepped into the hidden chamber. But instead of lighting the lanterns, Kent turned back, an odd smile curling the corners of his mouth, his eyes fixed on Tad's. "Look at this," he said.

He turned the switch on the lamp and an amber glow suffused the room. But it wasn't merely a glow — no, it was far more than a gentle light that emanated from the lamp.

It was as if the lamp had illuminated a whole new dimension within the chamber.

As if guided by an unseen force, Tad stepped into the room and moved closer to the lamp.

He reached out and tentatively touched its shade.

And as he did, he heard the familiar chorus of murmuring voices.

He was back.

Back in the hidden room.

The voices sounded almost as warm as the soft light of the lamp felt, and finally that single voice deep inside him that had warned him away from this place fell utterly silent.

He was where he belonged.

The voices wanted him here.

Why? Why did they want him here?

He looked up at Kent and Eric, and once more stroked the lamp shade, this time almost caressing it. "This feels like leather," he murmured, his voice sounding loud and foreign in the small room.

Eric shrugged, barely hearing Tad's voice as he looked at the room in the soft glow of the lamplight. But it wasn't just the light that made it different from the last time he'd been here. "It's all of us," he whispered, almost to himself. "It feels different with all of us here." Moving as if in a trance — or as if he were being directed by some unseen force — Eric dropped down and sat on the floor by a stack of books, opening one of them.

Kent, too, felt the subtle difference the light — or Tad's presence — had made. He

began moving slowly among the boxes as if searching for something, but neither knowing nor wanting to know exactly what he sought.

But he would know it when he found it.

Tad finally lifted his fingertips from the lamp shade and, like Eric and Kent, gazed around the room. The soft amber light seemed to focus on something in one of the far corners.

A box.

A long box, white, like the kind flower shops used for roses.

It didn't seem to fit in this room full of old, dusty things.

As Tad approached it, the voices grew louder, and though there were no words — at least none that he could understand — Tad knew they were guiding him.

They wanted him to go to the box.

Why? Why do they want me to have the box?

He touched the box, and one of the voices seemed to rise above the others.

Gently, he picked it up and brought it to the table.

He moved the ledger, still open to the page where the purchase of the lamp shade was recorded, to one side.

Silently, responding to the voices, Eric and

Kent joined him.

Tad ran his hands over the top of the box. It seemed to vibrate, as if pulsing from some energy hidden within.

He reached down to lift the lid, but something — something unseen and unheard — stopped him just before he touched the cardboard. As his fingers hovered a fraction of an inch above the box, Kent laid his own hand on top of Tad's.

"Not yet," he said.

Then Eric's hand covered Kent's as he breathed three words: "It isn't time."

Tad closed his eyes and listened to what the voices were telling him. They were right.

Whatever was in the box, its time had not yet come.

Eric could hear the music long before the pavilion came into view, but as soon as the path turned and they stepped out of the woods and into the park, they saw it, lighted up like something out of Disneyland. It stood perched out over the lake, the sunset forming a perfect backdrop for its ornate white latticework. Tiny white lights covered not only the roof, but every post as well, and from beneath the floor, brilliant lights made the water itself take on a mystic glow. The band was playing an old Beach Boys

song, and though it wasn't quite dark yet, there were already at least a dozen couples on the dance floor.

And lounging against one of the railings, passing a bottle concealed in a brown paper bag back and forth, were Adam Mosler and Chris McIvens. As soon as Mosler caught sight of Eric, he whispered something to McIvens, and both of them fixed a surly stare on him. Eric sensed Tad stiffen on one side of him, and could almost feel Kent's fist clenching on the other.

"Uh-oh," Tad said quietly. "I told you guys we shouldn't have come."

"If we didn't show up, people would think we had something to do with whatever happened to Ellis Langstrom," Kent said. "Besides," he added, nudging Eric, "we know Cherie is going to be here, and if Cherie's here, Kayla will be, too." He leered at Tad, and unable to pass up the opportunity to taunt him, he added, "Which means at least two of us will be getting lucky." Then he looked around with an exaggerated air of bafflement. "Gee, I wonder which two it will be?"

Tad felt himself flushing in the gathering darkness. "Up yours, Newell," he growled, which only elicited a snicker from Kent.

"Ooh, tough guy! If Mosler comes after

us, will you defend me? Please?"

"If he comes after us, we'll just ignore him," Eric declared. "We're here to dance, remember?"

"Can't we fight, too?" Kent demanded, then relented. "So here's what let's do. Before you and I close in on Cherie and Kayla, let's find a girl for Tad."

Tad rolled his eyes. "Fat chance."

"It's all about attitude," Kent said, and led the way up the ramp to the pavilion dance floor. "You've got to act like you own the place." He found a vacant spot along the pavilion railing, leaned against it, and scanned the crowd, deciding that if he didn't see Kayla, he might actually try to find a girl for Tad. Assuming, of course, that Tad liked girls at all, which Kent suspected he didn't. Maybe, he thought, he should look around for a guy for Tad. But what if Tad hadn't figured out he was gay yet? Better stick with girls, at least until Tad figured himself out. "Plenty to chose from tonight," he whispered into Tad's ear. "You know these locals can't be satisfying the demand."

As Tad pointedly ignored Kent's goading, Eric saw Cherie and Kayla walking up the ramp. He was about to move toward them when Adam Mosler and Chris McIvens stepped in front of the girls, intercepting

them before they'd reached the main floor. Eric's jaw tightened as Mosler talked to them, not letting them pass. Then Cherie said something that made Adam step back as if he'd been slapped and brushed past him.

Kayla followed, jerking away from Chris McIvens when he reached out to stop her.

Cherie scanned the crowd, spotted Eric, waved, and started toward them.

"Uh-oh," Tad said quietly, reading the expressions on the two local boys' faces as they watched what was happening. "Now there's going to be trouble."

"Not for me," Eric said, grinning, and a moment later Cherie leaned against the railing next to him and he turned away from Tad and Kent to focus his entire attention on her. "Hey, I was hoping you were going to be here tonight."

"It was me who asked you to come, remember?" She let her hand brush against his as the band started a slow song. "Want to dance?" Her hand slid down his arm to his hand, and Eric let himself be led onto the dance floor.

"Pricks!"

Adam Mosler spat the single word as if it were as foul as the wad of tobacco jammed

in the corner of his mouth, then gritted his teeth as he watched Cherie lead Eric Brewster onto the dance floor. "Who do those bastards think they are?" He grabbed the bottle from Chris and sucked down a gulp, wiping his mouth on his sleeve. The vodka burned through his throat to feed the fire already raging in his belly, and he could feel the strength of his fury building. His eyes shifted unsteadily to Brewster's friends, and he elbowed his companion as he saw Kayla rubbing up against the big dumb football player. What was his name? Newhall? Newell — that was it. Kent Newell. In his mind, Adam switched the *e* in Newell's first name to a *u,* then snickered drunkenly at his own joke. "Moving in on your territory, too," he said as he passed the bottle back to Chris.

McIvens drank a couple of swallows without taking his own furious eyes off Kayla. "I should kill the bitch."

"Not her, asshole," Adam said, his voice slurring. "It's all their fault."

"Yeah," Chris agreed. "You're right."

"Who the hell do they think they are, waltzing in here and tryin' to take over everything? They really think we're jus' gonna let 'em get away with it?"

"No way," Chris agreed. He took another

swig from the bottle, then passed it back to Adam.

As the band played and Eric and Cherie danced, Mosler and McIvens kept pouring more fuel onto their already blazing rage.

Cherie put her hands behind Eric's neck as he circled her narrow waist with his arms and drew her close. They moved together to the gentle rhythm of the music, and the faintest wisp of a breeze came off the lake.

The evening was starting to feel perfect — exactly the kind of evening Eric had imagined hundreds of times when he'd been stuck in Evanston while Kent and Tad had been up here. But now, finally, he was here, too, and with Cherie Stevens in his arms, and the music playing, and the lights — even the lake itself — glowing, and the sweet summer breeze wafting over him, he wondered if it could get any better. Then, as he swept Cherie into a turn and drew her still closer, he saw Adam Mosler glaring at him, fists clenched. His whole body tensed, and he moved his lips close to Cherie's ear. "You think Adam's going to make trouble?"

She shrugged and snuggled closer against his chest. "Who knows? He and Chris have a bottle, and sometimes Adam gets mean when he drinks."

"Think maybe we better chill for a while?" Eric asked, hoping she'd say no even if it meant winding up in a fight with Adam.

"I think we should just ignore him."

Eric did as he was told, closing his eyes and letting the warmth of Cherie's body spread through him.

"Okay, that's it!" Adam Mosler growled, draining most of what was left of the vodka into his mouth. "Son of a bitch's got his filthy hands on my girl."

Chris McIvens reached for the bottle. "So what are you gonna do?"

Adam surrendered the almost empty bottle. "I'm gonna kill him," he said, and started unsteadily across the dance floor.

McIvens finished the vodka and threw the empty bottle into the lake, then followed Adam as he pushed his way between the dancing couples, going directly toward Cherie Stevens and Eric Brewster. But when he got there, instead of spinning Brewster around and smashing his fist into his face, Adam merely tapped Eric on the shoulder.

"I'm cuttin' in, man."

Eric turned to see Mosler glowering at him, his face twisted with rage, his eyes bleary from alcohol. "I don't think so," he said softly. Out of the corner of his eye he

could see other couples stop dancing to watch, and he silently prayed that Kent and Tad were among those watching.

"Why don't you just go away, Adam?" Cherie said.

Adam ignored her, fixing his eyes on Eric. "I want you to leave my girl alone."

"I'm not your girl," Cherie said, grabbing Eric's hand. "Come on, Eric, let's just go."

"Not so fast," Adam growled, putting a hand on Eric's chest.

Eric balled his right hand into a fist and his whole body tensed as he braced himself for the first blow, but just as Mosler drew his arm back to take a swing, a sound rose above the music.

A scream.

The music faltered, then stopped.

Adam Mosler, his fist still poised to strike Eric Brewster, hesitated, and then, as another scream and then another came from the water side of the pavilion, his arm slowly dropped to his side. "What the f—" he began, rocking unsteadily as he looked around. "Wha's goin' on?"

Eric ignored Mosler as he followed Cherie toward the railing at the far end of the pavilion, where people were gathered. They pushed their way into a narrow opening at the rail and looked out over the water as

someone else cried out. At first he saw nothing, but as someone a few feet away pointed, he looked down.

He wasn't sure what he was looking for, but then he saw what looked like a pair of tennis shoes floating almost under the pavilion.

The crowd behind Eric pressed forward, and he felt the railing give slightly.

Below him, the tennis shoes disappeared for a moment, but then they were back, and as Eric watched, they drifted away from the pavilion.

Except the shoes were not simply floating.

They were attached to legs.

Legs clad in black jeans.

With the glowing water rippling around them, the legs floated up, followed by a torso, and then a head.

The body floated facedown in the water, its right arm and hand stretched out, as if reaching for something.

There was no left arm.

As the crowd gathered at the rail stared down at it, the outstretched right arm began to sink and the body rolled over.

As screams rose around him, Eric could neither move nor look away from the terrifying specter in the water. Cherie began to sob, and he put his arm around her, draw-

ing her close against him.

The corpse continued to roll, and finally lay faceup in the water. The body was fully clothed — even the shirt was still tucked into the jeans, and for a moment, just an instant — Eric had the feeling that it wasn't a corpse at all.

That it was moving.

That someone was playing some kind of horrible joke.

Then he realized it wasn't a joke at all.

The body was real.

It was dead.

And it wasn't moving.

It only appeared to be moving, because the shirt was rippling with the hundreds of crawdads feasting on the mortifying flesh beneath it.

The face was almost eaten away. Nothing remained of the eyes but empty sockets, the nose and lips reduced to shredded scraps of flesh and skin, and even the cheeks were mostly gone.

Four of the creatures were picking the meat from where the missing arm had been torn away.

Images flashed through Eric's mind:

The bloody knot on the heavy branch in the woods.

Tippy's guts hanging out of her belly.

And his own hands, plunging deep into the steaming entrails of —

His supper rose in his gorge, and he struggled to keep from adding his own vomit to the carnage in the water. Cherie was clinging to him now, crying into his shoulder, and he wanted to look away, wanted to look anywhere but at the grotesquery floating in the water, but he couldn't. As if held by some unseen force, he kept gazing down into the empty sockets that had once held Ellis Langstrom's eyes.

And even in their absence, those eyes accused him.

Merrill Brewster gazed numbly out the window of Ellen Newell's car as Ellen slowly pulled out of the dance pavilion parking lot, which was jammed with police cars, an ambulance, and what seemed like the entire population of Phantom Lake. Eric was next to her in the backseat, and she was clutching his hand so tightly that her fingernails were digging into his flesh. But it didn't matter. All that mattered to her was that he was there, and he was safe, and he was holding onto her hand as tightly as she was holding his.

Merrill had known something was wrong when Ellen had called less than an hour ago

and said she wanted to go with her to pick up the boys. Her refusal to talk about what was going on during the short drive to the pavilion had been enough to set off every alarm in Merrill's head. Then, when she saw the flashing red lights of the police cars and the ambulance, her alarm had escalated into terror, and she'd grabbed Ellen's arm. "What's happening here?" she'd demanded.

"They found Ellis Langstrom's body," Ellen replied. Knowing exactly what Merrill's next question would be, she answered before Merrill could even ask it: "Our boys are all fine."

Merrill had leaped out of the car before Ellen could park, frantically searching the crowd for Eric, but was stopped by a line of yellow tape and more police officers than she'd thought Phantom Lake had. Then everything had taken on a dreamlike quality. The crowd was silent, and the strobing police lights, flashing red and blue, cast a surreal glow over the scene. I'm going to wake up, she thought. I'll wake up, and I'll be on the sofa at Pinecrest, and everything will be all right.

And then Merrill saw Carol Langstrom, and she understood that it truly was a nightmare, but that Carol wasn't going to wake up.

Rusty Ruston was holding Carol as she sobbed, keeping her from going down to the water's edge. He tried to walk her back up toward the parking lot, but she struggled, finally found her voice, and screamed as she jerked away from Ruston and stumbled down to the spot by the lake where Ellis's body was being zipped into a black bag. As Carol wailed her grief into the night, two medics loaded her son's remains onto a gurney.

Two women broke through the crowd, and got to Carol just as her legs gave out and she slumped to the ground. They sat with her on the lawn, holding her, rocking her.

Merrill stared at the spectacle of the distraught woman and felt a pang of guilt at her relief that it was someone else's son who had died rather than her own. A moment later, though, her fear for Eric overcame everything else, and she began pushing her way through the crowd, panic tightening its grip on her with every second that passed. Finally, after what seemed an eternity, Eric, along with Tad Sparks and Kent Newell, appeared at the top of the pavilion steps, and a moment later Eric was in her arms.

And she hadn't let go of him since.

Eric was barely aware of his mother's grip

on his hand. Rather, the image of Ellis Langstrom's lifeless, colorless visage hung in his mind, and no matter where he turned, all he saw was that ravaged corpse. Beyond the corpse, flickering at the edge of his consciousness, were other images.

A bloody stick, thick and heavy, lying half concealed beneath a bush in the forest.

A hacksaw, its blade stained red, in a hidden room in the carriage house.

And fragments of dreams — dreams of things that couldn't have happened.

A numbness almost as cold as death itself began to spread through him. Should he tell anybody about all the things churning through his mind, all the images that seemed to taunt him from the darkness outside the car?

But what would he say?

What *could* he say?

After what seemed like an endless ride, the car at last pulled up in front of Pinecrest. Ashley Sparks, who had stayed behind with a sleeping Marci, waited on the front steps, and as everyone piled out of the car, a babble of barely heard conversation began to swirl around Eric.

His mother, asking Tad's mother to put on a pot of coffee.

And saying she was going to start to pack.

"Pack?" he heard Ellen Newell say. "Why?"

"What do you mean, why?" his mother replied. "I'm going home, that's why! I'm certainly not staying here after a boy's been murdered."

Murdered.

The word seemed to reverberate in the silence that fell over the group huddled in the foyer of Pinecrest, then Ellen Newell spoke again, her voice taking on an edge of authority that finally cut through Eric's numbness.

"We don't know that anybody has been murdered," she said. "And certainly nobody's going anywhere, at least not tonight." She began herding everyone into the kitchen, where Ashley Sparks was filling the coffeemaker.

"Poor Carol," Ashley sighed, shaking her head as she added ground beans to the machine and turned it on. "I'll call her tomorrow."

"I'm calling Dan," Merrill said as she picked up the phone. "And if I'm not driving home tonight — which I'm perfectly capable of doing — then none of you are going anywhere. You're all staying here with me. Understand? All of you. I will not be alone in this house with just the kids."

Ellen and Ashley exchanged a look, then nodded, knowing that argument would be useless, at least for tonight. "So we'll all stay," Ellen said. "The boys can sleep in Eric's room, and I suspect the rest of us won't sleep at all, given how strong Ashley makes her coffee."

Merrill managed a wan smile and dialed home. To her relief, she heard Dan's sleepy voice after only two rings, and she took the phone out onto the terrace, where only Dan could hear her.

"Does anyone know exactly what happened to the boy?" Dan asked, when she finished telling him what had happened at the dance.

"No, not yet," Merrill admitted. "The thing is, he was just Eric's age and —"

"And that doesn't mean a thing," Dan cut in. "For God's sake, Merrill. Don't make the discovery of a single body into a serial killer. You don't even know what happened to him yet."

"I still want us to come home," Merrill said, her voice flat. She heard Dan sigh, could actually picture the look on his face, and knew that if he were here right now she'd want to slap him. How could he be so dismissive? Then, as she glanced back into the kitchen and saw Ashley and Ellen sit-

ting at the kitchen table chatting as if nothing at all had happened, she expanded her frustration to include them. How could *all* of them be so dismissive?

"Kevin and Jeff and I will be up in the morning," she heard Dan saying. "I know exactly how you're feeling, and I certainly agree that it's a terrible thing. A tragic thing. But it doesn't have anything to do with us, and there's no reason to let it destroy our summer."

No reason to let it destroy our summer? Doesn't he realize it already has, at least for me?

"Dan, I'm not —" she began, but again he didn't let her finish.

"There's one more thing," he cut in. "Marguerite has had some kind of a family emergency and had to go down to Springfield. She'll come up with us next week."

Merrill chewed a cuticle. Marguerite's presence might at least have made the isolation more tolerable, but it didn't really matter since they'd be home before Marguerite got back from Springfield, let alone all the way up to the Phantom Lake. At least they'd be home if she had anything to do with it.

"I'll see you in the morning, honey," Dan said, his voice taking on a note that told her the conversation was over, at least for now.

His next words confirmed her interpretation of his tone: "If there are decisions to be made, we'll all make them together over the weekend."

Merrill sighed, knowing his mind was made up. "Well, at least everybody's spending the night with me."

"Which is a very good idea for all of you. How are the kids holding up?"

"The boys are traumatized, of course. We all are, except Marci, who's been asleep since eight."

"Well, things always look better in the morning. Our plane arrives at eight."

"We'll be here."

"Love you."

"Love you, too." Merrill clicked off the phone and looked out over the calm lake and the stars that were reflected in it.

Tonight, though, she found nothing at all serene in the view.

Tonight, all she wanted was to be as far away from Phantom Lake as she could get.

Shivering even in the warmth of the night, she turned and went back inside the house.

The amber glow seemed to draw Eric through the darkness like a moth to light, and he moved toward it until finally he came to its center. Now it seemed to spread directly from

him, moving out into the darkness in every direction.

He turned, and the surrounding darkness dissolved into the walls of the hidden chamber.

Tad and Kent were at the table.

The lamp was on, and now Eric saw that it, not he himself, was the source of the warm amber glow.

And it seemed to shine brightest not on him, but on the long white box that sat in front of Tad and Kent.

Tad looked at Kent, who nodded, and then Tad lifted the lid off the box.

An acrid stench rose up from the box and burned Eric's nostrils, and though his stomach heaved, he couldn't look away.

Inside the box lay a strip of putrefying meat, turning green beneath the crawling maggots that swarmed over its surface.

Kent and Tad were also gazing at the rotting mass, then Tad reached into the box and slowly lifted it out.

As Eric watched, Tad scraped a few maggots away, letting them fall back into the box like so many fat, squirming grains of rice.

Tad lifted the object higher, tilting it first one way, then another, letting the light play over its glistening surface as a greenish slime oozed from the mass and ran down his fingers and hands to his wrists.

Then, as Tad turned the object again, Eric saw the hand that hung at one of its ends.

The skin had been peeled off, leaving bloody fingernails at the tips of skinned fingers.

Tad was holding Ellis Langstrom's severed arm. He gazed at it almost reverently for another moment, then sighed and brought it to his mouth.

Tad's teeth sank deep into the decaying flesh, ripping a large piece loose. He chewed for a moment, swallowed, then opened his mouth for —

Eric jerked awake, his heart pounding, his pajamas soaked with perspiration.

"Jesus."

Though he whispered the single word, it seemed to echo through the room as his heartbeat slowly evened out.

He looked around. Kent was still on the floor, snoring softly. But Tad —

He heard retching sounds from the bathroom and saw the light under the bathroom door. Getting out of bed, he moved to the door and slowly pushed it open.

Tad was on his knees in front of the toilet, and as Eric stepped inside, he reached up and flushed the toilet, then wiped his mouth with a wad of toilet paper.

"Y-You okay?" Eric said, wondering even

as he spoke if perhaps he himself was about to vomit, too.

Tad looked up at him, his eyes filled with a horror Eric had never seen in them before.

"I was eating it, Eric," he said, his voice breaking as he uttered the words. "I dreamed I was eating Ellis's arm."

CHAPTER 22

As Dan Brewster's gaze wandered over the group gathered around the big table in the Pinecrest dining room, he wondered how it was that only he, Kevin Sparks, and Jeff Newell — who had worked long hours all week, then gotten up before dawn this morning to catch the flight to Phantom Lake — looked even faintly ready for a weekend of anything but sleep.

His wife's face was pale, Ellen had dark circles under her eyes, and Ashley had obviously been crying. As for the boys, Kent was sitting quietly, pushing the scrambled eggs Dan had made for everyone around on his plate as if they were turnips or lima beans or something else he hated. Eric wasn't even bothering to poke at his food, which sat undisturbed in front of him. And Tad was even paler than Merrill, and looked as if he might throw up at any moment.

Marci, it seemed, was the only one at the

table with any interest in food at all, but she was far too small even to make a dent in the platters of bacon and waffles that he had produced. Finally, it was Ashley who managed to meet his eyes.

"I guess we're not what you were expecting to find this morning, are we?" she asked, her voice as bleak as her gaze.

Dan reached over and put a hand on hers. "Are you going to be all right?"

She forced a wan smile, fresh tears threatening to spill down her cheeks, then took a deep breath. "I will be — of course I will be. I just keep thinking about poor Carol." She shook her head dazedly. "I can't even imagine how she must be feeling."

Merrill pushed her untouched breakfast plate a fraction of an inch away, and now her eyes, too, fixed on Dan. "I want to go home," she said, her voice as flat as her expression. "That's all I want."

Jeff Newell, about to take a sip of coffee, put his cup back on its saucer, and when he spoke he chose his words carefully. "Don't you think that's —" He hesitated, then went on. "— well, a bit premature? I mean, we don't even know what happened yet."

Merrill Brewster shifted again, her eyes boring into Jeff. "A boy is dead. What else has to happen?" She glanced first toward

Ellen Newell, then Ashley Sparks. "Surely you don't really want to stay here, do you?"

Ashley took a deep breath, then looked directly at her. "Carol Langstrom is my friend," she said, keeping her voice steady by the sheer force of her will. "I've known Carol and Ellis a long time, and she's going to need her friends right now." She hesitated again, as if knowing how much her next words might hurt Merrill, but then went on: "So no, Merrill, I'm not going anywhere."

"But —" Merrill began, but Dan, moving his hand from Ashley Spark's to his wife's, shook his head.

"Nobody's going home, sweetheart," he said softly. "At least not right now."

"But the sheriff was here, Dan!" Merrill said, pulling her hand away from his. "He was asking the boys questions about Ellis right after he disappeared."

"The sheriff?" Dan echoed, turning to Eric. "Am I missing something here? Do you guys know something about this?"

Eric shook his head. "We hardly even know him. One of his friends told the sheriff about something that had happened Monday night, that's all."

" 'Something'?" Dan echoed. "I think you're going to have to do better than that.

In fact, I think you're going to have to tell me exactly what happened, and exactly why the sheriff wanted to talk to you about it."

Reluctantly, Eric told his father the whole story of what had happened on the way home Monday night, and when he was done, he spread his hands helplessly. "That's all that happened. And even if we'd wanted to go after them, it wouldn't have been Ellis Langstrom. It would have been Mosler. He —"

Kent and Tad looked across the table at him and shook their heads, and Eric cut whatever he was about to say short and shrugged. "Mosler was the worst," he finished. "Langstrom was just sort of going along with him."

Dan studied the boys carefully. They looked traumatized, but they didn't look guilty.

"Do they even know what happened to the Langstrom boy yet?" Jeff Newell asked.

After a short silence, Kent Newell finally spoke. "One of his arms was missing."

Tad Sparks put his napkin to his mouth as the acid from his empty stomach rose in his throat.

"Honey, are you all right?" Ashley asked.

Tad took a breath. "I — I'll be all right." He sat back in his chair and stared down

into his lap.

"One arm missing sounds like more than an accident," Dan said. "But it doesn't necessarily sound like murder — maybe an animal attack or something." He turned to Kevin Sparks and Jeff Newell. "Either of you know the sheriff up here?"

"I've met him a couple of times," Kevin said. "Nice guy, as far as I can tell."

"Then let's pay him a visit this afternoon," Dan suggested. He turned back to his wife. "Here's what we're going to do. We won't make any decisions right now. First we're going to find out exactly what happened to the Langstrom boy, and what's going on. And we're certainly not all going to pack up and leave here while there's an investigation going on — not after what Eric says happened Monday night."

"I don't care —" Merrill began, but Dan held up his hand.

"This was a terrible tragedy for everybody," he said. "But it's not the end of the world." As Marci stood up to take her plate to the kitchen, Dan grabbed her and pulled her down onto his lap. "Besides," he went on, "I need to see my little girl in the Fourth of July parade."

As Merrill saw the happy grin that spread over Marci's face — the first happy expres-

sion she'd seen so far today — she decided that Dan might be right.

Perhaps they should stay, at least until after the Fourth.

And maybe nothing else would happen.

Rusty Ruston took a deep breath, then opened his office door to admit Gerald Hofstetter, the florid-faced, redheaded publisher of the *Phantom Lake Times,* and Ray Richmond, who had been the town's mayor for more years than his boyish looks should have made possible. From the moment Richmond called him to set up the meeting, Rusty had been certain that sparks were going to fly. Sure enough, as soon as the office door closed behind them, the mayor came right to the point.

"I think we all need to talk about Ellis Langstrom's death," he began, looking directly at Hofstetter. "Particularly given our dependence on the summer trade." Gerald nodded and smiled benignly, but Rusty saw him readying himself for what they both knew was coming next. "I want to know," Richmond continued, "whether I can count on the *media*" — he looked pointedly at Gerald — "to be sensitive to the town's needs."

"The public has a right to know," Gerald

countered blandly, the very neutrality in his voice causing a muscle in Ray's jaw to tense in frustration. Whenever Hofstetter used that tone, Richmond knew he was planning something particularly inflammatory.

"We don't know *anything* yet," Ruston interceded. "All we know is that Ellis was drunk the last time his friends saw him. What happened after he left them is a matter of speculation."

"And speculation," the mayor said, "is exactly what we don't need. There's enough of it on the streets already, and the last thing we need is for the newspaper to start in, too." He turned to Ruston. "How long before we get the autopsy report?"

The sheriff shrugged. "Depends. There was the missing arm, and a pretty nasty head injury, but there was no definite evidence of foul play — no obvious bullet wounds or anything like that. If the coroner's not too busy, I think we'll have it within a few days."

"I'd hate like hell to have someone else die because we were worried about a little speculation," Hofstetter said, once more using the tone that never failed to get the mayor's back up.

"We're not going off half-cocked on this, Gerald." Ruston laid his pen down on the

desk and folded his hands. "And nothing you print before we know exactly what happened is going to change the facts of what happened."

"But if it turns out it *was* a murder —" Hofstetter began, but this time Ray Richmond cut him short.

The mayor leaned forward. "I know you remember what happened when the Hanovers' granddaughter was murdered. This town almost died, and we all know it was largely because you kept spreading it all over your damn paper, even when you didn't have anything new to write about. So you sold papers, but the summer people all left."

"And in the end, my advertising revenues dried up, too," Hofstetter said. "I'm not a bad guy, Ray — I'm on your side. I want what's best for this town, just like you. I just don't want you to hobble me, and if Ellis Langstrom was murdered, the people in this town have a right to know it."

"Then I'll tell you what I'll do," the mayor said. "I'll give the coroner's office a call, and see if I can get Bicks to burn a little midnight oil and get us his report. I'm not asking you to bury the facts. I just don't want you to stir up a panic before we know if anything really happened."

Rusty looked up at the sound of the outer

office door opening to see Kevin Sparks walk in along with another man. He tilted his head just enough to alert the other two men. "Here we go," he said as he rose to his feet and moved toward the door.

Hofstetter and Richmond both turned around to look. "Who're they?" Richmond asked.

"Kevin Sparks, one of the summer people from The Pines," Rusty said. "I spoke with his son and two other Pines boys when Ellis first went missing. I'm assuming the other guy is the father of one of those boys."

"What do they want?" Hofstetter asked.

"I can only guess," Rusty sighed. "You two want to stick around to find out?"

"Sure," the mayor said, putting on his best campaign smile for the benefit of the people who kept Phantom Lake's standard of living one of the highest in the state.

Rusty opened his office door, beckoned Kevin Sparks inside, and shook hands with Dan Brewster as Sparks made the introductions. As soon as Rusty heard the name Brewster, he remembered the family's bloodied and mutilated cat.

And he remembered praying that there was no connection between what had happened to that cat and Ellis Langstrom's disappearance.

And he remembered talking to the boys, and his impression that they knew something they weren't talking about.

And now two of their fathers were here.

Rusty introduced the two men to Gerald Hofstetter and Ray Richmond, then Dan Brewster came directly to the point.

"We're concerned about what happened to the Langstrom boy."

Ray Richmond's brows rose a fraction of an inch. "We were just talking about that ourselves. Tragic — absolutely tragic."

"We're certainly not here to argue that," Dan Brewster assured him. "The question is, does anyone know how he died?" He scanned the three men, then decided to lay his cards on the table. "Frankly, my wife is terrified, and wants to pack up the family and go home." He gave the sheriff, the mayor, and the newspaper publisher time to glance at one another, and he read their expressions perfectly. "The last thing this town needs is a panic. So the question is simple. Is there any reason to panic, or not?"

Rusty shot Hofstetter a warning glance, then turned his attention to the visitors. "What evidence we have so far points to an accident," he said carefully. "We'll know more when we get the coroner's report."

"And until then," the mayor said, "we're not engaging in any speculation."

"That strikes me as eminently political," Dan said, softening the slight sarcasm of his words with a grin. "Maybe you should come down and run for mayor of Chicago — we could use some discretion down there." As Richmond visibly relaxed, he went on, "So, behind closed doors, does anyone have any idea how the boy lost an arm?"

Ruston's expression tightened, and the mayor said nothing. The newspaperman, though, leaned back against the wall and folded his arms across his chest. "That's the sixty-four-thousand-dollar question," Hofstetter said, ignoring the look the mayor shot him and fixing his gaze on Ruston.

"And I wish I had an answer for it," the sheriff said. "The body'd been in the water too long for me to even guess. If he'd been waterskiing, I'd say that was a possibility, but if he'd been skiing, he never would have been missing. Beyond that, I just don't know — it takes a lot to rip off an arm. A bear could do it, or a mountain lion."

"And until we hear from the coroner, let's not waste our time guessing," Ray Richmond cut in, heading the sheriff off before he could bring up the possibility of a wolf pack and scare everyone off before July had

even started. As Ruston subsided into silence, the mayor turned to Dan Brewster and Kevin Sparks. "I wish we knew exactly what happened to Ellis," he went on. "We have accidental deaths all too often, what with the water sports in the summer and snowmobiles in the winter, and I'm sure we'll get to the bottom of this one soon. Right, Rusty?" As the sheriff nodded, Richmond extended his hand to Dan and shot Hofstetter an unmistakable look. "Pleasure meeting you folks, and I hope the rest of your summer is less eventful than it's been so far."

With Hofstetter preceding him, Richmond made his exit, certain that Ruston would say nothing that might upset either of the summer people.

Two minutes later Dan and Kevin were back on the street, and as Ruston watched them go, he was certain of only one thing.

Whatever it was that those kids hadn't told him, they hadn't told their parents, either.

But what was it they were hiding?

And how was he going to find out?

CHAPTER 23

The atmosphere of grief hanging over Carol Langstrom's small house on Beech Street was almost palpable as Rusty Ruston climbed the three steps to the front door and rang the bell. He waited a few seconds and was about to press it again when he noticed that the door was slightly ajar. Easing it open, he leaned in, saw a knot of people in the small living room that opened off the tiny foyer, and stepped inside.

Leaving the door exactly as far open as when he'd arrived, he glanced down the hall toward the back of the house, saw three familiar faces among the half-dozen women who had managed to pack themselves into the tiny kitchen, and decided Carol was more likely to be at the center of the group in the living room than trying to make order out of the milling throng in the kitchen. He took off his hat as he stepped through the archway, glanced around for someplace to

put it, and wasn't surprised to see that every flat surface in the room was already filled with an array of casseroles, salads, cakes, and pies, as well as platters filled with cheese and crackers, cookies, muffins, and half a dozen varieties of pickles and olives. It seemed as if every woman in town had responded to Ellis's death by heading directly to the kitchen.

Carol Langstrom herself sat on the sofa in front of the fireplace, a box of tissues next to a teacup on the coffee table in front of her. Next to her was a woman who looked familiar, though Rusty couldn't immediately identify her. Carol appeared to have aged ten years in the past two days, yet she managed a wan smile when she saw him.

He dropped into a squat so his eyes were level with hers, and took her hand in his. It felt cold and clammy, and all the strength seemed to have drained out of it. "How are you holding up, Carol?" he asked.

Her gaze fixed on him for a moment, then wandered over all the women whose soft murmurings had slowly fallen silent as they realized the sheriff had arrived. They were now looking at him, one or two even edging closer to make certain they could hear whatever he might have to say. "I had no idea I even knew this many people," Carol

said, her voice breaking. "Let alone that they were such good friends."

"That's because *you're* such a good friend," Rusty said.

Carol's eyes glistened with fresh tears.

"I've spoken with the coroner," Rusty went on, dropping his voice in the hope that only Carol would be able to hear him, but knowing it was futile. "He's going to do the autopsy this weekend."

"Autopsy?" Carol parroted the word as if it had no meaning to her at all.

"Whenever there's an unattended death, the state requires an autopsy," Rusty explained.

Carol stared at him a moment, and when she spoke, her voice was flat and the words were not a question but a statement. "So you'll find out that my baby was murdered." There was a pause, and then she added "Will you find out who killed him?"

Ruston chose his next words carefully. "At this point I don't know what the report will show, Carol. We'll have to wait and see. But I have every reason to believe that Dr. Bicks will be able to tell us exactly what happened. We're doing everything we can until we know the exact cause of death."

Carol took a deep breath, seemed to come to some kind of a decision, and finally let

the breath out in a long sigh. "Can I bury him?" she asked, a sob breaking her voice. "I should do it on Monday." She took another ragged breath, and her eyes beseeched Ruston. "Can I bury my baby on Monday? Please?"

Rusty nodded, and spoke more to the woman seated next to Carol than to Carol herself. "Tell the funeral home to call the coroner's office. I'm pretty sure they'll be able to —" He hesitated, then forced himself to finish the sentence. "— pick him up tomorrow, late in the afternoon."

The woman nodded, then held out her hand. "I'm Ashley Sparks," she said. Ruston's eyes widened, and Ashley explained. "I met Carol years ago — actually, I think I was one of her first customers."

Carol reached over and took Ashley's hand, squeezing it affectionately. "The very first." She turned to Ruston, dabbing at her eyes with a Kleenex. "I still have her check framed on the wall over my desk. And I should have all the rest of them up there, too — I think she single-handedly kept me in business that first summer." For the first time since Ruston had arrived, a genuine smile finally curled the corners of Carol Langstrom's mouth. "I'd buy something one day, and Ashley would come in the next

morning and buy it from me." She squeezed Ashley's hand again. "The morning I opened, I didn't even have enough cash left for food for our dinner, and even though a lot of people came in that day, Ashley was the only one who actually bought."

"That's not true," Ashley interrupted. "I remember a little Spode figurine that Sandy Banks bought —"

"That was so badly damaged that I could only charge three dollars for it," Carol shot back.

"You should have charged twenty-five, which I told you at the time. You were selling everything so cheap I felt like I was robbing you. Why do you think I kept coming back? I recognized a sucker when I saw one!"

Carol shook her head in defeat and turned back to Ruston. "The sad part is, she's right. But what she's not telling you is that she started making me sell things for what I could get for them instead of ten percent more than I'd paid for them. God, I was so dumb until Ashley came along — she should be running the shop herself."

"And put in the hours you do?" Ashley said, pulling back in an exaggerated show of horror. "No thanks! I'd much rather mind your business than my own." She turned to

Ruston. "So now you know far more about me than you ever wanted to know, unless you're as much of an antiques freak as Carol and I are. It's nice to meet you. My husband —"

"Actually, I met your husband earlier."

She nodded. "He dropped me off here on the way to your office. I trust he and Dan Brewster didn't make too much of a nuisance of themselves?"

"They were no problem at all," Ruston assured her. "And thanks for being here," he said, his eyes shooting toward Carol Langstrom for an instant.

"I couldn't be anyplace else."

"Okay, then," Ruston said, rising to his feet and wincing at the pain in his knees.

Carol stood up, too. "You'll call me?" she asked. "As soon as you hear anything at all?"

"Of course. You'll know everything almost as soon as I do."

Carol sank back onto the sofa as Rusty made his way to the door. "I can make it until Monday," she said quietly. "This is Saturday. I can make it until Monday."

"Of course you can," Ashley replied, once more taking Carol's hand in her own. "We'll just take it a day at a time. We're all here to help you do whatever needs to be done."

Carol gazed once more at all the people who had come to her aid. "I keep thinking about all the things that need to be done, and I keep making all these lists in my mind, and —"

"And you don't need to take care of anything right now. You don't need to think about cooking, or cleaning, or anything else. We can take care of everything."

"Everything except the shop," Carol sighed.

"The shop?" Ashley echoed. "Why are you worried about it? You'll leave it closed over the weekend — all week, if you need to."

Carol shook her head. "And lose the busiest weekend of the summer? I can't afford it, Ashley — I've got so much inventory in the back room I can hardly move around in there, and if I'm closed next week it'll all sit there for the rest of the summer. And I can't afford to just keep it all in inventory."

"Then I'll do it," Ashley said.

Carol stared at her. "You?"

"Didn't you just tell the sheriff I could run it as well as you? In fact, didn't I hear you tell him I *should* be running it instead of you?"

"But —"

"No buts," Ashley declared. "I'm not really doing you much good sitting around

here holding your hand, and Lord knows you've got enough people in the house that you don't need me. So until further notice, I'm running the shop. I'm assuming the key is in the usual place under that awful Chinese import urn you think makes such a great planter?"

Carol's eyes narrowed. "How do you know where the key is?"

"I found it one day when I was poking around. So that's that — I'm running the shop until you feel like coming back. Deal?"

"Are you sure?" Carol asked, her eyes again glistening with tears.

Life would go on, even after Monday.

Ashley nodded. "Whatever you need, we'll take care of it."

"I wish —" Carol began, then cut off her own words as she felt herself beginning to sink back into a morass of grief.

"I know, honey," Ashley said softly. "We all wish it. But these things happen, and all we can ever do is try to cope."

"I know," Carol cried, "but why did it have to happen to Ellis?"

No one had an answer for that question, and it hung, unanswered, in the air.

CHAPTER 24

Eric cast the spinner out from the dock, watched it arc through the air and splash into the water, and slowly reeled it in. Yet when a big bass rose out of the depths to nibble at the lure, he barely even noticed it, let alone tried to jig it into snapping at the hook. Instead he merely sat down on the dock, let his bare feet dangle in the water, and reeled in the rest of the line. Next to him, Tad was still rummaging through the tackle box, supposedly looking for just the right lure that would bring a nice walleye home for dinner, but in reality paying no more attention to the fishing gear than Eric was to the fish that had nearly taken his hook. For his part, Kent Newell was sprawled out on the dock, staring silently up at the cloudless sky.

No one who happened to look down at them from the house would suspect that there was anything on their minds other

than fishing and lying in the sun. But Eric's stomach was still faintly queasy from the nightmare he'd had, and out of the corner of his eye he could see that Tad's face was still pale from the violent nausea his own version of the dream evoked. And though Kent hadn't actually said anything, his very silence this morning had told Eric that he had something on his mind.

Then, as the spoon on Eric's line came out of the water, Kent said: "I had a dream last night."

As Tad's head snapped up and their eyes met, a cold knot formed in Eric's stomach.

Kent sat up, pulled his knees up against his chest, and wrapped his arms around them. When he spoke again, his voice was little more than a whisper. "I dreamed that Ellis Langstrom's arm was in that box." He looked first at Tad, then at Eric, knowing he didn't need to tell either of them he was talking about the white box they'd found in the hidden room yesterday.

"S-So?" Tad stammered, refusing even to meet Kent's gaze now.

"So have you guys ever wondered how come Dr. Darby took all that stuff apart?"

It was the last thing Tad had been expecting Kent to say, and now he finally looked at him. "Took it apart?" he repeated. "What

are you talking about?"

"All of it," Kent said. "The table that was missing a leg. The hacksaw frame with no blade."

"M-Maybe they weren't even together when he bought them," Tad suggested, but even as he spoke the words, he knew they rang hollow, and even though he was looking at Kent, he could see out of the corner of his eye that Eric was shaking his head.

"They wouldn't ship the table with only three legs, would they?" Kent asked. "I mean, if they were going to take the legs off, they'd have taken all of them off, right?"

Tad said nothing.

"And what about the scalpels?" Kent pressed. "Who'd put them in another box if you were going to send the doctor's bag anyway?"

Tad shrugged, though his skin was starting to feel cold and clammy despite the warmth of the day. "Okay, so let's say he took them apart. So what?"

Kent's eyes flickered between Tad and Eric. "Haven't you guys noticed that ever since we started putting that stuff back together, things started to happen?"

There was a silence as the full meaning of Kent's words sank in.

"Tippy and the scalpels," Eric finally

breathed. "And the hacksaw — we put the blade in the hacksaw, and Langstrom's body was missing an arm."

A fresh wave of nausea broke over Tad as the still fresh memory of last night's nightmare leaped up in his mind.

He'd been sitting at a table.

Jeffrey Dahmer's table.

And he'd been eating —

Tad's stomach heaved, but he'd eaten so little for breakfast that nothing came up but the foul taste of bile.

"And I keep thinking about the lamp," Kent said. "We put it back together, too."

"You think maybe something else is going to happen?"

Kent shrugged. "How should I know? But doesn't it seem like we should at least figure out who Darby got it from?" When neither Eric nor Tad responded, Kent went on. "Maybe if we can figure out what's gonna happen, we can figure out how —" His voice faltered, then he looked away.

"You mean maybe we can figure out how to keep ourselves from doing it?" Tad finally said, his voice shaking.

"We didn't do anything," Kent said. "All we did was have a bunch of dreams!"

"The *same* dreams," Tad argued. "And if we didn't have anything to do with Tippy or

402

Ellis Langstrom, how come we all dreamed about it?"

"I don't *know!*" Kent flared. "And neither do you. All I'm saying is we should find out."

"And how are we supposed to do that?" Tad demanded. "Just go online and Google lamps and murders?"

"No," Kent shot back. "We go back in that room and look in the ledger. We find out where the lamp came from, then start looking in those books Darby put in there." His gaze shifted from Tad to Eric, then back to Tad. "We have to go back in there and find out who owned the lamp. And I have to find out what's in that white box."

"No way," Tad said.

"We have to," Kent repeated. "Besides, what if that box is empty? What if my dream didn't mean anything at all?"

Tad's jaw clenched — the last thing he wanted to do was go back in that room. Not today — not ever! But what if Kent was right? What if the box was empty?

"Come on, Tad," Kent said, sensing the other boy wavering. "We have to go."

"You can go back in if you want, but Eric and I aren't," Tad said, but his voice was hollow. "Right, Eric?"

Eric shook his head. "I think Kent's

right," he said softly. "We all have to go. We can just go in there, find out those two things, and come right back out."

Kent stood up. "C'mon," he said to Tad. "Nothing's going to happen. It's just a room."

Five minutes later they stood in the secret room, bathed in the amber glow of the lamp. As the now familiar voices began to whisper at the edges of their consciousness, a serene calm fell over all three boys.

The white box sat quietly waiting on the tabletop, exactly as they had left it, but none of the three made the slightest move to lift its lid.

It was still not time.

Eric drew the journal closer to him and slowly turned the pages until at last he found the entry he was looking for.

The entry that identified the lamp.

"E.G.," he whispered, reading from the ledger. "The lamp came from Plainfield, Wisconsin, from the estate of someone with the initials E.G." He closed the ledger and looked at the stack of books on the floor. Surely one of them had an index.

Eric picked up the first book on the stack, then the second.

With the third one, he finally found what

he was looking for, and as he began to scan the pages at the back of the thick volume, names seemed to leap out at him.

Names he'd already found on the Internet.

Jeffrey Dahmer, who had once owned the table on which both the ledger and the white box now sat.

Patrick Kearney, who had cut up boys Eric's age with the hacksaw.

Jack the Ripper, who had kept his surgical instruments in pristine condition.

And listed under *G,* in type that seemed almost to leap off the page, he found the name he was looking for.

Gein, Edward, p. 72.

Eric turned the pages back until he came to the right one, and found himself gazing first at a photograph of what looked like nothing more than an old farmer.

Then he began to read: " 'Edward Theodore Gein,' " he said softly as both Tad and Kent listened in utter silence, " 'also known as the Plainfield Ghoul, was a serial killer and a grave robber who made unspeakable items out of his victims' body parts. When he was arrested in 1957, police found a disemboweled and beheaded woman strung up and dressed like a deer, hanging in his kitchen. They also found

bowls made of human craniums, a box full of noses, a belt made of women's nipples, female genitalia in a shoe box, the carefully stuffed and mounted faces of nine women on his wall, and furniture and lamp shades made from human skin.' "

"Lamp shades," Tad echoed.

"Made from human skin," Kent breathed.

Involuntarily, Eric's eyes went to the lamp shade that was glowing with an ethereal light in the shadowy room, then to the other object that sat on Jeffrey Dahmer's table. "Open the box," he said.

It seemed to shimmer with an energy of its own as Kent's hands reached for it with the same involuntary movement that had taken Eric's eyes from the book to Ed Gein's lamp a moment before.

His fingers hesitated when they touched the cover, which seemed to vibrate with an oddly electrical charge.

He ran his fingers over it again.

Finally, he lifted the lid.

Nestled deep in the box, barely visible in the dim glow of the lamp, lay what must once have been Ellis Langstrom's arm. Now, though, it was nothing but an elongated object, dark brown with dried blood, chunks of flesh missing, as if they'd been

torn away by the teeth of some kind of carnivore.

The arm had no skin; every shred of it had been peeled down to the muscle and tendons — even the fingers had been carefully skinned, though the fingernails remained, their roots exposed to the light and air in a manner that was oddly obscene.

"Jesus," Kent whispered.

Tad gagged and turned away.

But Eric Brewster stared silently at the grisly object, a series of thoughts even more horrifying than the contents of the box reeling through his mind:

It's all of them . . . the killers are all here . . . they're here, and they're alive, and somehow we've turned them loose.

And there's no way to stop them. . . .

CHAPTER 25

Dan Brewster lingered over his coffee, gazing out at the overcast sky and the dead-gray surface of the lake, both of which felt like an exact match of the mood that had hung over the house since he'd arrived on Saturday morning. Even though it had been only two days ago, it felt like at least a week.

A gray and overcast week.

And now there was a storm forecast for this morning, which he hoped wouldn't actually occur when he and his family showed up at Ellis Langstrom's funeral this afternoon.

He glanced at Eric, who was sitting to his right, reading the front page of the morning paper. As silent this morning as he'd been all weekend, Eric looked as if he hadn't been sleeping much, and most of his breakfast was still untouched. "There anything you want to talk about?" Dan asked when Eric, sensing his father looking at him,

finally glanced up from the paper. Dan thought he saw something flicker in Eric's eyes for a fraction of a second, but then the boy shook his head and went back to studying the paper.

On the other side of the table, Merrill — still in her robe — was staring out at the gray morning, her chin in her hand, as silent as her son. In the strange quiet of the house, the sound of Marci's fork on her plate as she finished her sausage seemed preternaturally loud, and he saw Merrill startle as the clock in the hall began to strike.

"Nine," Dan said as the clock finished striking. "The funeral's at eleven." Merrill looked at him blankly, as if the words had no meaning. "The Langstrom boy," he said softly. "Ellis."

Merrill still looked as if she didn't understand, but then comprehension slowly dawned in her eyes. "You're not thinking of going, are you?" she asked. "We didn't even know him."

"Which makes no difference at all. The Newells and the Sparkses are going, and given —" Dan hesitated, his eyes flashing toward Eric, who was no longer looking at the paper but was now focused entirely on him. Marci, sensing that something might be about to happen, froze with her fork

halfway to her mouth. "Given everything that's happened," he went on, unwilling to refer directly to the sheriff's questioning of Eric, at least in front of Marci, "I think we have to make a good show of faith." His eyes fixed on his wife. "Call it a matter of community."

"I think Marci's too young to go to a funeral," Merrill said, carefully enough that Dan knew that she was looking for a way out for herself. He weighed the options, then nodded his agreement.

"I think you're absolutely right about that," he said, and saw relief come into his wife's eyes.

Marci went back to her breakfast.

"And I'll stay with her," she said. "We need to finish making her costume for the parade, anyway."

"Then it will be just you and me," Dan said, turning to Eric. When his son opened his mouth as if to argue, Dan cut him off. "You're certainly old enough to go," he said, then shot a glance toward Marci that made it clear to Eric that his next words weren't to be questioned. "And given all the circumstances, I think perhaps your absence might be conspicuous."

Eric's already pale face turned ashen, but he nodded. "Okay," he breathed, knowing

not only from his father's words, but from the look on his face, that no argument he might muster was going to get him out of going to Ellis Langstrom's funeral. But it wasn't just the idea of going to the funeral that had sent a chill through his entire body and was now making him feel as if he might throw up.

That was caused by something else: the terrible certainty that had been slowly coalescing inside him that somehow, in some way he couldn't quite comprehend, he and Kent and Tad were, indeed, responsible for what had happened to Ellis Langstrom.

Merrill stood with Marci on the front porch and watched as Dan steered the Lexus down the driveway. As the car disappeared, the first drops of rain began to fall from the leaden sky, and even though the morning wasn't particularly cold, Merrill wrapped her arms tightly around herself and felt suddenly, terribly, alone.

Not only were Dan and Eric gone, but so was everyone else.

Ellen and Jeff Newell had gone to the funeral, as had Ashley and Kevin Sparks, which meant that not only was the house next door empty, but so was the one beyond

that. Even though both houses were completely hidden by the forest anyway, she still felt as if she and Marci had been stranded in a strange and frightening wilderness.

Stupid, she told herself. For once in your life, just stop being scared of everything. Determinedly ignoring the knot that was forming in her stomach, she resisted the impulse to double lock the door when she went back in, and even managed to keep from going through the house to pull the draperies closed. After all, it was only a couple of hours.

Surely she could be alone for a couple of hours.

Besides, they had a costume to finish. The dining room table was already covered with fabric and patterns, and cardboard and glue and all the glitter and paint that Marci had decided was absolutely essential to her Statue of Liberty costume. All that was missing, in fact, was the costume itself, which Marci had insisted on taking to her room every night so it could be protected from even the slightest disaster that might befall it.

Dear God, Merrill prayed silently. *Don't let her turn out to be the same kind of scaredy cat I am!* Managing at least a small chuckle at her own silliness, she shook off enough of

her fear of being alone in the house to steer Marci up the stairs. "Run up and put on your costume so we can do the final fitting, okay?"

Marci ran up the stairs as Merrill put on the teakettle to keep her hands — if not her mind — busy on something other than her isolation.

Marci opened her bedroom door, stripped off her shorts and T-shirt, and lifted the dress gently off the chair she'd laid it over last night so she could watch the moonlight make the silver material glitter in the darkness.

This, she was certain, was going to be the best costume on the float, and maybe even in the whole parade.

Careful to avoid being stuck by the pins still holding it together, she slid her arms inside the sheath and lifted it over her head. A moment later it fell gracefully to the floor, and Marci turned toward the mirror over the dresser to adjust the sleeves and the neck so it would drape over her just the way the robe did on the real statue.

A flicker of movement over her right shoulder caught her attention, and Marci spun around, her heart suddenly racing.

The room was empty.

The window!

That was it — she'd seen something through the window!

Clutching the silvery material in both hands and lifting it high enough so she wouldn't trip over it, Marci went to the window and peered out. For a second or two she saw nothing but the rain streaking the glass.

Then, down on the lake, she saw it.

The man in the boat was there again. His hair was matted down by the rain, and so was his beard, but there was no mistaking who it was.

And he was sitting in his boat, right there in the lake, staring up at her.

As she watched in horror, his arm came up, and his hand stretched out as if . . .

As if he was reaching for her!

A scream welling up in her throat, Marci grabbed the front of the dress and ran.

Merrill's heart caught when she heard Marci's scream, and she ran for the stairs. But before she mounted even the first step Marci came flying down, the dress streaming, her face a mask of terror. Then she was in Merrill's arms, clinging to her, sobbing hysterically.

"He's out there again! He's out there in

the lake! And he was looking right at me, Mommy!"

Merrill hugged the little girl tight, smoothed her hair, and desperately tried to hold back the wave of panic that threatened to overwhelm her. Sweeping the crying child into her arms, Merrill lurched to the big living room windows and scanned the lake.

Nothing.

Nothing but rain falling softly on the terrace, the lawn, the trees, the water.

But no boat and no man.

"He was right over there," Marci sobbed, pointing to the edge of the woods just beyond the carriage house.

"Well, he's not there now," Merrill said, gently rubbing her daughter's back, trying to soothe her.

"But he saw me!" Marci wailed. "And he reached out like he was going to grab me!"

"It's all right," Merrill whispered, still trying to console her child even as her own heart continued to pound. "There's no one there, sweetheart. No one at all."

"But there was!" Marci insisted, sniffling. "There was, and he saw me, and I hate this place!"

Merrill silently agreed, and when Marci had finally settled down twenty minutes later — soothed by a cup of cocoa and a

promise of cookies as soon as the costume was finished — she moved methodically through every room of the house, checking the locks on the windows and the doors and pulling the draperies tightly closed. When she was finished, she led her daughter back to the dining room to work on the costume, but Marci's enthusiasm for the project had waned just as much as her own.

She looked at the clock.

Only an hour and thirty minutes to go until Dan came home.

CHAPTER 26

Rusty Ruston stood at the back of the small Lutheran church, which was packed with nearly every resident of Phantom Lake. The old wooden pews had filled an hour before the organ music even began, and as the service began, people kept on coming. Now the front doors were propped open, and a throng sheltered by a sea of umbrellas stood outside in the droning rain, listening to the service.

Flowers filled the sanctuary, and the closed casket was covered with a blanket of white roses, a large framed photo of Ellis propped on an easel in their midst.

Ruston tried to concentrate on what the pastor was saying, but the combination of Emil Lundgaard's mumbling voice and his own irresistible urge to scan the crowd for anything that wasn't as it should be, made following the service impossible. Though Fred Bicks had released Ellis's remains for

burial, Rusty hadn't yet received the official report, and though he — along with nearly everyone else in town — hoped the report would show an accidental death, his gut told him otherwise.

The missing arm was the problem. Ellis Langstrom could easily have drowned while drunk, or even fallen and hit his head. But a missing arm raised a huge red flag in Ruston's mind.

And if his instincts were right, then he needed to concentrate less on the eulogy and more on the possibility that if someone had, indeed, killed Ellis Langstrom, that somebody might very well have come to his victim's funeral. For what seemed like the hundredth time, Ruston scanned the faces he could see, looking for someone who looked nervous, or someone who seemed to be acting strange, or just for something that felt wrong.

All three of the boys from The Pines were there with their families, which didn't surprise him. Nor did it tell him anything, either about the boys' innocence or their possible guilt.

Ellis's entire high school class was there, of course, along with most of the rest of the school-age kids, at least the ones who were in middle school or beyond. Eudora Morri-

son — his own old English teacher — was sitting in the third pew next to Neal Barton, who was scheduled to retire from teaching math next year, though nobody expected he would give up coaching the football team.

And everybody was behaving exactly as he would expect them to.

The congregation rose for the final prayer, and Ruston bowed his head along with everyone else, then — also along with everyone else — remained standing while Adam Mosler, Chris McIvens, and four of their classmates strode to the front of the church to act as pallbearers for the short walk to the graveyard that occupied the acre next door.

Then, as the boys struggled to carry the heavy coffin down the aisle as if it weighed nothing at all, Ruston saw Adam Mosler's eyes suddenly blaze with pure hatred. He shifted his own gaze, and realized who it was that had roused Mosler's fury.

Eric Brewster, flanked by Tad Sparks and Kent Newell.

Ruston watched carefully to see how Brewster and his friends would react, and a moment later, as neither Eric nor either of his friends broke from Adam Mosler's fury, he came to a decision: even if Fred Bicks

ruled Ellis's death as something other than an accident, he wouldn't waste much time trying to prove that the boys from The Pines had anything to do with it. His judgment — honed by years of observing all kinds of kids — told him that had those boys been guilty of anything, they wouldn't have been able to meet Mosler's gaze at all, let alone hold it until Adam himself had to break it.

No, the murderer may indeed be here, but Ruston was nearly positive that he wasn't a resident of The Pines.

As the coffin, closely followed by Carol Langstrom, passed through the church's doors, the pastor spoke loudly over the sounds of people starting to put on their raincoats. "After the interment, please join Ellis's mother for a small reception in the parish house."

Ruston fell in beside Carol Langstrom as soon as she was out of the church and guided her to a folding chair under a tiny awning that had been set up at the grave site, then stood with the decidedly smaller gathering as the minister softly prayed, Carol Langstrom silently wept, and the six pallbearers lined up behind the coffin under identical black umbrellas.

The rain beat down as the pastor spoke his final words.

Carol stood up on trembling legs, touched the coffin for a moment, and watched silently as it was lowered into the ground.

It was finally over.

Murmuring softly, the crowd began to drift toward the parish house where Anna Lundsgaard would undoubtedly have laid out twice as much food as anyone could possibly eat.

Ashley Sparks and a woman Ruston didn't know walked slowly beside Carol, Ashley holding a large black umbrella. Carol was hunched over, as if the weight of Ellis's death was more than she could bear.

Ruston kept an eye on Adam Mosler and his friends, readying himself for whatever they might do now that the funeral was over, but the six merely handed their umbrellas back to the funeral director and walked away.

A red-eyed Cherie Stevens went with them, along with Kayla Banks.

Ruston had long ago learned to trust his gut instincts, and right now his gut was telling him that Ellis's murderer — assuming he *had* been murdered — was not among the mourners. But something had happened to the boy, and as soon as Fred Bicks's report was faxed to his office, he was going to have to start coming up with some

answers, or else answer a lot of fury from a lot of people.

And he was going to have to deal with both Gerald Hofstetter and Ray Richmond, at least one of whom wasn't going to like the coroner's report no matter what it said.

And, of course, there was Carol Langstrom. Rusty didn't care much about either Gerald Hofstetter or Ray Richmond, but Carol Langstrom was another story altogether.

She deserved to know what happened to her son, and whatever else occurred, he intended to give Carol the answers — and the resolution — she needed.

He looked up at the sky, hoping maybe God would be looking down on Carol Langstrom, but all he saw were ominous black clouds.

God, apparently, had no intention of giving him any help at all.

Whatever needed to be done, he'd have to do it himself.

CHAPTER 27

Chris McIvens jumped as Adam Mosler slammed his fist against the trash can on the corner in front of the Northwoods Café. Though it was barely seven o'clock and the sun wasn't even close to setting, the sidewalk was as deserted as the park across the street, and the very emptiness of the village made the sound of Adam's fist crashing into the metal sound even louder than it was. "What the hell was that all about?"

"Just pissed," Mosler growled, rubbing his burning knuckles and flexing his fingers. "God, I wish I had a car."

"Yeah?" McIvens asked. "And I wish I had a yacht, too. So even if you had a car, where would you go?"

Mosler's eyes narrowed. "Somewhere — anywhere. I'd get Cherie, and we'd just take off. Get the hell out of this stupid town."

"Yeah, right," McIven's replied, his voice mocking. "You and Cherie. In case you

didn't notice, she wouldn't even hang with us after the funeral. You might as well write her off, at least for the rest of the summer."

"No way," Adam muttered.

Chris McIvens rolled his eyes. "In case you hadn't noticed, she's hot for that Brewster guy."

Adam's fingers curled into fists as he remembered the way Cherie had been looking at Eric Brewster all through Ellis's funeral. "What the hell were those pricks even doing at the funeral? They didn't even know Ellis!"

"Get over it," McIvens sighed. "They'll be gone at the end of summer. If you ask me —"

"Which I didn't," Adam cut in, but he was no longer even looking at Chris McIvens. Instead he was staring out at the lake beyond the park. "What do you say we take my dad's boat out for a spin?"

Chris looked up at the sky. The rain that had been falling all through Ellis Langstrom's funeral had all but stopped, though the clouds still hung overhead like a shroud, which would probably be enough to keep anyone else from coming down to the village. He knew if they didn't do *something,* Adam would spend the next two hours bitching about the summer people. "Let's

go," he said, never noticing that Adam hadn't been staring at the lake at all.

Rather, he'd been staring at the little boat that was bobbing on the water off the point that separated the town from The Pines.

Eric put his fishing pole in a rod holder and zipped up his sweatshirt against the wind that had started blowing down from the north.

"I thought fish were supposed to bite when it rains," Tad complained.

Eric glanced up at the dark sky. Half an hour ago, taking the boat out had seemed like a good idea. Better, anyway, then just sitting around thinking about Ellis. But now that they were actually on the lake, he wasn't so sure how good an idea it had been.

The lake was empty except for a couple of old fishermen in their rain gear, sitting motionless at anchor in the midst of the wild rice that spread out from the far shore. Even as he watched, a brief rain squall made them vanish altogether. A moment later the squall passed, and once more Eric could see the old fishermen, as oblivious of the rain as they seemed to be of anything else. And yet Eric couldn't stop thinking.

He couldn't stop thinking about Ellis

Langstrom, and about the funeral, and about everything else. He reeled in his lure, then cast it out again, barely watching where it landed, and as he eyed Tad Sparks and Kent Newell, he knew they were thinking about the same things. "You think maybe something could have happened when we started putting all the stuff back together?" he asked, seeing by their expressions that they knew exactly what he was talking about. But when neither of them spoke, he went on. "I don't know, this sounds so stupid . . ." he began, but then let his words trail off, not sure he wanted to voice what he was thinking.

"What?" Kent asked. "Say it."

Eric took a deep breath. "It just seems like — well, maybe we helped the personalities of the killers who owned those things come back to life." He looked at Kent and Tad, who were staring at him as if he'd lost his mind. "Sort of," he added.

"Oh, man," Tad breathed. "That's just too weird." But in spite of his words, he shivered, and unconsciously pulled his jacket tighter.

The three of them sat still, staring at one another, none of them quite willing to be the next to speak. Then the far-off sound of an outboard motor droned across the water,

and all three boys looked toward its source.

A boat was coming directly toward them, running at full throttle.

A boat Eric instantly recognized. He quickly reeled in his line as it approached, praying he was wrong about what was about to happen. But as the boat raced closer and he recognized Adam Mosler standing at the wheel, he knew his first instinct had been right. "It's Mosler!" he yelled, and then Kent and Tad were scrambling to pull in their lines as Eric pulled the rope on the outboard.

The little engine didn't catch.

"Hurry!" Tad said.

Eric checked the choke and pulled again. Nothing.

Mosler's boat was bearing down on them, the roaring engine echoing across the silent lake.

Eric pulled again, and this time the little motor sputtered and then came to life.

Too late.

A split second before the prow of Adam Mosler's boat would have slammed into the side of their skiff, Adam suddenly cranked the wheel hard, his boat heeled into a tight turn, and a huge wake surged toward the little boat that was already all but overloaded by the three boys in it.

The pitch from the wake caught Tad standing up. He stumbled, tried to catch his balance, then collapsed into the boat, banging his head on the gunwale. "Sit down!" Eric yelled, and Kent instantly responded, dropping to the center bench and holding on to both sides of the rocking boat.

Eric crouched on the bottom, holding on to the tiller.

Mosler gunned the motor again, spun in a tight circle around them, and even in the gray light of the evening, Eric could see his eyes glittering with rage. Then he tore off to the north, turned, and came racing back, once again turning at the last possible moment, sending water cascading over the three boys in the rowboat and making it pitch and roll so badly it nearly capsized.

Then, on the third run, Adam cut it too close, and the stern of his speedboat caught the small outboard, wrenching it loose from the transom and sending a wash of water over Eric at the same time the boat rolled for the last time.

Eric lost his balance, his elbow smashing against the gunwale an instant before the boat capsized, dumping him — along with Tad, Kent, and all their gear — into the lake.

Adam, seemingly stunned by what had

happened, throttled back his boat, and for a moment he and Chris McIvens stared at the three boys thrashing in the water. Eric thought they were going to come back and help them, but then Adam gunned the engine once more, twisted the wheel, and a moment later the runabout was up on a plane, racing back toward town.

Eric grabbed a floating cushion and swam over to Tad, who was clinging to what was left of a Styrofoam cooler. Tad had a gash on the back of his head and blood was sheeting out of it and running down his neck. He seemed too dazed even to realize what had happened, but when Eric shoved the cushion under him, he managed to cling to it.

As Kent swam over to them, Eric looked toward shore. Pinecrest was nothing more than a small smudge of green lawn in the distance. "I don't think Tad can swim all the way back," Eric said as they bobbed in Adam's slowly calming wake.

As if to confirm Eric's words, Tad laid his head on the cushion, and his grip on it visibly weakened. Eric grabbed onto Tad's shirt. "We've got to get him back in the boat."

"I don't think we can even get it turned over," Kent said. "We'll be lucky if it doesn't

just sink. Let's see if we can get Tad onto it, then maybe we can push the boat ahead of us."

Together, the two boys towed Tad back to the overturned boat. Kent carefully hoisted himself on top of the hull and helped Eric muscle Tad up the keel. Though barely conscious, Tad gripped the slippery wood, then began to shiver, his lips turning blue.

Kent slid back into the water. "Push," he told Eric, grabbing hold of the broken transom and kicking his legs as hard as he could. Eric, a flotation cushion under his chest, worked his way up next to Kent, and then both of them were kicking, trying to move the overturned boat toward shore.

But the boat didn't move.

"The anchor," Kent said, realizing what was happening.

Eric moved around to the bow of the boat, groping inside the overturned hull until his fingers found not only the rope, but the rusty eyebolt to which the rope was tied.

Tied so tightly that Eric knew he wouldn't be able to work the knot loose.

Nor was there anything left with which to cut the rope.

"We'll have to pull it up," he called to Kent, and a moment later the other boy was beside him.

Once more climbing up onto the hull, Kent grabbed the anchor line and slowly brought it up while Eric did his best to keep the overturned boat from rolling so far that both Kent and Tad would be thrown back into the water.

Slowly, so slowly that Eric wasn't sure it was happening at all, the anchor began to come loose from the mud at the bottom of the lake. Then, at last, he felt the boat lighten, and as Kent kept pulling up the anchor line, he once again kicked hard.

The boat inched toward shore.

After a few minutes that seemed like much longer, Tad regained enough consciousness to cling to the rope while Kent slid back into the water to help Eric move the ruined skiff through the water. They swam in silence, kicking hard, gripping the stern of the boat even as their fingers, then their hands, and finally their arms, went numb.

As darkness was falling and Eric was about to give up hope that they would make it, he felt something beneath his feet.

"We did it!" he croaked as he stood up, the water now only chest-deep.

Moving around to the prow of the boat, he took the anchor line from Tad and pulled the boat far enough in so its gunwale stuck in the mud. Then, as Kent helped Tad get

to shore, Eric hauled the anchor out of the now shallow water.

But it wasn't just the anchor that came up. An ancient crawfish trap, its float — and the rope that tethered the float — stuffed inside the trap itself, appeared.

When they'd dropped the anchor, one of its tines had caught the trap. Even with the whole mess on shore, it still took Eric nearly a full minute to extract the anchor from the rusting trap. Meanwhile, Tad regained his strength, and Kent came over to help Eric.

Then he saw that the anchor, the float, and its plastic line weren't the only things that were in the trap.

There was something else as well.

As Kent picked up the old float and started scraping the slime away, Eric gazed silently at the other object that had fallen from the trap.

A moment later Kent had scraped enough of the slime from the float to read the single faded word that had been put on the float to identify the trap's owner.

"Jesus," Kent whispered. "Look at this." He held it out for Eric and Tad to see.

DARBY.

All three of them gazed at the float for a long time, then, though no one had said anything, they turned to the other object

that had been in the trap.

It was covered with rust and missing its handle, but there was no mistaking what it was.

The blade of an axe.

Adam Mosler and Chris McIvens sat silently in Sheriff Ruston's office, their heads down, their gazes fixed on the floor. "Tad Sparks had to have eleven stitches in the back of his head," Ruston began. "You two should both be on your knees thanking your lucky stars that none of them were killed."

"I — I'm sorry," Adam stammered, but Ruston didn't hear anything that sounded like genuine penitence in his voice.

"You're going to be a lot sorrier when those parents decide what charges to press." Ruston got up from his chair and walked around to the front of his desk. "Criminal mischief. Destruction of property. Reckless endangerment." He leaned back against the desk and crossed his arms. *"Attempted murder, three counts."* He let that sink in for a moment, then went on. "You're in serious trouble, Adam. Eric Brewster's father is a lawyer. A damned good lawyer."

Adam sucked in a ragged breath. "It was an accident," he whispered.

" 'Accident' my ass!" Ruston snapped, his

words lashing like the tip of a whip. "Fortunately for you, those same three parents have cool heads, and seem to think maybe at least some of what you two did could have been accidental. So here's what's going to happen. They're going to talk things over tomorrow, after all of them have had a chance to sleep on it, and see how the Sparks boy is doing. Wednesday is the Fourth, so they're not going to tell me what they've decided until Thursday morning. Which gives you two days to think about things, deal with your own parents, and hire yourselves an attorney." His eyes fixed on Chris McIvens. "And don't think for even one minute that just because you weren't driving the boat that you're off the hook. You're not." He wheeled back to Adam Mosler. "As for you, at the very least you'll be buying Pinecrest a brand new boat."

Mosler glowered up at Ruston. "That boat was a piece of shit."

"Well, the new boat you buy for them won't be."

Adam's features hardened into a sullen mask. "Those assholes killed Ellis."

"I don't think so," Ruston said.

"Why?" Mosler sneered. "Because they're rich?"

Ruston's eyes narrowed to a dangerous

squint. "If I were you, I'd start watching my mouth," he said softly, "otherwise Dan Brewster might just add a slander count to the rest of your offenses."

Ruston's phone rang once, and then the fax machine on the credenza behind his desk came alive. He glanced at the clock — almost nine-thirty. Frowning, he reached back and pulled the cover sheet out of the machine the second it finished printing, glanced at it, then peered once more at the two boys he'd been doing his best to scare some sense into for the last hour. "Out of here," he barked. "Both of you. And I don't even want to hear any rumors about you two, understand?" He held Adam Mosler's gaze until the boy finally broke, nodding his agreement to the sheriff's words. Ruston tipped his head toward the door and both boys bolted before he could change his mind.

As the door closed behind them, he reached out and picked up the next few pages of the report the coroner's office was faxing, knowing from the lateness of the hour that the news was not going to be good.

He scanned the pages, searching for the cause of death, and when he found it his stomach knotted.

Blunt force, trauma to the head, resulting in cranial fracture.

The details were even worse. Pieces of pine bark had been found embedded in the skin, the skull, and brain, indicating that Ellis Langstrom had been clubbed so hard that it crushed his skull.

His arm had been severed inexpertly by a saw, right through the bone.

The pages clutched in his hand, Rusty sank deep into his chair. How the hell was he going to tell Carol Langstrom how her son had died?

And how was Mayor Ray Richmond going to keep it from Gerald Hofstetter? He couldn't, any more than he could stop Hofstetter from printing the story.

Which, he was certain, would be the end of the lucrative summer season.

It wasn't just Carol Langstrom who was going to be battered by this report.

It was the whole town.

Beyond that, there was his own personal problem: finding out who had killed Ellis Langstrom, why whoever it was had done it, and how he was going to prove it.

Adam Mosler's accusation rose unbidden in his mind: *Those assholes killed Ellis.*

He remembered all three of them being at the funeral.

The perpetrator always revisits the scene of the crime.

He remembered thinking that those boys knew more than they were saying.

From the depths of his memory he recalled a book he'd read a long time ago, about two other boys from Chicago. What were their names?

Leopold. Nathan Leopold and Richard Loeb.

Best friends who had killed someone just to see if they could do it.

Just for the fun of it.

Was it possible that the same thing had happened here, only this time there were three boys involved?

Why had the fathers of two of those boys come into his office the next day? Had they been just taking the temperature of the local officials, or was there something they knew?

Maybe he'd been a little too hasty in giving those three boys the benefit of the doubt.

Maybe he ought to talk to them again.

Maybe he ought to ask them to come into his office, instead of going out to Pinecrest.

He unconsciously tapped the end of his pen on the report as he turned it over in his mind.

Seconds turned into minutes.

He kept tapping, kept thinking.

And he listened to his gut, which was still telling him that those boys had not killed Ellis Langstrom.

Who, then?

And then he remembered something Dan Brewster had said only a couple of hours ago, when he'd gone out to Pinecrest to hear exactly what had transpired on the lake that evening when Mosler and McIvens rammed the Pinecrest boat. He hadn't paid much attention to it at the time — he was far more interested in what Adam and Chris had been up to. But just before he'd left to pick up the two delinquents, Dan Brewster said his daughter had seen a scary looking man out on the lake in a rowboat that, at least according to his daughter, had something like a cross in the bow.

Ruston had known who it was right away, of course — old Riley Logan, who'd been living out in the woods for years, minding his own business except for his occasional forays into town to do some Dumpster diving.

And not causing anyone any trouble.

Yet now, as he reread the coroner's report one more time, Rusty Ruston found himself thinking about Logan.

And not just about Logan.

There was also the Hanover girl's murder.

Suddenly his gut was stirring.

Not churning, but stirring.

Trust your gut, he told himself.

Trust your gut.

CHAPTER 28

At precisely eight o'clock the next morning, Ashley Sparks parked her car in the small lot behind Carol Langstrom's antiques shop and found the key to the back door in the same spot where it had been "hidden" for at least the last five years. She was an hour early; that would give her time to go over the inventory book and familiarize herself with anything in the store she might not have seen before.

A square brown box — stained and battered — sat on the top step, and Ashley opened the door, turned off the alarm with the code Carol had given her, then picked up the box. Taking it inside, she put it on Carol's desk and started to open it. But even before she'd pulled the first of the interlocking flaps loose, she hesitated.

Why hadn't the box been taped shut? Surely it hadn't been shipped like this. It took her less than five seconds to find the

answer to that question: the box bore no label at all, which meant it hadn't been shipped.

Then why was it there?

The answer to that question came just as quickly: it was something personal that someone had left for Carol, not knowing it wasn't going to be Carol who opened the store. And if it was personal, she shouldn't open it.

Turning away from the desk, Ashley moved through the office door into the shop itself, savoring the fragrance of the store; it smelled like tung oil and furniture polish. She'd always loved that smell, ever since she'd been a little girl and started poking around antiques shops with her mother. But this morning there was a dark undertone to the familiar fragrance.

She found the light switches, then turned on all the lamps in the showroom to show off their ornate shades to best advantage, and in less than fifteen minutes, everything was ready. She'd adjusted the positions of at least three dozen of the porcelain figurines that were Carol's specialties, even moving one of them — a little boy sitting self-consciously on a toilet, his pants around his ankles and a surprised look on his face — into the restroom, certain that whoever

was the first to use the tiny chamber that day would buy the item. Just as she was about to take a tour of the showroom, she heard the back door open.

"Hello?"

A second later Carol Langstrom appeared in the doorway. Though dressed perfectly, Ashley could clearly see the lines around her eyes and mouth, and the pallor that her makeup didn't begin to cover.

"Carol? What on earth are you doing here?"

Carol smiled wanly, her sad eyes betraying the depth of her grief. "I can't stay home alone — not by myself. At least not yet. All I do is think about Ellis and what I could have done to keep him from going out that night." She bit her lower lip, and Ashley could see her struggling to control her tears. "I need to stay busy — I need to work. But not by myself." The look in her eyes threatened to break Ashley's heart. "You'll stay with me today?"

Ashley reached out and gently touched her friend's arm. "Of course." As Carol retreated to the office in back, Ashley followed.

Carol glanced around the office as if searching for something, though Ashley was fairly certain she was doing nothing more

than trying to distract her mind from thoughts of her son. Finally, her eyes came to rest on the unopened box on her desk. She gazed at it uncertainly, then turned to Carol. "What's this?"

Ashley shrugged. "It was on the back step."

Carol moved closer, then drew back. "Phew! It certainly smells strange." Reaching out with her hand while still trying to keep her nose as far from the box as possible, Carol opened two of the flaps.

The stench that Ashley had been only barely aware of a few moments earlier now poured forth as a sickening odor, and Ashley struggled not to gag. "My God, what is it? It smells like a dead animal!"

Carol peered inside. For just a moment she thought it must be someone's idea of some kind of strange art. There was what looked like some kind of wire construction and —

Oh, God!

Carol recoiled a step. "Call the sheriff," she said, her voice catching.

"The sheriff?" Ashley echoed. Holding her breath against the noxious odor, she edged close enough to look over the edge of the box.

What looked like scraps of some kind of

raw meat were hanging from whatever the wire had been formed into. She felt her breakfast rise in her gorge, and quickly closed the flaps of the box, putting a phone book on top to hold them down.

Only as the worst of the stench faded from her nostrils did Ashley finally pick up the phone and dial the number Carol Langstrom recited.

"That was on my doorstep," Carol Langstrom said, pointing at the box that neither she nor Ashley Sparks had been able to bring themselves to touch during the few minutes it took for Rusty Ruston to get to the shop.

"Where did it come from?" Ruston asked.

Carol shrugged helplessly.

Ruston moved closer to the box. "No label at all? No note?"

"Nothing on the outside," Carol said. "I don't know about the inside."

Ruston opened the flaps of the box, recoiling from the stench just as the two women had earlier. As Carol and Ashley automatically stepped back, he first looked into the box, then produced a pair of thin latex gloves from one of his pockets, put them on, and reached inside. Very gingerly he lifted the contents out of the box.

"Here," Carol breathed, opening the morning newspaper and spreading it over a tabletop. "Don't set it back on my desk. Set it here."

Ruston placed the object on the table, then stepped back, and suddenly both women had a clear view of what it was that had been left on Carol's back step during the night.

It was the bent and rusted frame of a lamp shade, whatever original covering it may have had long since stripped — or rotted — away.

Where perfectly sewn panels of silk or linen had once been stretched, there now hung ragged scraps of raw skin, held together by crudely tied pieces of string.

The skin had not been tanned; pieces of decaying flesh and rancid yellow globules of fat still clung to it, and the holes through which the string was unevenly laced looked as if they must have been made by an ice pick.

As Ashley struggled once again to control the nausea rising in her belly, a maggot dropped from the grotesque construction onto the newspaper. "My God," she said. Choking on the words, she turned away.

Carol Langstrom, though, stayed where she was, staring numbly at the object.

"Why?" she finally asked, her voice hollow. "Why would someone leave something like that on my step?"

Ruston ignored the question for the moment, carefully studying the hideous thing. He moved slowly around it, examining it from every angle.

And then Carol saw it.

A bluish mark near the top of one of the strips of skin.

A mark that looked familiar.

A terrible foreboding building inside her, Carol forced herself to look closer.

No!

Oh no, God no, please no.

But even as she silently screamed the prayer, she knew it would not be answered.

She knew what the mark was.

It was a symbol.

An old Viking symbol, called Thor's Hammer.

Ellis had had it tattooed on his shoulder.

And now she was staring at that tattoo.

A shriek rose in her throat and exploded from her mouth before she could stop it.

Ruston, jerked out of his reverie, moved instantly to her side, asking what was wrong, but there was no way she could speak.

All she could do was point at the mark.

At the tattoo.

At the skin from Ellis's missing arm.

"Ellis," she finally managed. "It's Ellis's tattoo."

Then she felt Ashley's hands on her shoulders, and as her knees weakened, she let herself be helped to a chair, too stunned even to think.

"Jesus," Ruston whispered. He studied the mark a moment longer, then carefully lifted the object back into the box, where Carol at least wouldn't have to see it. "You going to be okay?" he asked. Carol nodded, her face pale, her eyes fixed on some invisible place in the far distance. Ruston was fairly certain she wasn't going to faint, at least not right now. He took a deep breath, turning to Ashley Sparks. "I need you to show me exactly where you found this, Mrs. Sparks."

"It was right here, sitting on the step," Ashley said a moment later as she and Ruston gazed down at the steps behind the back door.

Ruston scanned the step, then the small parking area.

Then he spotted the Dumpster next to the building. "Okay," he said. "Thanks. Why don't you go see to Carol while I look around a little bit?"

Ashley turned and went inside, while Rus-

ton walked over to the Dumpster and lifted its lid.

It looked like Carol's shop shared the Dumpster with a couple of neighboring shops, one of which was the bakery, which Ruston knew regularly disposed of bags of bread and bagels too old to sell.

Too old to sell, but not to scavenge.

The Dumpster had not yet been emptied this morning, but there were no bags of baked goods — only garbage utterly unfit to eat — and Ruston knew of only one person who was known to go through the Dumpster.

Someone who, if memory served, also used to run a trapline up in the woods.

Which meant he would know how to skin an animal.

Or an arm.

Now Ruston's gut was truly churning.

Gerald Hofstetter refilled his coffee cup in the newspaper's front office, then looked out the big window and watched Billy Stevens in his cherry picker hang a Fourth of July banner from the tall pavilion roof. Rich Patrick was unloading a van full of folding tables into the pavilion where the Chamber of Commerce would be selling hot dogs, hamburgers, corn on the cob, and

everything else anyone might be willing to eat tomorrow at the big picnic. Rich's wife, Marge, and her whole Red Hat club were blowing up balloons and hanging quilts to be raffled off.

Al Stevens was setting up the fireworks scaffolding over by the footbridge. Hofstetter shook his head. Al Stevens and his incendiary devices were a disaster waiting to happen, given that Al's reluctance to stay sober consistently was combined with his seeming inability to work for more than five minutes at a time. Still, Al had been doing the fireworks display for almost thirty years, and so far, so good.

At least no one had died yet.

Gerald heard the phone ring on his secretary's desk behind him and felt a brief flare of hope that it was Ruston with the coroner's report, but a moment later that hope died as it turned out it was just his secretary's boyfriend calling for the fourth time that morning.

But then, as his attention reverted once more to the scene beyond the window, he saw something that made that brief flare of hope burst into full flame: Ray Richmond was crossing the street — actually, he was almost loping — and as he disappeared through the front door of the sheriff's of-

fice, everything about his pace, his posture, and his attitude told Hofstetter that Richmond was in full mayoral mode.

This wasn't just the grocer dropping in for a quick cup of coffee.

Gerald smelled news.

He left his coffee cup on his desk and grabbed a fresh pad from the bookcase.

Rusty Ruston was just dropping the privacy blinds on his office window when he saw Gerald come through the door, and he shook his head in resignation. "One guess who just walked in," he said to Ray.

"Hofstetter, of course," Ray replied. "I swear to God, that man never stops looking out his window." He shrugged. "Might as well let him in — he can't put out a newspaper until Friday, and by that time everybody will know everything anyway."

Rusty opened his door and waved Hofstetter in. Abandoning the blinds, he handed both men copies of the coroner's report, then settled into the chair behind his desk as they scanned it.

"Well," Gerald Hofstetter said, leaning back in his chair as he folded the report and slipped it into his notebook. "So much for Ray's nice little theory that an animal attacked Ellis Langstrom." His eyes fixed on the sheriff. "Any idea who did it?"

Ruston nodded as Ray Richmond, too, finished the report, tossing his copy back on the sheriff's desk as if it had suddenly become poisonous. "I do, indeed," he said. "And by the way, Gerald, I don't remember saying you could keep that."

"It's a public document, isn't it?" Hofstetter countered.

Ruston decided it wasn't worth a fight, especially given that in the end Hofstetter would get the report anyway. "I'm thinking Riley Logan is the man we're looking for."

"Riley Logan," Hofstetter repeated as Ray Richmond sat silently in his chair, his face ashen as he thought of what the report he'd just read could do to the town's economy. "What makes you think it was Logan?"

Ruston tipped his head toward the cardboard box he'd brought from Carol Langstrom's shop and placed in the corner of his office farthest from his desk. "You might want to take a look at that," he said, rising and moving to the box. "Someone left this for Carol Langstrom last night." He opened the box, wincing at the odor that rose from it, and stepped back so the mayor and the newsman could peer at the object inside.

"Mother of God," Ray breathed.

As both men backed away, Rusty donned another pair of latex gloves and carefully

lifted the grotesque lamp shade out of the box, turning it so that they could see the blue mark. "Ellis Langstrom's tattoo." Though he spoke the words softly, Ray Richmond looked as if he'd been struck, and even Gerald Hofstetter's face paled.

As Hofstetter started scribbling in his notebook, Ruston put the grotesque object back into the box and folded down the flaps. "I'm taking Derek Anders with me, and we're going to go get Logan and bring him in."

"Jesus Christ," Ray said, still shaken.

"You still haven't told us why you think Logan did it," Hofstetter said without looking up from his pad.

"We know he was locked up in Central State for a lot of years, we know he used to run a trapline, which means he could have done that" — he tipped his head toward the box again — "and I can't think of any other person who might have done it." Now he fixed his eyes on Ray Richmond. "Maybe he didn't do it," he added. "But we've got enough to bring him in and question him, and there's no way we're going to keep a lid on this. The best we can do is have him locked up, at least through the Fourth. Then we'll see."

Richmond and Hofstetter exchanged a

long look, and finally the mayor nodded. "Do what you have to do," he sighed. "And be careful, okay? Don't you be letting Derek Anders 'accidentally' shoot anyone. Understand?"

Ruston nodded. "Derek's on his way over. We know where Logan's shack is, and it shouldn't take long."

As Richmond and Hofstetter got to their feet and started out of his office, Ruston unlocked his gun safe and took out a shotgun.

Just in case.

CHAPTER 29

Eric gazed dolefully down through the shallow lake water at the wreck of the Pinecrest skiff. Sometime during the night, it had filled with water and sunk to the bottom, where schools of minnows had claimed it. Now, with Kent Newell standing beside him on the dock, the minnows seemed almost to be mocking them while he tried to figure out some way to haul the ruined hull back to the surface. Kent, though, appeared to be thinking about something else altogether.

"What do you think is the big deal Tad wants to tell us?" Kent asked, confirming Eric's suspicion.

Eric shrugged, then turned to look up the lawn and saw Tad himself emerging from the mouth of the path that led through the woods to his house, a large bandage covering what looked like at least half his head. "Here he comes," Eric said, nudging Kent. "And it looks like they must have sewed up

half his scalp."

"You okay?" Kent called out.

Tad shrugged. "It's not as bad as it looks." He reached up to touch the bandage, wincing at the pressure. "Okay, so it's not *quite* as bad as it looks," he temporized as he joined his friends on the dock. "Still hurts, anyway."

Kent cocked his head quizzically. "Well? What's the big deal you called about?"

Tad took a deep breath, glanced up toward the house as if looking for someone who might be listening, and dropped his voice almost to a whisper. "You aren't gonna believe what my mom found on the back porch of Mrs. Langstrom's antiques shop this morning."

An image rose in Kent's mind of a square brown cardboard box, dirty and stained. Despite the heat of the morning, a chill ran through his body. But the box wasn't on the back porch of an antiques shop.

It was in his hands.

It was in his hands, and he was carrying it.

Tad's voice began to fade, and the images in his head became more vivid.

He was walking through the woods, and though it was night and he could barely see at all, he was following some kind of invis-

ible path, moving quickly through the trees, never stumbling, never uncertain which way to turn.

Then, in the way things happen in a dream, he was suddenly in town, and setting the box down.

Setting it down on a porch!

With Tad's voice droning softly and indistinctly far away, Kent slipped deeper into the strange scene unfolding in his mind. Now he knew what was in the box — knew it without even having to unfold the flaps at the top and peer inside.

Knew it because he'd made the object himself.

Now he could feel the stickiness of blood on his hands as he stretched the skin of Ellis Langstrom's upper arm over the bent and rusty lamp shade frame. His fingers twitched as he watched himself pierce the skin with some kind of thick needle, then pull through the twine that would bind the bloody tissue to the wire.

Suddenly, Eric Brewster's voice jerked him out of his reverie, and he saw Eric staring at Tad Sparks, his face almost as ashen as Tad's after Adam Mosler's boat had rammed them.

"How did they know it was the skin from Ellis's arm?" Eric whispered, and Kent felt

his skin crawl once more.

What was happening? Was it possible that what he'd just been remembering wasn't a dream at all?

Was it possible it had actually happened?

His knees suddenly weak, Kent sank down on the dock.

How would he know everything Tad was saying? How could he?

"He had a tattoo on his shoulder," Tad whispered. "It was stretched out on the lamp shade."

"Oh, God," Kent said, something almost like a sob choking his throat. He caught his breath, then looked up at Eric and Tad. "I dreamed it. I dreamed I made that thing, and I was carrying it through the woods, and . . ." His voice trailed off at the memory of depositing the box on the back porch of the shop. Now he could see all the details — everything in the tiny parking lot. He fixed his eyes on Tad Sparks. "I remember setting it on the back step of her shop. Right by the Dumpster."

"Jesus," Tad breathed as he and Eric also dropped down onto the dock on either side of Kent.

Kent looked at each of them, searching their faces for something, anything, that would tell him they had shared the dream,

too. "Didn't either of you have it? The same dream, like we all had last time, and the time before?"

Tad shook his head. "I couldn't go to sleep, so finally Mom gave me a pill. And I had a headache, too," he added, once again touching the bandage covering the stitches in the back of his head. "I don't remember dreaming anything."

Kent turned to Eric, but Eric only shook his head. "I don't remember dreaming anything last night, either," he said.

Now Kent stared down at his hands, half expecting them to still be covered with blood. "It was so real," he whispered. "And the weird thing is, I didn't even remember it until you started talking about it. But as soon as you said your mom found something on the porch, I knew what it was. I could *see* it! It was like it was *real*."

The three boys gazed down into the water in utter silence for almost a full minute before Eric finally spoke, his voice hollow, quavering.

"We have to go back in there," he said, and neither Kent nor Tad needed to be told what he meant. "We have to take all that stuff apart again."

"No way," Tad said. "Something's wrong in there, and I don't want anything else to

do with it."

Eric shook his head. "We have to. Every time we put something in there back together, something happens. And if we don't take it all apart again, it's going to keep happening."

"You know he's right," Kent said softly as he saw Tad's resolve begin to weaken. "We need to go in there one last time."

"One last time?" Tad echoed. "And then we're done?"

"Then we're done," Eric agreed.

As Kent nodded, all three boys got back to their feet.

Unwilling even to touch the lamp that now held the shade that Ed Gein had long ago made from the skin of one of his victims, Eric lit the lantern they'd brought in after they first began exploring the tiny chamber and its macabre contents. As the mantle flared and the lantern light brightened, the fragmentary voices that had begun whispering to them even before they'd entered the outer storeroom now blended into a gentle chorus, and Eric felt his resolve weaken.

A glow of softer light imbued the room, and he turned to see that Ed Gein's grisly lamp was once more glowing, its amber light seeping into every corner of the cham-

ber, casting no shadows at all.

On the table lay the old and rusty hacksaw, and the medical bag with its scalpels hidden inside.

Yet instead of reaching for the bag to return its contents to the separate bundle in which he'd originally found them, Eric took an object from the deep pocket of his cargo pants.

A heavy object.

A heavy, rusty object.

Hefting the axe head in his hand for a moment, he gazed at it almost as if he wasn't certain what it was.

Then he set it on the table.

Then Kent, instead of taking the hacksaw apart to return the blade to the drawer in which he'd originally found it, was opening boxes, as if searching for something.

Tad opened the ledger on the table and slowly turned the pages as if reviewing everything they'd read before. When he was near the end of the book, he stopped.

At that same moment, Kent stopped roaming the room. He was facing an ancient wooden filing cabinet.

As Tad gazed down at the entry in the ledger, Kent stooped down and closed his fingers on the handle of the filing cabinet's bottom drawer.

Eric heard the chorus of voices grow louder, taking on a note of excitement.

He moved closer to the table and looked over Tad's shoulder so that he, too, could read the entry Tad had found.

5/11 acq LB axe (#114) frm Prince Bros Fall River. $24,550. Excellent cond.

Kent slowly drew the file drawer open and reached inside, his fingers closing on an elongated object wrapped in newspaper. He lifted it out of the drawer, stood up, and moved to the table. Setting it down, he carefully — almost reverently — began stripping away the yellowed wrapping.

A moment later a wooden axe handle lay before them on the old Formica-topped table.

It glowed in the amber light, almost sparkled, as if surrounded by a force they could see.

And a single voice — a woman's voice — seemed to emerge from the chorus.

The voice sounded happy.

Happy, and excited.

For a long time the boys gazed down at the axe head and its handle, still separated by almost a foot. The light from the lamp shimmered, and the air itself felt charged

with a strange energy.

"It's done," Eric finally breathed, his voice echoing softly.

As Tad and Kent nodded, Eric reached out to the ledger, but before he touched its pages, the other two boys' hands had joined his own and together they turned to the last page.

Upon it was written Hector Darby's last words:

I pray that some day someone stronger will finish what I have begun.

"Let's go," Eric breathed, backing away a step, but leaving the ledger open on the table. "We're finished."

As Eric extinguished the lantern, the lamp went out as if of its own volition.

The three boys moved through the small door.

Eric and Kent drew the plywood back over the opening.

And in the darkness of the once more hidden room, the axe head and its handle began to vibrate as if they felt their proximity.

The table trembled.

The scalpels rattled softly in their bag.

The lamp flickered on once more.

The voices rose in chorus.

And slowly, forces within the tiny chamber began their work.

As if guided by an unseen hand, the metal axe head moved toward the wooden handle.

They aligned themselves and moved still closer.

They touched, and the handle slid into the socket on the head.

The axe lay complete.

The trembling ceased.

The light extinguished.

All, at last, was ready.

CHAPTER 30

Logan had felt danger in the air even before he opened his eyes that morning.

The dog was restless in his bed, moving stiffly, shifting position, groaning and sighing.

The crow hopped endlessly around the perimeter of the cabin as if searching for something, but whatever it sought remained eternally elusive.

The animals, Logan knew, shared the air of imminent disaster that hung over the cabin, making it difficult even to breathe, let alone to think.

All morning that sense of danger — of something unseen creeping closer and closer — grew and expanded and gained strength, until at last Logan could remain in the cabin no more.

He needed to get outside, to escape the confines of the tiny structure, to elude the oppressive weight before it crushed him. As

he pulled the door open, the old dog struggled to its feet, panting heavily, and followed him out the door and down the well-worn path toward the lake.

Logan paused by the dead tree that had stood by the path for as long as he'd been here. Now and then over the years he had thought about cutting it down for firewood, but always changed his mind before even nicking its silvered limbs with the blade of an axe or saw.

Best to respect the dead.

He knocked three times on the ancient tree's trunk.

He felt a little safer then, as he always did after tapping the tree. Still, even in the morning air he felt the menace lurking just out of sight and out of hearing.

He moved more quickly down the path, then cut away from it entirely, thrashing through the brush until he found what he was looking for.

His breath gave out as he found his goal, and he sank low to the ground for a moment to wait for his panting to ease and for the dog to catch up.

And as he waited, he gazed up at the tree by which he crouched. It was the tree at whose base he'd trapped his first raccoon, so long ago he'd lost track of the years that

had passed. But he'd marked the tree by leaving a souvenir after he'd skinned and dressed the 'coon. He'd placed the animal's skull in the main crotch of the tree, certain that the spirit of the raccoon would watch over him if he didn't bury it in the cold earth, and that it would warn him of trouble before it found him.

As the years had gone by, the skull had weathered and whitened. It had been his totem, and somehow every other creature of the forest understood that.

Until this morning.

This morning, the skull was gone.

Maybe he was wrong!

Maybe it was still there!

Rising once more to his full height, Logan reached up to the place where the skull had rested, but his fingers touched only leaves and dirt.

He scrabbled brush away from the base of the tree, but knew even as he searched that it was useless.

The skull was gone.

It had deserted him. It had seen the trouble coming and left.

"Bad," he whispered, laying his hand on the old dog's head as it nuzzled against him. "Real bad . . ." His voice trailed off as he tried to think.

Which way to go?

What to do?

And then he heard it.

The sound of men coming for him.

It was a long way off yet, coming from somewhere on the far side of the lake, but there was no mistaking it.

A boat.

A boat with men.

Men coming for him.

"He told me," Logan whispered to the ancient dog. "Dr. Darby said the men would come. He said they'd come, but they wouldn't understand, and they'd send me away again."

Now Logan peered up at the scraps of blue sky that glinted between the treetops. "What do I do?" he whispered.

But there was no reply.

At his feet, the dog stirred, a low growl rising in its throat, and it swung its head around so its sightless eyes fixed on the boat that was now clearly visible to Logan and drawing steadily closer.

Abandoning the tree that no longer held his totem, Logan made his way back to the path. From behind, the drone of the approaching boat's outboard drove him onward, and by the time he came to the cabin, he'd far outpaced the dog.

He threw open the door and began to reach for the things he'd need.

A blanket.

Three stale rolls he'd found in the Dumpster behind the bakery. He broke up two of them and threw them to the floor for the crow and the dog, and the mice that he knew, by the tiny droppings they left, crept in when he was gone.

By the time he was ready to go, the dog had made it up the path, quivering and panting at the door.

"It's all right," he whispered as it sniffed the air. "It's all gonna be all right." But even as he whispered reassuring words to the dog, he knew they weren't true.

They were coming to take him, just like the time he killed that girl.

This time would be bad. Very bad.

And this time there would be no nice hospital, no Dr. Darby.

Leaving the dog behind and shutting the cabin door so it couldn't follow, Logan started up the hill toward a place he'd found a long time ago.

A cave that was small — much smaller than his cabin — but that was so well hidden he knew no one else would ever find it.

It was his safe spot.

There was no path to the cave. He'd seen

to that, always approaching it from a different direction, always leaving it by a different route from the one along which he'd come.

No path meant nothing to follow.

But Logan knew the way. Knew it in his heart and in his head and in his spirit.

He hurried now, moving quickly, but leaving no track, no sign that he'd been there at all.

When he reached the rocky outcropping, he carefully pushed the bushes just far enough away from the opening to the cave to let him wriggle in.

He reached back and replaced the branches so perfectly that they appeared not to have been moved at all.

At last he settled himself on the floor of the cave, to wait.

Everything was going to be different now.

He closed his eyes.

Soon he would know what to do and how long to wait.

Dr. Darby — or maybe even Jesus himself — would tell him.

And when the time came and he knew exactly what he was supposed to do, he would leave the cave.

Leave the last place of safety.

And he would do what he was supposed to do.

While Derek Anders picked up the painter from the floor of the old aluminum scow that served as Phantom Lake's sole police boat, Rusty Ruston shifted the outboard into neutral. Then he killed the engine and tipped it up so neither the water intake nor the propeller would foul in the mud and reeds that choked this side of the lake. Inertia and the small craft's own wake carried its nose gently into the weedy lakeshore brush, just far enough for Anders to catch a sturdy limb to pull it fully ashore.

"We sure hit the right spot," Anders said, pointing to a boat that was all but invisible in the tangle some thirty feet to their left. As Anders made the painter fast to a tree, Ruston gazed silently at the feature of the boat that was most visible — the weird wooden cross that for years had identified Logan to anybody who had ever seen him skulking about the lake.

"Well, at least we know he's here," Ruston said, once more checking the shotgun he hoped he wasn't going to have to use. In his entire career, Ruston had yet to shoot anyone, and right now he was praying that this wasn't going to be the day that record

was broken.

With the boat securely tied and their shotguns cradled in their arms, Ruston and Anders began walking warily up the worn path toward the cabin in which Logan had been squatting for so many years that everyone, even Ruston, thought of it as belonging to the old recluse. "Keep an eye out for traps," Ruston said. "If he spotted us coming, no telling what he might do." As he made his way slowly up the hill, he ruefully remembered the fantasies he'd entertained now and then over the years, when instead of being a nearly unnecessary sheriff in a backwater town, he was the kind of fearless crime fighter upon which TV series were based. Now, faced with the reality of what might lie at the end of this walk, he decided he'd never entertain such a fantasy again.

His gut just didn't like it.

Still, he plodded on, and was just beginning to find the slope a little wearing when he caught sight of the roofline of Logan's shack. He stopped short, his hands tightening on the shotgun, and knew Anders had stopped, too, could almost feel the former high school football star's bulk looming close behind him.

Suddenly, everything seemed quiet.

Too quiet?

Even the birds seemed to have fallen silent, as if they knew something was about to happen.

With Anders staying on his heels, Ruston moved slowly forward. Brush had been cut and trampled in front of Logan's shack, and a few trees had been felled, probably for firewood. Some of their branches still lay strewn about, like the bare bones of an animal after the wolves have torn it to pieces and devoured every scrap of edible substance.

He knew that crossing that field of dry branches would be a loud announcement of their approach and would let Logan slip unseen from the back of the cabin.

Without being told, Derek split off from Ruston, going quietly to the right, keeping behind trees. Ruston waited for him to get into a position from which he could watch the two sides of the cabin that he himself could not, then shouted loudly. "Logan!" he called, cupping his left hand to his mouth while he still gripped the shotgun with his right. "It's Sheriff Ruston! If you're there, come out of the cabin with your hands up." He dropped his left hand to the stock of the shotgun and waited.

Seconds ticked by.

Nothing happened. No sound, no flicker of movement from the shadowy interior.

Nothing.

Though he was already fairly sure Logan wasn't there, Ruston called out once more. "Logan! Show yourself within ten seconds or we're going to fire!" Then, as Anders raised his gun to his shoulder and took aim at the tiny shack, Ruston gestured frantically for him to hold his fire. Knowing Logan as long as he had, he was all but certain that if the man were in the cabin, the threat alone would be enough to flush him out.

Once again the seconds ticked by.

Once again nothing happened.

"Let's go take a look," he said loud enough for Anders to hear, nearly certain that wherever Logan was, he wasn't inside the cabin. "You go around the back and I'll go in the front. And for Christ's sake, make sure you don't shoot me, okay?"

Obviously disappointed that he wasn't being allowed to open fire on the house, Anders reluctantly lowered his shotgun and disappeared around the far corner of the house as Ruston crossed the twigs and branches to the front door, which was neither latched nor even quite closed. Standing to one side, he used the butt of the gun to push the door wider.

When still nothing happened, he stepped in front of the door and pointed his shotgun at the dim interior.

A dog growled from the corner.

"Easy boy," Ruston said, but the dog took a snarling step toward him.

"I'll take care of the dog," Anders said, coming through the back door at the opposite end of the cabin.

Ruston looked around. Clearly, Logan was not there. The shack was no larger than Ruston's bedroom, and looked like it was mostly a storage place for whatever the hermit had scavenged over the years. The floor was littered with some kind of crumbs, and a crippled crow that was pecking at them only glared up at Ruston before going back to devouring the crumbs. A few ragged items of clothing hung on nails haphazardly hammered into the cabin's rough walls.

Then the dog's snarling grew louder, and Ruston turned to look just as it launched itself at Derek Anders, who reflexively pulled the trigger of his shotgun in response to the attack.

The blast almost knocked down the flimsy walls of the shack, and Ruston's ears rang with the concussion.

The crow screamed, leaping into the air as its one good wing flapped wildly.

Ruston grabbed a filthy shirt from a hook, threw it over the crow, picked it up, and took it outside, where it immediately scuttled away into the brush at the edge of the small clearing.

Back inside the cabin, Ruston found Anders looking intently at something he was clutching in his right hand, the shotgun now slung over his shoulder. "Look at this," the deputy said, and a moment later Ruston found himself gazing at a yellowed newspaper clipping. "It was nailed to the wall over there," Anders went on, pointing at a nasty tangle of rags on a torn mattress that must have served as Logan's bed.

SUSPECT ARRESTED IN HARTWELL STRANGLING

MADISON — Riley Logan, a custodian at the University of Wisconsin in Madison, was arrested yesterday in connection with the strangling death of sophomore Melissa Hartwell. Hartwell's body was found in the Administration Building's custodial supplies closet last Thursday. Logan has been hospitalized several times in the recent past for psychiatric reasons. He is being held without bail.

Ruston's blood chilled as he read the article.

"And take a look at this," Derek Anders said. "It was on the same nail."

KILLER REMANDED TO CENTRAL STATE HOSPITAL

MADISON — Riley Logan was found unfit to stand trial in the strangling murder of Melissa Hartwell, a UW sophomore. Judge Thomas P. Sewell, after reviewing testimony from three different doctors including Hector Darby, who was hired by the state for the purpose of evaluating Logan, has committed Logan to Central State Hospital, where he will be held indefi

The rest of the story had been torn away, leaving only a ragged edge at the bottom of the clipping. "Hector Darby," Ruston breathed as his mind began to whirl with memories of the Hanover girl who had been murdered years ago, just before Darby's disappearance. "What the hell is going on around here?" he said, more to himself than to Derek Anders. He scanned the shack again, the litter of boxes suddenly seeming a lot more foreboding than they had a few moments earlier. "I think maybe we better

find out what's in all these."

Anders picked up one of the boxes and put it on the only table in the cabin. "Looks like medical files," he said after pulling open its top and lifting out a yellowed folder.

"Medical files?" Ruston echoed. "Whose medical files? What are they doing here?"

Some of the boxes were so old they were mildewed and rotten, and even the best of them looked as though they could collapse at any moment.

"Oh, Jesus," Anders breathed. "Take a look at this."

Ruston joined him and peered at the folder the deputy had just opened. More newspaper clippings were on the top, all about the Hartwell girl. Under those was a fat file folder with the Central State Wisconsin Psychiatric Hospital seal on the front and RILEY LOGAN printed on the tab.

"It's like he kept a scrapbook on what he'd done," Ruston said. "And no one ever told us who he was — not even Darby." He shook his head. "Let's take that box with us and get out of here," he went on.

Anders picked up the box, and a moment later Ruston followed him outside. He scanned the hillside, already calculating just how many square miles of wilderness Logan had disappeared into. And he hadn't

taken the dog with him, which could have meant one of two things — either he was coming back, or the dog would have slowed him down.

In all the years he'd watched Logan, Ruston had never before known him not to have the dog with him.

Which meant he wasn't coming back.

"We're not going to find him today," he told Anders as they started back to their boat. "In fact, right now I'd bet we don't find him at all."

Anders's brow furrowed. "Where's he gonna go?"

"Anywhere," Ruston replied. "But if he knew we were coming — which I'm damn sure he did — he'll know better than to come back. And he knows the wilderness a lot better than anyone else, which means if he doesn't want to be found, we won't find him."

"So what about tomorrow?" Anders asked, glancing worriedly back at the cabin, which was now all but invisible again. "It's the Fourth of July picnic. What if he shows up?"

Ruston fell silent for a moment as he thought about his options, and decided he didn't like any of them. If he started a manhunt now, he'd need an explanation, and any explanation he might come up with

— and the rumors that would inevitably boil in the wake of that explanation — would put an instant end not only to the holiday tomorrow, but to the rest of the summer as well.

And his gut was telling him that no matter how many men he put on the search, Logan wasn't going to be found.

"We'll add some extra deputies for tomorrow, and tell them to keep a special lookout for Logan. I don't think he's going to show up, but if he does, we'll deal with him."

As they got back into the boat a few minutes later and started across the lake, Ruston silently prayed that his gut would be as reliable today as it had always been before.

CHAPTER 31

Rusty Ruston moved through the parade staging area in the Phantom Lake High School parking lot, keeping his eyes and ears open for anything that might be amiss.

An hour earlier he had deputized ten members of the volunteer fire department, briefed them not only on what had been found in Carol Langstrom's shop yesterday, but on everything he knew about Riley Logan as well. "The main thing is to keep a low profile," he'd told them as he handed each one a walkie-talkie. "The last thing we want is to panic anybody. So what I want you to do is stay alert and report anything you see that isn't right. Anything."

He'd placed Derek Anders at the parade destination, and assigned the rest to various points along the route. Once the parade was over, they'd move on to the park, where most of the town would gather for the rest of the day, staying right through until the

fireworks went off an hour after sunset. The whole celebration needed to go off without a hitch, and Ruston fully intended to see that it did. It was going to be a long day, and the best he could hope for was that Logan had spotted him coming yesterday afternoon, been rational enough to know exactly what was up, and had taken off into the woods with every intention to keep on going. If that was the case — and Ruston's gut was telling him it was — then he, Derek Anders, and the rest of the deputies would have nothing more serious to deal with than a couple of sunburns and maybe a few fingers scorched on sparklers by the time the fireworks display was over.

Up ahead, Misty Kennedy, who had coordinated the parade every year for the last three decades, was waving her arms at the high school band director, telling him to keep his musicians in line and shouting orders at the float drivers, demanding that they check their order one more time. And everyone was ignoring her, just as they had every year for the past three decades.

Ruston checked his watch: 9:55.

Five minutes to showtime.

He walked through the high school musicians as they finally began falling into what passed as a formation, adjusting their

uniforms, chattering excitedly, and tuning their instruments to the best of their admittedly small ability.

Still, everyone loved the band, especially the parents of its members. The baton twirlers were warming up — only one flying out of control as Ruston watched — and the banner announcing the Phantom Lake High School Band was moving into place.

Then he began catching snatches of the kids' conversations.

". . . satanic ritual murder . . ."

". . . picked up hitchhiking by some pervert . . ."

". . . I miss him . . ."

". . . he was a jerk, but still . . ."

"Do you think . . . ?"

"Did you hear . . . ?"

"My mom said . . ."

So it wasn't the parade the kids were talking about at all, and Ruston sighed as he realized he should have expected it. The kids — the whole town — was nowhere near over the shock of Ellis Langstrom's death. Still, he'd hoped that today, at least, they'd be able to put their worry and grief aside long enough to enjoy the holiday for which Phantom Lake had been famous for almost a century. And judging from the size of the crowd, the rumors about what might have

happened to Ellis Langstrom hadn't spread too far, for it looked to Ruston as if half the people in the neighboring counties had come to join in the fun.

He pressed his thumb on the transmit button of his walkie-talkie. "Five minutes," he said.

Each of the deputies responded with "all clears," and Ruston began to relax.

Then he caught a glimpse of a ragged-looking guy with a shaggy head of hair on the other side of the Birthday Club float, and felt a shot of adrenaline squirt into his bloodstream. An instant later he was running, trying to keep the man in sight, dodging students, tubas, clowns, and bicycles.

He made an end run around the back of the drugstore's float, which appeared to be intending to bribe the judges with hot dogs this year, but by the time he got to the Birthday Club, the man was nowhere to be seen.

Slowing his pace close enough to a walk that it wouldn't unnecessarily alarm anyone, Ruston moved along the only route the man could have taken while keeping the float between himself and the sheriff.

There!

He had him now. He sped his gait just enough to close in on the man without

panicking anybody else, but just as he was about to lay his heavily practiced, if rarely used, "law enforcement" hand on the man's shoulder, followed by a spin that would end with the man pinned against the wall of the bank, the man turned around.

Fred Rawlins.

The manager of the very bank Ruston had been about to slam him up against.

Rawlins was wearing a shaggy wig and rags for some float — probably designed by his over-the-hill hippie wife — the point of which Ruston was certain would be lost on nearly everyone except Mrs. Fred, who had changed her name to Sunbeam Moonrise twenty years earlier, and had steadfastly refused to allow people to shorten it to "Sunny," thus relegating herself to being known as "Mrs. Fred" ever since.

Fred himself now smiled and held out his hand. "Hell of an event again this year, Rusty," he said, waving exactly the kind of small American flag his wife hated. "See you at the barbecue?"

Rusty Ruston shook the proffered hand, nodded, then stepped back as Fred climbed aboard his wife's float, which seemed to be trying to draw attention to the plight of the homeless. Sunbeam Moonrise had struck again, and Ruston wondered what Rawlins's

superiors in Madison would say when they heard their bank had sponsored a float honoring the people they wouldn't be caught dead loaning money to.

Not my problem, Ruston decided. His problem was to figure out some way to relax a little; he'd nearly spun the bank manager around and slammed him up against a wall, and he couldn't stay that edgy all day or he'd wind up hurting someone.

He had to calm down.

He had to trust his deputies to be his eyes and his ears.

He checked his watch.

Ten o'clock on the dot.

The band was lined up, and the drum major held his baton high. He gave a short blow on his whistle, and the band began to march out of the parking lot, the drum major strutting smartly. As the band turned the corner onto Main Street, they broke into an enthusiastic rendition of "Strike Up the Band" that was only slightly out of pitch.

The parade was officially under way, and, as always, the crowd began cheering with far more enthusiasm than Ruston thought the parade truly merited.

But that, of course, wasn't the point.

The point was for everyone to have a good time, and Ruston decided that the best way

he, too, could have a good time would be to go back and stand next to Misty Kennedy while she stood at the curb with her clipboard and stopwatch, trying to control the pace of the floats. The drivers were getting themselves under way either when they felt like it or when they got their engines running, whichever came last.

Following the band was Summer Fun's "Land of the Free" float, with Merrill Brewster's daughter Marci as the Statue of Liberty, wearing a costume that was far better than any ten-year-old Miss Liberty had worn in years and standing proudly in the center of what was apparently supposed to be some kind of immigrant ship.

With any luck at all, Ruston decided, the rest of the day would turn out just as beautifully as Marci Brewster's costume.

Finally, as "Land of the Free" cruised slowly by him with only a slight list to starboard, Rusty Ruston began to relax.

CHAPTER 32

Logan moved the brush away from the cave entrance and peered out, his rheumy eyes squinting against the sun that had risen high in the sky while he slept. He listened while he waited for his eyes to adjust to the glare, holding so still that even his breathing was silent. Only when both his eyes and his ears told him there was no danger lurking nearby did he finally wriggle out of the cave's narrow entrance to stretch his cramped muscles in the great expanse of the morning.

As the aching of the night began to ease, he crouched low, once again listening.

Nothing to be heard but a pair of jays, quarreling over some morsel of food they'd found.

Rising, he began making his way quietly down the slope toward his cabin, moving slowly, constantly casting his eyes and ears in every direction, searching the woods for any sign of men waiting to take him away.

Nearly an hour later he finally reached his goal.

The one-winged crow was perched on a stump outside the cabin door, and the moment it caught sight of him, it began bobbing madly up and down, cawing and flapping its wing.

"Shhh," Logan hissed, but the bird paid no attention, its scolding far from over. As the man headed for the door, the bird hopped off the stump and scuttled to the cabin, pushing through the door as soon as Logan cracked it open. As it disappeared into the cabin, the bird fell silent, and Logan felt a grim foreboding.

He pushed the door wider, and the sunlight flooded in.

His dog lay dead in a pool of black, sticky blood, his chest blasted open.

For more than a full minute Logan stood silently in the doorway, his eyes fixed on the corpse of what only yesterday had been his best friend.

A trick, he told himself. Has to be some kinda trick. Who'd want to shoot a harmless old dog?

But even as he formed the words in his mind, he knew they weren't true. "No," Logan whispered, finally moving into the cabin and dropping to his knees. He lifted the

cold, limp corpse and held it to his chest, cradling and rocking the remains of the animal as gently as if it were a baby. "Why'd they do that?" he murmured. "What'd they think you could do to them?" He buried his face in the dog's fur and breathed in the pungent smell of the only real friend he'd known in years. "I'm so sorry. So sorry."

Tears began to stream down Logan's face, and his gentle rocking turned violent. A moment later, still clutching the bloody corpse of the dog to his breast, his balance failed and he was rolling on the floor, his grief for the loss of his one true friend igniting the worries and fears and terrors that had been building up inside him ever since he'd discovered that Dr. Darby's demons had once more been set loose.

And now they'd killed his *dog*.

His poor, harmless, deaf and crippled old *dog*.

For a long time — he had no idea how long — Logan lay on the floor, sobbing. But slowly the emotional storm faded, and at last he sat up and wiped his sleeve across his face.

Everything, he knew, had changed.

Everything was wrong.

His most precious secrets were strewn across the cabin floor, and he knew he could

never live here again.

His eyes fixed on the crow, who was pecking at the last of the bread crumbs Logan had left for it on the floor yesterday.

"I'm sorry," he whispered, only partly to the crow. Now images were flitting through his mind. Images of the girl he'd killed so long ago, the girl he'd wanted only to love.

And Dr. Darby, who had tried to help him.

And the girl that Dr. Darby had killed. Logan reached deep into the dim recesses of his memory and found her name.

Hanover.

That was it. She'd looked like the other girl — the girl he'd loved — and he had been afraid she might die, too. But Dr. Darby had told him she wouldn't.

Dr. Darby had told him he was all right.

But then Dr. Darby had killed the girl and told him to make sure the demons stayed locked up.

Logan had watched Dr. Darby drown that night. He'd been out in his boat, fishing in the moonlight. He'd even tried to save Dr. Darby, but the water was too deep, and he hadn't been able to get to him.

He'd failed.

And now he'd failed again.

The demons were loose, and now even his

dog was dead.

And soon the men would be back, and they'd take him away.

But maybe it wasn't too late! Maybe there was still something he could do — something that would make up for all his failures.

Struggling back to his feet, Logan picked up the ruined body of his dog. "Come on, dog," he muttered. "Maybe we're not through quite yet."

Leaving his cabin for what he knew would be the last time, Logan carried the body of the dog down to the lake, never once looking back.

The crow, as if somehow knowing it would never see Logan again, uttered one final caw and then fell silent.

Logan settled the dog down on its bed of rags in the bow of the boat, just the way he had a thousand times before. The old dog looked as if he might simply be taking a moment's nap.

Logan stepped into the boat and pushed off, heaving the bow loose from the mud.

He rowed quickly but silently, hugging the shoreline, as he made his way toward Pinecrest.

The lake was almost unnaturally quiet; deserted of even a single other boat this morning.

When he came to his goal thirty minutes later, Logan slid the bow of the boat into the weedy cover twenty yards from the Pinecrest lawn and tied the painter to the branch he'd used so many times before.

"Shhh," he said to the dog. "Wait here."

Quietly, Logan moved through the woods that bordered Pinecrest until he was as close to the carriage house as he could get without leaving his cover. Already the voices were whispering to him, but this time he knew he could not fail.

He had one last thing to do, and this time the voices would not deter him.

He moved quickly from the safety of the woods to the carriage house door, but hesitated before he touched the doorknob.

What if he failed again?

Perhaps he should turn back now, go back to his boat, and follow where Dr. Darby had led.

But that *was* failure.

And this time, he was not going to fail.

This time he would do exactly as Dr. Darby had wanted him to do.

He gripped the doorknob, and as the voices grew louder he felt a new energy flowing into him from deep inside the building.

It was going to be all right!

This time he was not going to fail!

Shivering with anticipation, Logan opened the door and stepped into the darkness.

CHAPTER 33

Rusty Ruston was on his third circuit around the expansive lawn that sloped gently down to the pavilion beneath which Ellis Langstrom's body had been discovered only a few nights earlier. This evening, though, it was almost as if the tragedy had never happened. The pavilion itself was twinkling with thousands of tiny lights as dusk settled, and fireflies were starting to blink as well. A four piece band — the latest in a series of musical performances that had been going on all afternoon — was playing to a nearly full dance floor that was getting more crowded by the minute. The lawn itself had been transformed into a colorful patchwork of blankets as families from all over the county had settled in to eat the picnic supper provided by the Lions Club, then watch the best fireworks display north of Chicago, at least if you believed what Mayor Richmond had to say.

Under a huge oak tree near the edge of the lawn farthest from the pavilion, Derek Anders was throwing a ball to his toddler son, having apparently decided he'd had enough of the long day of constant surveillance. Two other deputies had obviously taken their lead from Anders, and were waiting for the fireworks with their families.

At least one of them looked as if he'd had one beer too many, but Rusty couldn't blame him; all of them had been on duty since early in the morning, and it was long past time for everybody to take a break, including himself.

Besides which, everything had gone off without a single hitch so far, and this was shaping up as the best Fourth ever, at least for the merchants in town.

"Here, Rusty, I made you a plate."

Ruston turned to see Rita Henderson holding an oversize Chinet platter piled high with barbecued ribs, potato salad, corn on the cob, and even one of Billie-Jo Jensen's huge biscuits, dripping with butter. His stomach rumbled loudly as he took it, making Rita raise an eyebrow.

"What a charming way of telling me you haven't eaten all day," she said, then eyed the crowd appreciatively. "But what a great day. It all came off perfectly, thanks in no

small part to you. You may rest assured that you have my vote next time you're up for reelection." She handed him a plastic fork and a napkin. "But right now it's time for a little relaxation."

Ruston smiled, and tried to force his eyes to stop wandering over the crowd searching for trouble that wasn't there. "Thanks, Rita," he said. "Maybe you're right." But just as he headed for an empty seat at a picnic table, he spotted Eric Brewster and Cherie Stevens holding hands as they moved carefully through the maze of blankets, heading for the lemonade booth.

Which wasn't a problem in and of itself, but Ruston's antennae still went up.

Quickly, he searched the area for two potential sources of trouble: Adam Mosler and Al Stevens.

Eric's rival, and Cherie's overly protective father.

Ruston spotted Stevens first; Al and his brother Billy were busy on the floating platform, putting the finishing touches on the fireworks display.

Deciding Stevens wasn't going to be a problem — at least right now — Ruston searched for Adam Mosler and found him leaning against a tree, glaring furiously at Eric and Cherie.

Ruston focused his gaze on Mosler, and as if by the sheer force of his will, the boy turned a few seconds later and looked at him.

They made eye contact, and even from twenty yards away, Ruston could see Adam start to deflate. Finally, the boy nodded, turned, and walked in the opposite direction toward the baseball diamond, where a game of softball was just winding down in the face of the dwindling daylight.

Good. He could enjoy his meal in peace.

He settled in at a picnic table with Rita Henderson and a couple of families with little children who moved over to make room for them both. All around him he heard the chatter of happy people. So far, the biggest problems had been a couple of sunburns and one skinned knee, only the last of which had even needed the ministrations of the first aid tent. So if Al Stevens could manage not to blow his fingers off tonight, this whole Fourth of July might just go down in history as the best yet, despite what had happened Friday night.

Real life could wait until morning.

He tore a bite of meat off a rib, then sucked the thick sauce off his fingers. "Now that is what I call good," he sighed.

On the other side of the table, a baby —

probably just a year old and still in its mother's arms — seemed to sense his mood. Gurgling and smiling, it stretched out its hand toward Ruston, offering him the remains of a potato chip that was clutched in its tiny fingers.

"Why, thank you," Rusty said, reaching out to take the chip from the baby. "Don't mind if I do. Don't mind at all."

The baby giggled happily, and Ruston decided that, at least for now, all was, indeed, right with the world.

Riley Logan stumbled out of the carriage house door into the gathering dark of the evening.

At the top of the lawn, the house was still quiet, still deserted.

But inside Logan's head, the voices still whispered. Now, though, one of them had risen above the others.

A woman's voice.

A woman who was speaking to him, telling him what he must do.

"Not here," she said. *"I want to go where there are people."*

Logan's grip tightened on the axe.

"I need to finish," the voice whispered. *"I need to finish it all."*

Logan moved toward the path through the

woods that would take him to town.

In the distance, somewhere beyond the treetops, he could see a glow in the sky.

Lights.

Lots of lights.

All the people would be there.

As many as she wanted.

"Yes," the woman sighed as he began moving toward the lights. *"Oh, yes."*

Eric Brewster wished he could sink into the pleasure of having Cherie Stevens next to him on the quilt his mother had brought from Pinecrest, and where they now sat with his family. He'd felt a pang of jealousy a couple of hours ago when he first spotted her talking with Adam Mosler, as well as a terrible feeling of disappointment that she was still hanging around with him. In fact, he'd felt a lot more jealousy, and a lot more disappointment, than he'd either expected or been willing to admit to Tad and Kent when they saw how he was looking at Cherie and started teasing him about it.

And he'd been even more surprised by how good he felt when she'd spotted him, cut her conversation with Mosler short, and come over to say hi, then stayed with him all afternoon, even as Adam Mosler started burning with visible anger. Indeed, he felt

good enough about it that he didn't even mind the leers Tad and Kent were giving him from the blankets they and their parents had spread next to the Brewsters' quilt.

But even Cherie's presence couldn't quite dispel the dark sense of foreboding that had hung over him all day, the strange feeling that there was something he was supposed to have done that he had failed to do.

Or — possibly even worse — done something he shouldn't have.

The problem was, he couldn't quite remember what he and Tad and Kent had done the last time they'd gone into the room that was hidden behind the storeroom in the carriage house.

He remembered clearly what they'd intended to do — that was easy. They were going to go into the room, take apart everything they'd put together, and be done with it.

But he couldn't remember taking anything apart.

Not the lamp, or the hacksaw.

Not even the scalpels from the medical bag.

But so what? It wasn't like anything that had happened was their fault! Certainly he hadn't killed Tippy, and Tad hadn't killed Ellis Langstrom, and Kent hadn't made a lamp shade

out of the skin from Ellis's arm!

All that happened was that they'd *dreamed* about those things.

But how could they have dreamed things they didn't even know had happened?

And that, he knew, was what had been wrong all day: he had a strange feeling that something else was going to happen, something that he and Tad and Kent could have prevented if only they'd done what they went into the hidden room to do. But had they done it? Had they done anything at all?

Or, even worse, had they done the *wrong* thing?

That was the thought that had been hanging over him all day, and now, as the dark of the night gathered around him, that thought was getting heavier and heavier.

"Hey," Cherie said, breaking into his reverie. "I know a great place to watch the fireworks from. You know the footbridge over the marsh? The one that leads to the path to The Pines?"

Eric nodded, and as he saw the sparkle in her eyes, his mood lifted slightly. Maybe, if they were alone in the dark . . . His spirits lifted even more as he considered the possibilities. "I know the bridge," he said.

"My dad helps put on the fireworks, and they always put the platform off the bridge,

so it's the best place to watch from. Want to go?"

Once again Eric nodded, but out of the corner of his eye he could see his mother already shaking her head.

"But we should all be together," Merrill began. "I don't want to lose —"

"It'll be okay," Dan cut in, cutting off Merrill's worries even before she'd finished voicing them. Then, certain her real fear was that Adam and his friends might gang up on Eric if they spotted him alone with Cherie, he said to Eric, "Why don't you take Kent and Tad, too? With all four of you kids gone, there might be enough space on the blankets for the rest of us to actually stretch out."

Eric looked at Cherie, who hesitated only a second before nodding, which was just enough to tell him she'd been hoping to be alone with him as much as he was hoping to be alone with her. Still, Tad and Kent would give them plenty of space, and at least nobody had suggested that they take Marci along, too. "Just make sure you come back here right after the fireworks are over," his father went on as he and Cherie stood up.

"No problem," Eric said as Kent and Tad got up, too. A moment later Cherie's warm

hand was holding his own as she led them all across the sea of people and blankets toward the path that would take them to the footbridge.

Riley Logan moved silently along the path toward town, hearing nothing but the voices that seemed to come not only from within his own mind, but from all around him as well.

The woman's voice was the clearest, rising above all the others.

"They never understood," she was saying. *"They never knew why I did it. They didn't care. It didn't matter about me. All that mattered was Father. Father and Mother. But they didn't care about me, either. Nobody ever cared about me."*

Logan didn't know if she was talking to him or to herself, but it didn't matter.

She was talking, and he had to listen.

Had to listen, and had to obey.

She fell silent for a moment, and when she spoke again, the tone of her voice had changed. She said a single word: *"Stop!"*

Then all the others fell silent, and Logan froze in his tracks and for a moment heard nothing at all.

Then a different sound came to his ears.

A sound from directly ahead.

Someone on the path.

A man.

A man who was singing tunelessly to himself.

Logan crouched low to the ground, hunkered down in the brush at the side of the path.

He smelled the man before he came into sight.

"Drunk!" the woman whispered. *"Just like Father!"*

The man came into view, his stumbling gait telling Logan the woman had been right.

"Stand up to him!" the woman commanded. *"Stand up and face him!"*

Logan listened and obeyed.

He rose to his feet and stepped into the middle of the path just as the man approached.

Startled, the man dropped the bottle of beer he held in his hand.

"Kill him!"

Needing nothing more than the softly spoken order to spur him into action, Logan swung the axe.

Its edge — honed razor sharp by Logan himself only a little while ago — sliced cleanly through the man's neck.

His head fell to the ground, the eyelids

twitching, the mouth gaping open in surprise and shock.

Then the corpse's knees buckled and it sank to the ground, blood spraying the trees, the path, even Logan himself.

Logan gazed down at the body, not quite certain what had just happened.

"Yes," the woman whispered. *"Very good. Perfect. That's one. But there are more. So very many more . . ."*

"One," Logan repeated, and now the entire chorus of voices came back and rose, washing over him and bathing him in ecstasy.

His hands tightening on the axe, he moved forward a few steps, guided by the voice of the woman.

Then he heard more voices approaching, young voices, and the hollow sound of footsteps on wood.

People were on the bridge!

Logan ducked into the woods and slipped down the bank to the dark, cold water of the marsh.

Quietly, he waded through the tangled reeds until he was directly beneath the bridge.

He stood silently, listening for the woman's voice, waiting for her to tell him what to do about the feet that were now scuffling

on the wooden planks above his head.

Kent and Tad sat perched on the bridge railing, facing the fireworks platform, while Eric leaned back against it with Cherie leaning on his chest. His arms were around her, his nose buried in her hair, taking in her fragrance with every breath.

Then, out of nowhere, he heard a voice: *"Not them. Not here. Not yet."*

Eric turned to look at Kent, his brow furrowing. "Did you hear something?" The look on Kent's face told him the answer to his question even before the other boy spoke.

But it was Tad who said, "A voice," and slipped off the railing to stand next to Eric. "A woman's voice."

Now Kent, too, was off the railing and peering away into the darkness.

"I didn't hear anything at all," Cherie said.

"Hurry! I want to do it! I want to do it now!"

"Oh, Jesus," Tad whispered. "Where's it coming from?"

"What are you guys talking about?" Cherie demanded.

The three boys only looked at one another, a terrible dread falling over them as the voices — the voices they'd never before heard outside of the secret room in the car-

riage house — grew louder.

Louder, and more demanding.

Logan slipped through the water as silently as he had moved through the woods, and only when the bridge was well behind him did he finally climb the bank to stand at the edge of the lawn.

The lighted pavilion — and a thousand people — lay before him like a scene from a dream.

"Yes," the woman whispered. *"There they are. All the fathers and all the mothers! It's time. It's time to make them pay for not caring about me!"*

Logan's grip once more tightened on the axe.

With Lizzie Borden's spirit guiding him, he would, indeed, make them pay.

CHAPTER 34

The spiraling light of the first salvo of fireworks glittered into the sky, and a moment later the darkness of the night was shattered by the blindingly white petals of a sparkling chrysanthemum, its brilliance in the darkness punctuated by the thundering boom of the rocket's explosion.

But Eric Brewster barely noticed.

Something terrible had happened!

He could feel it — feel the pain of it almost as if a blade had been plunged deep into his own belly. And yet the pain wasn't inside him — it was somewhere else, somewhere nearby.

As the second rocket exploded in the sky, another stab of agony slashed through him, and for an instant he froze, every muscle in his body going rigid in response to the searing pain.

Next to him, he heard Tad Sparks gasp, but it wasn't the kind of ecstatic sigh that

was rising from Cherie Stevens's throat. Tad's gasp was the sound of shock, and when Eric turned to look at him, Tad's eyes were wide and his mouth agape.

"She's doing it," Tad whispered. *"She's going to kill everyone!"*

As if in response to Tad's whispered words, a voice suddenly howled in Eric's mind — a woman's voice — the same voice he'd heard a moment ago. But now she was no longer whispering.

Now she was screaming!

"Kill her! Kill her now! Do it! Do what I say!"

Then another voice, a choking voice. "Five," the voice whispered.

Another scream, but this time not from inside Eric's own mind.

Then another choking syllable.

"Six."

The third rocket burst overhead, but now Eric was utterly oblivious to what was happening in the sky. Instead he was running, his feet pounding on the ground, Tad and Kent racing after him. In an instant they were off the footbridge, and in another they had burst out of the woods onto the crowded lawn.

More rockets ignited the sky, and now the crowd was roaring with delight, but inside Eric's head there was only one sound.

The sound of someone dying.

Laurie Kingsford gazed raptly at the explosion of fire, her two-month-old baby cradled against her breast. Only as the brilliance of the red, white, and blue flag began to fade did she finally look down into Ben's tiny face. Her mother hadn't wanted her to bring the baby at all, but Laurie had been so sure that her baby would love fireworks as much as she herself did that she'd ignored her mother's warning. And she had been right — little Ben was staring straight up into the sky, his eyes so wide that Laurie could clearly see the reflection of the fireworks in his tiny pupils. As the sky brightened with the next salvo, Ben's eyes looked like they were filled with swirling gold dust, and Laurie decided that she would watch the rest of the display only through the eyes of her baby.

That would be something to remember the rest of her life.

But a second later, before the burst of fire overhead had reached its zenith, the glittering reflection suddenly vanished from Ben's sparkling eyes and Laurie could feel a looming presence just behind her.

Turning, she started to look up, but it was already too late — blessedly, Laurie didn't

even have time to see the axe slashing toward her head, let alone realize what was about to happen to her.

In an instant it was over.

The axe head slashed through Laurie's skull so cleanly that the back of her head merely fell away, almost as if it had never been a part of her at all. Her expression was barely affected — perhaps, had anyone been looking directly at her, they would have seen a hint of surprise in her eyes. But even if it was there at all, it was gone in the tiniest fraction of a second, and as the light overhead reached its peak, the light of life in Laurie Kingsford's eyes was snuffed away.

Ben, still cradled in his mother's arms, began to scream, but his crying was quickly drowned out, first by the ecstatic cries of the crowd as they watched the fire in the sky, then by his mother herself as she tumbled face forward, her breasts pressing against his tiny face, her blood streaming over him from the unholy wound that only a moment ago had been the back of her head.

Logan gazed unseeingly down.

Above him, the brilliance of the sky finally began to fade.

Inside his head a woman's voice pealed with laughter.

"Seventeen," he said softly.

Then, as Laurie Kingsford slumped in a pool of her own blood, Logan moved on, already searching for the next target of Lizzie Borden's axe.

Eric stumbled, grabbing the back of his head where the searing pain sliced through his brain as if by —

— as if by an axe!

He heard a dull voice. A dead voice.

"Seventeen."

But the voice wasn't like the other voices — not like the voices he'd heard when he was on the footbridge.

This voice was real!

As the pain started to fade from his head, he looked around, frantically searching for its source. But there were people everywhere — crowds of people, all of them staring up into the sky.

Then Eric saw him.

The man from the boat — the boat with the huge cross mounted in its bow.

The man with the wild gray hair and the full beard.

The man who was now swinging an axe back and forth as if cutting wheat with a scythe. But instead of grain and chaff falling to the ground around him, this reaper

was leaving a grisly trail of pain and terror.

And death.

Now a babble of voices was rising in Eric's head, but one single voice — the voice of the woman he'd heard on the bridge — rose above the rest.

"Yes!" the woman cried every time the axe slashed through flesh and bone. As the carnage grew and one victim after another fell beneath the bloodied weapon, a note of ecstasy crept into the woman's voice. *"Yes,"* she moaned. *"Oh, yes . . ."*

Again and again the axe flashed, and Eric watched in horror as glimmering droplets of blood played among the fireflies swarming from the trees and embers falling from the sky.

And over it all — even over the howling voice of the woman whose ecstasy rose with every strike of the blade — another voice rose.

A voice keeping careful count of the dreadful carnage.

"Seventeen . . . eighteen . . . nineteen . . . twenty . . ."

Logan's feet took on the same cadence as his voice as he trudged through the crowd, the axe swinging back and forth with every stride.

One after another, people fell away, the slickly bloodied steel slicing as cleanly through bone as the flesh that enveloped it.

"Don't stop," the woman moaned. *"Don't ever stop. . . ."*

Yet even as she spoke, Logan paused to wipe the blood from his face before it blinded him completely.

"More! More!" the woman howled. *"Keep going! Kill them all!"*

Logan swung the axe again, ripping it through the top of a young boy's head even as the child raised his arms to fend off the weapon.

"Twenty-eight."

All around Logan, people cheered at the spectacle in the sky, unaware of the massacre that was closing in from behind.

"There! See them? The mother and the father and the little girl!"

Though the fireworks were exploding every second now and the cheers of the crowd were all around him, Eric recognized the voice in an instant.

Recognized it, and knew that only four people were hearing it.

He himself, Kent Newell, Tad Sparks . . .

And the man with the axe.

The unseen spirit behind the howling

voice seemed to rise above all else, and suddenly not only did Eric hear her voice, but saw with her eyes as well.

Saw the people she had just chosen.

"My family," she was raging now. *"My mother and my father and my sister. My sister Emma!"*

But the little girl Eric was seeing wasn't her little sister at all, and her name wasn't Emma.

Her name was Marci.

And she was his own little sister.

"Kill them," Lizzie Borden's voice implored. *"Kill them now!"*

Merrill Brewster slipped her arm around her daughter's shoulders and drew her close as they gazed up at the spectacle in the sky. As the fireworks built toward their finale, she tried to remember ever having a more perfect Fourth of July, but even as the question formed in her mind, she knew the answer.

Never.

The day had been perfect, and she finally understood that Dan had been right — whatever had happened to Ellis Langstrom had nothing to do with her or her family, and for once she hadn't let her fears ruin the summer for everyone.

515

As if reading her thoughts, Marci grinned up at her. "Now aren't you happy we didn't go home yesterday?" she asked.

Merrill smiled down at Marci, who was still dressed in her costume as the Statue of Liberty. "Very happy. Happier than you'll ever know."

"Kill them!" Lizzie commanded. *"Kill them now!"*

Logan lumbered toward the family that was still a dozen paces away, the steady stream of flashes from the sky lighting his way, the slashing axe, which was flickering as if lit by a strobe.

"Thirty-three. Thirty-four."

Eric charged past the screaming, bleeding people whose cries were all but ignored by the mob whose attention was still focused on the spectacle in the sky.

"No!" he howled as Logan moved closer to his family, the axe rising high above Marci's head while inside his own head Lizzie Borden's voice screamed for more blood.

More death.

Ahead of him — just out of his reach — the rag-clad man stood poised with Lizzie Borden's axe over his head, and in another moment —

A surge of panic triggered something deep inside Eric, and then he was leaping forward, his arms outstretched, the single word he'd uttered before now erupting from his throat with enough force to rise above the volley of fireworks that were pouring into the night sky as the finale began.

"NOOOOO!"

With an unnatural strength that came out of nowhere, Eric seized Logan's arm and whipped him around.

Logan's eyes — dead black orbs — fixed on him.

"Kill him!" Eric heard the voice command, and this time knew it was his own death she was demanding.

Jerking free from Eric's grip, Logan raised the axe again.

But then he hesitated, and a faint glimmer flashed in his eyes.

"Kill him!" the voice screamed.

Now Kent and Tad appeared out of the crowd, hurling themselves on Logan, trying to bring him down, but the old man held his stance as if braced by some unseen force.

Eric grabbed at the axe handle — slippery with blood — and wrenched it free from Logan's grip.

The voice howled: *"Yes! Yes! You do it! I*

killed my family. Now it's your turn!"

Eric's eyes flicked toward Marci, who had finally turned away from the glory in the sky and now beheld the horror all around her. Her face paled and her mouth opened wide, but no sound came out.

Eric tore his eyes away from his little sister to look once more at Logan.

Their eyes met.

And their gazes held.

And in that moment when their eyes held each other's, Eric understood everything.

Logan, his eyes finally coming back to life, nodded.

Tightening his grip on the axe, Eric raised it, then brought it down, sinking it deep into the old man's shoulder.

Logan staggered, but held his stance, and as blood began to gush from his shoulder, he spoke.

Spoke so softly only Eric could hear.

"Thirty-eight."

Time seemed to stand still, and once more the eyes of the boy met those of the man.

Once again, the man nodded.

As the voice inside his head screamed out against him, Eric raised the axe a second time, and plunged it deep into Logan's gut.

Again the old man staggered, and this time he sank to the ground.

"Thirty-nine," he whispered, as Kent and Tad fell on him, pinning him to the spot where he lay.

Eric was trembling now, and as he stood over the fallen man, he felt a terrible cold enter his body. The voice of the woman was still screaming, but the other voices were starting to fade away. And the man on the ground — the man he'd already struck twice with the axe, was staring up at him.

For the third time their eyes met.

For the third time, the man spoke. "Do it," he whispered. "End it."

As Kent and Tad held him down, Eric raised the axe a final time, then brought it down, its head swinging in a great arc before slicing though the old man's neck to sink deep into the ground beneath the blood-soaked lawn.

"No!" the last, lone voice sighed inside Eric's head. Then it fell silent, and Eric stared down at the severed head. The features were almost invisible behind the blood-matted beard, but as the fireworks above began to fade away, Eric was certain he saw the lips move.

"Forty."

The single word echoed in Eric's mind, but then, as the last glowing embers fell

from the sky, silence finally fell over him, too.

The voices vanished.

Then, very slowly, the sounds of reality returned.

All around him, Eric heard people howling and screaming, but this time it wasn't because of the fireworks from above.

Now it was because of the horror they were discovering all around them.

But inside, all was still quiet.

No more voices shouted in his head.

He looked down at his hands, still clinging to the bloody axe.

His legs began to tremble.

He took one stumbling step toward Tad and Kent, but his legs wouldn't work, and he sank to the ground, every ounce of his strength drained away, every scrap of energy gone.

He barely felt the quilt his mother wrapped around his shoulders, barely noticed as someone took the axe from his hands.

"It's okay," he heard someone say as he took a ragged breath and struggled against the terrible exhaustion that held him in its grip. "You did the right thing. He would've killed us all."

The night began to close around him, and

for a moment Eric continued to struggle against the gathering darkness, but then he gave in and let himself fall into the embrace of sleep.

Tonight, no bad dreams would come.

EPILOGUE

Eric Brewster made a right turn off the highway, following the sign for Phantom Lake. Though it had been only five years since he, Kent Newell, and Tad Sparks had been up here, nothing looked the same.

Or at least it didn't look the way he remembered it.

Last time he'd been up this far north, it had been with his parents and his sister, and they'd been intending to spend the whole summer at the lake.

Instead it had been barely two weeks.

Two weeks that were still, even after five years, etched in his memory as vividly as if they had happened only a week ago.

Except that even though the memories were vivid, he still wasn't exactly sure what had really happened.

"Just three more miles," he announced, breaking the silence that had hung in the car for the last hour — an hour during

522

which, Eric was sure, Kent and Tad had been as involved with their memories as he had been with his own. Yet so far none of them had even mentioned the real reason they were here, just as they had maintained a near silence about those two weeks through their last year of high school and the four years of college that had followed.

The same near silence had hung not only over the three boys, but over Eric's family as well. That Fourth of July had been hardest for Marci. For more than a year she had awakened almost every night with nightmares about a wild-eyed man with a flowing beard coming after her with an axe, waking the whole family with her screams. But eventually the nightmares lost their power, and she hadn't even mentioned one in the last few months.

His mother, on the other hand, was still trying to overcome the terror those two weeks had instilled in her, and even now refused to leave the shelter of their home in Evanston for even a single night.

Nor would she talk about what had happened, covering her ears if anyone even mentioned Phantom Lake.

But now, as Eric, Kent, and Tad drew closer to the lake, the atmosphere in the car changed. Kent and Tad both sat up and

began looking out the windows, putting their memories behind them, at least for a few minutes.

Tad leaned forward between the two front seats. "Remember Cherie?" he asked.

"Of course I remember her," Eric said, almost too quickly.

"That's probably why he was so hot to come on this trip," Kent said, knowing even as he said it that Cherie Stevens had nothing at all to do with them coming up here.

"Did you two stay in touch?" Tad asked.

"She called me a couple of times," Eric said. "But after that . . ." His voice trailed off as he searched the landscape for something that looked familiar, but saw nothing.

It had been too brief a time, too long ago.

"She's probably married to that dweeb and has five kids," Kent said.

"Adam Mosler," Eric breathed.

"Yeah," Tad said. "Adam Mosler. God, what a jerk. Suppose she still works at that ice cream shop? And what do you bet Mosler's working at the gas station?"

Eric shrugged as he maneuvered the car into the bend that would feed them directly onto Main Street. "We're about to find out."

But as they came out of the bend and the village appeared before them, nothing looked any more familiar than it had when

they'd gotten off the highway a few minutes ago.

The Phantom Lake they had expected to see had vanished.

Vanished almost without a trace.

The buildings were still there, of course, but they looked nothing like they had five years earlier.

At least half of them were boarded up, and even those that weren't had a weather-beaten, unkempt look to them. Paint was peeling, exposing graying wood beneath, and what awnings were still in place were sagging, torn, or both.

In spite of the warm summer day, there were no crowds of tourists wandering the streets.

No one wandering the sidewalks with an ice cream cone in one hand and shopping bags in the other.

No blankets on the pavilion lawn.

No picnicking families on vacation.

No children splashing in the water, no one waterskiing.

The marina held only a couple of fishing boats, both of which looked as worn and tired as the village itself; all the other slips were vacant.

A sodden mass of trash lay mounded against the base of the pavilion.

Unconsciously, Eric slowed to the pace of a funeral cortege as they crept along the deserted street.

"There's the ice cream shop," Tad said softly, pointing. "Or at least that's where it was."

Sheets of plywood now covered the plate glass windows, and the peeling sign hung askew.

In the next block, they spotted another sign on another vanished business, one that had faded even more than that of the ice cream shop, but was still barely legible:

CAROL'S ANTIQUES

"Jesus," Kent breathed. "What the hell happened to this place?" Yet even as he asked, he was fairly sure he knew the answer.

The same thing that had happened to them had happened to the town. Except the three of them had been able to leave right away.

The rest of the town had not.

"I wonder how long it took?" Tad asked, knowing that all three of them were holding the same thought, just as they had since childhood.

"I don't know," Eric replied. "But I know

who could tell us. If she's still here." A few seconds later he turned into the library parking lot, where only one car sat by itself.

Less than a minute later they pulled the library door open and went inside, their footsteps echoing in the silent building.

The librarian's nameplate still read MISS EDNA BLOOMFIELD, just as it had five years ago, but no one sat at the desk.

"Hello?" Kent called.

A small voice came out from between massive shelves of books: "I'm here!" Then Miss Bloomfield herself appeared, patting her hair nervously. She was exactly the same as Eric remembered her, but even older and tinier. She hurried toward her desk, rubbing her hands briskly as she sat down. After adjusting the single pencil that sat on the desk, she looked up at the three young men. "Oh, my goodness! We don't often get patrons anymore. I tend to talk to myself, so I didn't hear you come in."

"We were wondering if maybe you could tell us exactly what happened here," Kent asked. He glanced at Tad and Eric, but when neither of them said anything, he spoke again. "Our families used to come here when we were kids, and now —" He hesitated, but found no better way to say it. "It looks like the town's been deserted."

Edna Bloomfield sagged visibly in her chair, and when she replied, she didn't quite meet their eyes. "It was something that happened about five years ago." She shook her head sadly, took a deep breath, then went on, but now her voice was barely audible. "Twenty-four people were killed," she whispered. "And I don't know how many more were hurt. It was terrible . . . just terrible." Finally, she managed to look directly at them. "The town never recovered. First the tourists stopped coming — I mean they just stopped, overnight — and the people started moving away."

"The crazy guy," Eric murmured almost to himself. "The one with the axe."

Miss Bloomfield's head bobbed and she bit her lip. Then she took another breath, straightened herself in her chair, and folded her hands on the desk. "It was a horrible thing," she said. "But I'm an optimist, and always have been. The town will come back to life. All things have their cycles."

All things have their cycles.

The thought sent an icy shiver down Eric's spine. Then, seemingly out of nowhere, a question came from his lips. "Whatever happened to the axe? Do you know?"

Kent and Tad glanced at each other uneasily.

"Now, why would you want to know that?" Miss Bloomfield replied, but before Eric could formulate a reply, she leaned forward as if to confide some kind of secret. "But it's the strangest thing! The axe simply disappeared." She spread her hands wide, as if still barely able to believe it. "Right out of the sheriff's office. One day it was there, the next day it wasn't." She shook her head, her expression turning sorrowful. "Sheriff Ruston lost his job over it, of course. It was quite the scandal. And, I guess that was the beginning of the end, really. The thought of that terrible axe still being out there somewhere . . ." Edna Bloomfield's voice trailed off, and she shuddered as if a draft had just chilled her.

"But you stayed," Tad said.

"I wouldn't know where else to go," the ancient librarian replied. "I suppose when I die, they'll close this old place, at least until Phantom Lake picks up again."

"What about Cherie —" Kent Newell began, then faltered and looked to Eric for her last name.

"Stevens," Eric said.

"Did you know Cherie Stevens?" Miss Bloomberg asked, brightening.

All three nodded.

"The last I heard of Cherie, she and her husband had moved to Minocqua. Now, what was the name of that nice young man she married? Not that terrible Mosler boy, thank heaven. I always thought he was trouble. If you ask me, I've always thought he must have had something to do with . . ."

As Edna Bloomberg prattled on, Eric wandered away, knowing deep inside himself that whatever Adam Mosler had done over the years, he'd had nothing to do with what happened that night.

Kent Newell and Tad Sparks thanked the librarian and slipped out, joining Eric on the front porch. Edna Bloomberg's voice could still be heard until the heavy library doors swung closed behind them.

Eric's arms felt like lead as they got back in the car. Suddenly, he wished he'd never suggested this trip; it would have been better at least to remember the town as the beautiful place it had once been before that awful Fourth of July when everything changed. And yet even as he wished he hadn't come, he knew the trip wasn't over yet.

He still had to at least try to find out what had happened all those years ago when he and Kent and Tad were plagued by night-

mares that turned out not to be illusions at all, but twisted refractions of things that had actually happened.

But how had they happened?

What had caused them?

"What now?" Tad asked. "And where are we going to stay? I don't think there's even a motel here anymore."

"Let's at least go out to The Pines and take a look around," Kent suggested. "I bet it's still the same. Then we can get a room down in Eagle River or someplace."

Eric took a deep breath and started the car. Going out to The Pines — no, going out to Pinecrest — was what this trip was all about anyway. Though they hadn't talked about it — not directly anyway — all of them had known that was why they had come all the way up here: to try to make sense of something that he — that *all* of them — only vaguely remembered. But if he didn't remember those things — if he didn't close that particular chapter — it would haunt him for the rest of his life.

Perhaps it was different for his friends, he thought. Tad was headed for graduate school at Northwestern next year, and Kent was taking a research job in Salt Lake City. But he hadn't quite decided on the next step of his future yet, and he knew why.

There were things he had to put to rest before he could go on.

Steeling himself against the heaviness that threatened to paralyze his arms, he steered the car out of town.

The entrance sign to The Pines was overgrown with weeds and green with moss, its carved letters barely legible. As Eric drove slowly down the long lane, they could see that a few of the houses — a very few — had been kept up, but the rest looked as if they'd been abandoned for years.

Kent and Tad said nothing as they passed the summer homes that had been so inviting only five years ago but now crouched in the forest, empty and sad. The farther they drove, the deeper the melancholy that hung over the area imbued the car, and when they finally came to the gates at the head of the long Pinecrest driveway, Eric almost changed his mind about turning in. Yet going back to Pinecrest wasn't something he — or any of them — could avoid. Whatever lay at the end of the drive, he had to come to grips with it.

Had to know.

Had to remember everything that had happened, or dismiss what memories he had as nothing more than the dreams they

seemed to be.

"What are you waiting for?" Kent asked, and nudged Eric's arm.

Eric turned into the driveway and drove to the house.

It stood as solid and as foreboding as the first time he'd seen it, but even with the first look, he knew there had been no one living in the house for years. The lawn was choked with weeds, and long-dead branches still lay where they had fallen years earlier. The wind had piled leaves against the front door; the fountain was choked with a vile-looking muck.

Despite the warmth of the summer day, the house and grounds felt dark and cold.

Eric parked the car and the three of them got out, their eyes going instantly to the old carriage house.

"Remember the nightmares we used to have up here?" Tad said in a voice so quiet that his words were almost lost.

Kent nodded and began walking toward the carriage house, and without a word, Tad followed.

Eric hesitated a moment, his gaze shifting toward the edge of the woods where a handmade cross still tilted over Tippy's tiny grave, then he, too, started toward the old

brick building.

The outside door still scraped along the concrete when Kent opened it.

Deep in Eric's mind, a memory stirred.

A memory of voices.

But not voices, really. Something that sounded like voices, but without any distinct words. Now, as the door opened wide, Eric listened.

And heard only silence.

Slowly, reluctantly, he stepped into the shadows of the carriage house and turned right.

Toward the storeroom.

A moment later they were there. Eric could feel Tad and Kent right behind him, feel the same tension emanating from their bodies that was making his own feel as if it was almost vibrating.

He reached out to touch the doorknob, his mind already filling with memories of what lay on the wooden panel's other side. Just before his fingers closed on the knob, he hesitated, his fingers tingling in anticipation.

Anticipation of what?

Energy!

Yes, that was it. There had been a strange energy in the doorknob five years ago. An

energy that had run through his whole body and amplified the voices that seemed to whisper to him out of nowhere.

He forced his hand to close on the knob.

Nothing.

No voices. No energy running through his hand as he gripped the doorknob.

Nothing at all.

"It all feels so different," Tad whispered.

"We're not kids anymore," Kent said. "Maybe we imagined it all."

Eric opened the door and turned on the light.

Everything was exactly the same. The same jumble of furniture, the same piles of cartons stacked against the walls.

Even the photo album still sat on top of the little desk in the corner.

And the sheet of plywood was still against the far wall, just as it had been the first time they came into this room.

And now Eric remembered what lay behind that sheet of plywood.

A door.

A sealed door they never should have opened.

"I don't believe it," Kent breathed, slowly scanning the contents of the room. "It's all exactly the same. Exactly." He walked over to the photo album and turned a couple of

pages. "We were probably the last people ever to be in here."

"Remember how weird it was?" Tad asked. "It always seemed like we lost track of time when we were in here. Hours and hours."

"We were kids," Kent said, waving Tad's word's dismissively away. "Come on — let's move that plywood and take a look in the other room."

Neither Eric nor Tad moved.

"Maybe we shouldn't," Tad said.

Ignoring Tad's words, Kent grasped the sheet of plywood and pulled it, sliding it along the wall.

And all three of them froze at what they saw.

Instead of the open doorway to the tiny chamber that they were certain lay behind the plywood, all they saw was the faint outline of a small doorway that had been filled in with brick.

Brick that looked like it had been there for decades, not mere years.

Kent gazed uncertainly at Eric and Tad. "Didn't we unbrick this?"

Eric said nothing, his own mind still grappling with the same question.

"Maybe the whole thing was a weird dream," Tad said. "Could that be?" He walked forward and put his hand on the

bricks. "This looks like old mortar — I mean, really old."

"We should open it up again," Kent declared. "I'll bet that's where the axe is — right back inside there with all the other stuff." He stepped toward the door.

Suddenly, Edna Bloomfield's words echoed in Eric's mind: *All things have their cycles.*

"No," he said, reaching out and putting a restraining hand on Kent's shoulder. "Let's leave it alone."

Kent turned, his brow furrowed. "Leave it alone?" he repeated. "Why?"

"Let's just leave it," Eric said. "Let's just leave it all and go."

"I'm not exactly sure what happened when we were inside there," Tad said when Kent still seemed unconvinced. "I don't remember a whole lot about all of this. But I remember the nightmares. I remember the nightmares, and I never want to have them again. I think Eric's right."

Still Kent hesitated, putting his hand on the bricks and running his fingers down the poorly mortared joints.

And as he watched, Eric had a déjà vu flash.

A flash of Kent, his expression as mesmerized as it looked now. But in the flash, Kent

wasn't running his fingers over mortared bricks.

He was running them over the surface of a cracked Formica tabletop.

More images flashed through his mind: scalpels, and blood streaming from a gaping wound. A rusty hacksaw. A severed arm.

And a lamp shade.

A lamp shade made of —

As if to shut the images out of his mind, Eric grabbed the edge of the plywood and shoved it back across the doorway, knocking Kent's hand away.

Kent jerked back. "Hey!"

"Let's go," Eric said, his voice suddenly hard. "Let's go right now."

He held the door for Kent and Tad, and when they were in the open doorway, Eric took one last look around the storeroom.

Then he flicked off the light and closed the door firmly behind him.

But as he started back toward the car that would take him forever away from Phantom Lake, he turned and looked back at the carriage house one last time.

And wondered how long it would be before the next cycle began.

ABOUT THE AUTHOR

In the Dark of the Night is **John Saul's** thirty-third novel. His first novel, *Suffer the Children,* published in 1977, was an immediate million-copy bestseller. His other bestselling suspense novels include *Perfect Nightmare, Black Creek Crossing, Midnight Voices, The Manhattan Hunt Club, Nightshade, The Right Hand of Evil, The Presence, Black Lightning, The Homing,* and *Guardian.* He is also the author of the *New York Times* bestselling serial thriller *The Blackstone Chronicles,* initially published in six installments but now available in one complete volume. Saul divides his time between Seattle, Washington, and Hawaii. Join John Saul's fan club at www.johnsaul.com.

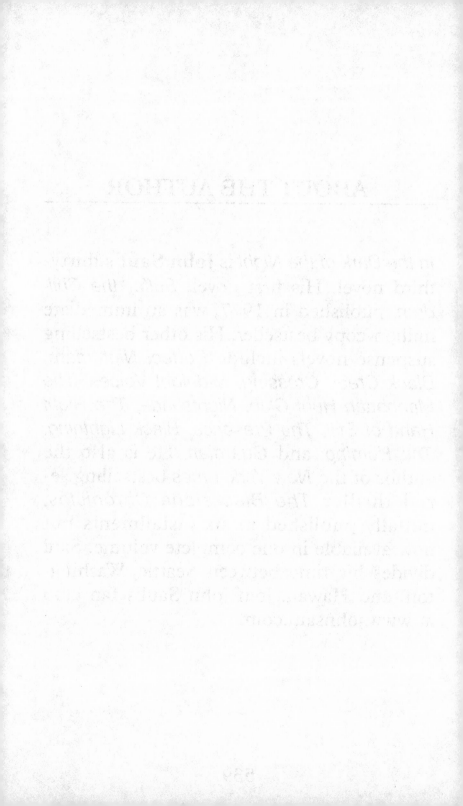

The employees of Thorndike Press hope you have enjoyed this Large Print book. All our Thorndike and Wheeler Large Print titles are designed for easy reading, and all our books are made to last. Other Thorndike Press Large Print books are available at your library, through selected bookstores, or directly from us.

For information about titles, please call:

(800) 223-1244

or visit our Web site at:

www.gale.com/thorndike
www.gale.com/wheeler

To share your comments, please write:

Publisher
Thorndike Press
295 Kennedy Memorial Drive
Waterville, ME 04901

FICTION

4/07